ROSIE ANDREWS was born and grew up in Liverpool, the third of twelve children. She studied History at Cambridge before becoming an English teacher. Her debut novel, *The Leviathan*, was an instant *Sunday Times* bestseller, going on to become one of the bestselling debut hardbacks of 2022, and has been short-listed for the Goldsboro Books Glass Bell Award, the HWA Debut Crown Award and the Books Are My Bag Readers Award for Fiction.

She lives in Hertfordshire with her husband and daughter.

THE PUZZLE WOOD

Rosie Andrews

R A V E N ❧ B O O K S
LONDON · OXFORD · NEW YORK · NEW DELHI · SYDNEY

RAVEN BOOKS
Bloomsbury Publishing Plc
50 Bedford Square, London, WC1B 3DP, UK
Bloomsbury Publishing Ireland Limited,
29 Earlsfort Terrace, Dublin 2, D02 AY28, Ireland

BLOOMSBURY, RAVEN BOOKS and the Raven Books logo are
trademarks of Bloomsbury Publishing Plc

First published in Great Britain 2024
This edition first published in 2025

A catalogue record for this book is available from the British Library

ISBN: HB: 978-1-5266-3737-6; TPB: 978-1-5266-3738-3; PB: 978-1-5266-3740-6;
WATERSTONES SPECIAL EDITION: 978-1-5266-7949-9; GOLDSBORO: 978-1-5266-7950-5;
EBOOK: 978-1-5266-3695-9; EPDF: 978-1-5266-3696-6

2 4 6 8 10 9 7 5 3 1

Typeset by Integra Software Services Pvt. Ltd.
Printed and bound in Great Britain by CPI Group (UK) Ltd, Croydon CR0 4YY

To find out more about our authors and books visit www.bloomsbury.com
and sign up for our newsletters

For product safety related questions contact productsafety@bloomsbury.com

To my husband and JEA

From scarped cliff and quarried stone
She cries, 'A thousand types are gone:
I care for nothing, all shall go.'

Alfred, Lord Tennyson, *In Memoriam* (1850)

PART 1

To Mr Drake, Abingdon, Oxfordshire:
16th May 1852
Hereford

It is with regret that I write to inform you of the death of your wife's sister, Miss Emily Murphy, in April of this year. Miss Murphy was employed as a governess by my client, Sir Rowland Bridewell, of Locksley Abbey, Herefordshire, and the Bridewell family has undertaken to see to her committal. They hope to satisfy you that everything that could have been done was done properly, and to reassure you that Miss Murphy's trials were not prolonged. Although the condolences of strangers will be no great comfort, I beg you to accept them, and those of the Bridewell family, on this occasion of your loss.

Yours truly,
F. Lewis, Attorney at Law
Lewis, Putnam & Bird

To Mr Lewis, Hereford:
20th May 1852
Abingdon

I write on my wife's behalf. Mrs Drake has received your communication, but we remain unsatisfied that we have been provided with a proper understanding of the circumstances. Though it could not be known to you, my wife and Miss Murphy were long estranged, and her residence in Herefordshire was not known to us (neither were we aware of Miss Murphy being unwell). I must, therefore, apply to you for further particulars, and would be gratified by your giving this matter your swiftest attention.

Yours respectfully,
William Drake

To Mr Lewis, Hereford:
23rd June 1852
Abingdon

It is more than a month since I first wrote to you concerning my wife's sister, Miss Murphy, and I am yet to receive news, a state of affairs which is entirely unsatisfactory. One cannot help but wonder at the delay, and ask whether this might not be part of an effort to sustain a deliberate scrimping on the facts. As a fellow man of business, you will be mindful, I am sure, of the economical use of time, and will appreciate that the quickest route to resolution will be the full disclosure of the events that led to Miss Murphy's passing. In a fortnight's time, if I remain unsatisfied, I will pass this matter to my attorney. We are determined to know the whole truth.

Yours respectfully,
William Drake

DEATH NOTICES

Unexpectedly, of Mr William Drake, 4th July 1852. Mr Drake, the well-known pottery merchant and local philanthropist, of Abingdon, Oxfordshire, was in his fifty-second year. Mr Drake established the poor school at Frithford, and was a valued member of the Baptist Church. All who knew him must mourn his passing. He is survived by his wife.

To Mr Drake, Abingdon:
6th July 1852
Hereford

Being but recently returned from business overseas, I only now find myself in a position to attend to your letters. I beg forgiveness for the delay, and hasten to explain matters.

In the first instance, my client felt moved to avoid exposing his daughter, a child of eight years, to notoriety. He was concerned bringing the incident to public notice would be further injurious to her. In the second, Sir Rowland at first believed Miss Murphy to have no surviving relations, and only in the aftermath of the tragedy was it disclosed that, in fact, she had one sister living. My client then feared that knowledge of the circumstances would be most acutely distressing to your wife, and it was his initial judgement that the details of Miss Murphy's death should not be known abroad. However, it has since become clear that any attempt, even where motivated by kindness, to obfuscate the truth risks more harm than it confers benefit. I have therefore secured his permission to send on a copy of the death certificate, countersigned by a doctor. The original resides with the Hereford Register Office.

I can only offer my further condolences to you, and especially to Mrs Drake. I would beg you to consider that, since the proverbial horse has bolted, and the likely outcome of a more candid disclosure between husband and wife will be further grief, it might be advisable for you to impart this news with the disturbing particulars removed.

Yours truly,
Fitzhugh Lewis, Attorney at Law
Lewis, Putnam & Bird

CERTIFICATE OF DEATH

When and where died: *15th April 1852, Locksley Abbey, Herefordshire*

Name and surname: *Emily Frances Murphy*

Sex: *Female*

Age: *25 years*

Occupation: *Governess*

Cause of death: *Self-inflicted*

Signature, description and residence of informant: *Sir Rowland Bridewell, Locksley Abbey, Herefordshire*

When registered: *18th April 1852*

Countersigned: *Frederick Sidstone, MD*

REQUIRED as GOVERNESS, having several years' experience, to a single child, girl, aged eight years. Applicant must thoroughly understand her business. Able to teach the usual strands of an English education, including music, needlework, French, arithmetic and use of the globes. A respectable, honest person, of good character. Satisfactory references. Paid at ten pounds per quarter. Direct to Mrs Parry, Housekeeper, Locksley Abbey, Herefordshire.

To Mrs Parry, Housekeeper, Locksley Abbey:
16th October 1852
Oxfordshire

In response to your advertisement in The Times, *I propose myself as a candidate for the position described. My situation is that I spent five happy years as private governess to an Oxfordshire family, but find myself needed no longer, as the boys are for school. Before being taken on by my current family, I was employed as a daily governess in Mayfair, where my charge was a girl. I served the family for three years, and was entrusted with all aspects of providing a typically English education, including the teaching of music, needlework, French, arithmetic and use of the globes. I am able to provide good references, and to travel into Herefordshire immediately.*

Yours faithfully,
Miss Catherine Symonds

I

The Black Mountains, Herefordshire
2nd November 1852

The last swallows were leaving. They flew swift and low, the dark gloss of their feathers glinting in the late-afternoon sun. Catherine was stiff and tired, eager to use the water closet, but the journey showed no signs of hurrying itself. The trap continued its rumblings over stones and tree roots, with one bad jolt forcing her to champ down on the soft flesh inside her cheek. She tasted coppery blood and tutted in annoyance, but the driver, Parry, huddled beside her in an ancient greatcoat, kept on exactly as before. She was inclined to tell him to take more care, but was acting the part of a lady, and a lady didn't do such things. Everything depended on playing her part well.

Every few minutes, her right hand moved to bother the spot beneath her lambskin glove where her wedding and mourning rings used to sit. The rings, a plain gold band and a diamond solitaire, were safe in her trunk, rolled up in a pair of stockings, but without them her hands felt bare as bones, and each repetition of the unconscious movement probed a mordant guilt because, having made her a wife only a year earlier, William, her husband, was dead. And what was worse, much worse, it was all her fault.

When she wasn't worrying at her fingers, her hands strayed inside her reticule to fuss the pages of her letters. These sheafs of paper were like an anchor, reminding her why she was here, and of a plan that allowed no room for error. They insisted that dwelling on William in the here and now was a mistake. To distract herself, she bit sharply into her cheek again, exploring the damage with the tip of her tongue. It felt ritualistic, pain as a forfeit.

She looked about her. Steadily over the last few hours they had climbed from the rolling Herefordshire plain into the hills. Now they were well above the flat sameness of those English fields, and rattled through tunnelled lanes lined with hedgerows of shining black bryony and wild rosehips, moving up and down with the shape of the land, but still gradually gaining in height. She remembered how, from below, these peaks had loomed like tidal waves, green-shadowed, hulking shapes crowned by a band of stubborn cloud. She had thought them unscalable, but now she realised the slope was flattening. The sturdy pony wheezed up a final stretch of ground as Catherine's bowler-hatted companion, stinking of tobacco and old-fashioned wash-fear, urged it on with flicks of the whip, and every few minutes sipped something pungent out of a tin flask.

'Is this the old Roman road?' she asked.

'It is,' came the reply, in a voice containing a noticeable burr.

She tried to orientate herself. They had to be well to the west, near the border with Wales, but she could not be more specific. Her father had lacked the means to send her to school past eight or nine. Their mother had taught her and Emily at home until she became too ill to do much at all, but later, after her own marriage, Catherine had picked up books in William's library. She recalled a map showing a great earthwork barrier running right down between the Irish and the Severn seas. These were embattled lands. Maybe this forest was there then. Maybe it remembered.

Inwardly, she snorted. Such nonsense. She wasn't here to dwell on the past. She would do better to rehearse her story.

She was Catherine Symonds. The Christian aspect of the name was her own, and the surname had leapt out to her from one of William's books. She was twenty-seven years old. A character? Yes, she had forwarded it. She hoped it hadn't gone astray? Of course, she would write immediately and have a replacement sent. It might take a couple of weeks to arrive, but if her prospective employer felt otherwise satisfied, it hardly made sense for her to return into Oxfordshire. *Very good, sir. I'll see to it straight away.*

She had practised in front of the mirror until her jaw ached.

The ruse was simple. When the idea had first taken shape, she had hardly expected it to work, but only five days after sending her proposal she had received a reply from the housekeeper at Locksley Abbey. The letter made the place sound very isolated. Mrs Parry advised that she was the only candidate, that it was the only big house for miles, and collection would be arranged for her at Hereford. Good, she had thought. The fewer people, the lower the chances of being caught. With only a few days to cover her tracks, she had concocted a story of a poorly cousin, and chosen a remote location in the north for the residence of this unhappy woman, so that if Mrs Catherine Drake was never heard of again, people would say, 'I heard she went into Yorkshire.'

The deception was worryingly thin. Even if it didn't arouse immediate suspicion, it wouldn't outlast a few weeks, and would unravel quickly when her character didn't arrive. But it offered a window of time. A narrow one, but a window, still, in which she might discover the truth.

The trap leapt again, the wheels throwing up a clod of earth, soft and damp, on her skirts. She brushed it off, then thought with horror of her appearance and did her best to clean her gloves against the side of the cart before straightening her bonnet, unseated by the wind, against her dark hair, careful to touch the fabric with the tips of her fingers only. As she turned her head, she noticed a smooth track branching off into the trees. It looked a fair prospect: better, at least, than the intolerable ruggedness of the road they were on. 'Is there no more gentle route, Mr Parry?' she asked.

He gave a short shake of his head. 'No other at all,' he said. 'Except the mine road, for coal. That one joins this.' She didn't think she imagined his disapproval; his lips flattened into a line and his brows lowered over his pitted nose at the thought of leaving the track.

'I didn't know there were mines here.' It accounted for the smell. They rumbled through a fading greenwood of oak, ash and beech, after rain, and all should have been wet leaves and rising musk, but something grittier rode the wind, something that might be explained by a band of men, not far away, perhaps digging right beneath her at this moment. She couldn't help picturing them huddled in small groups in the black damp, striking rock, dragging things long buried into the light. 'Are they deep, the mines?' she asked.

'Getting deeper. The master thinks they'll pay in the end.'

'And you don't?'

There was a long pause in which she glanced to her side and saw his face was set gravely, then he said, 'Sir Rowland don't answer to me. Might need to answer to Lady Anne,' he added. 'It's her father has the money.'

'Who is her father?'

'Uriah Caplin. A fortune in cotton. He's cheese-paring,' he added confidentially, though Catherine wasn't sure what he meant. He seemed to realise he had been indiscreet, and was silent for a while.

'Did you ever work in the mine?' she asked, after a few more minutes.

He spat over the side of the cart. 'Not me. I've worked at the big house since the old master's time.'

'Who was he?'

'Sir Maurice.' Then he added, 'My lad's a collier, mind.'

A son. She saw him in her mind's eye: bulbous-nosed, as big and unimaginative as his father, dirty with a slick of candle-lit sweat. They rolled on. The trees gathered thicker and the wind whistled through the branches. 'Did the wood grow over the mine?'

'Wood's always been here,' came the answer.

Rounding a bend away from the wind, they drove straight into the sun. It breathed gold over the tops of the trees. Nothing moved. She had the odd feeling that the forest observed their passing. There was something she didn't like about it. It was all too much. Even the vanishing flash of a squirrel's tail would break up the endless mottled green. Then, as if in answer to a prayer, a sudden baying rose over the hill. Startled, she said, 'What's that?'

'Master's dogs, driving the stag down,' Parry said gruffly. 'Don't go near 'em, if you want my advice. They're vicious as wolves.'

She hated the thought of being chased and worn down to nothing. Cornered. Anxious, she changed the subject. 'Are we near the house?' Another surge of agitation, stronger than the first, accompanied this thought. She wasn't ready. She could not carry this off.

'A few more miles.'

How many times, she wondered, had Parry driven a young woman of no family up these tracks, warned her to avoid the dogs, shared gossip about his employer? How many govern-esses of Locksley had there been before her? 'Did you know my predecessor?' she asked. He looked confused. She tried again. 'The governess before me?' Some obscure emotion clouded his grizzled face. 'Why did she leave her post?' She had to be careful, even with him. Rumour of Emily's fate would not have reached her in Oxfordshire. Not if she were who she claimed to be.

Parry's answer, though not a surprise, was brutal nevertheless. 'She didn't. She's dead.'

For some moments she could hardly breathe. The din made by the dogs, ferocious and exuberant, grew nearer. Eventually, she managed, 'How sad.' This was how you were meant to talk about the death of strangers. Vaguely, with proper sympathy, but not with heartbreak.

'Such a little thing …' Parry began.

It seemed he would say more, but just then, fifty yards ahead, the treeline released a brown shadow, liquid-limbed. It leapt across the track. A stag. Nothing had ever looked so at home, like the forest itself had sprung into life. Parry let out a cackle, and she was treated to the sweetness of hops on his breath. 'Did you see?' she said, too late. Before she could finish her question, it was gone, and her heart clamoured to go with it.

But that was impossible. She had to travel this road. The alternative was unthinkable: to remain awake each night for the rest of her life, heart palpitating, reaching for what she couldn't quite remember.

Ten minutes later, they left the old Roman road, turning sharply to the south, and the banshee cries of the dogs drifted away as they crested the plateau before the higher peaks. The path became serpentine and overgrown. Then something else cut into the silence. A shout. Someone called out a reply, and a dog yapped. Every reminder that there were other people here, that it was not as isolated as she had thought, brought another stab of fear. Any encounter, no matter how small, meant some new chance of being discovered.

'Men coming down out of the mine,' said Parry.

They swung round and arrived at a crossroads. A thin stream trickled along next to the road, and a thick ribbon of trees obscured the path ahead. Parry whistled the pony to the side, then uncapped his flask. Between sips, he said, 'Wait here. The pony needs water.'

She was tense and sore all over. She wanted to move. Most of all, she wanted to find a trunk and squat down beside it. 'I'll go to the stream,' she said. 'Here, pass me the bucket.'

Parry fumbled his flask. His hand clamped down on her arm, and she was surprised to see something set deep in his bleary eyes, something like fear, which gave her pause. 'A woman shouldn't go about in these woods alone,' he said carefully.

For an instant she felt doubt, then shook him off. 'It's trees and squirrels, Mr Parry. You're not suggesting I'll come to harm?'

'Not *harm*,' he said, more carefully still. 'But my mother with the angels would skin me alive if I let a lady go off on her own through those trees. There are legends about the wood,' he added. 'You don't want to get lost in there.'

'What legends?'

'The wood's always been here,' he said, repeating his claim from earlier. 'It don't belong to us.'

Lightly, she replied, 'It belongs to Sir Rowland, does it not?'

But Parry shook his head and said gruffly, 'Bit of paper. You can't own …' He stopped, seeming more resigned. 'Can't expect you to understand, not being from here. You've got to have grown up here. You've got to know the wood. I …' But he wouldn't say more, and slumped back in his seat, clutching the reins.

She thought of the superstitions of countryfolk, ghosts and hoary-headed men of the forest, simple stories, but told so many times and changing so often over the years that Parry could not even explain what worried him. 'Well, I insist on going,' she said, in the end.

He sighed at her determination. 'Go with the stream down the slope quite a bit. It's easier to dunk the bucket over there.'

He pointed away from the sun and she observed. The stream bed looked deeper where her gaze fell, with clear water rippling over rock. It looked tempting enough to drink, but the channel was steep-sided, and the water's surface appeared nearly out of reach. Still, she would have to try it, as she wanted to drink — and see to other things — without anybody watching.

Parry leant back in his seat as the pony investigated dangling weeds with blunt teeth. 'Don't go too far off the path.'

She didn't answer, and climbed down from the cart. Following the stream, the ground was more sheer than she had expected, thick with whorled roots and rough growth, carpeted with yellowing ash leaves. The bucket smacked against her leg. She imagined its weight coming back up the hill and knew she mustn't go too far. She nearly gave up the idea of attending to the call of nature, but that need was urgent, so she looked back, deciding she was not yet distant enough from the road, and carried on. After a few moments, Parry was out of sight and the quiet beneath the rusting canopy allowed her thoughts to rake her again. What if this was all a terrible mistake? What if Sir Rowland saw through her concealments immediately? What if — and this was the worst prospect — the letters from his man in Hereford had told the truth, and none of this charade was necessary?

No.

She pressed her eyes closed. These misgivings were not useful. She would soon know whether the lie would hold. In the meantime, she had only to keep her nerve. Besides, there had never been any real doubt. Emily would never have taken her own life.

In the weeks since William's death, after her first reading of Emily's death certificate, she had asked herself the same question hundreds of times. She asked it again now: how could she be sure? She hadn't seen Emily in twelve or thirteen years.

If she cast her mind back to when they were children, she remembered their home in Berkshire, in a plain country town where people made bricks. She could conjure up its cattle market and Congregationalists, its grasping merchants, her father's painting studio, her mother's warm chest. She could see Emily there, too, a little shadow full of temper and wiles, and fierce, rare affection. But then, where she might expect her picture of childhood to expand, gain depth and perspective, it refused to do so. Her memories remained fractured things, glints on cut glass that rose up in the seconds before sleep, then faded into darkness. She could not remember the cause of her estrangement from her sister. Emily had left, she was certain. Her mother had died, and then her father … She knew, or had discovered, what had become of Gilbert Murphy, but the precise order of events evaded her. At some point in her middle teenage years, she had left home and entered service. But exactly why, or whether Emily had gone before or after that, she could not say. She only knew she had not heard from Emily again, and had given her up for lost until the letters from Lewis, Putnam & Bird. Now even Emily's features were hazy. Sometimes she would pass a mirror and see a particular expression occupying her own face, and think – *there*! She looked like *that*. But these moments of recognition were rare and fleeting.

She had never really questioned these frayed edges. She assumed everybody lived with similar gaps and the pernicious guilt that went with them, and they did not seem strange until she began to consider some of the things she did not know: that she could not say where her sister had gone, or why, and she could not assemble the pieces of the puzzle of her own life. But still, she *knew*, viscerally, that Emily would not have killed herself. Someone at Locksley was lying, and she intended to see them brought to justice.

The stream split, flowing around a tiny eyot. One branch went nearly due west, down into the valley. She could have leapt across easily enough, but the ground that way was rougher, so she chose the other direction and went further into the thicket, treading a carpet of red and ochre leaves. She disturbed a drumming bird, just catching a flash of scarlet in its tail as it fled. Pausing by a sturdy oak, she rubbed her smarting back, looking about. Despite the changing season, her surroundings were dense and protective enough, so she attended to her clothing, pulling down her drawers and raising her petticoats. As she squatted, she thought about how Parry had called her a lady. Hardly.

She closed her eyes and listened to the warbling birds. There was a sudden breeze. It was welcome, flooding her lungs with air. She corrected her undergarments, then walked into the current. Emerging from the canopy, she found herself on a downward scree of rocky ground between the edge of the wood and a steep precipice, below which snaked the long road they had just climbed. She moved to the edge and looked down. The distant fields reminded her of her father's landscapes.

Without warning, Emily's voice sounded in her ear – *they're as flat as a rat under a hackney cab*. Memory, usually so parsimonious, grew unexpectedly lavish, bringing back her sister's clever fingers daubing vivid streaks of canary yellow and moss green on to her father's mundane efforts, giving animation to what had been committed to canvas without it. She saw her father, staggering drunk, stinking, pretending not to notice how the work was improved by the changes. How it had come to life without him.

Above her, an arrow of geese swept over the forest. The wind hurried off their harsh cries, and took her recollections with them. Turning away, she began to scramble back up the slope towards the treeline, and slipped.

2

'Hey!' someone shouted. Strong arms came about her middle, and she was waltzed away from the edge. The hands that released her as she was grounded looked like an old man's, as lined as a map, blue-scarred, with prominent knuckles and nails whittled down. She smelt sweat, dust and paraffin oil.

'All right, miss?' the newcomer asked. 'I've soiled your frock.' He revealed two dirty palms, holding them up as if in surrender.

He was perhaps twenty. He stood before her in sturdy boots and blackened canvas trousers, bare-chested, too young to have much hair on his body, with his cheeks and forehead sparkling with the earth's dust. In some way, clearly, she entertained him; though he tried to hide it, a half-grin made him impish. She smoothed her skirts, resenting his relaxed stance. Why did men get to do that? To look so comfortable in their bodies even as they uncovered them, when women carried such a burden of fabric? She stood straighter. He was not going to see her embarrassment.

'I was fine,' she said churlishly. 'There was no need for interference.'

This wasn't William's estate. Supercilious wouldn't work here. Flatten yourself. Be no one.

'Don't know about that, miss,' said the young man, undaunted. He looked about them, back up the wooded steep towards the road, then away, into the thicker mass of trees. 'But you don't want to be in this wood on your own.'

She said, more softly, 'I came down for water. I'm travelling with Mr Parry.'

'I'm Ned Parry. Parry's my dad. He thought you'd wandered off. Sent me down to find you.' At some point he had picked up the bucket from where she had left it, and said, 'Shall I fill this up? Don't know what he's about, sending a lady in here.'

'Why, is it haunted?' she said, not bothering to hide her scepticism.

He frowned. 'The forest comes round thick. I wouldn't want a woman on her own out here.' He glanced up at the slope again, his brows knitted together.

'It would be easy to get lost here,' she admitted.

Ned pointed to a place to collect water, and whistled as he bent down. 'Is it for the pony?'

She was so thirsty she could drink her own spit, but nodded. She wasn't going to drink from a bucket in front of him. That could get back to Sir Rowland. Even something as innocuous as that could raise his suspicions.

'Not thirsty?' he asked.

'I drank earlier,' she lied.

'Then the pony gets the lot. It's lucky, that one, out here in all this,' he said, gesturing to the trees. 'I handle the pit ponies, up at the mine. That's no life for an animal.'

It took her a moment to realise what he meant. 'They send ponies underground?'

'They do. Not women, not no more, or girls, not below ground. But ponies, they do. Just the little ones. Sometimes they take them down in harnesses. They wouldn't go otherwise, see.' The last words were said quietly.

'Then our pony is lucky, as you say,' she said, suddenly melancholy at the thought of the doughty beasts being lowered out of the sunlight.

Ned smiled again. 'You're working for Bridewell?' He didn't say *Sir Rowland*, she noticed.

'Yes.'

'Bet he takes the price of water out of your pay. I know a girl at the Abbey, and she says he's tight as a gnat's jenny.' He flushed. 'Sorry, miss.'

'Never mind.' To improve matters, she said lightly, 'Your sweetheart is at the Abbey?'

'One of them is.'

She laughed, unable to help herself. 'Scandalous!'

He strode along easily, one hand in his pocket. 'To tell you the truth, I met my real sweetheart in the West Country. There's no better place in the world. I'll go back one day.'

'But your father is local, isn't he?'

'That's right. I spent some time with my mother's people out there. But the work dried up. I'm not interested in mining. It's horses for me. I'd like to go into business for myself, as a horse-trader. Not that working for Bridewell will help me there. Like I say, he's tight. Don't say I didn't warn you.'

'I won't.'

She was breathless by the time they got back to the trap. Parry climbed down and offered Ned his flask. Ned took a deep draught. After a few seconds, the older man scowled and snatched it away from his son. 'Didn't have to empty it, did you?' Ned just laughed.

The two men talked quietly while a short procession of people came down the track from the crags above. Men and women walked together, with some ragged boys bringing up the rear. Like Ned, most of the men went bare-chested. Her eyes fell to the muscles of their torsos and the dark fuzz of their body hair. They wore wide-brimmed hats or flat caps like a uniform, but there was no clear rule for hair – long or short, shaggy or thin. To her surprise, the women carried sacks like the men, and wore trousers with tattered aprons tied over the top. Some had leather belts with hooks attached, and two of the sturdier amongst them dragged wheelbarrows. The lines that etched their foreheads were deep and ingrained with dirt. Blue scars like Ned's marred chests, arms, and legs where the trousers rode short. Most were as thin as cords. They watched her like she watched them. The children pointed at her dress, the one she hadn't thought too fine for a governess. Nearing the trap, still staring, they unbuckled their belts and settled across the path. They seemed happy to sit anywhere. From pockets and bags they pulled tins of bread and cheese, which they ate in a hurry.

Behind her, the pony slurped the water and Ned's hands wandered in its mane. He spoke to his father. 'Had to do for two of 'em today. Black lung. Poor creatures couldn't go no further.' Parry didn't answer, and Ned's fingers worked the rough hair.

A hard voice came across the stream. 'Time!' The workers started to rise, but Ned kept his back to the speaker. The call came again. Catherine peered through the trees, searching for the owner of the voice.

Parry held out his arm for the bucket. 'You'd better go, lad. Dowle doesn't like being kept.'

'Bugger him,' muttered Ned.

'Time!'

At last, the speaker moved into view. He was big, sporting an auburn thatch across his chin and throat. As he approached, those on the ground shuffled away, but one young boy was too slow and caught a cuff across the back of his head. The victim scrambled to join his fellows, calling to a black terrier, still yapping, 'Coke! Here, boy!' Dowle came on. He walked with a slight bow to his knees, but still dwarfed the others. Stepping over the water, he adjusted a pipe in his heavy-jawed mouth, revealing leonine teeth, and stopped, hands deep in the pockets of his twills, close enough to the cart that the watching workers saw the target of his impatience: Ned.

Ned shot a glance at his father. 'Harris called a meeting tonight,' he said. 'We're—'

'Shut up,' said Parry gruffly. 'Till you reach home.' Ned nodded, he and his father gripped hands, then separated.

Dowle herded the others with curt orders. The women strapped themselves to the carts and the men shouldered sacks of tools or coal. 'Ned Parry, if your arse isn't at the head of this line in ten seconds, I'll have your ticket,' called Dowle. Turning to the cart, he eyed Catherine, saw the mud on her skirts, and smirked.

'Turd-arsed prick,' muttered Ned, into the pony's mane. He no longer seemed to care if Catherine heard. 'Today he—'

But Dowle was reaching into a leather satchel by his side. Before Ned could move, Dowle was thumbing through a small notebook, squinting like he could hardly read it. He took out a stubby pencil. Seeing this, Ned straightened. 'Coming, aren't I?' he said, giving the pony a final pat. The pencil scratched the paper. Ned said, 'Mr Dowle, you can't change what I got today, that's against regs.' His face glowed. Dowle carried on. Ned said, 'You can't change that!' He looked round. 'Lads! Tell him. What I got is what I got, isn't it? Can't be changed now.' Twenty pairs of eyes drifted to the ground, and the confidence drained from Ned's words.

Dowle scraped his tongue across his bottom lip. His eyes showed a piggy cunning. 'Not what it says here.' He held up a square of pale green paper, black with fingerprints and ink, covered in indecipherable marks. Ned seized it.

'This isn't right,' Ned said, glaring at the numbers. 'I hewed seven shillings' worth today. I worked my arse off.' He looked up from the paper. 'Mr Dowle, this isn't right.' He sounded more conciliatory, but a rancorous undertone clung on.

The overman spat, some of the liquid webbing his beard. 'It's right,' he said. 'We get this load over before sundown, or I'll do the same tomorrow. And next time you think of moving slower than a stuck shite, you'll think again, won't you?'

Now what passed over Ned's face was ugly. He clenched his teeth and breathed hard out of his nose. 'We deserve better than you,' he said impetuously.

Dowle stalked within three paces of the cart. Catherine's breath caught in her throat, Parry twitched, and Ned watched his aggressor with a mixture of contempt and fear. Next to Dowle, he looked very young. There was a space into which he could have stepped back, but he didn't. For a second or two, Dowle ground his hand against his chin, then he struck out, hitting Ned below his right eye socket. Blood erupted and Ned shouted, bringing his palm to his face. Dowle paused, then kicked Ned near his groin, forcing another cry. Parry jerked in his seat, almost involuntarily, but Ned grunted, 'Leave it.'

Don't do anything, Catherine told herself. But what could she do anyway, even if it were possible to intervene without ruining her own plans? Dowle was a juggernaut. The overman drew back his arm for a second blow, Ned cringed, and Dowle jabbed like a boxer, splitting the collier's lip. Catherine couldn't help what she did next. As Dowle seized Ned's collar, she shouted, 'Leave him alone!'

Stupid, so stupid, she thought, even as she got between them. You weren't supposed to make trouble. At least not for yourself.

Dowle paused, considering his new opponent.

'You won,' Catherine said softly. 'He's not fighting you.'

Dowle weighed her up. She was a woman, and so below him, but by her dress and manner, nearly a lady, and so above. In reality, Catherine thought, governesses had no influence over anyone, which was why she travelled in a dirty cart, fetching buckets of water. Still, she guessed the overman knew little about governesses. She drew herself up straight, assuming the expression she was meant to be avoiding, the one she used to wear when her servants looked at her like she might still be one of them.

Behind them, Parry dipped his arm into the footwell of the trap and came out with a rough cloth, which he dampened and handed to Ned for his eye. Ned winced with its sting.

'Get back in line,' Dowle said finally, apparently deciding he had done enough to press home the lesson.

The blood-soaked cloth muffled Ned's response as he fell in with his fellows.

Parry clicked to the pony. As they drove on, Catherine turned on him. 'You didn't stand up for him,' she said, furious. 'That man's a brute and you did nothing.'

Parry shook his fuzzy head.

'What?'

'You don't know what you're saying, girl,' came the resigned answer. 'You can't fight the overman. You'll learn, if you're round these parts long enough.'

Behind them, the line of men, women, boys and carts lumbered by, and out of sight.

3

Coming here was a mistake, Dr Arthur Sidstone realised, as Sir Rowland's face turned puce and his balled fist descended on a hardwood desk piled high with letters and invoices. His words were flecked with spittle. 'My God, if you had said "Frederick Sidstone" when you arrived, you would have been out on your ear. I should throw you through those doors right now. Your grandfather? The pompous old devil.'

Arthur glanced at the double doors opening on to the east terrace. They were paned glass, rather heavy. He winced, regretting his slip a few moments ago in mentioning his grandfather's involvement. Some men were silver-tongued. Not him. Every time he opened his mouth, it seemed, it was to propel a foot into it.

He had only been in Sir Rowland's study about ten minutes before things went downhill. Arriving on time with an appointment for a short interview, he had produced letters from Sir Monty Cottrell, chairman of the county canal syndicate. Arthur's grandfather, Frederick, had doctored to the villages around Locksley and Hern for decades before his effective retirement earlier in the year, so Cottrell had not hesitated to give an endorsement to his grandson, though Arthur had been in the Indies from a young man, and Cottrell had never actually met him. He had only been back on English soil these three months.

Still, the device had been necessary. Sir Rowland was known to be a snob, unlikely to hear the petition of a lowly medical man just to be a good neighbour. Now Arthur had seen the baronet had a bad temper as well, it seemed even less likely they would reach an accommodation.

A few minutes earlier, he had been ushered in by the housekeeper, who knocked on the study door several times before the occupant barked, 'What?'

It was early afternoon, long-shadowed outside but not yet dark, nor particularly cold, but the study blazed with a huge fire, and candles and oil burnt in the chandelier overhead. The result was that the room was far too hot, but Arthur was not encouraged to hand over his coat; the housekeeper, when he turned to hear the click of the door, had disappeared.

He stood poker-straight, trying to look self-possessed as Sir Rowland looked him over before scanning the letter. Folding it, the baronet said, 'What can I do for you, then?'

Arthur related the beginnings of the problem. He had learnt that much of the forest around Locksley, including the area known locally as the Puzzle Wood, was to be cut down and the land sold off.

'So?' came the brusque reply.

Cautiously, he explained that not only did his grandfather's cottage sit on the forest's southern boundary, but the trees themselves were ancient, the site of folktales from his childhood, part of the landscape for as long as memory served. In short, he wished to know whether the wood could be saved. This last hope was uttered a little awkwardly. The wood belonged to Locksley absolutely, and its owner could do with it what he liked.

'What's this to you?' asked Sir Rowland. He rose and opened a lacquered drinks cabinet, arranged glasses, then poured whisky for himself and angled a second glass towards Arthur, who shook his head, adding thanks. With his back to his guest, Sir Rowland drained the glass without ceremony.

'Well,' began Arthur, 'the wood is old and …' He realised he had not planned what he was going to say. 'There are said to be several unusual features – cairns and barrows, and the like, and some of the oldest trees in the Borders, and we felt …'

This was where he made his first mistake. At *we*, Sir Rowland turned sharply. He glanced down at the letter again. When he spoke, his voice had tightened. 'Cairns and barrows? You're a Sidstone? Of Hawk's Leap Cottage? He sent you, then?'

Arthur had not intended to lie, just to wait until he and Sir Rowland had built up a rapprochement, but it was too late now. He shook his head. 'Not sent me. But I'm here on his behalf.'

His discomfort grew. He had known since setting out from Hawk's Leap that he could not tell the complete truth, that his grandfather was not just exercising an old man's prerogative in disliking the realities of progress. For reasons his grandson did not fully understand, Frederick Sidstone was truly afraid. He spent hours and hours with his books each day, dwelling on the matter of Locksley, the wood, and the mine beneath. Arthur was certain he took sedatives to quell bad dreams. But when he had tried to discuss it, and work out more precisely what his grandfather was afraid of, Frederick had shaken his head and busied himself with his papers. So, after giving the matter much thought, and wanting to ease Frederick's mind, finally Arthur had decided to come here today and make a last-ditch appeal to the baronet.

He had no intention of telling Sir Rowland any of this. He suspected the root of his grandfather's terrors was no more than a countryman's long love of myth and superstition, married to the creeping imperatives of age, but these details were not the baronet's business.

Sir Rowland, pouring himself another glass, said, 'You know the old puddle duck attended my wife last year? Not that he made a bit of difference. He made things worse, if anything.'

Arthur hadn't known, and now wondered why his grandfather had not told him. 'I suppose I—'

'Look.' The baronet reached into a drawer and pulled out a bundle of letters, flinging them one by one on the desk. 'The Society of Antiquaries, the Monmouthshire Association, the British Archaeological Association, the Cambrian Society. Years of this, I've had. His letters are like a plague of locusts, demanding I refrain from cutting down trees on my own property, that I put an end to the mining operation.' He pointed at one of the papers. 'Here he is rambling about spirits and relics and God only knows what else. He's a cracked pot.'

Arthur, never quick with words, especially in anger, found himself tripping over his tongue. 'Well, I don't—'

'You're here under false pretences, not showing your hand except in error. It's not the behaviour of a gentleman. Now I know the reason. You can tell your grandfather to refrain from sending more letters – as you can see, I have enough to manage.' He threw Cottrell's letter on the pile with a last sarcastic flourish.

'I should leave you, sir,' said Arthur shortly. 'I'm sorry to have taken up your time.' He looked at the stack again, having had no idea there were so many, regretted coming, and was relieved at the thought of getting away.

Sir Rowland was still on his feet, turned towards the French doors. He stared into the grounds, muttering something about it getting late, and needing more lights, and at that moment, two figures entered the study.

The first slipped in like a shadow, the top of her head hardly brushing the handle. She was about eight years old, mousy hair tied back tight, and wore a stiff white collar below a saturnine frown. Behind her, wearing lees-of-wine, the shade a little too bright, came a tall woman with fair curls below a receding hairline. She was as pale as Sir Rowland – or as he was before his shouting fit. Wispy brows framed protuberant eyes, which darted between the two men at the windows. Her mouth was ill-made, but she had a handsome, straight nose, not unlike the baronet's.

'You knew I wasn't to be interrupted, Grizel,' said Sir Rowland, barely looking over his shoulder. 'Take her to the nursery, won't you?'

'She will not go.' Arthur wasn't sure he liked the scowl she directed at the child, who regarded her father in silence.

'What do you mean, *will not*?' Arthur expected the child to shrink away, but she didn't. 'Are you in charge of her or not? She'll do as she's told or I'll have Mrs Parry thrash her again. What has she done, anyhow?'

'She has assembled a large collection of mice and released them in the kitchen, to the terror of the servants.'

'I was studying them,' said the little girl stolidly. 'They're all different, you see. Different weights and shades. Some are fawn-coloured, but some are more like silver, or even red. But they escaped from the box,' she said, her sentence ending on a wistful note. 'I tried to catch them again, but they were too quick.'

'They couldn't have escaped the box,' came the woman's sharp reply. 'Mice can't open boxes for themselves.'

'They can, too,' said the child, her lowered brow the very match for her father's. 'I watched them and they worked together to lift the lid. They're clever.'

Arthur suppressed a smile.

'See how impudent she is, Rowland?' said the woman, in frustration.

'Take her back upstairs,' the baronet said, with a sigh.

'You won't punish her?' asked Grizel.

'Reprimand her as you see fit.'

'I won't stoop to thrashing her myself – that's a servant's job,' she complained, her voice reaching a whine. 'You must tell Mrs Parry—'

'You don't need my permission to instruct the servants,' came the answer. Arthur wondered whether that was true. What was her position, really? He had spent nearly every holiday in this valley as a boy, but didn't remember a girl living at Locksley. Sir Rowland addressed her by her Christian name, so she wasn't a governess or companion. She had bristled at the idea of thrashing the little girl, not for its own sake, but because she thought it beneath her. And she had a look of the Bridewell family, yet Sir Rowland's discourtesy suggested a more distant relationship. Perhaps she was a cousin, he decided.

A sheen was visible on Grizel's upper lip. Arthur became more aware of the heat in the room, every bit as uncomfortable as the sultry days he had hated in the East. Grizel's eyes flitted between the two men. 'She has been telling tales again, Rowland, and now her nonsense has disturbed the staff.'

'Not now.' Sir Rowland's voice was sharper.

'We can't let her carry on putting such stories about. You should lend me more authority with her, Rowland. You know how I'm a slave to her every need, and I really think—'

'I'm not the least bit interested what you think. I've told you, a new governess arrives this afternoon, and will take over Georgie's care.'

Hurt twisted her lips. Arthur could see now that she was older than he'd first thought. Fine lines around her mouth placed her at least in her mid-thirties. She said, 'Must you be so unfeeling? I want what is best for Georgie, and believe I am much better placed than a governess—'

'Grizel, I have a *guest*. Take her out of my sight.' During this time, he had not looked at the child once. Arthur, though he had little experience with children apart from the occasional lethargic infant, felt it a shame.

Grizel mumbled to herself as she retreated, guiding Georgie by her shoulder.

'Grizel?' Sir Rowland said.

'Yes?' came the reply, hopeful.

'The passages are still too dark. Tell Mrs Parry to light more candles. And more logs on the fires. There's an arm coming loose on the entrance-hall chandelier. Get it mended. The whole house is to be brightly lit. I don't want to see a single shadow.'

Hearing all this, Arthur felt beneath his collar. Not exactly out of the top drawer – it had been a long time since he had money for new clothing – it felt damp and clammy. Smoke from the chimney stung his eyes. The wind must have shifted direction, but the fire kept up its ardour.

Grizel seemed pleased to be given a purpose. 'Yes, of course,' she said, nodding. The door closed behind them.

Arthur, still keen to leave, retrieved his hickory cane and looked about for his hat, relishing the prospect of fresh air.

'Wait! Perhaps I was too hasty.' The baronet's voice was cajoling.

Arthur waited as his host sank back into a leather chair and released a breath. 'Look, things have been rather fraught. Do you know the estate's position?'

'No.'

Sir Rowland eyed a portrait above the fireplace. Its subject was a man, one vaguely familiar to Arthur. He realised he was looking at the Bridewell patriarch, Sir Maurice. His grandfather used to talk about him, and Arthur half-remembered him from his boyhood, a tall, well-built figure on horseback, not unlike the son. Now, as he examined the face that loomed above them, he thought he saw more than he had then: a cruelty about the mouth, perhaps, something arrogant in the eyes. But he might have been imagining both.

Sir Rowland said, 'My father has taken up his retirement in Italy, so I am yet to inherit outright.' He turned away from the painting. 'But he prefers me to use the title, and has handed me full control; he does not expect to return to England, so it's up to me to improve Locksley's fortunes.' His brows knitted together. 'I don't know how much your grandfather told you of my wife's condition, but she is unwell, confined to her rooms in the west tower. There have also been –' there came a pause '– incidents. A few happenings that have set me on edge.' He rearranged some papers, and Arthur felt the older man was avoiding his eyes. 'The colliery is a full-time concern, and Mrs Wingfield is struggling to manage my daughter.'

Perhaps she was his sister after all if she was expected to care for the child, Arthur thought. Strange that his grandfather had never mentioned a female child of the old baronet.

Sir Rowland continued. 'That's why I engaged a governess, to give Georgiana more stability.' He halted a few moments. 'Look,' he said again, 'there's something you might help me with.'

Warily, Arthur nodded. 'Go on.'

'I need a capable man to take on a problem.' He left the chair and paced the oriental rug. 'The mine isn't yielding as it might. I employ a foreman, Dowle, but it's far from ideal. We're isolated here, and there are few men of the better cloth, so I have to make do with Dowle's sort. The truth is, he's too close to the type of man that makes a collier to progress my interests.'

Arthur spoke hesitantly. 'I know nothing about mining.' He felt the sting that came with telling lies. He did know about mining – not as much as a collier would, but as much as a man who had lived with colliers and doctored to them might. But he could not tell Sir Rowland of his experiences. The gentry here had not forgotten the disarray of thirteen years ago; it would be dangerous, even now, to admit his brief flirtation with Chartism. 'Is there any reason you wouldn't look into this yourself?' he asked.

'I'm stretched thin,' answered Sir Rowland, a fretful note entering his voice. 'My father is away, as I explained. My father-in-law has been ill, and my daughter has had a difficult time. Truly, it's an advantage that you're not a collier. This is better suited to your abilities.'

Without warning, impressions entered Arthur's head. Roughened palms beneath nimble fingers; blackened nails; the sweet, strong smell of sweat on skin. He applied all his effort to push them away, blurting out the words before he could help it: 'What sort of man makes a collier, then?'

'A low man. A man good for digging in dirt, not politics.'

Carefully, Arthur nodded, but said, 'I wouldn't know where to begin.'

'What have you been doing in the East? The army?'

'Batavia. My grandfather had contacts in the Governor-General's office. I was able to get a medical post out there.'

'Why did you go? Couldn't get work here?' chuckled Sir Rowland.

Arthur hated this sort of teasing, the quips and verbal swordplay his host had probably mastered at school, then in parties of landed young men who never tired of pricking at one another. 'I ...' he began, not knowing what to say.

But Sir Rowland waved away his own questions. 'I'm joking, Sidstone. Pull the poker out, there's a chap. When did you head out?'

''Thirty-nine.'

'A difficult year,' said Sir Rowland. He looked up at the portrait again. Then he said, 'After Newport, my father's heart went out of being a landowner. Too many of his friends and their families were threatened by the sort of men I employ now – perhaps some of the very same men – and the prospect of revolution – a real revolution, not just a petty uprising – came too near. He wanted his seat in the sun.' He paused for a moment, and Arthur did too, remembering the events of that febrile year. 'So as I said, I need a man like you. The miners are organising again.

One of the pit men, John Harris, is definitely involved in stirring things up. I'm determined to allow no agitating and I'm opposed to any sort of collectivism. If they want to harp on about wages, secret ballots and the like, they can – it's a free country – but they can find employment elsewhere. They're paid enough – too well paid, if you want the truth – and it leaves them looking for trouble. I want to remind them this is Monmouthshire, not Boston or Paris. Or Newport, for that matter.'

This speech roused unwelcome emotions, but Arthur managed to cover them and said, 'I'm not sure what you think I can do to help. I know next to nothing about mining. And you've been clear that you don't regard me exactly as a gentleman, so can I assume, by extrapolation, that the action you wish me to undertake is ungentlemanly?'

Sir Rowland skirted the desk, stood alongside Arthur and put an arm about his shoulders. Now he was closer, Arthur could detect a slight odour of stale perspiration. 'Come, now. I spoke in temper. I know you're the right sort, in fact the very man for this job. And it would be paid. Not practising yet, are you?'

Arthur admitted he was not. 'I returned from the Indies so recently, I haven't had a chance to develop much of a clientele.' It was true: his purse was a sorry-looking affair. Any money offered by Sir Rowland would be a help.

'So you're perfectly situated to take this on for me,' said Sir Rowland.

'*This* being what, exactly?'

His host raised two fingers. He gripped the first. 'One, Dowle. Is he thieving? Is he the man to run my mine?' He shifted to the second. 'Two, name the men working against me in secret, along with any other information you can gather about their plans. Answer those questions for me, as my deputy, with my permission to go anywhere and ask anyone anything, and I'll sit down with your grandfather on the Puzzle Wood. I can't make promises. We're entering lean times. Clearing the forest would allow a railroad to move the coal more cheaply, and permit a new section of canal. Progress can't be sacrificed, but I'll listen, and we'll see if a compromise can't be reached.'

Finally Arthur agreed, but couldn't help thinking, with a degree of dread, of miners and their secrets. As Sir Rowland offered a drink and this time he accepted, a dull feeling at the base of his stomach said he would think better of it.

4

Catherine's ears rang with the howls of the dogs. She looked away from the stag with her stomach heaving as Sir Rowland, a hard satisfaction in his face, plunged his hunting knife deep into the sinew of the animal's neck. He pulled. Its eyes rolled back in its head as it died, shuddering. Catherine felt outside herself, as if someone else had watched it reel and stumble, and now waited for its muscular form to fall still.

The trap had descended the steep valley, crossing a small arched bridge over a rocky riverbed. They had climbed a track on the opposite side, eventually joining a cedar-lined drive approaching Locksley Abbey. Rather than taking her straight to the door, Parry had suggested he should first find Sir Rowland. They had circled the grounds behind the Abbey and now stood on the edge of the deer course, an expanse of meadow sloping eastward, towards the river. From here, her first full view of the house was from the back. She saw a sprawling place nestled in a dip between two forested slopes. A mock-turreted tower faced west, part of an older, red-brick structure that seemed to lurk behind the newer sections. The whole thing had a faded grandeur about it. She felt a sadness, but was not sure whether she was coming to it, or if she had brought it with her.

She had dismounted the cart and waited a hundred yards from where Sir Rowland stood with several men. Parry mumbled to the pony, which stomped and snorted, unsettled by the slaughter. The stag must have bled out quickly, but to her tired eyes the flow of blood appeared impossibly sluggish, and the patch around the fallen beast was black as tar. The huddled brown form taunted her, the rawness of the scene disturbing some memory – she could not hold on to the feeling, but had a sense of having witnessed something like it before.

It's nothing.

How tired she was. And so thirsty.

Before their arrival, the stag would have been flushed out and hemmed in by the dogs, but they had been called in by Sir Rowland, each handed off on a heavy chain to be held by shabby-coated men.

'What are they?' she muttered, almost to herself, but Parry heard.

'Alpine mastiffs,' he said, watching as she counted five of the huge creatures hauling at their chains, long-legged and brindle-coated. Parry said their names: Zeus, Apollo, Dionysus, Tartarus, Morpheus. He explained, 'Old Sir Maurice brought them back from his travels. He showed their dam in Liverpool. They say they're the biggest dogs either side of the border.'

Catherine could believe it. They were truly enormous. As if their size alone didn't make them fearsome, someone had hacked away the soft parts of their ears, giving their heads a skull-like appearance, emphasising their black, drooling mouths. *Don't go near 'em*, Parry had said. She would take that advice gladly.

A few seconds earlier, once the quarry was exhausted and came to open ground, Sir Rowland had taken his shot. She had seen it. They had pulled to a halt not far from where he stood with the gun steadied against his shoulder. He was not alone, but accompanied by a dark-haired man, tall and oddly dressed for a hunt, in the high collar of a stockbroker or bureaucrat. The tall man had leapt back as the stag lurched past with the dogs in pursuit. She heard its exhausted grunts, as rhythmic as pistons, as it tried, with increasing desperation, to evade their snapping jaws on all sides. After a few minutes its laboured sounds became hoarse; it tired and stood at bay. Sir Rowland hit high. The creature convulsed as he bent over it holding his knife. Rising a few moments later, he laughed toothily and clapped his companion on the back with his free hand before wiping the bloodied blade on light-coloured corduroys. She noticed the tall man's smile was thin.

Then she watched the animal. Part of her thought it might spring up roaring, and life effervesce again in its veins, but there was no miracle. The dogs surged, then were held back as the oldest keeper came on with his knife, hauling the kill on its back, gaining access to the heart and entrails. Then, as Sir Rowland noticed their arrival and strode towards the trap, the weapon came down again and the reek of blood and innards filled the air. The keeper's motions were quick, businesslike; his was a curt, practical violence.

Sir Rowland had passed off the gun to one of the handlers. Sweating beneath a fair, unruly widow's peak, he rubbed a sleeve against a prominent nose. He was handsome in a sportsman-like fashion, with full beard and sideburns, but fleshy, suggesting he dined too well. The high colour of exertion had begun to die back, and as he got closer, she saw how, despite the smile plastered on his lips, over the rest of his face a pallor held sway.

The dark-haired man followed him up the slope. Next to Sir Rowland, he looked out of his element. He had a mournful expression, but the longer she observed, the more this seemed native to him; more, anyway, than Sir Rowland's conviviality.

'Parry!' The baronet panted. 'Should have gone the long way round.'

Parry tipped his hat. 'Beg your pardon, sir,' he said. 'Didn't know you were still out.'

The dogs were salivating, the air heavy with the tang of dung and blood. 'Magnificent, aren't they?' Sir Rowland said, turning his gaze to the pack and addressing his gangly companion, who nodded politely. 'My father bred them, but I've appreciated them still more since the Rising – an Englishman never knows when he might need to defend his castle, eh?' He winked, and the tall man's mouth twitched in another thin smile. Catherine noticed something in that smile – sadness? – at the mention of what she was sure had to be the Newport Rising, when vast numbers of Welsh colliers had rebelled against their masters. It had to have been at least a decade ago. She wondered why he looked like that. He certainly did not seem to share the baronet's grim pleasure at the sight of the dogs.

The host glanced back at the stag. 'Well, he gave us the runabout. Still, he's caught now.' He looked Catherine over, evaluating. She wanted to hide, in case he saw … But that wouldn't work. She had to pass his test in this moment, or it was over. She ducked her head, raising her eyes as far as his chin. Beneath his bluff exterior, she thought she detected strain. 'You're Miss Symonds?' he said.

'Yes, sir.' *Be still*, she ordered the cawing, scratching panic inside. All she had to do was inhabit her role, be exactly what he expected.

There was something about the way he looked at her. Something that just notched the strands of her memory, and pulled them. As if she had seen him before. But that could not be.

He said, 'Take Miss Symonds in by the east door and show her to my study.' He paused, noting her dusty attire. 'I will attend you shortly. Come, Sidstone. We'll finalise things before we dine.'

Her heart was in her throat. Surely that could not be the extent of his scrutiny? Just this? As they turned away, she looked down at the mud on her shabby dress. It was perfect, she realised. She was the very incarnation of an impoverished governess.

As Parry led her away, behind them the pack fought over the entrails, and she shuddered.

Later, with her open trunk sitting in front of the door, she collapsed on the bed, her corset loosened, feeling the springs of the mattress digging into the lines of her body. It was too hot. The whole house seemed full of fires and glaring light. She could still hear the mastiffs in their kennels, their racket too high to be kept out completely by the thin casement.

She let her eyes close.

Across the nation, on country estates, in townhouses, young women like her lay down just like this, on lumpy mattresses on iron-framed beds, planning for the vicissitudes of an existence without capital. They were women of education and birth. Their fathers might be gentlemen and curates, but they had no fortune. Like her, they had dragged their own trunks up a progression of narrowing staircases, past the best rooms, then the rest, while a po-faced housekeeper warned them not to burn too much coal. Then, on being admitted to a poky room abutting the attics, they allowed the door to creak shut and realised they were at the mercy of others, dependent on their good opinion. Trapped.

But she wasn't trapped. She had bought the cheap trunk for a purpose. She did not rely on the pittance Sir Rowland proposed to pay, and money lay concealed in the lining paper, stuffed in stockings beside the letters Lewis, Putnam & Bird had sent to William. This last was a risk. She had nearly left the bundle behind, but if there was to be any hope of the police investigating matters at Locksley, she had no choice. She had to be able to prove her identity. The letters demonstrated her relationship with William and her connection with Emily, and Emily's connection with Locksley.

Yet thinking of the letters made her think of William, and wish them a thousand miles away.

It was useful being someone else. It allowed her, sometimes, to forget what she had done. Why William had died. He had been so good to her, so much better than she deserved, but in the end she had stretched his love for her beyond its breaking point. What he had discovered …

Standing, she moved to the trunk and slammed it shut, tightening its buckles and turning the key in the lock. Hauling it across the boards, she managed to squeeze it under the bed. Now it was contained. Good. She needed her focus on what she had come here to do. No matter what, she would discover what happened to Emily. Then perhaps she would be able to forgive herself.

She sat back on her heels. When she had entered the room she had been numb, hardly aware of her surroundings, but now she examined them. Hers was a small chamber on the nursery passage, at the join of the south and west wings. The air smelt faintly of mildew, and her nostrils were tickled by floating dust. It was papered as if it had once been part of the nursery, in a childish pattern of leaves, moths and cocoons. From all four walls the insects stared at her, their eyes artificially huge, wings dark and shining. A moth's cocoon was made of skin, she remembered distantly.

There was a connecting door so she might go in and out to Georgie, and a low, deep-set window. Apart from the bed and fireplace, the room's contents comprised a single wardrobe, a hip bath and washstand, a desk complete with scratches and ink stains, and a spindly plant on the sill next to a water jug, bone dry with a dead spider huddled at its base. Considering this for a moment, she took the key to her trunk and placed it in the plant pot, half-buried in the parched soil.

As she paced the creaking boards, other thoughts consumed her. She revisited every word uttered since her arrival. The most innocuous revelation might be fatal. Had she given anything away to Ned, or the Parrys? Had she looked at Sir Rowland's stringy guest in the wrong way? All the means by which she might have betrayed herself rose up to taunt her, and in response she slowed her breath to a crawl as her physician had taught her after William's death, when she found it was the only thing that stopped the guilt tightening her chest until she thought she, too, would die. Covering her mouth with her hands, she sucked in air through her fingers, rationing it like a drowning person.

You're just a governess, she told herself. Beneath their attention. She had to keep her faith that they would overlook her.

She thought of her meeting with Sir Rowland about an hour ago. In his private study, her new employer had offered her his hand. Looking at it, she had recalled how his fingers had dripped with the stag's viscous blood, but now they were clean and smooth, the nails filed to neat half-moons. Extending her own gloved hand, she had imagined that, somehow, in touching her, he might recognise the shape of the other, sense her clinging shadow, but the contact was brief and absent of any spark of knowledge.

The study was dark, masculine, with thick Eastern carpets and wing-backed chairs of pea-green leather. The Bridewell crescent, a bull facing a stag, adorned a relief carving below the mantelpiece. She picked out a motto: *nec terra nos tenere potest.* The words seemed familiar, as if they should mean something to her. *Terra*, she knew, was something to do with the earth ... But she could go no further.

The fire blazed too hot, and a few escaped embers lay on the hearth. She noted a globe, a fruitwood desk littered with paper, and above that, a portrait of someone long-backed and stern-looking, attired in the fashions of the previous century. She soon realised he resembled Sir Rowland. Most of the other pictures were of horses with burnished coats, surrounded by liver-coloured dogs. Between the frames lay faded vermilion paper mounted with heads and bodies. Scaly piscine flesh, feathers in the russet hues of autumn, and summer-velveted antlers crowded her as Sir Rowland looked down at her letter. He read, then regarded her over the rim of his eyeglasses.

'Good,' he said, after several long seconds. A brief frown passed over his face. Was he going to ask for her character? 'You can start immediately?'

'As soon as you like, sir.'

Sitting in the shadow of the bay window, he kept turning his head, gazing out towards the dark hills like he was looking for something, or waiting. Between these bouts of watchfulness, he asked about her family. She navigated this well enough, telling him about her birth and parentage, the progression of her parents to Heaven, and – with this being her only real falsehood – their prompt pursuit there by her only sister.

Sir Rowland gave over a few moments to curriculum. '*Qui vous a appris à parler français?*'

'*Ma mère.*'

'Use of the globes?'

'Yes, sir.'

'You know your Bible?'

'I would hope so.'

'And the usual girls' ...' he paused, flourishing his right hand, 'accomplishments?'

'I'm competent in drawing, needlework and deportment, sir.'

He nodded. 'Georgie needs a gentlewoman to show her how to conduct herself. It's all very well having Mrs Parry, and Mrs Wingfield, but ...' He removed his eyeglasses and set them down, looking out of the window for some time as she waited. At last, he regarded her again. She expected he saw what he wished to see: respectability, relative youth, some measure of health and, most desirable of all, self-containment. Here was a neat, continent sort of woman. One who would not need management. Yes, she saw him decide; she would do. Tapping his fingers on the arm of the chair, he said, 'Will you take the position?'

'I will, sir.'

'Do you have any questions?'

Questions rattled about, eager to get out and press him, but she denied them. 'No, sir. I'm sure the ways of the house will become clear to me in time.'

Satisfied, he rose and rang a bell, then picked up a decanter a third of the way full of something the colour of rich dark wood. He placed a heavy glass on the desk and poured a glug of the liquid. Then he turned to her. 'You'll have a drink?'

'What?' The word was out before she could stop herself as his odd question echoed in her mind. Like the Latin, she felt it had some greater significance than she understood. But how could it? She had never been here before. She recovered, saying, 'I mean, no, sir. I won't, thank you.'

'One more thing,' he said with his back to her. 'My wife.' He faced her again, and his cheeks were as pale as bleached bones. She had a feeling – and she could not have justified it – that he was somehow out of his depth. Her father used to look like this when bills arrived, she remembered, and was startled, for she had not realised she knew that. She had thought those memories beyond her reach.

He continued. 'Lady Anne is poorly disposed. She keeps away from the world in the west tower. She is not to be disturbed.' Catherine nodded. 'As for my daughter … You'll find she is given to mischief and telling lies. Do not set store by what she says.'

'No, sir,' promised Catherine. This was interesting. What might such a little girl have to lie about?

'And don't roam the grounds at night. The dogs are out after sunset. They'll obey me, and more often than not Parry, but otherwise they're a law unto themselves.'

She thought, uneasily, of the men dragging the straining hounds away from the hunt, and their bloody jaws as they snarled at their fellows. 'Yes, sir.'

Sir Rowland's hand appeared to shake a little as he swallowed a mouthful of whisky, grimaced, then looked up as a knock sounded. 'You'll join us for dinner this evening. Usually you'll eat in the schoolroom, but this evening Dr Sidstone joins us, as well as Mrs Wingfield, my father's ward.' He stopped, then added, 'Mrs Wingfield is recently returned from Ireland.' He did not sound pleased about this, but before she could think about it, there was a second knock. 'Enter,' he said.

The door opened and Catherine observed a middle-aged woman in a dark, plain dress, with a large chatelaine of keys at her waist. Everything about her was spare and economical: neat nose, ungenerous mouth. If you took away fifteen years, she would have been handsome.

Sir Rowland said, 'Take Miss Symonds to her room, Mrs Parry.' The housekeeper inclined her head. 'Four for dinner, plus Georgie. Did you see to the fires, and the lights?'

Mrs Parry glanced at Catherine, then spoke smoothly. 'The fires are lit, sir. The chandelier is to be mended this evening.'

'Good,' he said shortly. He indicated the decanter. 'Top this up, would you?' She took it. 'Did Mrs Wingfield see you about Georgie?'

'After discussion with Mrs Wingfield, I confined Miss Bridewell to her room and administered the switch twice to the back of her leg,' said Mrs Parry, in the same unflappable voice.

Sir Rowland nodded. 'See that all the lights are on before we sit down to dinner,' he said. 'And be sure to see the windows are closed properly. Several were left ajar again this afternoon.'

Catherine followed the rustling taffeta of the housekeeper's skirts. The house drew in as they ascended its floors, the passageways shrinking down to tunnels. It was older than she had realised, with walls of thick stone, dark with panelled wainscot. There were so many paintings – grouse and knickerbockers, beaters, ponies, prey and predator riding over moors and coverts – she thought they had to be concealing damp, or cracks. There were family portraits, too, though fewer of these, and the ones she noticed were mostly of men and solemn-looking children. Once or twice, as they hurried by, she noticed a dark shadow where something had occupied the wall, but been removed.

Mrs Parry swept ahead of her. 'On Sunday afternoons you will be free, other than keeping Miss Bridewell out of mischief. The schoolroom is on the same corridor as the nursery. Miss Bridewell is expected to make use of the area during the day, and not stray into other parts of the house. You will use the schoolroom if you need somewhere to sit in the evening. If there are problems with the child, see me between five and six o'clock in my study. You must come to me, not the master, and certainly not Lady Anne. Mrs Wingfield should be treated as a member of the family, and not relied upon in your work. There is an order here. You won't mind my saying that, in my experience, the worst disruptions in a house occur when people stray out of their right place. But you've done the job before, so I'm confident we will understand one another.' Catherine imagined Mrs Parry's nostrils flaring as she spoke. 'Each evening you'll bring Miss Bridewell to the drawing room for six o'clock, where she will spend time with her father. During that hour you will ready the schoolroom and nursery for the following day's work, and then supervise her bathing and bedtime. You will be served a meal in the school-room, rather than the servants' hall. You will pin your hair. You will wear gloves. You're dressed well enough,' she conceded, turning up a flight of stairs to the second floor, and sweeping her eyes over Catherine's gown, 'but you will wish to launder that. If you prefer the work to be done by the house, that can be arranged, and the cost deducted from your pay. You'll see to your own needlework. We are proud to keep a small staff, just myself and Edie apart from some occasional maids, and you'll kindly remember that she answers to me, and not obstruct her work. Both she and Cook come in daily, and Cook will see to any essentials if you go down to the kitchen – cocoa and so on. If you would like tea, this will be deducted.'

Mrs Parry gestured that Catherine should go before her. The stairs spiralled upwards in steep, bare stone, and now they passed walls without panelling, flaking with green paint. It was colder up here, and from somewhere there was a breeze, winding through labyrinthian passageways. As they climbed and went round corners, Catherine felt faint with hunger, conscious of her dry throat. They came to a junction, startling a plump young woman with wisps of fair hair escaping a housemaid's cap, fiddling with a window. She stepped down from the window nook and stumbled, righted herself and stood back against the passage wall, wringing together hands with stubby, bitten nails, angry with reddened skin from her work. Catherine saw her eyes were puffy and the whites coloured, as if she had been crying.

'Edie,' said Mrs Parry sternly. 'What are you doing?'

The young woman's cheeks flamed as she curtseyed. When she looked up, Catherine saw she had a slight squint. 'I tripped, Mrs Parry. Beg your pardon – I wasn't expecting no one to come round so fast. I was seeing to it the windows were shut, like the master ordered.'

Mrs Parry snapped, 'Stop mooning about and go and get changed for service.'

Nervously, Edie nodded and scurried away.

Tutting, the housekeeper closed several windows along the passage as they went. 'Inexperienced staff must be shown a firm hand,' she said with a sniff. 'Edie is young, and disappointed in matters of the heart. It must not disturb her work. I will expect you to follow my example with the servants. Good Christian principles at all times, and they can't go too far wrong.'

Wondering what Edie had done to risk *going wrong*, but knowing she could not ask, Catherine asked instead, suddenly curious, 'Does the household attend church?'

Mrs Parry stiffened. 'No doubt we would like to, but it is a small living at Locksley, and regrettably vacant.'

'Did the minister retire?'

'He was ill, I believe, and went back east. He had people in Derbyshire.'

'Surely it must have been possible to find a replacement?'

'The distance can be off-putting to some.'

'How do you manage without regular services?' She realised, too late, she was asking too many questions.

Mrs Parry sniffed again, imperiously. 'As best we can, between ourselves and the Lord.' She gathered pace, and they rounded a corner into a thin corridor. 'That will be your room, there,' she said. 'But you should meet the young lady.' She halted outside a door. 'Here is the nursery.'

Mrs Parry's body blocked Catherine's view as she turned the handle. Her gasp as she swung the door open was sharp. 'What on earth ...' she cried out, and moved aside, treading slowly, as if trying to avoid broken glass. From behind her, Catherine was able to see the cause. Hair. The boards were strewn with it. Brown and soft, it carpeted the otherwise orderly room. In the centre, perched on a stool with booted feet raised off the wreckage, a little girl, about eight years old, hummed some melody – Catherine thought it was familiar – and clutched a pair of ornate silver sewing scissors. Her hair was cut away in a ragged, patchy cap, close about her skull.

'What have you done, child?' said Mrs Parry, her composure shaken.

Georgie Bridewell answered with more calm than was reasonable for a small girl caught in such naughtiness. 'I told you to cut it, Mrs Parry,' she said.

'Why, of all the wayward and disobedient children ...'

Catherine moved further into the room. Georgie saw her, and her eyes widened. Some strong feeling rose up in her expression, and Catherine was suddenly terrified. It had not occurred to her — she was so foolish — that Georgie, of the entire household, would be most likely to spot a resemblance to Emily. She kept her face as neutral as possible.

'Hand me the scissors, Georgie,' she said quietly, holding out her palm.

In the pause that followed, mutiny leapt up in the child's eyes. Catherine did not repeat her instruction, and kept her arm upraised. As she wondered whether the sinner intended upon compounding her crime, the scissors clattered noisily to the floor. Georgie poked out her little pink tongue and jumped off her stool, running out of the room.

5

'But what is it, Rowland?'

'Soup.'

'Its ingredients evade me,' muttered Grizel Wingfield, making spirals in the pale liquid with her spoon.

Sir Rowland said irritably, 'It's Jerusalem soup. Leave it if it doesn't tempt you.' Turning to Dr Sidstone, he added, 'Cook hasn't been long with us.'

'Neither have any of the staff except the Parrys,' offered Mrs Wingfield in reply, allowing the slop to drip off her spoon. 'We seem to have some trouble keeping servants.'

There were five at dinner: Catherine, Sir Rowland, Dr Sidstone, Grizel Wingfield and Georgie Bridewell, sitting next to her aunt, and clearly in disgrace. She had not spoken since being discovered hiding near the back stairs, crouched in a nook between the gun room and the cellars. Every few moments, as if noting the child's ragamuffin state for the first time, her father glowered over the candelabra at her hair's wild, chopped appearance.

Just before they came through for dinner, Parry had dragged a set of tall ladders into the entrance hall by the great staircase, then mounted them gingerly. The meal was now disturbed by the noise of him mending the chandelier, and Mrs Parry's sharp directions. Catherine listened as they worked, enjoying the housekeeper's dictatorial tone.

But Sir Rowland scowled at the frequent interruptions. Speaking to Dr Sidstone, he said, 'Some of the staff preferred how the house ran in my father's time. He liked to spend money, along with some of his other … eccentricities.' He ate some soup, grunted, then wiped his mouth. 'But we can't be stuck in the mud. We can exist very well with fewer live-in employees. Cook comes in each morning, and even the maids are all hired from the village. The miracles of modernity, eh? But it does mean we have to withstand a certain amount of dilettantism when it comes to repairs.'

The doctor nodded. He nodded at everything, like a porcelain bobblehead.

Catherine looked over the centrepiece of ivy and water lilies at her charge. Georgie Bridewell seemed to have no interest in the conversation. She had not touched her soup, and instead held her spoon like a mirror. Her hair was cut close to her head in ragged lumps, as if she had shorn it in a frenzy. She resembled a naughty little sprite, a smile playing on her lips as she admired the results of her barbering. There was something about Georgie in this pose that lifted Catherine's spirits. She groped about for a cause, and realised, to her shock, that she was remembering.

They were in their bedroom in their home in Reading. Emily's voice had squeaked in outrage. 'I look nothing like Cousin Amelia! My hair possesses more shine, and is finer. Hers is as coarse as Pluto's nether-regions. And she needn't worry about dropping her spoon at dinner, for her chin could finish her soup all on its own!'

Catherine recalled how she had laughed uproariously in spite of herself, and called her sister a wicked thing.

She held the memory by its thinnest edges, and reached for more.

Another hard clatter came from the entrance hall as Parry dropped something, and Sir Rowland snapped, 'For pity's sake!'

The recollections vanished. She returned to her observations of the family. On seeing his daughter's hair just before

56

dinner, Sir Rowland had berated Grizel, asking how such a thing had been allowed to happen. 'You mustn't put the blame on me, Rowland,' Grizel had complained. 'Georgiana was in Mrs Parry's charge.'

'I'll have words with her,' said Sir Rowland, eyeing the housekeeper at the top of the stairs. He continued darkly, 'But if you can't contribute to the running of the household, it presents the question of why I tolerate you here at all.'

Embarrassed, Catherine had stopped between two side tables laden with French terracotta heads, trying to pretend she hadn't heard. As she glanced into the room, Dr Sidstone had his gaze fixed on a pair of ugly cherubs. He looked mortified.

She thought Grizel might flounce or weep, but instead the older woman giggled. It was a jarring, childish sound. 'You say the most amusing things, Rowland,' she said, and swept past. Georgie followed, then Sir Rowland, leaving Catherine in the entrance hall. She turned to watch Parry teetering at the top of the ladder. It was just too short, so he had to stretch to reach the arms of the chandelier.

'Care,' warned Mrs Parry.

Were they married? No, Catherine thought; the housekeeper was too contained, everything about her neat and controlled. She would never choose the man now atop the pyramid formed by the steps, his clothes still bearing the dust and mud of the road, and if she did, she would change him. Side by side, there was a similarity in their looks: dark hair, slight features, not tall. Brother and sister, she decided. That made Mrs Parry Ned's aunt.

As Catherine broke off some of her roll and chewed in silence, Sir Rowland told Dr Sidstone about the mine. 'My father sunk the shaft. Two hundred feet, almost. Not to exploit the coal seam — nothing half so sensible. He wanted to learn about the geology, the strata of the rocks and so forth. There was a fashion, if you remember, a couple of decades ago, for pulling out all sorts of debris and trying to discover the age of the Earth. It cost a fortune. Nearly bankrupted him, in fact, and was a near-catastrophe for the estate.'

Dr Sidstone nodded as his bowl was taken away.

Nobody spoke to Catherine, or seemed to expect her to volunteer anything. This was unsurprising – she was a woman and an employee. She was not expected to have opinions. But why an educated man, a doctor, needed to be so sycophantic, she had no idea. Perhaps he was of that spineless type that never agrees or disagrees with anything. Or maybe he wanted something. As far as she could tell, he had been in England less than three months. He could have had nothing to do with Emily's death.

Mrs Wingfield did volunteer her contributions. Dr Sidstone listened politely, but their host was visibly contemptuous, rolling his eyes. Catherine listened rather better, for her own reasons, and from what she could work out, Mrs Wingfield was a ward of the former baronet. She had only been here a year or so, and before that had been in Ireland, where she had been married. The reasons for her return were not yet clear. The obvious assumption would be that she was widowed, but why not stay in Ireland, where, presumably, she had a home and her own comforts? It was obvious Sir Rowland didn't want her here. Still, she had been at Locksley when Emily died. They had certainly known one another.

As the meal progressed, she thought through other lines of enquiry. Lewis's letter had implied that Georgie had witnessed the tragedy. Yet what precisely had Georgie seen? The death certificate said Emily had carried out the act herself, but how did the authorities know this? Where had it happened? Did nobody consider foul play? She couldn't press the child too much – that would arouse suspicion – but if she built a trust with her, she might be able to coax out what she needed.

What of Lady Anne? *Indisposed* could mean anything from pregnancy to a general intractability. It could mean she wasn't even here. Perhaps her separateness in her own wing was a ruse, and she had been shipped off to a smaller house, where Sir Rowland did not have to see her. She had a rich father, according to Parry. So did Lady Anne expect an inheritance, or were there brothers? If there was a title, that could not pass to a woman, but business interests might. It might be none of these things – Lady Anne might merely have disliked the role in which she had found herself, and chosen to lock herself away.

Grizel Wingfield said the housekeeper and her jack-of-all-trades brother had been here longest out of the servants. Though their involvement in Emily's death seemed unlikely, their innocence of it was by no means certain. She was curious, too, about why Locksley had a problem retaining its staff, and leapt to the simplest explanation, strengthened by Sir Rowland's words about his father's extravagance: money. William's estate – hers, now – was much smaller, but even he had kept a housekeeper, cook, valet, two footmen and various house and chambermaids. She had been resentful of the sheer mass of them, rendering it impossible to walk from one room to another in the peace of her thoughts without someone scurrying down a nearby staircase.

The Abbey, by contrast, was riddled with empty spaces and laced with stairs and passageways. She had passed a long corridor of staff bedrooms on her way down to dinner, doors open, and spied bare mattresses and dusty boards. Throughout the house, the neglect of professional repair mentioned by Sir Rowland was on display. Peeling strips of paper, scratched panelling, carpets thinning, and a film of dust on anything not used every day reminded the onlooker that there was no team of maids and footmen scrubbing, polishing, smartening here. Just the Parrys, with too much to do, and – from the sounds of things – bickering over the best way to keep the old place from crumbling as they rushed about stoking up the fires demanded by their employer.

She looked at Sir Rowland last. He was pink from the heat and his wine goblet, and cast furious glances between his daughter's scalp and the voluble Mrs Wingfield. He was the key to everything. How much could happen at Locksley without his knowledge?

She was distracted, and almost didn't notice Grizel Wingfield move her hand. Sir Rowland was pontificating about the general election. Georgie was fiddling with her napkin. 'Stop it, Georgiana,' said Mrs Wingfield, but Georgie's hands carried on working the linen. 'Stop that,' ordered her aunt again. When Georgie did not comply, Grizel's right hand slunk towards her, and Catherine watched as the long fingers sought out the child's upper arm and, through the thin fabric of her sleeve, pinched down hard, holding the grip for several seconds, until the skin turned white. Finally the little girl dropped the napkin, and Mrs Wingfield's hand darted back under the table. Georgie looked down at her garment and pushed up the cuff, revealing, to Catherine's dismay, a track of bruises on her inner arm, running purple and yellow all the way up to the crook of her elbow.

Mrs Wingfield smirked.

The baronet hadn't noticed. He was talking, animatedly, about the public finances. Catherine glanced at Dr Sidstone. Had he seen? She thought he had. He quickly hid his instinctive expression, but too late. She realised he was affected, and that surprised her; most men of his class showed an indifference to the ordeals of children.

Sir Rowland continued. 'They installed monkey closets on Bedford Street? I read about it in *The Times*. There's no money-wasting scheme that can't gain traction these days …'

The doctor didn't appear to be listening. He was watching Grizel Wingfield, who stirred her soup. But he said nothing.

Georgie's face had turned a shade whiter in the glow of the candles.

'Georgie, do you perhaps need to use the water closet?' Catherine asked quietly. Not quietly enough. Sir Rowland stopped speaking mid-sentence and arched an eyebrow.

Mrs Wingfield stared at Catherine. The pleasure had left her face. Her mouth was set. 'Miss Symonds, we are in the middle of a meal. It's hardly appropriate—'

To Catherine's surprise, Sir Rowland cut in. 'Don't interfere, Grizel.'

'I thought you would take my part against a *servant*,' Mrs Wingfield hissed. 'Father would never—'

This brought Sir Rowland heavily to his feet, silencing her. He balled and discarded his napkin so it fell sloppily against the centrepiece. 'Don't speak of *my* father,' he said, his face reddening further. 'I'm going to get some air.' He stalked out, muttering, and a moment later, Grizel Wingfield, covering a sob with her gloved hand, fled the room.

Noting the oddness of this exchange, Catherine filed it away and looked over the table towards Dr Sidstone, who was studying his pocket watch. 'Georgie, wait outside, please,' she said.

'But, Miss Symonds—'

'Do as you're told, please.' Georgie scowled, but complied.

They remained alone for half a minute as she held the doctor under a steady gaze. Eventually, he sighed, and said, 'What is it, Miss Symonds? You're watching me like a sparrowhawk.'

She considered whether to speak, then the words almost tumbled out. 'You saw the run of bruises on the child's arm.'

'Did I?' Morosely, he tapped his fingers on his wine glass.

'You had to have done.'

'Children are disciplined every day,' he said, shrugging. 'If the child misbehaves, what else can she expect?'

'Punishing for naughtiness is one thing,' she remonstrated. 'This was done for sheer spite, and obviously not for the first time.'

He looked up. His eyes were dark and melancholy. There was strength somewhere in his face, which she saw now was not unpleasant, though rather angular, with cheekbones etched high, but the rest seemed beaten down; in fact, she thought she had never seen anyone so defeated. 'What is it you think I should do about it?' he said.

'You could speak to Sir Rowland. He could intervene where I can't.'

'I can't help but wonder why, if you're so convinced of what you saw, you do not speak with your employer yourself.'

'You're a gentleman, and his friend. I'm certain you could influence him.'

In the too-bright candlelight, he looked nearer forty than thirty. He rubbed his eyes, blinked, then stood. 'My grandfather had a cat once upon a time: Tabitha. It, like you, liked to poke its nose into affairs not its own. It would go anywhere, and was completely fearless. My grandfather was very fond of it, and boasted of its escapades.' He adjusted his collar and tie, looking directly ahead. 'It was run over by a Tilbury gig on the road to Abergavenny.' Finished with his task, he glanced back at her. 'You cannot shape the world, Miss Symonds. It will always shape you, instead. How many like what remains, when the world is done with them?' He hovered for a moment, and she thought he would say more, but he followed the others from the room.

Unexpectedly, she felt cold, as if the temperature outside had plummeted. Perhaps someone had opened a door in the kitchen; yes, there, she could hear a noise – a howling. Sir Rowland's dogs again. It was a horrible din, that howling, skimming the edges of her nerves like a thin blade against skin.

But she gathered herself. With the others out of the way, this was her chance to question Georgie.

In the entrance hall, Parry swayed, applying the tip of a small knife to the chandelier. The ladder shifted beneath him slightly and he cursed. 'Time for that chain, Mrs Parry,' he said, steadying himself against the wood. 'Quick now.' At the balustrades, Mrs Parry was just in sight. She disappeared for a few moments, then re-emerged from the shadows, holding something in her hands.

Catherine pulled up her skirts and sat by Georgie on the bottom stair. She hesitated. She was eager to ask her about Emily, whether she had been happy here, whether Georgie had liked her, but the child's face was still pinched, and she rubbed the sore place on her arm. 'We can go and see Mrs Parry when she's finished, and see if she has some arnica for that,' Catherine said quietly. Georgie was silent, looking at the upper landing where Mrs Parry hefted the cast-iron loops of the new chain, passing the whole thing off to her brother, who pitched on the ladder.

'Why did you cut your hair?' Catherine asked. 'You wanted Mrs Parry to cut it?' Georgie nodded, her lower lip wobbling. 'Why was that?' she asked, more gently.

'When Aunt Wingfield brushes my hair at night, it hurts,' said Georgie finally. 'She pulls so hard, to hurt. But when I complained to my father, he said I was making things up again.'

'I see. Well, I'll be brushing it from now on,' she reassured her, thinking, briefly, that the only other hair she had ever brushed was Emily's. 'I don't pull.'

In the quiet that followed, Georgie gave a sniff and looked up. Catherine's gaze followed hers, and for a moment she stopped speaking as Mrs Parry came into view again, leaning over the ornamented balustrade. She had brought a small footstool, and perched on it to hold out more of the chain to Parry, expecting him to liberate her from its weight. But Parry was slow.

Catherine felt something on the air, a presence. Something surrounded her, sank into her, and made her feel suddenly as if she were underground, suffocating. Her throat closed tight, or, despite seeing nothing in the gloom beyond the house-keeper, she would have cried out in warning. From her place in the hallway she heard no sound, but, leaning out over the high space of the stairwell, Mrs Parry did appear to hear something. The housekeeper cocked her head towards the dark of the upper passageway beyond, diverted by something out of sight. Catherine only saw her look — so imbued with dread! — for an instant.

The next moment was as brief as Parry's impotent shout, but later Catherine would remember it dragging for an eternity. She would see it in her dreams, the housekeeper slipping her foot-ing, the chain unbalancing her, unravelling. Mrs Parry's mask of dismay turned to shock, she shrieked, and as she tumbled over the rail, her hands clawing at the air, Catherine blenched, and pulled Georgie quickly to her chest.

The impact was blunt and heavy. The chain landed first, then the form of the woman, in a heap of dark taffeta, organic, ghastly, and still.

6

'There's evil in this house,' insisted the governess. Her face was pinched and drawn. Arthur handed her a mug of brandy, but she left it to one side and said, 'Something at work that none can see.'

He had dug through the dry pantry for the spirit, preferring those few seconds away from her. Wrapped in a shawl borrowed from the servants' cloakroom, her teeth chattering, she was a frustrating witness to what had just taken place. But his discomfort in her presence was more than that; her terror was contagious. Though in his profession he could not help being used to death, and in the minutes after Mrs Parry's fall he had transitioned from dinner guest to physician without much difficulty, he was more vulnerable to the governess's fear in this moment. He felt it slipping over him like a knot, throttling something inside him.

Perhaps, he decided, it was how her words echoed his grandfather's. They were not the same – Frederick did not claim there was evil at Locksley, but *something at work*, that was closer. Something outside their understanding.

Since Arthur's boyhood he had heard talk about the world before Christianity, the world of the Mabinogion, its venerable kings, druids and sages. He remembered, unexpectedly, the dogs of Annwn, the spectral hounds of the Underworld that pursued the souls of mortal men and were a portent of death. The tale reminded him of Sir Rowland's slavering pack outside, circling the house – guarding against what threat?

'It was just an accident,' he said. When she shook her head, he went on firmly. 'Yes, an accident. A horrible thing to happen, certainly, but—'

'No!' Miss Symonds's voice rang out. 'She saw something,' she avowed. 'It terrified her.'

He placed himself opposite her at the servants' table. He felt odd. The feeling had chased him all day, ever since arriving at Locksley, a prickling discomfort in his own skin. But now he wondered if that wasn't a distortion, rather like Miss Symonds thinking Mrs Parry had been frightened by something *before* she fell, instead of because she was falling. A trick of the memory. Someone had just died, and *now* he felt odd. Yes, he thought. That was it.

'Drink that and you'll feel better,' he said. 'It's the fright, you know.' She looked like she would say something else, but then sipped the warming liquid, cradling the cup near her mouth.

As they shared the silence, he searched his recollection. He had been walking the passageway between the hall and the back stairs when it happened, trying to judge whether Sir Rowland intended to rejoin the party, and whether it would be considered impolite to leave. He had not seen Mrs Parry fall, only heard it, a blunt impact that would have alerted him even if Parry had not been shouting, or the little Bridewell girl sobbing. He had attended several patients after falls, though none had died before today, yet had never heard the moment of collision itself. It was unlikely, if ever he heard it again, that he would mistake it for anything else.

When he had reached Mrs Parry, he had recoiled, letting out a harsh oath at the violence before him. Then he had stood for a short time, looking down. Anyone seeing him might have thought he was in shock, but his medical brain was taking over. 'Get her away,' he ordered the governess, indicating Georgie Bridewell, who stood staring at the bloody sprawl until

Miss Symonds ushered her off. Kneeling, he checked for signs of life, knowing people could and did survive falls from worse heights, but the housekeeper had taken the full force against her cranium, and her skull had smashed like the top of a soft-boiled egg. The pink-grey matter of her brain was visible beneath the shattered bone. Putting his fingers to the site, he found it warm, with blood seeping copiously from the injury. Her eyes were open, but breath had departed, and there was no pulse.

Parry was descending the ladder too quickly, unsteady on his feet. Arthur helped him with the final rungs, trying to draw him to the side, but he would not go, and it was wretched to see him kneel by his sister, calling her name. He held her hand and rubbed it between his, and when Sir Rowland arrived at the scene, demanding to know how it had happened, the servant was red-eyed and could not answer.

Miss Symonds had taken Georgie Bridewell to her room and placed her with Edie, the housemaid. When she came back down, whey-faced but calm, the governess had described what she had seen. 'She looked into the middle distance, down the passageway on the upper floor. She was trying to hand the chain to Parry for the repair, but whatever it was she saw, it affected her terribly, and then she fell.'

'But there was nobody there?' asked Sir Rowland. 'Nobody touched her?'

'I didn't see anyone touch her. But there was *something* there, something that frightened her badly.'

'Of her own volition, then,' said Sir Rowland stolidly. He spoke in Arthur's ear. 'She's had a shock. Usually I would not look well on someone spreading rumours, but hardly her fault in this case. A terrible thing to witness. I've known Mrs Parry for many years. Could stand a drink myself. Still, better get her moved first.'

'I suggest we manage that side of things,' said Arthur. 'I don't think it would be right to ask Parry ...'

'What?' came the reply, distracted, and then, 'Yes, quite.' The baronet frowned, observing the bloody disorder created by the fall. 'I'm not sure we can lift her without ...' Finally, he said, 'There's likely to be some tarred canvas in the coach house. Let's bring that in, and we'll take her to the undercroft.'

They walked with a lantern across the gardens at a quick pace, moving up the gentle slope. In the coach house attached to the stables, they rooted in the dark. The block was large, but only two or three horses nickered around them in their stalls.

'It's a big place,' Arthur observed, groping for something to say. 'You could stable three times as many horses, if you chose.'

'I don't keep as many as my father did,' agreed Sir Rowland glumly, as together they dragged the canvas out of its box, checked its condition and, taking an end each, began to roll it up to carry back to the house. 'We couldn't justify the expenditure once he was finished with his tenure, nor of the wages either. Just a single groom sees to them now, from the village. I can change that,' he added, with a touch more passion, and a note Arthur thought was triumph. 'I'll get everything here back to how it ought to be.'

'Shall I take the front end?' asked Arthur, curious about the source of Sir Rowland's unexpected confidence, but unwilling to pry too much into another man's business affairs. Sir Rowland, still carrying the lantern, agreed.

The canvas was cumbersome and their return to the house was slow. Something about their rhythmic steps made him feel better, perhaps now they had real work to do. The sky was clear. He looked up at familiar stars, then Jupiter high in the east, Mars hinting red as deeper night fell. They were about halfway before he heard a deep snarl, and then another, somewhere just ahead. He stopped moving abruptly. Behind him, Sir Rowland cursed. 'It's just the dogs, man,' he said. 'What is it with some men, that they don't like dogs? They won't harm you while you're with me. Morpheus!' he snapped into the shadows.

Arthur was about to object that it wasn't that he disliked dogs. It was just that in this blackness, in possession of the knowledge that they were set to guard against strangers, he could not enjoy the sounds rumbling from their throats.

In response to Sir Rowland's order, one of them stalked into the light. Earlier, when the animals had hunted the stag, Arthur hadn't got quite so near them as he did now. He held his breath as it slunk past him towards its master, and he realised the thing nearly reached his hip. It was huge, broad-backed and muscular. He could well believe creatures like this had been bred to hunt lions. At least its snarls relented as it found Sir Rowland, who gruffly ordered it and its fellows to their bed. Instantly obedient, the pack, led by the fearsome Morpheus, went off towards the kennels.

In the hall, they levered Mrs Parry into the canvas, wrapped it with care, and transported her down the back stairs into the undercroft.

'I'll report it, of course, and contact the coroner,' Sir Rowland grunted as he lowered her to the floor. 'But nothing moves quickly in these parts. We might be waiting days.'

The two men stood for a few moments, confronting this thought, catching their breath. It was dark and cold. Arthur disliked leaving the housekeeper's body here, so alone, but it would not do, either, to have her in the main house. Not with a child present.

He realised, as he looked down on the covered shape, just illuminated by the glow of the lantern, that Sir Rowland was issuing short, half-repressed sobs. Arthur had seen men cry like that when given a hopeless diagnosis; he knew all there was to do was to wait for it to end.

'Excuse me,' said Sir Rowland, turning his back and placing an arm against the bricks. Arthur swung the lantern the other way as the baronet's body shuddered.

'It's quite natural,' he said awkwardly.

A moment later, the baronet withdrew his arm, took out a handkerchief and blew his nose. In the silent dark of the undercroft, the sound was nearly obscene. 'I don't know what came over me. There have been things that—'

'Think nothing of it,' said Arthur. He didn't like Sir Rowland's proximity, nor his confiding tone. He felt the sudden desire to distance himself. He was slightly ashamed of that sentiment, but it was there all the same.

Sir Rowland continued. 'I've known her since ... Well, as far back as I can remember. Mr Parry, too. I was planning to retire them together; set them up, you know. There's a cottage near Pantygelli I had my eye on. I was just waiting for the estate's finances to ...' He trailed off.

Surprisingly generous, thought Arthur. 'That sounds kind,' he said. 'It's a pity it didn't work out.'

'That's the worst part,' said Sir Rowland. 'I hadn't said anything – tonight somehow didn't seem the moment – but I received word from London just before dinner: my father-in-law is dead. I'm a rich man.' He spoke flatly.

So Lady Anne would mourn two souls tonight, Arthur thought. Did she know? Had anybody carried news of the accident to her rooms? 'Please accept my condolences,' he said formally.

'Save them. He was an old bastard,' said Sir Rowland. He sniffled, and gave a humourless laugh. 'But his money will be useful. It will provide Parry with a retirement, though he'll have to go on his own now.'

They trekked back upstairs.

Now, Arthur regarded Miss Symonds across the kitchen table. In spite of the strange feeling of being watched that had dogged him all evening, which was still strong, he was confident the fall was an accident. The housekeeper had been engaged in something unfamiliar, the circumstance in which most accidents took place. No one had been near enough to prevent the incident, and she had mis-stepped. His view led him, unfortunately but inexorably, to the opinion that Miss Symonds – who, after all, had not known Mrs Parry well and had only arrived this afternoon – had a whiff of the hysteric about her.

She had finished the brandy. 'Why don't we get rid of that?' he suggested.

They went through to the scullery. The back of the house was stifling, with the stove stoked far too high. Normally, he reflected, in a big house like this, after even a modest dinner with guests, he would expect to see a small herd of servants scrubbing and polishing, their chatter audible from the family rooms. Instead, all was silent. Mrs Parry's absence filled that silence, and he felt, for a moment, unutterably sad.

'She has a nephew,' Miss Symonds was saying. 'Parry's son. He works at the mine. He'll have to be informed.'

'Parry will tell him, I'm sure,' said Arthur. 'It's late, though. Perhaps it will wait until the morning.' He thought of his task tomorrow, at the colliery. He might end up meeting the Parry lad himself. 'But don't think of it now. Try to rest.'

'I can't,' she said, gathering the shawl around her. 'I have things I have to do, that I must find out …'

He sighed. 'Miss Symonds, I would not recommend you begin accusing your employer of doing away with his housekeeper.' He took the mug to the deep sink and cast away the few drops remaining, thinking how he hated the stench of brandy. 'You'll recall my anecdote about the cat? I was only half-joking.' He turned to face her. 'Look, there really is nothing to suggest it was anything other than—'

She cut in. 'Do you know another woman died here? And Sir Rowland covered it up?'

'I'm sure he did nothing of the——'

'Her name was Emily Murphy. She was the governess here before me.'

He frowned, thinking of her recent arrival. 'How do you know this?'

She shook her head energetically. He took this to mean she would not tell him. He said, 'Try to focus on your work, Miss Symonds. That's the best advice I can offer.' He rinsed the mug, shaking out the drops. 'I'll be riding back to Hawk's Leap tonight, and tomorrow I'll visit the colliery on business for Sir Rowland,' he told her. She looked up, her face suddenly curious. He did not elaborate. 'Don't worry about the Parry boy – I'll make sure he hears the news.'

'You won't stay the night at Locksley?'

'No!' He realised, with an itching discomfort that felt out of place in the thoroughly ordinary setting of the servants' hall, he did not want to sleep here. Indeed, he could think of nothing he wanted less. At this exclamation and its unspoken admission, Miss Symonds looked slightly mollified.

But as he left the hall, her voice echoed in the big space, following him. 'You know something is not right here, doctor. You know it, just as I do.'

7

Frederick would be pleased, Arthur thought, at his apprentice's efficiency. Even unused to such bloody scenes as he was, and out of practice given the long journey from the East, he had managed the aftermath of the accident well enough, shielding the ladies from the horror as much as possible, and had reckoned quickly with the unfortunate truth that nothing could be done for Mrs Parry. Yes, he decided, he had acquitted himself as his grandfather would expect.

Why, then, did Miss Symonds's words still resonate?

You know something is not right here.

Why had he been so eager to get away?

The period on which he congratulated himself, an interlude of around half an hour between first kneeling beside Mrs Parry, and he and Sir Rowland removing her body, neglected those few seconds beforehand in which he had stood nearly frozen, looking down at her crumpled form. The scene before him had seemed curiously stretched, if such a thought made sense, as if the hideous sight were the focus of some sort of tableau; a draw for the eye, with things happening elsewhere that he did not understand. And he had felt more impotent, he conceded now, than he liked to admit, seized by an emptiness into which other forms of awareness had crept.

Now he was away from Locksley, he could recognise what he had denied to the governess, that despite his careful words to her in the servants' hall, in those moments before acting, he had felt something else besides paralysis. But what? *Something.* Nothing he could justify in conscious thought. But it was the oddest thing, he realised. What had come to him in those instants of utter stillness was, in a strange sense, motion. He had heard a noise that could not possibly have been present: the sound of rustling leaves.

But surely it had been just the shock, the noise no more than his blood rushing behind his eardrums.

It was gone now.

As he went along, the lanterns that rose and fell with his saddle did something to illuminate the way. The low-slung moon did a little more. In spite of the darkness, he was in no danger; he knew these paths, knew where the late birds roosted and where the vixens screamed. He had been a boy here. He was a man now, and something more prosaic than woodland spectres disquieted him, or at least a little. He kept thinking of Mrs Wingfield's behaviour to the girl, and his own reply, when the governess had begged him to act.

Why did it bother him so much? As he had told Miss Symonds in the dining room, children were struck every day. If he had a farthing for every slap or slippered backside he had received as a boy, he would be dressed like an emperor tonight, not in this decaying coat.

But the thought persisted like an infuriating ditty that, once heard, would not be dismissed. Mrs Wingfield had not just disciplined the child as Sir Rowland had encouraged. She had clearly been hurting her for some time. He had dismissed that.

What had the world done to him? Had it really turned him into someone who would see a small child pinched, deliberately and to inflict pain, and say nothing in challenge? And why? Because he wanted something from Sir Rowland? Because he was afraid? Was he every bit the coward Miss Symonds said he was?

The unwelcome palpitation when she had suggested he stay overnight at Locksley had not quite disappeared, and the sense he had had all evening, the feeling of not being alone, had returned. And in returning, it had grown, and taken on a more specific form. For some reason, the day's events had made him think of Barnabas, and the night they had walked to Newport in the rain.

It was at Barnabas's urging. It was only fifteen miles. Both men were young and strong. Arthur, who would do anything for his friend, had quickly agreed to his request, but once in the cellars of the Maypole, some distance outside the town, he found himself regretting it. Belligerent voices mingled in the musky air. Though he had picked up some Welsh in his two years in Monmouthshire, the voices were so heated that a lot of the meaning passed over his head. Beside him, Barnabas, his features cramped in concentration over his lightly stubbled chin and spotted red neckerchief, listened, and ate an apple.

The air was close with pipe smoke. A hundred workers gathered elbow to elbow, with doors bolted and shutters closed. These were ironworkers and colliers, sawyers and shopkeepers. A few old soldiers had drifted in. Every name was taken down in ink. Every person who passed the door had someone to vouch for them. To the outside world, no meeting was taking place.

The cellar roof dripped tepid water on Arthur's head, and his stomach was raw. Barnabas could hardly stay seated on the bench they had found, and drummed his palms against his knees, jiggling his legs in that restless way he had about him. As he did so often, he suggested his friend might keep still, but Barnabas returned in his soft mountain voice, 'Quiet, Arthur. I'm trying to hear.'

At the front, the sharp-elbowed vied for position as the speaker held his listeners in thrall. He spoke Welsh, oscillating between mellow reasonableness and a booming sonorousness, but Arthur missed a lot. Barnabas, born and bred here, began to translate as Arthur eyed the bottom of his tankard.

The speaker, John Hogall, the publican, was a balding giant in a bottle-green coat. His subject was how things would be when there were no more masters. 'Now is the time. They've turned tail: the managers, the bankers, the shopkeepers. Any that remain will not stand in our way. It's clear the working man must rely only on himself, not on the promises of those in superior situations, as milky and delicate when they are made as when they are broken!' A cheer greeted these words. 'But do not be afraid! Though you cannot give your faith to the landlords, you can still give it to your fellows. Look about you! Look each man and each woman in the eye. Promise them if any is killed, their family will be provided for. And ask yourself, if met with force, *am I prepared to die?*'

Arthur watched Barnabas. His friend was just twenty, coltish, possessed of a certainty Arthur admired but couldn't replicate. In the gloom of the cellar, the sharpness of his friend's cheek caught the light, and twines of dark hair fell in his face. He was muscled, a farm boy as much as a haulier, returning each summer to his home in Cardiganshire to help bring in the harvest, and finding work on the coalfields where he could. Arthur knew his family struggled, but Barnabas wouldn't accept offers of money. 'No,' he had said, the last time. 'It's for the employers to pay a wage we can live on, not for you to hand out charity. And watch: we'll make them do it.'

But Arthur thought his friend was wrong. He knew the owners used the colliers ill, but a sense of the importance of law and order prevented his heart being with the cause. He was no believer in anarchy, and certainly not violence. He hoped the Chartists exaggerated their intentions. Perhaps once the beer ran out, everyone would go home and sleep it off.

He whispered to Barnabas, 'If the Chartists take Newport, even if they seize the bridge, even if some of the soldiers come over, without a real plan, they will fail. And there will be the devil to pay.'

'We're already paying him, Arthur. Some of us more than others. People can't live like this. Don't worry. Once Newport is taken, other places will follow our lead.'

Arthur sighed. He wouldn't be here if not for Barnabas. They hadn't been friends longer than a few months, but already a deep affection existed between them. One wouldn't know it from events tonight, but they were generally of one mind about everything. Barnabas's sudden passion had taken him by surprise.

Only months after his studies concluded in London, his parents had died of the typhus. After dealing with his father's small estate, without siblings and with few connections, Arthur had found himself adrift. His grandfather had suggested he come to live with him in Herefordshire, acting eventually as his replacement. He had considered the offer but, with a notion of making his own way, had eventually declined, and travelled about looking for a place. Soon, he had found himself in Newport – *Casnewydd*, Barnabas would say, though his grandfather insisted on its still older name: *Caerleon* – where he had stuck out like a sore thumb. But he had weathered the stares, the whispers behind his back, and had haunted its taverns, spending the little money his father had left him, until someone had suggested a position in Pontypool, doctoring to a mining village. He had been here over a year now, becoming familiar to the locals, earning their trust, and making friends, as he had with Barnabas. He had grown to feel oddly at home. But tonight, for the first time in months, he felt his otherness. There was a current of anger beneath the words of the crowd, underpinned by a history he did not share.

'Will you march with me?' shouted Hogall. Barnabas was on his feet. The noise was such that even Arthur, knowing such meetings were taking place all over the coalfield, could believe it was coming: revolution.

The assembly rushed up the stairs and Barnabas seized Arthur's wrist. His hand was warm and his smell – light beer and sweat – was strong. 'Come, Arthur! No more great men!'

With a deep sensation of dread, Arthur pulled the collar of his greatcoat up over his jaw. Barnabas saw his fatalism and laughed, leading him out through the back door. Around them, whooping men and women danced, careless of the rain. Barnabas skipped a step or two beneath the hanging maypole, his dark hair shining, his shirtsleeves soaking wet. There was something fey about him. Arthur wanted to pull him back to his rooms, toast bread and drink coffee, and talk of ordinary things. But as the men and women moved off together in a stream, he knew that wherever Barnabas went, he would go too.

He was just over a mile from the cottage by the time the strange feeling faded, and the memories with it. He rode south to the high point of Hawk's Leap, where his grandfather's cottage overlooked the drop. Thin clouds tussled with a nearly full moon as he edged his mount around the black of the wood, and below, the dark river moved quietly. This was the land Sir Rowland would sell. Its loss would break his grandfather's heart.

By the time he had got the horse put away, it was late. He expected Frederick to have gone up, and was anticipating climbing into bed when he saw the parlour windows were lit. He went to the back door, appreciating the warmth as he entered the scullery, then frowned at a print on the rug. As his eyes adjusted to the dim space, he saw a pair of boots covered in grime. The cottage walls were thick Silurian stone, but the parlour door was open. Frederick sounded like he was enjoying himself, a hint of claret running through his words as he told a story. Arthur had heard the tale before. It was about Locksley Abbey, and its relic.

'... and there it stayed, in the Ark. When Nebuchadnezzar sacked the Temple in 587 BC, the Ark was stolen. It was thought the Rod was taken. But the Locksley version of the tale says that this was not so – the contents were saved by King Josiah of Judah, and taken to a secret chamber, where they survived many centuries to the fall of the city in 1099. The invaders waded up to their knees in blood, but the Rod found sanctuary with a surviving group of elders, who intended to smuggle it to Alexandria. At the last they were betrayed, the Rod was discovered, and seized.

'There followed a fight for custody of the relic, and the victors then made the long journey overland, via Constantinople. Their prize changed hands more than once, and at some point became divided. The tale has it that at least one of these fragments ended up, around 1130, in Limoges, in the possession of a simoniac dealer. This is where our monks of Locksley come in. One Brother Peregrine, who, if we are charitable, feared it would again be lost, stole it back, and fled to England. Some years later, Peregrine became Abbot of Locksley, and, *hey presto*, the object was revealed, in a reliquary, bedecked in ruby, sapphire and jet. The piece of the Rod of Aaron within, the monks said, would shoot out stalks and blossom as described in Clement's First Epistle, and once a century, though none gave it water or planted it in soil, produce a crop of almonds. Its power was said to be that of healing; and more! Of resurrection. It was said that it could give back what was lost.

'For about fifty years, the object fed the Abbey, drawing in the desperate and the dying. But there was never a verified account of any person being saved. Some reported respite from minor maladies – warts and agues and pustules – but, according to one of my contacts in the Monmouthshire Association, who recently came upon certain documents on the Welsh side of the border, they almost certainly defrauded their patrons, for there is a different explanation of the item's provenance, one hinted at in the confession of a young Welsh thief named Iestin, set down around the end of the twelfth century ...'

Arthur was exhausted. He had no intention of disturbing the discussion, though he wondered who Frederick had roped in to listen to his musings. He realised he was hungry, and observed the kitchen table piled end to end with leather-bound books and papers. Mrs Morgan, their daily woman, was not supposed to touch these stacks when cleaning, and Arthur had spent most mornings since he arrived back in England trying to work around them. Now he was seeing them with fresh eyes, thinking again of the bundle of letters Sir Rowland had flung upon his desk, wondering whether his grandfather's interests now flirted with obsession.

Putting things aside with care, he saw, across nearly every margin and spare inch of paper, annotations in a slipshod scrawl. He recognised his grandfather's penmanship, but it was distinct from the neat hand of the letters he had received every month in Batavia. It was not only sloppier, but appeared hurried, as if set down in a frenzy.

Once the space was cleared, he took a cold potato and leek pie, a recipe favoured by Mrs Morgan, off the sideboard. He noticed his grandfather had not touched it, and wondered if his stomach might be troubling him again. When he had finished two slices, he heard their mystery guest give a cheery goodbye, then the front door closing. He sat for a few minutes with his pie, mulling over what he had undertaken to do.

He had told Sir Rowland he knew nothing about mining. He had had no choice. If it became known that he was the same Arthur Sidstone who doctored near the Pontypool works before the Newport Rising, and marched with the Chartists, his life here would lie in tatters. The chance to save the Puzzle Wood would be gone. So he would go to the works. He would speak to Ned Parry if he could. But if he recognised any of the colliers, or found that any of them had marched on the Westgate thirteen years ago, he was damned if he would give his new patron the name of a single man. Finishing his meal, he mused that he had been guilty of enough betrayals. Enough blood stained his hands already.

8

Frederick had not retired as he had thought. 'Arthur, is that you?' He was boiling a kettle as his grandfather entered the kitchen carrying several books beneath his arm. 'You're back late.'

The purpose for which he had gone to Locksley seemed suddenly distant as, gravely, he related the horrific events of the evening. 'My goodness,' said Frederick, when Arthur described the fall itself. He pulled at grey whiskers. 'You saw it happen?'

'No.' He thought of his dispute with Miss Symonds. 'I was elsewhere. I ... heard it.'

'What was she doing to lose her footing like that?'

'Assisting in the repair of a chandelier.'

'Sir Skinflint had his housekeeper climbing ladders, did he?' This was said wryly, without any surprise at his adversary's stingy nature.

'Something like that.' Arthur pushed the remnants of the pie towards Frederick.

The other man demurred. 'I'm not hungry.'

'Will you have tea?'

With an absent-minded nod, Frederick said, 'How did the new governess take it?'

Arthur considered his answer. When they had spoken after dinner, Miss Symonds had struck him as calm, collected, a little mutinous; not at all the type who would believe in ghosts or spirits. Then, after the accident, she had spoken of evil, and seemed very much more shaken. 'She was upset. She seemed to think it had something to do with an earlier death at the Abbey – the previous governess. Do you recall when that was?'

Frederick was busying himself with milk and sugar. 'In the spring, I think, or a little later ...'

'What do you remember of the circumstances?'

His wording suggested the possibility of a lapse in memory, and elicited a frown from the older man. 'She hanged herself in the woods behind the house.'

Arthur winced. He hated those cases. 'You're confident it was self-inflicted?'

Frederick frowned. 'What else? I examined her and signed the death certificate myself.' Closing his eyes as he dredged up further details, he said, 'I don't recall there was any dispute about it. The coroner was away, and Bridewell saw to the arrangements. There was no family. I spoke to Mrs Parry, who said the Murphy girl was *a little forward*. Parry didn't seem to have noticed much. He said she was a pretty thing, then returned to his gin flask.'

'Was she pregnant?' Arthur asked, raising a cynical eyebrow.

'Not so it might have been detected.'

So if Sir Rowland was importuning her, Arthur thought, there was no proof. 'And then you and Sir Rowland quarrelled,' he said, remembering.

'Yes, the fat chatterjack. But that was about Lady Anne.' Grimacing, he reached down and rubbed his stomach. There was an audible rumble from his mid-section.

'You're sure you won't eat anything?' Arthur asked, concerned. Frederick had always enjoyed a robust appetite but lately had lost weight.

'I had a little something earlier.'

'I noticed you had a dinner guest.'

His grandfather nodded. 'If you had put your head around the door, you would have found yourself the bearer of bad news, for it was young Ned Parry who came.'

'The collier?'

'The same. The lad's interested in the Puzzle Wood.'

'I didn't know you knew him,' said Arthur, thinking of the young man with sympathy. There would be sadness in his house tonight.

Frederick said, 'We spoke in passing on the road a few weeks ago, and he asked how the wood got its name.'

'How was that?'

'I'm certain I've told you before: the monks of Locksley took their leisure here, so "puzzle" may be a corruption of *pausare*. A place of rest. After that, Ned wished to hear all about its history, so I suggested he called on me.'

'Seems an odd area of interest for a miner,' Arthur said, thinking of men he had known.

'Only if you have fixed ideas about what a miner should be interested in.' His grandfather reached into one of the books and took out a letter. 'We were speaking of this, which I received just yesterday.'

'What is it?'

'Part of my correspondence with Cardale Musgrave, of the Monmouthshire Association.'

Sir Rowland had also received letters from that group, Arthur remembered. 'So this is about the wood?'

'That's right,' Frederick said, sipping his tea.

Torn between his own tiredness and the knowledge that he had to find out what his grandfather was so worried about, Arthur said, 'Are you going to tell me what's in it?'

'A history. One which all but confirms what I have long suspected, and in light of which,' he said, 'it would be unthinkable for the wood to be cut down.'

He handed over the letter and Arthur unravelled the meanings of the tight-knit loops and curves. The handwriting was tortuous, but eventually he understood the whole.

To Dr Sidstone, Hereford:
30th October 1852
Church Stretton, Shropshire

Humbug! All along, the Peregrine casket was humbug! Allow me to congratulate you on being first to see it. I have taken the trouble of copying for you a confession of one Iestin Roberts, or Robbets. The original would have been stored with the records of the early assizes and almost certainly has not survived, but this facsimile is extant in an unofficial chronicle of the life of St Peregrine. It was rescued by chance after the suppressions, and – until recently, when it was passed to the Association – was in the keeping of the Earls of Hereford. Roberts was a Welsh thief who came over the border sometime in the late twelfth century, only to be caught in his thievery and hanged at Hereford in 1200. Before that, it appears he broke into the Abbey with the intention of removing the Peregrine reliquary, and employing the relic in saving his mother, who was dying. He became convinced it would only work if the fragment was first liberated from the custody of the monks, because … Well, I won't spoil the surprise. See for yourself (I have smartened up the translation a little!).

On a separate sheet, Musgrave had written out the thief's confession.

March 1200

My mother had blood in her humours. She would not live. I confess I went to the wood and lay down like in a dream. In that sleep, I departed my body, and he came to me. He said the relic came from the wood, and the monks stole it. If I returned it, my mother would still die, but he would put the breath of life back in her. So I did. The monks hunted me, but I knew the wood. I escaped. I took the casket and pulled the thing out. It was not much, like a shrivelled bit of horn. I buried it in one of the old places as he told me, then hid. They took me on the second day and charged me with wanting to sell the casket, but that was a lie, by Christ's blood. Now I will hang. But just as he said she would, my mother lives. Let it be known, when I was taken up, the bailiff pulled my teeth to make me tell them about the casket, but even when they knew it was empty, he did not ask about the relic. I was in such pain that I would have told them but he never asked. From that I know my dream was true, and the monks did not know its nature.

Musgrave continued the story.

What to make of all this? No record exists, of course, for Iestin's mother, so whether she lived much past her unfortunate son or not, we will never know. But this episode remains instructive. It tells us, firstly, that there was an old belief in the animating power of the wood, and secondly, that there was an enduring opinion amongst the lower classes, where such rumours always survive longest, that the monks did find something precious in there. Nothing, or something? In either case, the monks christened it the Rod of Aaron, and commissioned a reliquary to hold it, but they did not believe in its potency. This is corroborated by Iestin's final words: when he was arrested, nobody cared a whit about the relic. It was the casket they wanted. That was itself seized during the suppressions of 1539, but Iestin's confession suggests the item — whatever it was — remained in its hiding place in the Puzzle Wood, and, more likely than not, has since rotted away there. The relic taken by the Commissioners was probably nothing more than an ordinary piece of wood, or a section of

*stag's antler. As you know, the casket sits now in the collection
of the Duke of —shire. But it's a fraud, a bejewelled fraud, and
you, my friend, were on to it all along!*

    C.

'Well, what do you think?' asked Frederick, taking the letter
back. Arthur glanced at Frederick again, marking, as he had
done more than once in recent weeks, that his collar and cuffs
were not fresh, and that he had not shaved cleanly. The hand
that clutched the letter, Arthur saw now, had uncut nails, brown
beneath the tips, as if its owner had been clawing in the dirt.
Probably, in his enthusiasm for the story and for his papers, his
grandfather had simply been forgetting to wash his hands.

'Think of what?' he said tightly.

'Iestin's story. It tells us the Puzzle Wood is a nexus where
ancient powers resided. They might still. They must not be
disturbed. The wood cannot be sold, and the mining must
stop, too.'

Arthur sighed. He didn't like to dampen his grandfather's
passions, but this couldn't go on. 'The only thing this tells us is
that old men like to gossip.'

'No,' Frederick said, shaking his head. 'Rumours about the
wood have circulated for as long as I can remember. Longer –
since my father's father's day, and further back than that. It's
always been a strange place. And you mustn't doubt that in this
world there exist older truths than most people care to recognise. I do not deny the Bible, but that is no reason to close off
consideration of other potencies. To do so would be dangerous.'

'The thief said it cured his mother,' Arthur pointed out. 'It
doesn't sound especially dangerous to me.'

'That's because you don't recognise the cost of dabbling in
things you don't understand. Power like that described here is
capricious, Arthur. Darkness and light, death and life, they are

sides of the same coin. You can't barter with them like a cod merchant. There might be a greater cost than you understand when you stick your hand in the barrel. And what you do not understand, you should leave alone.'

But this was false; Arthur understood death all too well.

Life, and death. He felt, suddenly, that he could look over his shoulder into the dark and see Barnabas standing there, smiling and straight-backed, laughing at a joke his more serious friend had not intended to make. This illusion was so intense he could not decide whether it was pleasurable or agonising, but still, more than he had ever wanted anything, he wanted it to stay.

Yet he felt the familiar disquiet that arose on any occasion when he thought of those days. His solution, as it had been for thirteen years, was to barricade the subject. He said crisply, 'Look, we're talking about events that took place centuries ago. It's a matter of historic interest, but I'll have no truck with legends.'

As the fear in Frederick's eyes was replaced with sadness, Arthur suspected his own feelings were understood. 'But maybe they will have truck with you, boy. Somewhere, here at Locksley, in this very Nemean wood, there existed a pagan shrine. The monks found it. Without asking leave, they took something from it. Something formidable.'

'It's no secret there were temples built by the Romans, all over—'

He was shocked when Frederick snapped, 'Not a *Roman* god – those itinerant shapeshifters! No. The first deities of these islands were not worshipped from within bricks and mortar, and nor did they follow the Eagle to these shores. They were here before it, raised up from civilisations older than the Anglo-Saxons; older, perhaps, than the Britons.'

'Of course,' said Arthur, not a little hurt by Frederick's tone.

His grandfather went on. 'The relic taken by those monks was some object belonging to, or associated with, the shrine of one of those ancients. It must be left alone. Sir Rowland must allow what is buried to remain *in the past*.'

Arthur's head hurt. 'I always thought the purpose of your correspondence with Musgrave was to arrange to excavate—'

'No!' came the urgent reply. Then Frederick rubbed his grey temples, his voice strained. 'Once, maybe, I thought …' He stopped. 'It must be left alone,' he repeated.

'This is all very well,' Arthur said with a sigh, thinking of the present facts and seeing no point in arguing, 'but we're unlikely to secure Sir Rowland's co-operation with this.' He indicated Musgrave's letter.

A silence followed.

'What is it?' Arthur said, growing frustrated.

Frederick grumbled, 'There's little point trying to open a mind sealed so tightly shut.'

'That's hardly fair—'

'I wonder what you would say if I told you … No, I mustn't draw you in.'

'Why not share whatever it is, you can call me obstinate and narrow-minded, and then I, at least, can go up to bed?'

Frederick shifted uncomfortably, glancing down at his hands. 'Very well. I will. It was shortly before Newport, before you left for Batavia. I was riding more then, seeing clients in Hern and over the pass, and I had cause to go through the wood frequently. It happened that one night I was riding home late – I had attended a birth and the child had finally come just before midnight – and I cut through the wood, very near Locksley. I was …' He nodded, as if acknowledging a truth. 'I was indeed tired, but not so tired that my mind would conjure up phantasms, no. At first, I heard, rather than saw.'

'Heard what?'

'Music. Dim and ethereal music, drifting through the trees. I felt sure I must have nodded off in the saddle and proceeded to pinch myself, and, in due course, the music faded. I rode on, certain I had been dreaming. Then, as I crested the hill and began to ride down towards Hawk's Leap, I looked back; it was high summer, clear, but late, and the wood was dark, the sky studded particularly bright, and over the entire canopy I saw it.' He paused, seeming to look inward, remembering.

'What?'

'A black shape rising. An impossible shape; it was enormous, so opaque no cloud could conceal it.'

In spite of all his long years of observation and medical training that told him that only the things he could see, feel and replicate could be relied on, in spite of knowing Frederick's story was absurd, the hairs on the back of Arthur's neck stood on end. He kneaded the skin fretfully, and said, 'What happened then?'

His grandfather answered calmly. 'It remained in my sight for several seconds, but seemed to dwindle, then it was gone.' He watched Arthur from under his bushy brows, rubbing his temples. 'You'll think this nonsense.'

Arthur shrugged. That it was nonsense was the only conclusion that could be reached by a man of sense, but he didn't need to say it. 'What do *you* think it was?'

Frederick paused for a long moment. 'Perhaps nothing at all. Perhaps I imagined it.' He rapped the letter. 'But this, Arthur, this tells me I did not contrive the sight. There is *something* in the Puzzle Wood.' Arthur did not reply, and Frederick went on, in a more level tone. 'All I wish to do is protect the wood. To get Sir Rowland's promise that he will put a stop to his folly, and stop disturbing what he should not. To do otherwise will see the end of him, mark me.' He waved Musgrave's letter, seeming calmer at the thought of Sir Rowland's defeat.

Arthur sighed. 'Well, I did go to see him, anyway. That's why I was there this evening.'

His grandfather leant in. 'And what did the good baronet have to say?'

Carefully, he answered, 'There's a chance we may reach a compromise.'

'How?'

'He wants me to investigate some behaviour at the colliery. He feels things aren't as they should be.'

'Nor will they be. Coal! This far north?' Arthur was relieved to hear a more characteristic scepticism return to Frederick's voice.

'There is at least some. They have a full operation there.'

'A few threads might be found,' Frederick conceded. 'Not enough to make it worth destroying the hills. I can't believe you agreed to it. What if he finds out why you were in the Indies?'

'He's more concerned about the colliers. Besides, if you want him to change his mind, we don't have a choice, do we?' He was annoyed. He had gone to Locksley to argue on his grandfather's behalf. He had only taken the commission from Sir Rowland to make that argument more persuasive.

Frederick looked up sharply. 'He hasn't asked you to do anything odious?'

'No.'

Frederick replaced the letter in the book. 'You're a mite too gentle, Arthur. You need to be able to tell a man to go to the devil. It's my fault. I should have injected more backbone in you.'

'I'm going up to the colliery tomorrow after breakfast,' Arthur said, getting to his feet. His tone was short, but he was irritated at the reminder of his earlier cowardice, and badly wanted his bed. 'If I see Ned Parry in the morning, I'll pass on your condolences.'

'Don't do me any favours,' said Frederick, ruffled.

The two men bade each other goodnight more coolly than usual, and retired.

9

The wind picked up, whistling in the casements, tinkling the panes in the glasshouses. In her high-up room, Catherine watched the flickering oval of her candle lower inch by inch through the dark. She listened to the settling creaks of Locksley's ancient timbers and the call of an owl outside, accompanied by stranger sounds from night birds she did not recognise. Somewhere downstairs a clock chimed midnight. Still she did not sleep. Gradually, as she shifted on her front, and back again, then on her side, the wilder noises of the evening died away; but, circling the house, the mastiffs howled louder and louder. Even later, once the dogs had given up and bedded down, her ruminations robbed her of sleep. However hard she tried, she could not remove the imprint of Mrs Parry's expression from her consciousness.

After the accident, she had watched as the body was taken away by Sir Rowland and the stiff figure of Dr Sidstone. Minutes later, Edie had appeared with a pail and cloths, wrung out some of the hot water and sunk to her knees to soak the tiles in rusty suds. Looking on, Catherine had wanted to take a cloth and help, but couldn't risk Sir Rowland seeing her lower herself to such a task. She had watched, not without sympathy, as the sobbing Edie scrubbed the dark blots from the chequered floor.

Long after her charge should have been asleep, Catherine settled Georgie in her bed. The little girl was pale and quiet, her skin clammy. They had found a pot of arnica balm in Cook's stores, and applied the aromatic salve lightly to the bruises.

These were worse than Catherine had first thought, running all the way up her arm. Georgie had said nothing else against her aunt, and it was all Catherine could do not to question her further about Emily. *What happened to her? What do you remember from the day of her death? Who liked her, who resented her?*

But Georgie wouldn't trust her if she did. She had no reason to disclose anything to her new governess. She might even tell her father.

Catherine closed her eyes, holding Georgie's cool hand lightly in hers. The outline of a song danced in her head. She thought perhaps her mother used to sing it, and tried harder to remember, focusing until the words floated near enough to pluck them out of distant time. The melody came back strongly, but she recovered only a scant few lines.

> *Nous n'irons plus au bois,*
> *Les lauriers sont coupés.*
> *La belle que voilà,*
> *La laiss'rons nous danser.*

The words seemed to have some other inspiration than memory. Something about this place, she felt, had reached in and lifted them from their prison of flesh and bone. Georgie seemed to like it. Eventually, beneath the gentle tune, her breathing slowed and her eyelids lowered. The little girl drifted off more easily than Catherine expected. She waited until Georgie was properly asleep, then washed and retired to her own bed, leaving the inner door ajar.

She was not as lucky as her charge. Each time she closed her eyes, she saw it again – not the fall, but the rictus look that had arrested Mrs Parry's face as she stared into darkness at something in the passageway that *should not have been there*. In the dim, cold room, that word – *something* – made itself better known. Its ramifications did not escape her, and neither did she did think she was the only one to contemplate them. She remembered Sir Rowland's paleness, her inexplicable feeling that he was drowning in plain sight. What did he know about this place that she didn't?

She thought again about Dr Sidstone, the stringy physician. *Just an accident*, he had said. No. Mrs Parry's death was connected with Emily's, somehow. There had been a presence on that landing. The housekeeper's expression before she fell had spoken louder than words. But who? She tossed and turned, her mind racing as she realised she could only say for certain that she, Georgie and Mr Parry had been downstairs. Any other person in the house could have been on the landing. She had to be wary, and not let her mask slip for a moment.

In the early hours, still unable to empty her thoughts enough to sleep, she got out of bed and paced the room. A coiled discontent sat heavy inside her. There was something wrong in this house, exactly as she had told Dr Sidstone, but even as she thought of her words to him, she flinched; of course the colourless physician thought she was hysterical. He might be cowardly but he wasn't stupid. When women spoke of nebulous evils, educated men smirked behind their handkerchiefs and snuffboxes. It had always been so.

A sudden flurry of raindrops spattered the glass as a harder gust of wind blew down from the hills. She rubbed the goose-pimpled flesh of her upper arms and stared into nothingness. It was a long time before she saw something move. Or not move, exactly. A light winked and weaved. Close or far? It was hard to gauge its distance and impossible to see anything other than the light itself, but it blinked on and off, not rhythmically, but skittishly, and she could imagine that whoever held it moved in and out of the trees.

She watched it for a time, wondering who could be out there with a lantern at this hour, and what they were about. A minute or so passed, then, just as it had been kindled without notice, it was gone. It did not drift out of sight or ebb away; it was snuffed out. She waited for it to reappear, scanning the darkness, trying to distinguish between the blackness of the wood and the line of the top of the slope, but she could not, and it did not return. As the clock downstairs crept towards a drizzly dawn and chimed five times, she crept back beneath the coverlet, huddled low, and finally found herself able to sleep.

She woke stiff from a bed not her own. Disorientated, she perceived that she was no longer between her own sheets in Abingdon, and lay still for a while to gather her thoughts, remembering all that had happened. As she roused herself fully, she rose and lit a small fire in the grate in the schoolroom, before checking the nursery.

Georgie was sitting up against her pillow. Her ragged short hair flickered in the light of Catherine's candle. Deciding not to mention the dreadful events of the night before, Catherine assessed her. Her temperature and appearance were normal, so she said she would come back presently and eat breakfast with her, then took a few moments to toilet and hang the few dresses she had brought. Afterwards, locking her trunk again with care, she returned the key to the arid vase on the sill and returned to the nursery.

Georgie's eyes followed her around the room as she neatened a cushion on a chair, then went to the mantel and examined its cluttered collection of jars, in sundry sizes, as if the little girl had scavenged them over the years from used-up jams and chutneys. A brass magnifying glass was buried in between them.

She picked up a jar, reading the label's endearingly childish penmanship – *Coleoptera: Adephaga: Gyrinidae* – then held the magnifier and peeped through the glass at the dark grey, shining shell.

'It's a water beetle,' she said, recognising its fishy eyes. Scanning the line of captured creatures, she said, 'Did you catch all of these yourself?'

'Yes.'

Looking at the water beetle more closely, she had to admire its perfection, and the detail of the thing, from the long, jointed front legs to the bristles on its hind legs that allowed it to swim. How gracefully its pattern fitted it for its task, she reflected, in a moment of awe. How did it know its own needs so well?

'I kill them with chloroform,' revealed Georgie, disturbing her governess's concentration. Catherine glanced up at her, surprised. 'It's all right,' the child reassured her. 'There are lots of them in the pond, and it's necessary if I'm going to know what each of them is.'

Now Catherine did not find the collection quite so endearing, and returned to her tidying. The room wasn't much of a nursery, she decided, as she went about. There were hardly any toys. She had always imagined a rich little girl would be inundated with presents from distant godparents and devoted aunts – dolls and marbles and dainty tea sets – but Georgie Bridewell seemed to have to invent her own forms of amusement, making do with chloroformed insects and sketchbooks in place of the things a child should have.

After a while, as her governess folded a fringed blanket, Georgie said, 'I didn't dream it, did I? The awful thing that happened.'

Abandoning her task, she sat heavily on the end of Georgie's bed. 'No. You didn't.'

'She really fell?'

'Yes.'

'And she didn't get up again?'

'No, Georgie. Some injuries are too awful for people to recover from.'

Georgie frowned, looking puzzled, like she was deciding something. After a few moments, she nodded to herself, picked up a riddle book from the side of her bed, and became engrossed in its pages.

A harried Edie came to Catherine's room at around seven o'clock. On a tray, she carried a macaroni dish, a slab of bacon, two rolls and a pot of tea. The maid's eyes were rimmed with red, her fair hair untidily pinned beneath her mop cap. She had slightly overlapping front teeth. Catherine recalled how Ned Parry had joked of several sweethearts at the Abbey. She had seen no other candidate young enough, so he must have meant Edie. Had this been what Mrs Parry had meant when she said the young woman was disappointed in matters of the heart? She remembered, too, how Ned had said he had his real sweetheart tucked away elsewhere. It was a shame, but the handsome young collier was flirtatious, she decided, and perhaps that had been enough to convince the maid that they were in love.

'Edie.' The young woman jumped at her own name. 'I didn't mean to startle you,' Catherine said.

'No, I ...' Edie smoothed her skirts. 'I am a bit fretful,' she admitted. 'Especially after last night.'

'What happened was so distressing, wasn't it? We can talk about it if you'd like. If it would help,' Catherine added carefully.

Edie poured tea, the slop of brown liquid over the tray betraying her upset. She lowered the pot, shaking her head. 'I'm fine, miss,' she insisted. 'No point talking on what's done.'

'Why don't you take some tea?'

'No, I must be getting on.'

'Who's to know?' Catherine said coaxingly. 'Here.' She poured steaming tea into a cup. 'I'll find another mug for Georgie.' She added milk and a lump of sugar, and Edie picked it up and sipped to test it, then drank it down quickly, wincing at the heat.

'I suppose you liked Mrs Parry?' Catherine asked. She couldn't see how this would be true, but Edie's dismay seemed real.

Edie replaced the cup delicately, and nodded. 'She was strict, miss, but not unkind.'

'I understand she had an affectionate family.' Catherine sipped her tea. 'Mr Parry and his son, Ned, who must be very upset. If he knows, that is,' she added, troubled at the thought that he might not. 'Perhaps I ought to call on him.'

'How do you know Ned Parry?' Edie's voice had changed, become taut, and Catherine glanced up to see the housemaid watching her out of puffy eyes, the look within hard and suspicious.

'We met on the road, just for a few minutes,' Catherine explained.

Edie took this in and said, with a prickly dignity, 'Ned lives with Mr Parry at the gatehouse, and he'll know by now anyway. There's no need for you to do anything, miss.'

Catherine nodded, then spoke low, so Georgie might not overhear on the other side of the door. 'This isn't the first tragedy to happen at Locksley, is it?'

Edie frowned. 'I can't think how you'd know that, miss.'

'I'm certain Mrs Parry told me.' She felt guilty, but the woman was dead and could raise no objection to the lie.

Softening at the mention of the housekeeper, Edie said, 'Not the first, no.'

'How did it happen before?'

'I couldn't say. I've only been here a few months. My dad's a collier,' she explained. 'Sir Rowland let most of the old servants go last spring, then found he needed someone to do the beds and meals and fires after all. He sent word there was work for me. But I didn't know Miss Murphy.'

'Still, I would have thought a young girl like you, knowing everyone in the village and at the mine, and here at the Abbey, would find people told her things. Did you hear nothing at all?' She measured her tone as she spoke, careful to sound merely eager for gossip.

Edie looked away and brushed a strand of hair off her face, hesitating. She said, in nearly a whisper, 'I heard she was a beauty. She wasn't liked by the mistress, or not much, anyway. And liked by the master a bit too much. But that's all I know,' she said, pausing at the door. 'Truly, it is.'

'Well,' said Catherine lightly, wondering where Edie heard what she knew, 'what wife in her right mind wants a pretty young woman in the house?' She kept up a confidential, catty air, as she had done as an under-housekeeper when being less than discreet.

'Exactly so, miss,' said Edie, nodding. 'Can't blame the mistress. It's one thing when a husband takes a fancy to a serv-ant – different when it's a young lady like yourself.'

'Does Lady Anne never come out of her rooms? Surely she would want to be vigilant if Sir Rowland ...' She left this sentence unfinished, arching an eyebrow to convey her meaning.

But Edie shook her head, her confidences at an end. 'You like to talk, miss, but I must shift to my work.' She hurried off with a pattering step. Over her shoulder, she called, 'I'll bring hot water in a bit.'

As she and Georgie shared the macaroni, Catherine thought about Lady Anne, the one member of the household she had not met, and whose character she had no way of studying. Edie had been right; a wife did not need to be wicked to resent the presence of a vivacious young woman in her home. Far from it. Thinking of her own marriage, not passionate or long, she knew, if children had come, as they had both wanted, she would have picked out their nurses and governess herself. She would have been a fool to do otherwise.

Beneath everything else, constantly, she thought of Emily. A beauty, Edie had said. But Catherine only remembered her sister's looks as a child. Emily, or at least the grown woman she would have become, was a dark shadow somewhere at the back of her mind.

With breakfast finished, Georgie rocked back and forth on a wooden horse, one of the few toys in the nursery, watching out of the window as Catherine readied herself. She used a kettle of warm water and a basin, with a linen sheet for drying, and, once she had made herself presentable, encouraged Georgie to do the same. As the little girl scrubbed her face and hands, she decided they would start work in the school-room. Sir Rowland expected teaching to begin immediately. He would be reassured if, bending his neck around the door, he were to see his daughter with a slate and chalk in her hand, and the new governess supervising arithmetical problems. But once the midday meal was done, she would have Georgie give her a tour of the house.

She looked through Georgie's dresses and found a dark velvet, a bit small, but that would do. Gently, she eased it over the child's petticoats, feeling consternation at the way the little girl had hacked at her hair, and how more than one red cut crusted her scalp. 'Usually in the afternoon we would do French grammar,' she said. Then, as Georgie's face fell, she said, 'But this afternoon only, you can show me Locksley.'

Georgie rocked in the saddle for a few seconds, seeming animated by the prospect of no French. 'Arithmetic this morning,' Catherine warned, drawing a frown. 'But first, let me tidy up your hair.'

She remembered the scissors she had confiscated, and located them. Taking care, she neatened the fuzz of dark curls into a short cap. When she had finished it was tidy enough, though austere against the child's delicate features. She realised Georgie was pretty in spite of her solemnity, without much of her father's coarseness about her. 'There,' she said. 'Much better.'

Georgie was quick in her learning, but easily distracted. The problems Catherine set every half hour were completed in a silent hurry, seemingly without difficulty, but soon she grew bored and began to be naughty, scratching her slate or drumming her feet, then trying to slope away towards her collection of jarred beetles. Catherine avoided the urge to scold her; it was better for Georgie to have something to do than dwell on the events of the previous day. At the end of the second hour, she allowed her charge to put the arithmetic aside and take up her sketchbook instead.

'What's this one?' Catherine asked, observing the strokes of the child's pencil as she sketched the outline of a slender black creature with pincered jaws.

'*Ocypus olens*,' came the quick answer. 'Devil's coachman.' Georgie bowed her head in concentration, her tongue protruding slightly to the side of her mouth. The drawing seemed to come easily to her, and, when engaged like this, she was an undemanding companion. Catherine began to enjoy watching her work. There was something soothing about the quiet tapping noise, with neither governess nor child feeling much need to talk. The time passed quickly.

They started the tour in the early afternoon. The day had not mellowed, but rather grown colder, and Catherine threw a dark red shawl over her dress. She took a candle, as the morning had been promising but now the clouds had begun to congregate, and the house lay in shadow. She and Georgie rounded their heads into each chamber. Her impressions of grandeur passing into neglect deepened as they went along. As they moved through the Abbey, the house grew darker still. Here, as downstairs, oil lanterns burnt brightly, but their task was more difficult. Soon it began to rain, making the rooms chill and melancholy. She stopped, looking out of the windows, considering how different everything looked once the sun went into hiding. From the north wing she could survey the back of the house. Beginning with a green-tinged terrace, the gardens sloped upward. Cypresses guarded its boundary, and behind these lay the wood, its thick canopy shielded by a pall of mist. Nearer, she made out the glasshouses, rain glancing off their ironwork, and a gravel path running through a sunken garden before it roughened, going off up into the trees.

Emily must have walked these corridors as Catherine did now, although perhaps more joyfully. She imagined her sister shunning the house, preferring the grounds, playing in the spring sunshine with Georgie between the glasshouses and the beds. Had she and her charge cut across the grass, and wandered into the wood, or embarked on quests to add to Georgie's collection of beetles? Since Catherine arrived she had fought a singular feeling of being her sister's shadow, a postscript in a story over which she had no control. That sensation was very strong now.

Georgie led Catherine down the passage. These other rooms were mainly for guests, hardly used. Catherine was glad to leave them and explore the south wing, containing the senior female servants' rooms – although it seemed only Mrs Parry had been actually accommodated here, with an adjoining study – and, Catherine thought, noticing the insult, Mrs Wingfield's suite.

'I suppose you try to avoid this part of the house,' she suggested to Georgie, who passed her aunt's doors on tiptoes.

'Aunt Wingfield likes me to stay in the nursery. But when Miss Emily ...' She stopped, shaking her head, pressing her finger to her own lips in reprimand. 'No,' she whispered. 'You are not to talk of it.'

'What?'

'I'm not to talk of it,' she repeated. 'I promised.'

Catherine held the child's shoulders before realising she gripped too hard and the ends of her fingers had whitened.

Georgie was flinching. Withdrawing her fingers, which suddenly resembled claws, she was ashamed.

'I'm so sorry.' Georgie's lower lip trembled. 'But who did you promise? Your aunt?' Catherine eyed Mrs Wingfield's doors, wondering where the tall woman was.

Georgie's look had changed. She resembled her father: pale and guarded, aware of something she would not share. Catherine could not tell whether she, or something else, had ushered this fear into her expression.

'Georgie!' she called out, as the child turned and ran down the dark corridor, quickly vanishing from sight.

10

Even as she called to her charge, Catherine kept her voice low. It would not do for her employer to see she had already lost control. Passing into the west wing, she realised Sir Rowland's rooms were probably here, and presumably this was the way to the tower, where Lady Anne abstained from her own life, and her daughter's.

She peered into alcoves that housed ebony elephants with curving tusks and birds under bell jars, and stood on her toes to look behind a carved Chinese chest. She could no longer hear footsteps. Probably Georgie had stowed herself away amongst the furnishings. *Come out*, she willed. Pulling aside the thick curving drapes of hunter's green that separated her from the window seats and the driving rain, she murmured the child's name as she searched the passage end to end. At the next turn, as she looked into the gloom, a shadow skipped ahead, then vanished from sight.

'Georgie! Come back here!' she whispered furiously, but was answered only by the soft noise of a closing door ahead, and the unmistakeable click of a key turning in a lock.

She hurried through passageways that seemed to be getting darker and more chill. Now she and her candle were brighter than their surroundings, and she progressed slowly at the centre of her own small sphere of light, hearing only the swish of her dress against her legs. After a while, she came to a meeting of three ways, and saw she might go on, deeper into the west wing, or turn right down a staircase forty or so yards ahead. The final way went left, beneath a sturdy stone archway, through which a set of double doors was just visible, nestled in the wall. She hesitated, considering the arrangement of the building, then went left, under the arch.

These had to be the doors to the west tower. She was drawn to them. They seemed older than anything else she had seen at Locksley, their ancient oak lengths cracked and desiccated. But something about them was disquieting, too; standing there, she felt odd, as if she had just missed someone, whose thin echo remained. She put her free hand to the door and spread her fingers. The wood was surprisingly cold. A heavy lock was embedded in the timber. No key. She pushed lightly, testing, but their securing from the other side must have been the noise she had heard, because both doors held fast.

But was it her charge who had snuck within? Georgie shouldn't be here, and Catherine could not rap on the doors, or call out to her. This was Sir Rowland's unbreakable rule. She could not gainsay it without losing her place.

She imagined the little girl slinking past these rooms, desiring only her mother's arms. Lady Anne seemed to have chosen her own isolation and abandoned her daughter to the care of governesses and servants. No wonder Georgie was wild.

If her charge had locked herself behind these doors, Catherine would have to wait for her to come out. She could do that in the nursery. But Georgie could still have run the other way, down the passage. Carrying on, she went into each room. They were family bedchambers, papered in pink daphnes or white and gold leaf. She scurried in and out as quickly as she could, opening wardrobes and checking under beds. She had never felt more like a servant than she did now, entering spaces without permission, checking over her shoulder for their rightful owners.

The final door opened on a room rich with the scents of old wood and leather. It was very dark, but a thin beam of light stole in over the drapes. She skirted the wall and opened them, allowing in the light; then, turning, realised she had walked into a menagerie. Floor to ceiling, the room teemed with life. Or rather with death.

Birds, their feathered skins stretched over wire frames, stood mounted on a gathering of wooden plinths. A coven of ducks and a surly-looking owl were arranged in stiff upright poses meant to suggest vigour and breath. A pelican, leaning askew, reached for a waxy fish dangling on a wire. He would never catch it. It would never get away. They would remain forever in their predatory dance. The room felt disused, everything robed in a slick of dust, but quickly she realised it was not so; someone had been here. Works on zoology, botany and geology, edged in carmine, had been taken down from the shelves, and cases lay open on a walnut table without the grainy film that lined everything else. She ran her fingers over the wood, noting a partitioned tray of pinned butterflies and moths, their wings soft in brown and orange, their little black bodies speared through. Eggs were stored in soap and cigar boxes, their curves of pastel green, blue and pink resting in soft wool cradles. Some were the size of a woman's closed fist, others gleamed like tiny, breakable pebbles. Beside these, an ivory escutcheon held minerals, each sample labelled in an elegant hand. The words were alien – *pyrite*, *malachite*, *gismondine*, *spectrolite*.

'Better be careful, Red Riding Hood.' The voice came from the doorway. Some definition was missing from the consonants. She turned to see Sir Rowland leaning against the frame. His hair, which yesterday had been slicked back with a pomade, was roughly tousled. Smells clung to him: tobacco and, if she were not mistaken, port wine.

She recovered herself. 'Sir?'

'In the story,' he said. 'She strayed off the path and ended in the wolf's belly.'

'Yes, sir,' she said meekly, hoping he wouldn't ask about Georgie. She made to walk by, but he caught her arm, his fingers gripping her shawl. 'Sir!' she said, trying to move back into the room. Was this what happened with Emily? Was what Edie had taken to be forwardness really a familiar, sordid tale of a rich man unable to keep his hands to himself?

'Where is Georgie?' he asked, his mouth too close to her ear.

'Resting,' she lied. 'A midday sleep is good for a child. Sir Rowland, would you please release my arm?'

He did, but blocked the doorway, looking as if seeing her for the first time.

He knows.

But he seemed to have other ideas. 'If you are interested enough to come in here, let me show you where my father's interests lay.'

'I must be getting back to Georgie, sir,' she said, with pretended regret.

'Nonsense,' he said. 'Stay. Look.'

He went to the shelves and took down three or four more works, handling them roughly, dropping them on the table alongside the collectors' cases. He stared as if he wasn't sure how they got there, as if he had only just remembered where he was. She took a step back and absorbed the titles: *Buffon's Natural History*, *Philosophie zoologique*, *Essay on the Theory of the Earth*, *Views of the Architecture of the Heavens*. They gave her an odd feeling of memories drifting just out of her grasp. No. It was nothing, just a fancy of similar things once lived.

'Look at all this,' Sir Rowland said, waving a hand at the birds, the eggs, the pinned butterflies and moths. 'His obsessions. I should set light to all of it. Except the rocks. Those I'll dump in the ocean.' He spoke with a bitter fervour.

She looked about, thinking this had to be where Georgie inherited her love of collecting. 'Many men like to curate things from the natural world, do they not?'

He scoffed. 'He kept a whole house of this rubbish. It's all in the attics. Meteorites, cowrie shells, endless sketches of lice and fleas and aphids. All without use.' He dug into a crate, disturbing shredded newspaper, and pulled out something that he tossed up and down in his hand. 'Here,' he said, throwing it.

She caught it at the last instant. His gift was about the size of a turnip, pale, smooth and cold. Her fingers moved over its hard ridges, and it took her a few moments to understand what she was holding.

A skull.

She recoiled, but as her hands sought their own knowledge, she found herself touching long, curved teeth, letting the pads of her fingers explore deep orbital cavities and the high bones of the forehead. It had never been a person. It had belonged to some sort of ape. She breathed again.

'There are endless piles of this stuff,' said Sir Rowland darkly. 'Bones and eggs, and drawings of every sort of creature imaginable.'

'Why did he collect it all?' she asked.

Sir Rowland took the skull back, examined it for a few seconds, then threw it down with a sudden power. It cracked, rolled, and came to rest beneath the wired pelican. He took several steadying breaths, and looked around the overstuffed room.

'He was always buying books and maps like they cost no more than candles, as if we had nothing better to do with our capital.'

She let him talk. Clearly, Sir Rowland had got himself into the mood to share his thinking; she wasn't going to stop him.

'Then, soon after the upheavals of 'thirty-nine, he decided to retire to Naples, and leave the estate in my hands.' He waved an arm, bleakly, at the pelican and its waxy prey. 'His passion just died. I'll never know precisely why. I tried then to be rid of it all. I thought Anne's father would take some of it off my hands – he and my father were very thick, when my father was here, and their interests ran together, but …' He stopped, seeming to think better of his chattering tongue. 'Then, when Grizel went to Ireland, I thought to ship some of it over to her there, but her husband had about as much interest in that as he did in her.' He trailed off, gazing at the clutter. 'Now I must work out what to do with it.' Running his hands over the stack of books, he opened a cover and read aloud from some scribbled words. '"He who is God by nature converses with those he has made gods by grace, as a friend converses with his friend, face to face." St Symeon. And St Irenaeus: "If the word has been made man, it is so that men may be made gods." Do you believe, Miss Symonds, that one thing can become another?' he asked, almost idly, but the fear she had detected earlier had leaked into his stance, and his hands shook against the blue leather of the book. It was called *Vestiges*, with some longer title she did not have time to read.

A *vestige*. That was something left behind. Like a clue. Like a sister.

'I don't know what you mean,' she answered.

'My father would talk about the philosophers. Heraclitus, Plato. *Nothing ever is. Everything is becoming*,' he intoned. 'My mother called it blasphemy, bade me shut my ears, or God would hear, and abandon me. That's the question on the rack in all these books,' he said. 'Has God abandoned us, Miss Symonds? Does he hear our cries, our prayers, our little …' he paused, releasing a humourless laugh, 'struggles? Are we unique in his Creation, or are we, after all, just a few paces beyond the beasts of the field? My father made it his quest to discover whether we are, as scripture might suggest, God's beloved children, or whether we have mischaracterised Nature, deceiving ourselves that She has some special interest in us, when in fact She is wholly impersonal, red in tooth and claw.'

'You talk of things beyond my competency, sir,' she said.

Seeing how he stared, as if his eyes burnt out his sockets, she feared he was mad. Some struggle raged inside him. He ran his fingers over the binding of another book. She thought he might tear the thing apart as a frightening momentum entered his words. 'Transmutation. *Evolutio*. The unrolling of the scroll of Creation. Men transforming into something new. These ideas convulse the world. They were my father's obsession. He believed – though I never saw sense in it – that if the scientific men are right, and the globe is older than we have thought, and we have changed as part of the physical world, then God, too, must be part of that world, just another step on the ladder. He believed we might transcend our material existence and see God face to face. He maintained there was no reason anything might be regarded as impossible. Man's lifespan, his awareness of spirit, life and death themselves, all were part of a progress. With enough time, or pressure, anything could change into anything else, as coal becomes diamonds; and in light of those considerations, why should we regard anything as miraculous? Why should we say Christ was anything but a man?'

She hardly parsed his words, but it was as if she had heard them before. The feelings they evoked slithered up inside her like earthworms. She had never been this conscious of her ribs, her heart encased within them, her dry tongue, the tread of blood behind her eardrums.

'I'm not sure I understand you, sir,' she said, feeling faint. 'Mine was a simple Church education.'

'That's why I chose you,' he said, staring down the book. 'I want Georgie to have a good Sunday School knowledge of the Bible. It's not healthy for girls to be exposed to such ideas.' He placed a single finger against the spine and pushed it away. 'You're a modest woman, Miss Symonds,' he said, sounding more alert. 'What should I make of that? Is it a veneer for my benefit? So many of your sex, you see, are not what they seem.'

Inside she was panicking, but answered levelly. 'I seek only to provide a proper education for Georgie, sir.' When he grunted, she added, 'Might I ask if there is anything I ought to look for in her? For instance, is she likely to speak about what happened to Mrs Parry?'

Sir Rowland went to the window and pulled aside the drapes, staring out. She had the sense he was watching for something. He murmured words not meant for her. 'All quiet now. No lights at all.' Then he turned back, distracted. 'You should know the facts, I suppose. One of the servants will only let it slip.' His mood seemed to dip further. 'Georgie witnessed another death not long ago.'

She had not expected him to tell her himself. 'How dreadful,' she said. 'Might I know what happened?'

He returned to the table, stroking a wing on one of the butterflies with surprising delicacy. 'We don't know exactly. She was taken into the woods by her governess to play. At some point they were separated. When my daughter was recovered many hours later, Miss Murphy had taken her own life. Georgie was found with the ...' he inhaled deeply, seeming to wrestle with how to describe it, 'the body,' he said, in the end.

Her heart hammered. Georgie might have witnessed it. 'Was there an inquest?' she asked.

'What?'

'I meant to say, was there any investigation?'

'Everything was done properly.' His voice had changed again, the confidences removed. Perhaps he saw he had revealed too much. His fingers coaxed the crêpy membranes of the butterfly's wings away from the backing paper, and crushed them. 'Best be getting back to the path, Miss Symonds, if you wish to avoid the wolf.' He gave a pained half-smile, and nodded towards the door, steadying himself against the table as she went.

II

In the morning, Frederick's mood had improved. He ate a hearty breakfast and seemed to have forgotten the mutually churlish note on which they had parted the night before. As they ate, Arthur remembered something his grandfather had said. 'I ought to have checked – did you say you and Sir Rowland quarrelled about Lady Anne, as well as the wood?'

Chewing his toast, Frederick said, without embarrassment, 'It was my opinion, after Georgiana Bridewell was born, that Lady Anne ought to refrain from the marital bed.'

'Sir Rowland can't have been pleased,' Arthur said.

'As you'd imagine,' came the dry response. 'He approached me on the very day of Miss Murphy's death. He wanted me to look at his wife again. Well, I didn't see why I shouldn't take his money, so I consulted with Lady Anne.'

'What was the matter?'

'The same as ever it was. She's tiny, with a crooked pelvis. The child almost killed her.' He sipped, shaking his head. 'But between you and me, I'm convinced Lady Anne was quite relieved.' He laughed so suddenly he lost some of the tea, then wiped his whiskers clear.

Arthur flushed, returning to his newspaper. 'There's nothing else wrong with her?' he asked.

'Nothing at all. I write everything down,' Frederick said. 'I always have, as you know, and I remember the case distinctly.'

It was true. Frederick kept thorough notes on all his cases.

They finished eating without much further conversation. Arthur started for the colliery after breakfast, advancing north-west from Hawk's Leap. Soon he was out of the wood and on the upland flats, using a cane, gauging his way across wet moorland overspread with purple grasses. As he pushed on in the face of a persistent drizzle beneath a writhing band of cloud, he estimated his destination was an hour's rough hike away. That was fine. He enjoyed walking. He had hated his dozen years in the soupy damp of Batavia, all insatiable mosquitoes and fishy reek, and harboured no dislike of the fresh cool of the border hills. Yet he found he could not shake off the sensation of being out of consonance with his surroundings. His grandfather's talk of gods and Celts – as rum as it all was – had done its work, and he was dogged by two things as he picked his way over the soggy moor: his grandfather's ghosts, and his own.

In Newport, that night thirteen years ago, they had gathered in twos and threes in a glut of rain, and shared news in anxious voices. Some carried pikes and cudgels, but others buried empty hands in their pockets, or sheltered pipes with shivering palms. Arthur, shifting his feet to squeeze some of the water from his boots, had wondered whether the rain presaged disaster. Perhaps not in Wales, he had thought, eyeing the unrepentant sky. They had marched up to their laces in water, then halted between Risca and Cefn. Rumours passed like wildfire as they awaited other men from across the heads of the valleys. After about an hour, the column broke into groups, some finding sanctuary under the eaves of the buildings, others lingering on the outskirts, eager to be off. Waiting wore everyone's patience thin. Some began to make suggestions: search the houses, drag shirkers from under their beds and force them to stand with their friends. Soon, the sound of pikes putting in windows broke through the rain. A dog yelped, then fell silent, and a boy cried for the dog, his racking sobs forming a small part of the night's clamour.

Arthur and Barnabas claimed a doorway, settling in with their boots half-buried in mud. The spot stank of manure. Barnabas didn't seem to notice their sordid surroundings. 'Once we control the town, it will be a base for what comes next. A wider rising right across the country. We'll be able to speak to Parliament from strength, to force the authorities to hear our petition and accept the Charter. We might even get a hearing from the Queen.'

Arthur was more concerned with Barnabas understanding the danger of what they were about to do. Holding his lantern in one hand, he used the end of the scything knife he had received at Newbridge to scratch a crude diagram in the frame. He created a simple outline of the road towards Stow Hill.

'This is the Westgate Hotel, here. If the Chartists gain control of the hotel, it will act as a signal for a wider rising, in Newport and then beyond the town.' He thought, remembering what had been said in the tavern. 'They'll take the turnpikes, block the roads and apprehend the mayor too, I expect. They'll try to take the workhouse,' he said, pointing north of the turnpike gate. 'They say there are weapons there.'

'Arms for two hundred men,' agreed Barnabas, with evident satisfaction.

Arthur did not want to argue. He didn't point out the brutal truth, that even though they were thousands now, not hundreds, they still did not have enough weapons to win. 'There's gunpowder in the warehouses here,' he said, pointing with the knife. 'But not undefended. They're not fools. The authorities will know of the march by now. They'll send word to Bristol for more soldiers, maybe even to London.'

Shaking his head, Barnabas said, 'That doesn't matter. The Westgate can be held against hundreds – maybe even an army.'

With more patience than he felt, Arthur said, 'Yes, and that's good for the rebels if they can take it, but disastrous for them if they fail.'

Barnabas, hunched beneath the dripping arch, flinched. Arthur knew why; *the rebels*, he had said. Not *us*. *Them*. After a few moments, Barnabas said flatly, 'No one is forcing you to be here.'

He hated what he heard in Barnabas's voice: pity, laced with contempt. 'Leave with me,' he said. 'We could go to Abergavenny, or Brecon. My grandfather lives near Longtown. This madness will pass, and we'll be—'

'Pariahs, as we should be if we betray our friends,' interrupted Barnabas, the criticism cutting through Arthur as his knife had cut through the wood. He crooked his neck and stared out from beneath his hat. 'Just go, if you're going.'

'I won't leave you.' He took a furtive glance around. Men with rifles milled about, guarding the way out of the village. 'I don't even know if I could.' He looked again at his sketch. 'But if this goes on, we'll soon march down the hill towards the Westgate.' He drew breath. 'All I'll ask is that you stay out of the front ranks. Keep to the middle of the column.'

He reached for Barnabas's sleeve, but his friend pulled away. 'You ask me to let others stand where I will not.'

'I ask you not to run towards your death!' Arthur hissed, conscious of the nearby glow of pipes, fearful in case someone overheard.

A shape passed their doorway, a man, wearing oilskin, with a long face covered in pockmarks. He stopped to spit, and stared, seeing the coldness between the huddled pair. When they were alone again, Arthur couldn't voice his true feelings. The words seared his throat. This was a world that would only spit his sentiments back at him. A world that would not change for him, no matter his desires.

More than a decade later, these ghosts followed him like foot-pads. They crept out of the shadows of his mind and whispered in the damp grasses. Their presence could be heard in the growling *kaa-kaa*s of the crows overhead, as if they mimicked the laughter of violent men.

Gradually, his path joined the colliery road. Each day, he knew, the hewers and banksmen trekked up from the rows of cottages that spotted the lower valley. They came up the drift road, a walk of more than five miles, though some, like him, took the quicker, steeper route. Of course, by now it was nearly nine in the morning; the miners would have left their cottages by four, carrying just bread and cheese, with tins of tea or beer. They would have been underground since before sunrise. Silence reigned over the hills.

But within a few more minutes he heard the voice of the colliery – shouting and pistons, neighing horses and dragging wheels. As he walked into the shadow of the works, it was as if someone turned back the clock on his life. Everything felt so familiar. He joined the tramroad and passed men mending a section of the single rails. Two were young, the third older, short and wiry, with a beard reaching his chest. As he approached he saw their silent communication: *here's a one, look sharp*. Their humour was indiscernible unless you knew where to look: a crinkle around the eyes, a returned smile. Two heads went quickly back down. But the bearded man looked over Arthur's greatcoat, and his walking boots, too little used.

'Good morning,' Arthur said. 'I'm on the hunt for a Mr Dowle.'

'Tried the gates of Hell?' muttered one of the younger men, and his companion let out a hard laugh, interrupted by a cough. Phthisis, Arthur thought. Early in its progression. The older man hitched his belt and glowered until his juniors returned to their work. Arthur saw his right hand was clawed and he hefted the crowbar with his left.

'Which way to the office?' asked Arthur.

The man continued to stare. His face was pockmarked with old scars. After several long seconds he offered a nod in the direction of the gate. 'Next to the lodge. Not sure he's in there. I tried once already. If you see him, tell him there are men looking for him.'

'Thank you,' said Arthur. 'What's your name?'

'Harris.'

The man Sir Rowland was worried about. An agitator? A leader, certainly, from the way the younger men deferred to him.

'I'm here on Sir Rowland's behalf. If your business with Mr Dowle is urgent, I could raise it with him.'

Harris's gaze hardened. 'No, sir,' he said. 'I'll come by and by.' He looked Arthur up and down again. 'Have I seen you before?'

'I'm newly arrived in Herefordshire.'

'Still,' said Harris slowly, 'I know your face.'

Flustered, Arthur shook his head. 'I was here as a boy. My grandfather is Frederick Sidstone, the doctor.'

'I know the doctor,' said Harris. 'Still, I've seen you somewhere.'

He had only just arrived, and already someone had said the worst thing anyone could say: *I know you. I know your face.*

'You'll want to get that cough seen to,' he told the younger man. 'Come and see me when you can – no charge.' He received a wary nod for his pains.

As he was about to walk away, he thought of Mrs Parry, and said impulsively, 'Is what happened at the Abbey yesterday generally known?'

Harris understood immediately. 'Word came from the Parrys,' he said shortly. 'Bad business, that.'

Arthur assented, then lowered his head and walked off. Soon, he saw a brick engine house, a pit lodge that sheltered the shaft, the headgear, and the bank, where coal was dragged by the pit brow workers to the weighing house. Towering above the squat buildings stood the upcast chimney, in red stone.

As he entered the pit yard, a distinctive smell hung in the air. Sulphur, from the blasting. He walked over stony ground, passing tubs and whining cartwheels, wanting to cover his ears against the crank of the pistons, shovels scraping, the noise of trams full of rubble for slinging on the looming heap behind the works. But there was a slowness about everything. Too many men on the surface, and little urgency about their activity. Were they dragging their feet? Was this what Sir Rowland had meant by organising? It was a simple way to disrupt the work, to do everything as lethargically as possible.

He found Dowle quickly. A row was breaking out, and he was in the eye of the trouble.

'I tell you, Mr Dowle, there's firedamp, very thick,' said a fellow near the overman. 'The candles were blue-capped. It's a bag of foulness down there. The struts are rotten.'

'Bollocks,' said Dowle. 'I was down with the lamp first thing. The struts were replaced a month ago.'

Some men murmured refusals. One, braver than the rest, called out that there should be a proper fireman on the shift, then another demanded Dowle call the inspector.

'That'll take days,' said Dowle aggressively. 'But step forward, anyone who doubts my word.'

Nobody moved.

More workers drifted on to the pithead. Most were young, only a few over fifty years. Some were just boys, squatting on their hamstrings. Arthur remembered from Barnabas that it would be their job to manage the air doors and carve the windways to prevent firedamp, the perilous gas the men were anxious to convince Dowle was present. Was it? Or was this a pantomime to impede the work? He looked around and saw Harris standing away, near the gates. Eventually, Harris stepped forward and the others fell silent. Harris faced Dowle.

'I say there's firedamp down there. We've heard bubbling. We won't work unless you test it.'

Dowle's face was full of anger. 'Hear this: any man not wanting to work the day won't hear argument from me. Not from Stephen Dowle. But he as takes that path doesn't return tomorrow. And those as don't return, don't keep their cottages. Sort out who between yourselves.' He kicked a clod of dirt as he stalked off towards one of the buildings. Arthur was forced to follow.

The watchers drifted away, breaking up into twos and threes. One delayed to pick up his tools from the floor, then overtook Arthur with a blunted mandril on his shoulder, turning to look at him as he went. He was young, perhaps no more than twenty, with dark hair and a black eye, which caught Arthur's attention. His heart leapt in his chest as he saw a bone structure that was fine, masculine, everything about it full of intelligence and potential. He was so like Barnabas it was crushing. Then, with a look somehow older than his age, almost pained, the boy walked into the lodge.

A stream of men in checked flannel and black round-crown hats with ends of candles stuck in the brims went off in one direction, and Dowle in the other, towards a short iron staircase leading to what Arthur presumed was the office. Arthur quickened his pace. Dowle had just slammed the peeling blue door behind him when he caught up.

He knocked.

'What?' came a growl from within.

Picking up his cane, he rapped smartly three times. The door was thrown open.

'What the—' Dowle stopped, taking in Arthur's manner and apparel. His eyes narrowed, his voice running colder. 'Who might you be?'

Arthur introduced himself.

Dowle shook his head. 'No one called for a doctor.' He looked at Arthur's boots and the muddied hems of his trousers, then smirked. 'Certain you have the right place?'

'If we might sit down, I'll explain why I'm here.'

Dowle extended an arm with theatrical subservience. 'Be my guest.'

12

Catherine had evaded Sir Rowland, but Georgie still evaded her. The little girl knew the house better than her governess. Deciding to check the lower floors before returning to the nursery, Catherine descended the back stairs, watching for a flash of plum-coloured velvet. The house was cold and shadowed. Things were left undone, curtains closed, oil lamps and gasoliers unlit. As she walked, Catherine felt the first stirrings of hunger. She wondered whether the kitchen staff were here, and began to see how Mrs Parry had held the delicate balance of the house in place; now she was gone, things had begun to unravel.

Catherine had never been an enthusiastic housekeeper. She had understood her task: to maintain the hours and orderliness of the house and attend to the comfort and convenience of all, appearing unruffled, in control every minute of the day. She had done her job well. Then she had caught William's eye, and seen how he, a greying widower, admired her looks. Every time she walked into a room he grew nervous, shuffling things around and requesting things he didn't need – ink, when there was a full well, coffee he let go cold. But that was nothing. A woman doesn't have to be very admired to attract that sort of attention. Youth and any slight prettiness will do the trick, and so she ignored it, not wishing to lose her place. It was when William asked her to read to him in the evenings, and asked about her family, that she knew his interest had deeper roots. She related some of what she remembered. She was not a particularly honest woman, so she kept some things back. She told him her mother had died of consumption, which was true. Her father, an artist, had struggled with his nerves, which was almost true, and they had been reduced gradually, inexorably, into poverty. That was certainly accurate enough.

'Where is your father?' William had asked one night, firelight dancing on his thinning hair. He looked tired, and she sensed his loneliness at the end of a long day. He drew his chair close and leant forward, his expression warm.

'I don't know.' That was the first real lie.

'What happened to your sister?'

'I think she went into service.' She hesitated, her memories flickering far and near. 'I can't quite remember,' she said, in the end, with a frustration she tried to keep out of her voice. 'She was two years younger. When she decided to leave, I believe I had already found work. I seem to remember –' but she didn't, not quite '– that was how it was.'

'Was this before or after your mother's death?'

'After.' Again, she was uncertain. Everything about the past drifted on an unreliable sea. Had her mother died first, or had Emily left before that end? When her father was taken away, was this as a result of her mother's death, and Emily leaving, or had these things happened before? How could she have forgotten so much?

'This isn't normal, you know,' William commented, in bed, a week after they married. His fingers drew little circles on the skin between her forefinger and thumb. She stared at the decorative mouldings lining the ceiling. 'People don't just forget most of their childhood. Something must have happened to make you fly from your memories like this.' Did a hint of suspicion enter his voice? A realisation that he had rushed into marriage, and that, really, he knew nothing about the woman lying next to him?

'I thought everyone forgot things,' she said lightly.

'Oh, they do,' he admitted. 'But not like this.'

She missed William, she realised, as she passed unnoticed down the servants' corridors. Though he had been grey and so much older, and it had been his fate to be unexciting, he had been kind. Anything she wanted was his pleasure to provide. He had lavished money on her, spoiling his young wife with jewellery, dresses and furnishings. Her enjoyment of this generosity wasn't just material; she had liked being first in someone's heart, preferred for once. It was a novel experience, for her father had preferred Emily, and her mother, too, she believed. Why wouldn't they? Emily had been clever, gay, charming. Everything she wasn't. Again, this knowledge seemed to have crept up on her. She wouldn't have been able to articulate it this morning when she woke. It was as if this house, or this place, had the power to remove stones in the walls her memory had constructed.

She didn't find her charge, so hurried up the main stairs, following the route she had walked a day earlier with Mrs Parry. The nursery door was open. 'Georgie?' The room was empty, but a little jar of iridescent beetles was toppled over, and the dead creatures gleamed in a patch of sunlight on the wooden boards. She shivered. Someone had opened the casement. As she neared to close it, she cast her eye over the grounds and spied a flash of movement on the far edge of the lawn, just before a sprawling rhododendron. Black boots, plum velvet, white petticoats. She considered shouting, but that would only draw attention. She would have to go down. Sighing at the child's wilfulness, she pulled the window shut and went to fetch her cloak.

She gasped as her door swung open. The room was alive with white.

It took her a moment to see it was feathers that spiralled through the air to the floor, not snow, and a further moment to make sense of the other things she saw. Her eiderdown had been dragged from the bed and viciously slashed, and its feathers lay soiled with earth. She didn't understand, then realised the plant on the sill had been pulled up by the roots, stamped on, its dried leaves scattered. In the middle of the detritus, the silver scissors she had taken from Georgie winked up at her. She rushed to them, picked them up in shaking fingers, and stowed them away in the pocket at the front of her dress.

The door to the passageway was ajar, though it had been locked from the inside. So Georgie had run away from her, arrived here and destroyed her governess's room; then, hearing Catherine coming down the corridor, run outside, just as Catherine had entered to survey the wreckage of her things.

She was aghast. How could a child do this? It wasn't just naughty; it was malicious, like something a wild animal might do. She checked herself, taking deep breaths. It would not help to jump to conclusions. But what other explanation existed? That someone else had done it, and Georgie had come in and found it like this? Knowing she would be blamed, she had run away rather than explain herself? The only other person who might act in this way, from what she had seen, was Grizel Wingfield, that coiled ball of spite. This malice was just what she would expect from her.

But then there was Georgie, who was said to be wild and deceptive, who knew where she had put the scissors, and had seen where she had stowed the key to her trunk.

The trunk.

Her blood ran cold. She rushed to the bed and dug beneath the frame. The trunk was still closed, but the key was in the lock. As she dragged it into the light, a pair of furled stockings fell from the leather lid. She had not left them out. She unravelled them, running her fingers through the wool. *No*, she thought, discarding them, yanking open the box. The lining paper was ripped. She fumbled inside the tear.

They were gone. Her wedding rings, her letters, her money. All gone.

Someone had them, she thought, pacing her room. Someone was pawing through them right now, connecting the threads. Could she run? How long would it take her to walk out of the valley? She might be caught in the grounds with the dogs. She would be hunted down, dragged back to face Sir Rowland. What if he had them already?

No, she thought, with gritted teeth. It must be Georgie. There was still time.

She went downstairs and slipped out of the back doors. The wind was higher now, ruffling the tops of the trees against an iron-grey sky. She searched the garden with exaggerated calm. All the way down the terrace, scanning the evergreen rhododendrons, she looked for movement. Detecting a rustle, she spun about, but it was just a cat scrounging the bedding borders. Further down the carriageway, still in sight of the windows, she kept to the periphery on a track overhung with dark fronds of pine, then passed the flinted outbuildings that housed the mastiffs. She was relieved to see them confined behind their metal grid, but they kicked up a racket as she went by, making her blood colder as she recalled how they had slavered, and surged towards the stag.

Still, she had other reasons to be fearful now. Someone had her letters. When they discovered she had been married, and understood that letters sent to Mrs Drake and her husband from Sir Rowland's own solicitor were in her possession, they would call in the constable. It would be over, and she would never know the truth.

Her only hope was that Georgie had taken them, but not been interested enough to read them. Even if she had, Catherine might yet convince her the letters were part of a game, or that they belonged to someone else altogether.

She neared the edge of the garden. Here, on the fringe of the wood, the grass grew longer, the orderly feeling turning to wilderness. Clambering over a shoddy stile, she found herself at the bottom of a slope, and took her first steps beneath the trees.

With each footfall, she carried the knowledge she had gained from Sir Rowland: Emily had died here. In these woods, her sister had tied a rope about her own neck, and taken her own life. This idea felt too heavy. She considered for the first time, as her boots sank into the damp undergrowth, whether that might be why she had been unable to accept it. Had her grief brought her here? If she stepped back, and forced herself to believe what she was told, even if she couldn't understand it, would that bring her peace?

A little way up the slope, she turned to view the Abbey. The trees were thin, the sun sinking behind the house. Sunset was still some way away, but the contours of the valley made the hour seem later than it was. The building stood in deep shadow. Her eyes fell on the west tower. Something – or so she thought for a moment – moved at its window: a shape, obscure, just the suggestion of a body outlined behind glass. Or perhaps it was nothing.

She still had to find Georgie. The path took a widely curving circle through patches of dog mercury and leathery, browning fern. The going got rougher, the ground swelling in irregular hillocks, their tops grown over, bottoms garnished with dark-loving moss. She crossed miniature valleys and fallen trunks, and again, the feeling of walking in someone else's footsteps overwhelmed her. Had Emily walked this exact path? Did she shove aside the same branches and trip over the same roots? As Catherine wondered these things, she stumbled in a dip, turned her ankle, and cried out in pain. She tested it with her weight. It burnt, but she could go on.

She rested for half a minute. Then, thinking she was far enough from the house to take a risk, she called Georgie's name aloud. Her voice rang in her ears.

Nothing.

A sharp wind bit. She was beginning to strain her eyes to see through the trunks and past their hazy crowns. She could no longer pass freely along the path. Had she gone too far? Georgie could be anywhere. There was no guarantee she had not slipped by on her way home. Catherine decided to double back, and followed the track around, eventually emerging into a clearing, shaking off leaves and twigs.

The clearing was about thirty feet across. A vast yew, almost hollow, split down the middle as if by lightning, stood at its centre. It might have grown in the heart of this forest for a thousand years. With the great branches of purpled bark seeming to weave around her, she was arrested by a sense of them as unchanging, and the tree being of this moment, but also not; it was evergreen, a thing of all times. And there was more: a flush of recognition. She *knew* this place. But it was not from imagining her sister scaling its trunk and branches to commit her terrible act. The feeling was sprung further down, deep inside. It was knowledge rather than a suspicion: that she had seen this exact place, and this exact tree, before.

She had been here before.

But there at its base, on a bed of poisonous scarlet arils and dark, needled fronds, lay Georgie, curled like a kitten, her back set against the massive trunk. Heedless of the lichen soiling her dress, she seemed to cling to the tree, and it to her.

'Georgie.' There was no sign she heard Catherine, and no sign of the letters. 'Georgie,' said Catherine, with heartfelt relief, at least, at finding her. 'For goodness' sake, come here. You'll catch cold.'

Georgie's eyes were open, but she did not acknowledge Catherine's presence. Catherine knelt amongst the roots and lichen, gently turning Georgie's face to hers. The child was shivering, and Catherine soon realised she was shaking, too. She forgot about the letters, the violence done to her room, as a cold certainty crawled over her.

'Is this where it happened?' she whispered, not daring to look behind or above.

But Georgie did not answer. She hardly seemed to register that she was no longer alone. In a timbre slightly deeper than her own voice, she said, 'She's still here.'

A slow creak sounded.

Catherine steadied herself on trembling knees.

The sun was behind the tree. With one hand, she shielded her eyes against the descending beams. It was almost too bright to make out each angular bough. The silhouetted shapes bled into one another. It was so easy to guess at form, to conjure, but she thought that, beneath the crook of one of the branches, something dark swayed back and forth. She brought up her other hand, shading her sight. The shape ended in a pair of boots, dangling four feet from the earth.

Her scream rent the air.

And as she screamed, the wood gave something back.

She remembered.

13

The sisters occupy opposite ends of the bed, Catherine on her front with her fist beneath her cheek, gazing at the boards, Emily on her back. It grows dark, the fraying nets turning rust-coloured with the last light. There is a lamp, but no oil, and no money for more. Sighing, Catherine burrows into the thin mattress, and pushes Emily's cold feet away. 'Your toes are in my face.'

'Then I consider myself lucky you don't have Cousin Amelia's chin, or they'd be lost altogether,' Emily says. Catherine snickers. The girls' laughter is overloud in the silent house. Father is still out, Catherine thinks. She has been listening more than an hour.

'Let's say our prayers,' she suggests.

'To the devil with your prayers.'

'Close your eyes.'

'They're closed.'

'Definitely?'

'Yes.'

'No peeping?'

'I wouldn't dare.'

Catherine joins her hands and closes her eyes: 'Our Father, who art in Heaven, hallowed be Thy name. Thy kingdom come ...'

'Do you think Father will get his commission tomorrow if he goes to London?'

Catherine scowls. 'We're praying.'

'But do you think he will? I'd die for a new dress.'

Catherine lowers her hands, thinking of muslin and ribbon and laces. She clears her throat and carries on. 'Thy will be done, on Earth as it is in Heaven.'

'He's only done two paintings this year. I should think we're practically destitute. But if he can manage this one, we'll be able to hire Jenny again. We could have guests. We won't have to pretend we're already dining out.'

Catherine sighs into the dusk. 'You must resign yourself, Emily. Father no longer enjoys popularity amongst those who can pay for an artist's time.'

'Then I'll make money myself. My painting is every bit as good as his,' declares Emily fiercely. 'Better than his used to be, before …' She stops.

'Before he turned into a human gin sponge?'

Emily snaps, 'Whatever you say. But I can copy his dullard histories blindfolded, and compose my own pieces. Better pieces. You watch: I'll buy my own dresses. Of scarlet silk, with lace petticoats.'

Catherine wants to talk of these things, and of the future, but jealousy makes her snipe. 'Because the world cries out for female artists?'

Emily is not boasting. She is just thirteen, but her work shows luminous aptitude. She accompanies their father, or used to, when there were the funds, to exhibitions. She remembers everything. She purloins his cast-off canvases and primers, leftover poppy-seed oil and pigments, and retreats to the attics to spend hours with the key turned. Her imaginings are of the play of light on moorland grasses, windswept landscapes inhabited by solitary trees, and wandering heroines on lonely shores. These scenes are alive. Catherine feels them in her body: the soft, frigid white of snow between her toes, their play of warmth and shadow on her skin. She understands Nature is vast, and she is small.

But some of Emily's compositions are darker. They shriek of anger and pain. Their subjects crawl and contort themselves, do violence to one another, and strive for dominance over the elements. These make Catherine shudder, and turn away.

Emily rarely finishes her paintings. She abandons them for lack of supplies, then conceals them beneath worn-out sheets and ancient linens brought by their mother from Wales. Catherine has only seen them at all because she suffers from an excess of curiosity.

'The world is changing,' Emily says, with sudden passion.

'Name even one woman artist of renown.'

'Mary Moser. She was a founding member of the Academy. Kauffman, another.'

Catherine doesn't recognise the names. After a moment, though she feels pious saying the words, she changes the subject. 'Dresses are not everything, you know. What's important is that we are kind. That's what God wants.'

The rejoinder is tart: 'God wants you for a schoolmistress by the way things are going.'

A schoolmistress. Sand desks, slates and knitting. Ruling the backsides of unrepentant brats as they recite their grammar. She shivers, reaching for the sandbag she has warmed on the range. 'I'll enter service. Then there will be no cooking.'

Emily snorts. 'Who wants to be a servant? I'd rather work in the biscuit factory.' She laughs as if this decline is not a real possibility.

'Then we had better pray Father gets the commission,' Catherine says. 'And that he can keep the money long enough.' She thinks of the bottle their father brought home the previous evening, bright green and full. This morning it was half-empty.

'Yes, let's do that,' says Emily. 'Let's pray for God's mercy on we poor girls in need of bonnets. Come – put your hands together. For mercy.'

Father is late to his toilet. His shirt and waistcoat are yesterday's laundry, he stinks of Old Tom and sweat, and is deceived by his faith in the power of a perfumed oil to cover it. But his distraction makes it easier for Emily to cajole him into taking her to Hyde Park, to meet a man Father admits he knows only a little.

'Leonard Cox attended the Hunterian School,' he says, combing down bushy sideburns. 'Knows a lot about phrenology and things like that. He has good contacts – men with money, who might take a project from me.'

'What's phrenology?' asks Emily, passing over a pot of unguent.

'He's been in the United States, studying the terrain. He's a member of the Royal College,' continues their father, ignoring the question. 'He knows up-and-coming men in philosophy, transcendentalism and so on. This meeting could lead to other commissions for men of high reputation.' He sounds gleeful.

'What's transcendentalism?' asks Emily.

Catherine runs the syllables over her tongue as she tidies the carnage around them. *Tran-scend-ent-al-ism*. She has no idea, and she doesn't care. She cares only about whether Cox will part with enough money to pay the butcher, the fruiterer and the baker, before they all end up in the Oracle poorhouse.

'I can come, then?' says Emily, still badgering, and he nods. Catherine sighs. All her sister has to do is pout like a frog to get what she wants out of him. He is too lazy, or too dulled from the night before, to resist.

She questions her father. 'Will taking Emily not mean double the price for tickets? Wouldn't it be better if we saved that money?' Behind their father's back, Emily, tying her worn bonnet strings beneath her chin, sticks out her tongue. He does not seem to hear. 'Well?' Catherine says, with a note of impatience.

'Don't keep after me, girl,' he snaps, in the end. 'It's going to come right. You'll see.'

She spends the day alone. The long summer hours pass slowly, and it's dark when Father and Emily return in a hackney cab. Father hasn't taken a cab for years. She opens the door to see Gilbert Murphy, artist to the gentry, half-supported by her sister, reeling like a flag in a high wind.

'Get him inside. Quickly,' she says, her eyes darting up and down the lamplit street. 'Why would you let him get like this in public?' she hisses, pulling him in by his jacket and nearly losing her grip. He staggers through into the hall, hitting one wall, then the other.

'He took me to a beer house after he met Cox,' Emily says. 'I waited outside, but I saw all the people and the landlord called me "pet".' She looks up, slyly smiling. 'I met Cox, too. And Uriah Caplin, who has a great fortune.'

'I don't care if you met the Pope.' As she declares this, their father is meandering up to the first floor and Emily sits on the bottom stair unlacing her boots. Her petticoat is grubby. She looks younger than her thirteen years, her green eyes glowing.

'He got the commission,' she says, throwing her head back against the stair. 'Mr Cox liked me. He'll pay thirty guineas for the painting. We're going tomorrow.'

Certain Emily must have misunderstood, Catherine says sharply, 'What do you mean, liked you?'

Emily cocks her head, pleased with herself. 'He said I was *divine*.'

'Perhaps you misheard, and he said you were a *swine*.'

'Put your claws away! You're to come, too. They're sending a carriage.'

Wealthy gentlemen do not send carriages across southern England for starving portraitists and their shabby daughters, she thinks. 'Father is going to paint, but what has that to do with you? Are you to sit for the painting? And why would I want to go to Bloomsbury?' She does want to go, terribly, of course.

'It's part of the bargain for the painting,' Emily says vaguely. 'I won't have to do much. Just sit while they commune with the sublime.'

'There's no point talking to you,' Catherine mutters, and pushes past Emily, heading for the stairs.

Father wrestles with his shirtsleeves on the far side of the bed. Between them, her mother dozes on faded pillowcases in a yellowing cream nightgown. Earlier, Catherine administered more of the laudanum than usual; twenty drops were taken before Jeanette Murphy's pain receded and she floated away. Her father rocks on his feet, and turns. 'Eh?' he says, as if she had spoken.

'Did Mr Cox give you money?' She stays near the door. In these moods, her father is easy with the back of his hand.

'Gi-munny?' He stumbles against the chiffonier.

She speaks slowly. 'Did he give you money?'

'Later,' he slurs.

'Then how was the hackney paid for?'

'Eh?'

'Never mind,' she says, eyeing his overcoat. What is left will be in his interior pocket. She'll wait until he crashes out on the bed, then take it.

Father is up early, calling for bacon and eggs. They have no bacon, nor eggs. It's bread and coffee, and he is lucky at that. She says nothing about the money – she left enough to allay his suspicions. The remainder is hidden away beneath a loose floorboard in the attic, rolled in a pair of stockings.

'What does Mr Cox want you to paint?' she asks, pouring coffee.

Grandly, he says, 'It's not a painting, exactly. It's more fluid than that. We will talk and carry out a few simple steps of preparation, and then see what happens.'

She brushes specks of sugar off the cloth. 'What sort of preparation?'

'Just a few theatrical things. They want to dress Emily up like a muse. They have some half-baked theory about accessing a higher state of being.'

'But what exactly do they want her to do? Are you painting her?' A bad feeling leads her to persist where she would not usually question him. His vagueness worries her.

'Nothing to concern you, girl,' he says gruffly. 'But you'll come along to help your sister. Keep her company.'

'Of course. And who are the other men?'

He preens. 'One is Uriah Caplin, the importer. The other is Sir Maurice Bridewell. He has some interest in naturalism, is a collector and so forth.'

'I'll be back in a moment.'

She takes the stairs two at a time. She smells leathery carbolic soap, and a hint of steam, and crashes into their bedroom, where Emily reclines in the tub, her long hair dark and wet.

'What do they want with you?'

Emily spouts water from her mouth, rubbing her eyes. 'What?'

She goes to the tin hip bath and falls to her knees. Emily sits back in alarm. 'You must tell me exactly what passed between Cox and Father.'

Emily sighs, poking slender toes out of the water. 'Oh, *that*. Father told Cox about my talent.'

'And then?'

'They talked about Cox's interests. I can't remember the word, but it was something about using some sort of fluid –'

yes, thinks Catherine, Father said *fluid* '– and opening up a line to something or other. Why does it matter? I'm cold. Can you pass me my things?'

Catherine looks about for the chemise. 'Did they say you were to bathe?'

'I ... I don't remember.' Emily looks guilty, then rallies. 'But really, I think you are just envious because Father took me with him, because Mr Cox and his friends want me to take part in their experiment ...' She glances away, knowing she has said more than she intended.

Catherine withholds the chemise. 'What experiment?'

Emily rolls her eyes. 'Nothing improper. Cox and his friends believe there is some sort of power of Nature, and that I'll see it. Then I have to paint what I see.'

'You? Not Father?'

'Yes. It only works if you're ...' she hesitates, 'young.'

'And for *your* painting, these men are going to pay thirty guineas?'

'Why wouldn't they?'

'How could you be so stupid?'

'Excuse me?'

'You're not going,' she says flatly.

Emily stands, water falling off her. 'I am, and you're coming, too.'

'Miss Symonds!'

A mist of rain lay on her eyelids. The autumn evening was cool and damp. The voice grew louder, drowning out her memories. She tried to hold on, but Emily's voice and the premonition of disaster it kindled grew more distant, sliding away like oiled rope. She opened her eyes to see Georgie's wide eyes staring down, and the little girl's face coming into focus. 'Miss Symonds!' Georgie repeated.

She looked up, fearful of the dark shape, the booted feet moving back and forth like a pendulum. Her heart shrank, but she saw only knotted branches and scarlet berries.

The terror remained.

This was what she had kept from William – her horror that she was mad, that only lunatics forget their own histories.

She scrambled to her knees, realising she uttered some of these thoughts aloud. Her words, like her memories, were tattered. She pointed into the air, splaying her fingers. 'Georgie – don't look ... Did you see? Did it happen here?' Georgie had closed her eyes and was shaking her head.

'You must tell me.' Catherine pulled up her skirts and grabbed Georgie's shoulders. 'Did you see? Please, tell me you saw!' Georgie cried out. Catherine realised she was shaking the child like a rag doll, and she dropped her hands away. 'I'm sorry,' she said, her voice high and unsteady. 'I'm sorry.' Again her craving for answers overwhelmed her. 'But did you come into my room earlier? Did you take my things?'

The fright in Georgie's eyes grew. For a moment Catherine saw herself as she must look to the child – filthy with earth, hysterical. She sounded half-mad. Forcing her voice under control, she said, 'If you have taken my letters, you must give them back straight away. I promise you won't be punished.'

Georgie shook her head, adamant. 'I didn't take them.'

Before she could say more, she heard a gravelly bark, and a man's voice through the trees. 'Miss! Miss!' Parry had found them. She looked through the trees, down the slope. Before him, one of the giant mastiffs strained against its rope, dragging him along with its nose to the ground. As they neared the top, it began to howl. Parry cursed as it pulled him towards them.

Catherine got to her feet, brushing the earth from her dress and frantically shaking Georgie's velvet skirts. They couldn't be found like this. 'Quick,' she said, licking her thumb and rubbing the child's cheek clean. She brushed away wild strands of hair from her own face. 'We were playing in the wood,' she said. Seeing Georgie's stricken expression, she said, 'You're not going to get into trouble, I promise. It was just a game.'

'Miss Symonds!'

'We're here,' she called.

Parry entered the clearing. He was red-faced and puffy-eyed, and struggled to hold the dog as it pawed the ground and barked. Its snapping jaws were so close that Catherine moved Georgie behind her. 'Been sent to bring you back to the house, miss,' he said, his voice gruff. 'Trouble at the mine. Master wants everyone at their post.'

14

Arthur tried to ignore the business of the mine intruding on the draughty room, and returned his focus to the ink-stained ledger. He frowned in distaste at auburn hairs imprisoned in the book's spine, and the leavings of unwashed fingers. But the book spoke of the man. Dowle's office was in a state of disrepair, his idleness obvious as soon as Arthur walked in; the chair he sat in needed fixing, the locker had dents where someone had kicked or dropped it, and constant, unpredictable dripping from different spots in the roof distracted him from his task.

The overman had made a small fuss about the inspection. 'I'll need the run of the office for a few hours,' Arthur had said.

Dowle's ugly face crumpled in a scowl. 'What for?'

'Sir Rowland would like an opinion on the books.'

'Then let him come and tell me that himself.' Dowle snarled the words, showing rotten teeth.

'Perhaps he will, but you'll need to take that up with him. In the meantime, I have his permission.' He wondered whether Dowle might try to stop him physically, but finally the big man had stalked across the pit yard, leaving Arthur alone.

The ledger's contents, too, were messy and hard to follow. He worked things out gradually. The book recorded wages paid out, trade at the company shop, purchases of equipment, and – these sections having more rigour – deductions from the colliers' wages, and rent for the cottages. He noted how the wages fluctuated. That wasn't unusual, as the men would be paid according to how much they hewed. Barnabas had worked harder at the end of the month, less hard at the beginning, so Arthur expected some lean weeks. But the sums didn't rise as each month drew to a close. It seemed more arbitrary than that.

There was a separate section for production, showing coal mined and sold. These amounts went down over time, which tallied with what his grandfather had said: there might be some coal here, but not enough to sustain an entire village. That might explain the workers' surly expressions. There wasn't the work to go round, but they still needed to pay rent, burn coal and feed their families. This put them into arrears. The figures owed by each miner and his family to the colliery were higher than Arthur expected. Each name – Harris, Parry, Lewis, Preece – was recorded next to their wages. The ledger showed that nearly every hewing man owed the equivalent of several months' wages to the company store. There were deductions for mandrils, gunpowder, chisels, even for the 'service' of weighing the coal cut by each man's family, so he could be paid.

So, it appeared either there was no money here, or someone had an interest in concealing the amount being mined, possibly to siphon it off and sell it. Arthur didn't think the latter was possible without Dowle's knowledge. All it would take was one or two allies to help him move stolen property, or distract more scrupulous eyes while he did.

Certainly, money had poured in, even if not much coal had been brought out. That money, though, dripped out everywhere, for timber, canvas and tar for brattice work, a new cage, tubs and pit ponies, rat poison. The mine was costing a king's ransom to run.

He closed the ledger, wondering what he was going to tell Sir Rowland. There was no clear evidence of theft, only the suggestion the mine would not be profitable however much Sir Rowland might invest. Arthur spun out of the chair and searched the office, pulling open the desk drawers, rattling the safe and digging through the locker. This last seemed to double as Dowle's bin, piled with everything from crusts of hard bread to old trousers to depleted books of green paper, and at the bottom, a bottle of poison, unsealed. Arthur frowned. Arsenic should be clearly marked and under lock and key. Still, it was the man's personal locker, so he closed it, seeing nothing else relevant to his task.

He crossed to the door, cursing as he tripped over a crowbar leaning against a barrel. Outside, he watched as the men drifted across the yard. What would they do when the coal ran out? For a moment, they all looked the same; beneath the dust and muck were different faces, heights, colouring, but they moved in the same way, not picking up their feet, expending no more energy than they had to. They looked like people he had known before, and he felt it again – Barnabas, beside him, near enough to touch.

He remembered Barnabas's grave. He had only found it this year. A wooden cross sunk in the earth, marked with a short inscription. What had his grandfather said? That he could not barter with life and death. Yet he was aware, beneath the memory, of his own fierce desire for it to be otherwise. There was nothing he would not bargain to change what he had done.

He looked about the yard.

'You there!' he shouted, towards a passing shock of red hair. Its owner, a boy, turned. Arthur said, 'How old are you?'

'Eleven.' The lie was spoken with a brazen cheek, and a smile. His top right incisor was missing. He couldn't be more than nine or ten. A little black dog ran circles about his feet, yelping.

'Fetch Harris, would you?'

'We're about to go down, sir.'

'I'll make it right if you miss the descent. Go, find him.'

'Don't know where I'd find him, sir. He mumped off.'

'Right. Parry, then. Ned Parry.' It was the only other name he knew. Then, he remembered. 'No, he won't be here. He …'

But the boy had already run away.

Watching him go, Arthur knew no boy that young should be going underground. Sir Rowland would have to be told. He resolved to add that to the list after taking one last look about the site, then interviewing Dowle. But then the door opened, and one of the miners walked in.

Arthur recognised the face under the mop of dark hair. It was the young man he had noticed when he arrived. The pained expression had left his face, making the resemblance Arthur had seen earlier even stronger. Ned Parry was broader than Barnabas had been, and at some point someone had broken his nose, but otherwise the two might have been brothers. But Barnabas would be over thirty now, and the boy in front of him was just coming into manhood. He was muscular, not tall, clean for his line of work, dressed in fustian and wool that someone had mended with a loving hand. He wore a handkerchief round his neck, and over his shoulder carried the thin pick of the hewer. A lantern hung from a hook on his belt.

Arthur's discomfort made him stern. 'You're Ned Parry?'

The boy nodded without coming nearer. He was wary. To him, Arthur must have appeared like authority. Probably, as well as his upset about his aunt, he was worried about losing his job.

'I didn't expect to see you here today, given the tragedy at the Abbey,' Arthur began, awkwardly. He wanted to say more, but there were barriers, of grief and — yes, he admitted — of class. Somehow he felt his condolences would be taken as an invasion, an attempt to participate, and therefore unwelcome.

Ned shrugged.

'Mr Dowle wouldn't have let you take the day off?' Arthur asked. A humourless smile was the only answer he received. 'Well, sit down, won't you?'

The collier pulled up a stool and propped himself on it. His eyes darted about. 'Am I in …' He stopped. 'Will it take long? I'm the next man in the cage.'

'It shouldn't be long. It's to do with the mine, not you personally.'

Ned straightened, seeming to relax.

But Arthur found he could not let the moment go by entirely. 'Mrs Parry was your aunt?'

'My father's sister.'

'Your father must be very grieved.'

Ned leant back. 'He's taking it bad. He …' He halted, then started again. 'He drinks, you see. It's not really his fault. When I got home he was just himself enough to tell me what happened, then he fell asleep.'

Embarrassed by these private family matters, Arthur said, 'I'm sorry to hear it. But today I'm here on Sir Rowland's behalf. I need to ask you a few questions. Ideally it would have been someone else, but I'm new in these parts, and my grandfather, Dr Sidstone – the elder – mentioned your name.'

'I'll answer what I can,' said Ned. Then, more firmly, 'I won't put any man in trouble.'

'It's nothing like that,' said Arthur. 'I want to talk about the mine itself.' Ned nodded his assent. 'For example, how much do you earn?'

Ned ran his hand over the back of his neck. 'Not much, but I suppose I would say so.' An unexpected smile broke out over his face, and Arthur couldn't help but smile back, faintly. Ned thought again. 'I'm paid by the ton, and I work with the ponies. They pay separate for that, so …' He put out his tongue, thinking. 'Can't be quite a shilling a day,' he said finally.

'That little?'

Ned's face darkened. 'Dowle makes your time go up and down as it suits him.'

'I see.' That explained the rising and falling wages. So Dowle probably was stealing, but that money would be a trickle, only, and taken from the workers rather than embezzled from Sir Rowland. It was not enough on its own to prevent the mine being profitable. 'Are you one of the stronger hewers?'

'I'm strong,' Ned said simply.

'You work every shift you can, and work as hard as you can?'

'Yes.'

Arthur paused, thinking. He might disregard the petty punishments inflicted by Dowle on the men in his charge, but he could not ignore that the overall amounts of coal hewed were small, yet still Sir Rowland had invested in the mine as if the output would heat the whole of Newport. Thousands upon thousands of pounds had been sunk into this place. Did Sir Rowland expect—

He didn't get to ask his next question. Before he could speak, something shifted below him. The sensation was odd, beginning as a mere awareness that something was wrong, then the floor moved like a ripple in cloth. At almost the same time, from outside, a roar filled the air, and shook the walls of the lodge. Arthur locked eyes with Ned, watching the colour drain from his face.

Arthur's legs see-sawed beneath him as he tried to rise. Ned was already throwing open the door. Dust – a vast, crawling cloud of it, stinking with gas – billowed in, hot and foetid. Before Arthur could move, Ned had jumped down the four or five stairs to the yard. 'Come on!' Arthur dragged the lapel of his jacket over his face, followed, and stepped outside. The crude wooden staircase wobbled as he descended – though it might have been his knees – clutching the rail with one hand and the cloth with the other, choking on the smoke that invaded his throat and chest.

The sky had caught fire, and also, it was snowing, or appeared to be. He looked up. Smoke and ash billowed from the chimney, and a rain of black dust cascaded over the pit yard, settling, blurring his sight. The underbelly of the clouds, barrelling low against the hills, was bathed in eerie strokes of orange. He could hardly take a breath, the air was so close. Men rushed here and there, reduced to half-formed shadows, as others dragged themselves to standing, reaching for the outstretched hands that pulled them to their feet. Arthur thought there must be something wrong with him, with his eyes, and his ears. The inside of his skull still resounded with the force of the blast. Who was that who moved ahead, so fluid and quick? Just an outline against the grey air, a ghost … He put out his hand, clutched at nothing, felt the leaden ache of loss all over again. *Please, don't go. I'll be better this time* …

Coming to himself, he heard a scream, then harried voices, though the words escaped him.

'Let's go, Mr Sidstone,' called Ned again. The younger man's heels disappeared into the pungent whorl of smoke.

Arthur spotted Harris running to the lodge door, Dowle close behind him. Harris tossed a rope to Dowle, who caught it in his meaty fist. 'Where?' Harris shouted.

'The north headway,' came the reply.

'How many?'

'Forty-one.'

'Out of the way! Move!' Harris yelled. Arthur realised he meant him.

'Certain—' But he had already been shoved aside. He couldn't tell why he couldn't move faster, why his sinews were so dull and slow. He followed at a distance. He didn't know what to do. How could he help? Where was the threat? From the chimney? Directly beneath his feet? Had the danger passed, or could he expect to be blown to bits? His sense of self-preservation told him to flee. His conscience and his pride begged him to stay. He knew his skills would be needed, but this distant thought was beaten down by the urgency of his other feelings.

Then Ned was at his elbow, up on his toes trying to see over the heads of the others.

'Gear's gone,' someone announced, near the lodge door. Orders were issued for more ropes. Dowle stuck his head out, and shouted for brandy and tea.

'Can't go down yet,' said Ned. 'Not safe.' He frowned with concentration.

Arthur's voice felt thick and unnatural. 'Is there no other shaft? No chance the men might find their own way out?'

'Only the drift road, in the wood.'

'What's the drift road?'

'A second access tunnel, not a shaft. But that's the long way in. It's twisting and dangerous, and thin as a man is wide. Anyway, they've been trained to stay just where they are. If they're alive,' Ned added bleakly.

'Why?'

'Choke gas. It cuts off the air. They daren't light a flame. If they're alive,' he said again, 'they'll believe they're safer staying put than wandering around.'

'How likely is it anyone has survived?'

'Won't know until we get down there. God willing, it's not so bad as it looks.' But by the faces around them, Arthur could tell this was a thin hope.

Harris was directing the younger boys to safety, and Arthur heard him instruct one to go to Locksley. 'Sir Rowland has to send out for a minister. Then go to the village. Though they've probably heard.'

Dowle noticed Arthur, and beckoned him. 'You! You're a doctor. You'll come down with us.' It was a statement, not an invitation.

His mind filled up with the dark. He saw himself descending the shaft, the cage rushing by the rough-hewn walls, the light above shrinking into a pinprick of white.

They can't make you.

'I …' The smoky air constricted his chest. His knees were shaking. They watched him, waiting for an answer. He bore the weight of thirty stares. 'I don't believe I …' He wanted to say he would do whatever he could do, but that up here, on the bank, that that black cavity was no place for a man.

There was something in his peripheral vision, like a person moving right next to him. The footsteps that had dogged him all morning caught up, and the sense of an unseen presence was overpowering. Sweat and weak ale and apples drifted by. He turned, horrified, desperate.

There was only the imprint of his own boots in the mud, coated with ash from the tortured air.

Coward.

His breakfast rushed up his gullet. He leant to the side to release it, thankful for a chance to avoid their eyes. When he straightened, Dowle stared with a scorn he didn't bother to hide, but Ned's face was full of sympathy. 'It's not for every man,' Ned said quietly in his ear. 'Don't let them bully you.'

'No, I … I'll go.' He wiped his wet lips and breathed in deeply. 'I will.'

'He won't,' came another voice from the doorway. 'We'll need the doctor up here,' Harris said authoritatively. 'He can't do anything for anyone if he dies. Keep him up here and he can help when we come back.'

Relief made him throw up again. His stomach churned, and he was too hot, like in Batavia. Hot and alone in the middle of a crowd of strangers. 'Don't worry,' said Ned, as he choked. 'Let it out.'

The leaders retreated to the lodge to investigate the shaft. Arthur understood from Ned that the fire, fuelled by gas leaked from the collapsed rock, had to burn out before any rescue attempt could begin. The vents had to stay closed. Then, once any fire had died down, the pit would be reventilated, which would cause more delay. Any survivors would be likely to hunker down as near the pit bottom as they could, waiting for help.

The afternoon drew on. People brought tea, blankets, gin and stretchers. A boy handed out lamps as Harris walked from man to man, noting down the names of the missing in one column of a little notebook. Next to these, he put the names of volunteers. There was something affecting about the way Harris didn't have to ask, how they pressed him to let them go down, or merely nodded when the pen hovered near them.

Ned sat with Arthur. They drank tea out of steel mugs, leaning against the pit-yard wall. Arthur had given up trying to keep clean, and Ned was unrecognisable beneath a coat of ash and muck, disturbed only slightly by a light rain from the east.

'My aunt worked for Bridewell for forty years,' said Ned, after a while, flicking a stone into a shallow puddle a few yards away. His brow was set low. 'But she did a lot for us as well. We tried to manage, but without a woman in the house … I was always here, working, and my dad didn't cope well on his own.'

Arthur nodded. His own father had outlived his mother by a few years. That absence at the heart of his family had sucked out all the joy, and soon the will to live had gone out of his father, too. Illness had taken him not long after.

'When did your mother pass?' he asked.

'She didn't.' Ned's next stone missed and he launched another. It disappeared, rippling in the muggy water. 'She decided she didn't like him any more. Or me. Or not enough, anyway. I don't blame her. He'd get down about the war, and never having enough money, and he'd hit her. Not very often, but he did. I didn't do enough to stop it.'

'I'm sorry.'

'Me too.'

'Where did she go?'

'East to her people. I followed and found her, and worked there a bit, but in the end I came home. I couldn't leave my dad on his own. It wasn't good for him.'

'I expect it's not the best thing for any man to be entirely alone,' said Arthur, with care. 'But it's also important for each person to have freedom, and pursue their happiness according to their own lights.'

Ned laughed, an incongruous sound in the cheerless pit yard. It cut through what Arthur felt sure was his own pomposity. 'That's just something rich people say,' Ned said, chuckling. 'No blame. It's not your fault.'

Arthur felt deflated, but Ned continued before he could speak. 'I started in the mine. I was weak to begin with.' Looking down, he tightened his bicep beneath the faded cotton of his shirt. 'It takes time before the work stops hurting, and you harden up. Hour on hour of digging, delving, scraping, lifting. I grew used to it. To the dark, too, though that took longer.' The turn of his head towards the lodge as he listened to the men's voices lifted his jawline to the light, and Arthur saw how young he was, how sharp and strong were the lines of his face. 'Once, I was caught down there. Something caught fire, and caused a fall-in – smaller than this – in one of the lower galleries. Me, and two others. One was killed by the rubble. The other …' He whistled long and low. 'His chest did for him. It took three days of walking the windways, down and up again, without lamps. Three days of his lungs rattling in the dark. He gave up in the end. Sat down and wouldn't go a step further, though I begged and bullied him. I dragged him for a time. He still died.'

Arthur frowned. 'I thought …'

'What?'

'I thought you said the men were trained to stay put? Because of the—' He had forgotten the term.

'Choke gas.'

'Yes.'

'So we are.' He began to get to his feet. 'They'll send men down to look for you, and say if you aren't where the rock fall is, you must be buried in it. They don't keep searching. So that's what you do if you want to die.' He stood and kicked a stone hard across the yard. It hit one of the younger boys, who recognised anger when he saw it, put his head down, and walked on.

The air was clearing. Dowle came out of the lodge and confirmed that the cage and platform had been damaged too much to be used, and the men would find other means to descend the shaft. The volunteers got to their feet, shaking hands with their fellows, wishing each other luck. 'The cage is fearfully old anyway,' Ned explained. 'I'm always thinking the chain's going to snap. I'm sure it wasn't even new when Bridewell got hold of it.'

Arthur's mind returned to the ledger. There was something just out of focus, something that should have meant something. In the pandemonium wrought by the explosion, he could not pin down his thoughts.

Women were hurrying through the gates. They must have rushed up the hill, coming without hats, some even without shoes, dragging babies and little children, trailed by older lads and girls. Names filled the air – *George, Matthew, John, Alfred*. They gathered their boys like ducklings beneath the excesses of their shawls and surrounded the pit lodge. One, young and stout in a chequered blouse, approached Dowle at the door and clutched his arm.

'My Tommy, did he go down?' Dowle shook her off. She circled him, calling, 'Mr Dowle! Where's my Tommy?' The question came again and again.

Her voice faded as Dowle raised his hands. A hush fell over the assembly. One by one, Dowle called the volunteers forward. Ned saw, and shook his limbs in readiness. 'Come and stand in the lodge,' he told Arthur. 'You'll be needed.'

Inside, the air was noxious, and the space around them upended. One of the metal tubs had been taken off the rails, ropes dragged under and around it, and knotted tightly so it functioned as a makeshift basket. Above the pit, the ropes had been attached to the wheeled apparatus that would usually hold the cage, which lay on its side a few yards away in a heap of dented painted metal, rusting at the corners.

The fumes brought on coughing fits amongst the men as they lined up. Harris was first into the tub, Dowle second. Four others went in after them, but it wasn't full, and for a moment Arthur wondered why those who waited held back.

'Why aren't more going?' he asked Ned.

'It might blow again. If you go down with just a few, it means ...' He trailed off, but Arthur understood. Fewer to die.

'Space for one more,' called Dowle.

Ned clapped Arthur's sleeve. The group parted for him, the semicircle of men wishing him luck. Arthur thought he made a joke as he passed one of them, and got a cynical chuckle in return. Nimbly, he leapt into the metal tub. Arthur wanted to pull him back. He couldn't. He stood ten feet away as the men wrapped more ropes around their waists. These, too, were then attached to the apparatus. A cry of 'Stand fast' filled the air as the arrangement started to move and the men disappeared into the ground. Ned's tousled head went out of sight.

Arthur's mind filled with a symphony of images. The damp green and black of the dripping bricks, the shrinking aperture of blinding light as they were dropped into yawning fathoms, the dull rattle of the chains, the inrush of stale air from the deepest places. And the more he thought, and the lower they went, the more obscene it seemed to him. There was something rapine about these veins they had carved out in the earth, allowing the black gold to flow out. Perhaps it was as his grandfather often said: men had convinced themselves that they could act on the world without the world acting on them. But there were always consequences. Nothing was free.

15

As Catherine kept her distance from Parry and the snarling mastiff. She was in a daze. Georgie's shaking hand in hers seemed the only thing tethering her to the present moment.

Disturbed memories flitted about her like moths. The wood had returned them, and yet, for whatever reason, its giving had been interrupted, and now, as she reached for a deeper understanding of the past, she walked into a door swinging shut. What it had left her with, this fragmented knowledge, was the worst of all worlds, and dangerous. Who knew where it might lead?

Parry said little, but Catherine gleaned that there had been some sort of accident at the colliery, and Sir Rowland had called for his carriage before leaving the Abbey in what Parry called *a right hurry*. Hearing this, she raised her head to the sky, recognising that the air itself had changed, and felt smokier, dustier.

'I'm sorry,' she said impulsively, when they got to the stile. Parry turned about and looked out of pouchy eyes. She thought he had aged ten years. She said, again, 'I'm sorry about Mrs Parry. And for you and Ned, too. Is he at the pit?'

He nodded, and said gruffly, 'I'll go up when I've put this fellow away. Find out what's what.' The dog twisted round, lowering, and barked at Catherine, and he cuffed it, and went off to return it to its kennels.

The thought of Ned brought her closer to the present moment. He might be dead. That thought bothered her more than she had expected. She had met him only once, but had liked him. She was not unused to death. But there had to be something especially dreadful, she thought, about living each day knowing your child was hundreds of feet below the ground. Coming so soon after Mrs Parry's fall, it seemed fate had decided to turn a cruel eye on that family.

She glanced down at Georgie. Sympathy with the Parrys had nearly made her forget her own troubles.

But not quite.

Her letters were still missing. Georgie insisted she had not taken them. Did she believe her? Georgie might be naughty, but was she guileful? From the forthright way the child had cut her own hair, and her candid description of killing the beetles, Catherine did not think so.

That left Grizel Wingfield as the only person with obvious motive. She did not struggle to see Grizel as someone who would steal, or destroy things for the pleasure of it. Yet the implications of this were dreadful. If the older woman did have her letters, she would almost certainly have read them already. That meant Catherine was discovered, unless she could concoct an explanation Sir Rowland would believe, and in about the next minute and a half.

Any route was now a steep gamble, but outright denial seemed the best of the available choices. Sir Rowland clearly did not like his father's ward, or listen to her. And in any case, what good reason could Grizel possibly have to go inside her trunk? Surely a woman of her age would not sneak into an employee's bedroom and perpetrate such a spiteful crime? She thought about how she would say it, and arranged her face into an expression of artless shock. The letters must be forgeries. Nothing whatever to do with her, and she was mystified at their origin.

She had lied once, she thought grimly. She could do it again.

As Georgie climbed the stile, Catherine saw the tears in her dress, how it was soiled all over with mud, the petticoats ingrained with rust-coloured stains. They were hazy at the edges, as if they were … She froze at the sight, memories dancing just beyond her reach. She knew, though she did not know how, that she was thinking of blood. In this place, at a different time, white linen, and blood …

She stopped herself. She stood in full danger of discovery. She couldn't pursue these memories. She had to act, and now.

The dress would have to be mended. Thank goodness Sir Rowland had been drawn away. The accident at the mine was her friend in one respect, although it pained her to think it. She would hurry back indoors and get Georgie to the nursery, clean and respectable before anyone knew she had been missing.

She went round to the back door, but Grizel appeared almost at once on the threshold, like she had been watching out of the window. Catherine wondered whether she knew of the accident, because she did not seem disconcerted; her eyes were bright.

Catherine drew herself up as they reached Grizel, saying, with a gay smile, 'We were looking for leaf samples. I tripped. Georgie was kind enough to help me up. Clumsy of me, really.'

Grizel cast her gaze over their filthy attire. 'Come,' she said briskly. 'Something has happened at the mine. We will wait in the drawing room until we know what assistance might be required.'

Catherine protested. 'I'm sure Georgie would prefer to change.'

The other woman sniffed. 'When others are suffering, what is a little dust and bracken? Sit.'

In the huge room, Catherine was directed to a rosewood chair between the fire and a ticking bracket clock. Grizel insisted Georgie position herself on the Méridienne, beside her aunt. Georgie sat and fiddled with her bootlaces. Her aunt tolerated this for a minute before pulling her niece's hand away. She moved her into an upright pose and spoke to Catherine. 'You should pay more mind to her deportment. There is a corrective chair in the nursery; I suggest you make use of it.'

Catherine murmured that she would give it her full attention, then jumped at the quarter-strike of the clock. It was just past four. She couldn't settle, and looked about the room instead, noting an ugly ewer bedecked with apples, pears and cherubic behinds. She thought the room must have been redecorated in recent years. The paper was tasteful, a muted stripe that caught the light from the window. Above the fireplace, a square of more vibrant colour sat within the faded whole, as if something had been removed from the wall. She frowned, wondering what usually hung there, then looked up at the ceiling. It was lichen green, not very different in style to the drawing-room ceiling in the house in Abingdon. She took in the delicate gold-leaf cornicing, and counted six roundels positioned about a large central medallion, painted white. The shape was elliptical, with a distinctive fern pattern around its edge.

Her stomach churned from the strength of the feeling that she had seen this exact arrangement before. The clock ticked in her ears with vigour. The sense of recognition grew stronger every second.

But she still could not remember. However hard she pushed, the door was barred.

'Is something the matter, Miss Symonds?' asked Grizel.

She shook her head, breathing through her nose to control her impulse to vomit. Then she managed, 'I'm only concerned about the colliery.'

Grizel gave a drawn-out sigh. 'It is the fate of women to wait, to suffer without seeing. I'm certain we would rather know the full gravity of the situation. Then we can make plans. The Christmas fair, for instance. I can't help but fret that it will not be able to go ahead.' She sighed again at her own martyrdom. Despite her claim of suffering, Catherine felt sure this situation, her brother absent and Mrs Parry dead, was a form of ascendancy for Grizel.

She returned to possibilities. If it was Grizel who attacked her possessions, why? It was no secret she had resented Catherine's intervention at dinner the night before, but the reaction seemed extreme. Catherine considered again how she had pinched Georgie, how it had been so possessive, and at odds with reality, since Grizel seemed to have very little position here. Could that be it? She harboured a bitterness towards female employees who might outshine her? Catherine eyed her again, trying to decide whether she could be both a thief and a murderer. She was strong, with broad shoulders, and it was not hard to imagine her overpowering a smaller woman. But did she have the strength of a man? Was she strong enough to kill?

They sat in silence. Grizel rang the bell, and some minutes later Edie arrived. 'Try to be more prompt when I ring,' she said.

'Sorry, ma'am,' said Edie, breathing hard.

Just overworked, wondered Catherine, her housekeeper's instinct triggered, or doing something she shouldn't be?

'We'll take tea,' said Grizel.

'Ma'am.'

Edie scurried off.

'Silly girl,' said Grizel, unexpectedly, after a few more seconds of silence. Catherine looked up. She didn't say anything, and after another moment Grizel continued. 'She's been mooning after a boy at the colliery for months – Mrs Parry's nephew. It's affecting her work,' she complained peevishly.

'I see.'

They waited. Georgie prodded the flowered carvings on the end of the sofa. 'Leave that, Georgie,' said Grizel. The clock ticked too loudly. Then, just as Catherine dared to hope they would spend the rest of the afternoon in silence, her companion said, as if they had not stopped speaking, 'Yes, it is difficult, the impotence that accompanies being a member of our sex. I would far rather be at the colliery. But then, of course, it is raining.' She looked out of the window. 'No. I see it's gone off.'

'Yes.'

'It was like this the day Miss Murphy was found. Very overcast. Rain on and off, all day long.' She aimed a sly glance at Catherine. 'I know you'll have heard something of it. Who can match servants for gossip?'

Catherine nodded, but struggled to keep control of her facial expression. Was Grizel taunting her? Did she know her secret, or was she revealing more than she intended?

The tea arrived. It was a blessing. Having delivered the tray, Edie vanished, and Grizel reached for the urn, saying as she poured, 'Of course, it wasn't so dark. It was spring. I remember commenting to Rowland how fitting it was that she should be discovered at the yew. Apt. I wrote a poem about it that night, and read it at the committal. It was an odd whim of my brother's to have her laid to rest in the Bridewell vault. After all,' she said, looking at Catherine, 'she was just a servant, and she brought her trouble on herself. But of course, you don't know much of this, do you?' She handed Catherine a china cup.

'Nothing, Mrs Wingfield.' Her fingers flailed and burning liquid splashed on her wrist. Her throat felt full and tight, and a flush of distress raced up her chest. She willed her hand steady, forcing down a sip of the tea, letting it sear her mouth. She looked at Georgie, who had screwed her eyes closed. She said, 'Perhaps Georgie might be allowed to play in the nursery if we are going to talk of macabre things.'

Grizel replaced her cup. 'She will stay. She is fond of her aunt. Is that not so, Georgiana? How could she not be, with her mother absent?' The little girl flinched. Grizel's hand came to her shoulder, and her fingers pressed hard. There was a cruel look on her face, as if she enjoyed the child's reaction.

Hiding anger, Catherine said, 'Then let us talk of more cheerful matters. This service is very beautiful. Is it blue Saxon?'

'I think it must be,' said Grizel.

Catherine glanced again at the ewer. 'Did Lady Anne choose most of the furnishings?' This was a direct challenge. It said: *You are not the mistress here. You are a cuckoo in the nest. Pretending.*

Grizel replied, 'I was in Ireland for much of my brother's marriage.'

'What year were you married, Mrs Wingfield?' Catherine didn't care if she sounded impertinent. She knew she was returning spite for spite, but the other woman's cruelty had pushed her past her patience.

'Eighteen forty-one.' Grizel's mouth had flattened into a thin line.

'Was Mr Wingfield a gentleman?'

There was a long pause. 'He was a commissioned cavalry officer.'

'It's terrible when a marriage is over so quickly, and without issue,' Catherine said quietly. 'It must be hard to bear.' She sipped her tea, which had cooled slightly.

'A true cross. Yet, I suppose, being a governess, you must be resigned never to suffer in the same way.'

'Yes,' said Catherine. She drank, and did not allow her expression to change.

They sat late into the night. Edie brought a tray, and although Grizel told the housemaid to remove Georgie to eat with her in the servants' hall, she insisted Catherine remain. Around ten o'clock, they heard Parry's cart. Catherine jumped to her feet.

'Stay, Miss Symonds,' said Grizel.

'The news is bad, Mrs Wingfield,' Parry said, wringing his cap in the doorway, appearing hardly able to stand. 'There's forty-one still underground. Sir Rowland is still there, not expected back tonight.'

Catherine could not grapple with what she heard. Forty-one souls, buried in that darkness.

'What about your son, Mr Parry?' she asked.

'Still down there, miss, with the rescue. Grateful to you,' he added.

Grizel remarked that forty-one was a strange number and, as Catherine sat back down, said she thought the Christmas fair would, after all, be cancelled.

16

It was growing dark before Sir Rowland arrived at the colliery. Arthur watched as, with an expression of distaste, the baronet picked his way across the pit yard. He stood out like a sore thumb, dressed for a day of business. As he stepped into the glow of the gathered lamps, Arthur thought he looked much worse than when he had left him the night before. What had been pale had become almost colourless, and his eyes were hot with a hunted glare.

Sir Rowland said, sounding relieved, 'There you are, Sidstone. Where's Dowle?'

'Underground.'

The baronet observed the havoc around them. 'Damn the man. And damn this place. The sooner it's closed, the better.'

Trying not to betray his curiosity, Arthur said, 'I thought you wanted to make it pay.'

'It's a millstone. A cursed hole in the ground, I don't mind telling you.' The barely concealed condescension of the previous day seemed to have gone. Sir Rowland spoke to Arthur like an equal now.

'I see,' said Arthur. He was thinking of the workers, how they would live, where they would go. There seemed to be so many of them.

'How many dead?' Sir Rowland asked, removing his hat.

'We don't know. Forty-one men were down there, and seven more in the rescue. More are trying to get through via the drift road. I've sent a boy to Hawk's Leap for my grandfather, and supplies.' As soon he spoke, he wondered whether he should have omitted to mention Frederick. In fact, given his grandfather's state of mind, he half-regretted sending for him at all.

Sir Rowland seemed not to notice. 'What of Dowle? Is he robbing me?'

'Not of profits,' said Arthur carefully.

Sir Rowland heard the unspoken caveat. 'But?'

'He is robbing you.'

'How?'

'Money allocated for new equipment but not purchased. You invested money in a new cage?'

'That's right.'

'You'll see the old one still on its side in the pit lodge. And new struts and doors?'

Sir Rowland nodded.

'I'm willing to wager it will be discovered that those improvements were never made, and the money found its way into Dowle's pocket.'

'That would place the accident at his door,' said Sir Rowland grimly.

'If he comes back up, you should accost him.'

'The men mightn't like it.'

'I dare say the men don't like him much,' Arthur said. 'Although I must say, he's acquitted himself bravely enough today,' he added.

'Well, Dowle never lacked brute courage,' said Sir Rowland. 'But,' he said, looking about, 'the situation has changed. Nevertheless, I'm grateful. He won't rob me of another farthing.'

'No,' agreed Arthur. After a moment, he ventured, 'I hope Lady Anne is not very distressed.'

Sir Rowland coughed, sounding uncomfortable. 'Eh? No. Well, that is to say, she manages.'

'I'd be happy to give her something to calm her nerves.'

'Possibly. Let's get this dealt with first, shall we? But I'm grateful for your help. I'll certainly be telling my connections how you've obliged me.'

'It's nothing,' said Arthur. He realised he meant this. Sir Rowland's good opinion felt less valuable, somehow, than it had at the start of the day. He didn't care what the baronet thought of him now. He just wanted to go home, wash off the horror, and sleep.

His thoughts were disturbed by the sudden hum of activity in the lodge.

'They're back,' he said soberly.

As the two men approached the shaft, Harris, Ned, Dowle and the others scrambled from the tub, their faces black with dust and shuttered with exhaustion. Ned had something draped across his shoulders. One of his companions had carried up a small scrap of a mongrel, dark from nose to tail, and released it on the lodge floor, where it ran about Ned's legs, yapping. Arthur thought he had seen the dog before, but turned back to the tub. Ned ordered the terrier to lie down, and it did.

Ned had said he was strong. He proved it now, raising his burden easily over his head and down to the ground. Before Arthur could see, another man sprang forward and covered it with a blanket. It couldn't be one of the miners. Too small.

One rescuer called, 'We found him under a dram. A pony took the worst.'

A woman threw herself forward. It was the neat young mother Dowle had shaken off earlier. A cry escaped her, then a moan, as a murmur of sympathy mounted around the lodge. 'Just a boy,' someone said. Arthur caught the scent of seared flesh. Someone tried to pull the woman back and prevent her scrabbling at the blanket, but she held on, and as it came away, Arthur recoiled. He knew he had recognised the ratting dog. It had scampered behind the boy who had gone for Ned, just a few hours earlier.

Then the men's whispers of 'Shame' and 'Poor lad' couldn't be heard any more, because the mother was screaming, and the rest of the lodge had fallen quiet.

The boy must have met the blast sideways. Half his body had escaped the burns that had stripped the skin and flesh from his legs, torso and face, and that half was still covered by rags. His teeth chattered, his eyes were closed, and he breathed rapidly. If he were not covered, as if thickly painted, with the detritus from below ground, he would have been white and clammy, as he entered the distant state of nervous shock that so often precedes death.

'Let me through,' said Arthur, trying to force his way through the crowd. 'I'm a physician.' He saw Harris near the boy. 'Mr Harris, can you clear space here? I must do what I can.'

They finally pulled the mother away as Arthur set about his work, calling for fluids and more blankets. His movements were sure, fuelled by lessons learnt decades ago, yet he knew, even as he parted the boy's blackened lips, and heard no cry of pain and observed no change in his breathing, it was futile.

Around him, the rescue continued. The tub went down again, a second group of volunteers now standing in for the first. Only Ned volunteered a second time.

As Arthur bared the boy's chest, pressing down on charred and ruptured flesh, Sir Rowland's voice was heard. 'Dowle, in the office. Now.'

The overman spat and followed him.

Arthur spent twenty minutes trying to revive the boy as rumour hardened around them: none of the trapped men had any hope. It was over.

Afterwards, he stepped out to take the night air. He stood for a while, pulling breath into his lungs again and again, thinking about the boy's mother, her howls, and how, if things were only slightly different, her son would have been wearing short trousers at some newfangled school, learning his Latin and Greek, not holding open doors to allow the flow of air hundreds of feet below the surface of the earth.

He was still there when Dowle came out of the pit office with his ugly face locked in a grimace. The big man drove his foot into a barrel at the bottom of the stairs. It must have hurt, because he staggered, then picked up several half-bricks and threw them one by one at the clouded glass, smashing it. As the door opened, and Sir Rowland's reddening face appeared, he backed away. He threw the last brick at Arthur, who dodged the missile, then ran off across the yard.

Arthur looked at Sir Rowland, but the baronet shook his head. 'Let him go,' he said. 'The constable can pick him up. He won't get far.'

17

A hard morning rain pummelled the pit-lodge roof. Arthur went to the window and looked out on black, swollen clouds across the horizon. He rubbed bleary eyes, hardly able to see what he was doing, then stretched his arms against the edge of the desk and allowed his vertebrae to crack.

He had worked through the night. His knees and back smarted from the long hours of kneeling and bending over the stretch-ered bodies, and still the rescue crew brought up more. Ned remained at the top of the shaft, seemingly tireless. For all his youth, alongside Harris he looked every bit a leader, directing the others as they heaved their inert burdens, two men to each, and draped them with fresh cloths and canvases ready to be moved into rows for the attention of the doctors.

Frederick joined Arthur at the desk. The older man's lined face was tight with a restrained grief.

'Rest,' Frederick said, looking at the dead men. 'They're not going anywhere.'

'No,' he agreed.

'Here.' Frederick handed over a tin of water, keeping one for himself. They drank deeply. Though stale and warm, it was welcome on Arthur's parched tongue.

His grandfather put down his tin. 'The whole earth is at rest, and is quiet,' he said. His voice was so soft Arthur hardly heard it. 'But it trembled,' he added, more clearly.

It wasn't like Frederick to quote the Bible. Arthur looked at him, puzzled.

'It's the baronet's pride that's brought this on us,' his grandfather explained doggedly. 'If he hadn't been interfering with the wood, with powers he doesn't—'

Stifling a groan, Arthur broke in. 'Please, Grandfather. We've been over this. It was an accident. Mining is a dangerous business.' He crossed to the other side of the room. 'Can we drop the subject?' This wasn't the first time Frederick had raised the point, and Arthur was exhausted. The last thing he wanted to do was wander back into his grandfather's woodland realm of fancy.

Sounding ruffled, Frederick said, 'Certainly.' He sat down behind the desk. Arthur was sure he was sulking, and paced the room as he drank, trying to loosen his stiff muscles.

So far, twenty-nine men and boys had been brought up. With the exception of Tommy, they were between seventeen and perhaps fifty. Some had been identified, but not all. Ned had told Arthur that Dowle had not issued the miners with numbers, or even written down the number of the lamp held by each worker, so when, as in the case of the body before him now, he encountered one whose face had been almost entirely destroyed by the blast, leaving only blood and bone and burns, he could not be certain which of the missing it was. But he could make some inferences. He had removed the man's boots and seen he was in his middle years. He postulated that he was forty. That would rule out around half, and Ned and the others had named around ten more from sight. So he gauged that this particular victim could be any one of around ten others. He sighed. They would piece it all together in time.

He was uneasy with his own role in the night's events. His word had driven Dowle from the colliery, and his testimony meant the overman was to be hunted down. This didn't prick his conscience much. Dowle was a thug. Far worse, his own judgement, or at least partly his judgement, would see all these men seeking work in the months to come. He knew what he had said was true — there was not enough coal being weighed out here to keep so many employed. Sir Rowland was not wrong about that. But there was something about the way the baronet had turned on the head of a pin — moving from insisting the colliery could thrive, to calling it *cursed* — that told Arthur that he had been, in some way, part of a larger machination. The feeling was unpleasant.

Still, Dowle had definitely been stealing. In the hours since the explosion, Arthur had had more opportunity to observe the equipment. Nearly everything was worn past the point of needing replacement. The lamps were of the oldest type, their gauzes torn, the cases cracked. Above the shaft, the chain, like the cage, had fallen victim to rust. Even the red bricks of the lodge crumbled around their ears. Clearly, little of whatever money Sir Rowland had marked out for the colliery had been invested, and Dowle had controlled that money; therefore Dowle was guilty.

He drummed his fingers against a cabinet, unsatisfied. But before he could go over the facts again, the door opened, and Sir Rowland came in. He nodded to the doctors before moving to the shaft, where Harris and Ned were heaving the tub into place. They exchanged a few stiff words before he joined Arthur and Frederick.

'An unfortunate day,' he said, casting his eyes over the scene.

Frederick said nothing. Arthur was not used to this behaviour from his grandfather, who was usually gregarious, liable to forgive even the worst slights, but there were daggers in his eyes for the baronet.

'Baldwin's on his way,' said Sir Rowland distractedly. 'There'll have to be an inquest. With any luck, we'll have apprehended Dowle by then.'

Arthur looked at the horrors awaiting the coroner. 'If it's shown Dowle caused this, he'll hang.'

'Yes,' said Sir Rowland, without concern. 'And I thank you, Sidstone, for your part in rooting it out. I'm obliged to you.'

Arthur noted the set of his grandfather's mouth. 'Yes, you were right about Dowle.' He paused. 'And although it's not appropriate to talk of it at the moment, we should find time to discuss your end of the bargain.'

Sir Rowland frowned. 'Yes,' he said, avoiding Arthur's eyes. 'Look here,' he went on, keeping his voice low, 'there's been movement on that front. Sir Monty arrived here, you see, and, since it's my intention to close the colliery come what may, we've agreed the timing is too good to waste. Sir Monty still wants the Puzzle Wood for his canal, and now this land is to be made available, well, it makes sense to put it all together in a package.'

Arthur and Frederick exchanged glances. Beneath his whiskers, Frederick looked stricken.

'You're reneging on our agreement?' said Arthur, appalled.

'Hardly an agreement. We had a discussion, but there was no obligation. Nothing in writing. You did me a favour, and we will discuss suitable compensation.' He puffed up his chest.

'But you gave your word,' said Arthur. He felt an extraordinary anger bubbling inside him. He didn't care as much as his grandfather about the wood, but he cared about his grandfather. Sir Rowland's dismissal disgusted him.

'I wouldn't go that far. It was not a formal undertaking.'

'It was,' he said, in square contradiction.

Sir Rowland coloured, but gathered himself. 'This is hardly the time or the place,' he said, offended, and walked off.

The two men stood for a few seconds. Frederick replaced the cap on the water.

'He can't get away with this,' said Arthur, and made to follow.

He felt his grandfather's hand on his arm. 'Leave it, Arthur,' said Frederick, looking around at the huddled shapes of nameless bodies. 'He'll pay, but not now. Not now.'

Baldwin was shabby and spectacled, with raised shoes to disguise his stature. He licked his lips, which were rather dry, often. Though he had been driven up to the colliery in a cart and had only walked a short distance, he mopped a high forehead emphasised by a tonsure of greying hair. Yet despite this unprepossessing appearance, Arthur decided the coroner knew his business as he asked an efficient series of questions of Sir Rowland, then moved to the doctors to discuss the inquest.

'I charge you to perform full examinations, Dr Sidstone. You will be paid. Two pounds two shillings for each examination is the going rate. You can submit your expenses for my signature.'

'Very well,' said Arthur. He didn't like to think of money, not in this moment, but it would be a help, and certainly better than taking Sir Rowland's.

Baldwin nodded. 'Allow me to emphasise: the faster, the better. There'll be families concerned with interment, and frankly, I think we could all manage without any to-do.'

'We'll work as quickly as we can,' Arthur promised.

'And you'll have to testify.'

'Yes.'

Baldwin was leaving. Arthur accompanied him out. 'I'd like to ask you something,' he said hesitantly.

The coroner gave him a careful look as he opened the door on to the yard, and winced at the expectation of more rain, but said, 'Go ahead.'

'I'll walk you to your carriage.' They picked their way across the mud, avoiding deep pools of water. As they went, Arthur framed his question. 'This might seem a little strange ...' he said.

'You should get on with it before the rain begins again,' said Baldwin caustically.

'Speaking hypothetically, in a case of suspected suicide, if one coroner was unavailable, would you expect another to be called?'

Baldwin peered over his spectacles. 'Hypothetically?'

'Yes.'

'Not necessarily.'

'That surprises me.'

'As it might, if you've not practised as a rural doctor for a time. I understand you've been out of the country. But in fact it is not so surprising. The system is ... patchy. Some deaths are investigated, but in other cases people are keen to proceed with burial. If the death is not reported as suspicious, well ... We can't be everywhere at once.' They reached the gate.

Arthur thought for a moment. 'Would the suspected suicide of a young woman not be treated as more of a priority than, say, an accidental death, where the cause was more readily apparent?'

Baldwin scratched his moustache. 'You mean the Murphy girl?' Arthur did not answer, and the coroner looked about for his driver. 'There was nothing unusual about the case. It would not take particular priority.'

'You were away at the time?'

'That's correct. I had business in Sunderland with Sir Monty Cottrell. We have some shared interests there.'

'The trip was planned?'

The coroner's tone became impatient. 'Again, yes. There was no neglect of my duties. Why so much interest?'

Arthur shook his head. 'It's just idle curiosity.' The carriage approached, wheels slopping through the soft peaks of earth. 'I wish you good day.'

'Good day, Dr Sidstone.' Baldwin tipped his hat and left.

Trudging back, Arthur reflected that the conversation had revealed at least one point: Sir Rowland had known the coroner was to be away, and therefore when a death was least likely to be investigated. But it was not enough. Sir Monty might have told half the county about his trip.

In the lodge, Frederick bent over a man who looked asleep, his face grey beneath the coal dust. At a glance, Arthur would have said he died from asphyxiation.

Ned came to the door where he had stowed his pack. 'Dr Sidstone,' he said. 'Harris wants you behind the office.'

'Why?'

Ned shook his head. 'Don't know.'

'I'll just rest briefly. And call me Arthur, would you? I'm Arthur to a friend.'

At this, Ned grinned, unpacking food from his bag. 'Want some?' he asked, offering bread and some milk of dubious longevity. Arthur declined the milk, but accepted a hunk of bread. As Ned broke his own into pieces, he said, 'Sir Rowland's shutting down the mine, isn't he?'

'I ...' As he chewed and swallowed, he realised he had been desperately hungry. 'You heard him?'

'I'm not stupid,' Ned said. 'You can be strong as an ox, and work every hour, but if the coal is thin, it's thin.' He grinned again. His left cheek was dimpled.

When the bread was finished, Arthur ventured outside and realised Baldwin's anticipation of rain had been correct. It was even heavier, and he cursed the stinking sludge as he rounded the brick buildings, passing the sorting areas and silent equipment. But he had to go. Harris might have something to tell him about Dowle. What Arthur didn't know yet, the question he was avoiding, was whether he would pass this information on to Sir Rowland.

He peered, wiping water out of his vision, but couldn't see Harris. The only sound was the deep thrum of the rain and the squelch of his boots in the mire. As he rested his hand against the wall, he heard rapid footsteps, then something rushed at him from the right, and his face erupted in sudden agony. He gripped the bridge of his nose in both hands, swearing loudly. Through a haze, he saw Harris standing before him, his fist at his side. He had struck with his good arm, and flexed his wrist, as if it had hurt him as much as Arthur.

'What the devil …' Arthur grunted, his eyes streaming. He brought his hand away and looked down, seeing blood. 'What was that for?'

Harris was silent. Arthur met his eyes. They were not angry, but steady and sad. 'That,' said Harris, after several seconds, 'was because I know where I've seen you before.'

18

'You were at the Westgate?' Arthur brushed away a gobbet of blood from his upper lip, then wiped it on the wall. 'Christ,' he said disbelievingly. 'You hit me.'

Harris ignored this. 'I was in the column going down that infernal hill to take the hotel. And so were you.' But his posture had relaxed. He didn't look as though he was readying himself to strike again.

Arthur started to deny it, to say, *You have the wrong man. I was never there.*

He couldn't. Not only had he already admitted it, but the sense of a presence that had followed him out of the valley, and over the hill, had not dissipated. He felt he was under the eye of God. If he lied, it would be destroying something precious and fragile remaining in himself: the hope of one day being a good man. 'Yes,' he said weakly, blowing another streak of blood out of his nostrils.

Harris stepped back, allowing Arthur the shelter of the sloping roof. 'Why don't you tell me what happened? It might be a weight off you.'

'Why?' Arthur growled. But Harris was right. His secret had been a poison simmering inside him, all those years in Batavia. Even that one word – *yes* – was a relief to say. But it wasn't enough. He had to tell someone everything.

They sat on the wet ground as he and Barnabas had done outside Newport. 'You'll remember the rain,' Arthur said.

'We were wet, all right,' agreed Harris, peaceably. He took out chewing tobacco and offered to share. Arthur demurred, and began to speak, leaving out some of his gentler feelings. Picking up the tale after his fight with Barnabas, he described the hours after their parting.

'I was still furious, and scared. I badly needed to clear my head. I walked round the village, getting drenched through. Then a din started and the hills pricked with orange lights: it was the Chartists' signal to march down, into Newport, and take the Westgate. Another column was coming from the north. It took time. There were thousands of men. I started to wonder if Barnabas had been right, if it was not just a dream, and the rising was happening: first the workers would take the coalfields; then Wales; then England. But even I – who knew nothing of fighting – saw it would not work. Even with two thousand, five thousand, ten thousand, in the end, we couldn't win.'

Harris nodded slowly. 'I see that now. With that sort of attack, square on, the authorities would always have the better of us.' He seemed to come back to the present. 'What happened then?'

'I looked for Barnabas. I ran up and down. The road was narrow, thick with mist. I was trapped in the column. I pushed through because my blood was up. I was ready to fight anyone, even though I had barely been in a scrap in my whole life. Do you understand that?'

'Yes,' said Harris. 'It's a thing that happens in crowds. A sort of madness. Useful for a short space of time.' He chewed thoughtfully. 'You found him?'

'We reached the outskirts of Newport at daybreak. It was pouring with rain. I was still not near the front, but getting closer, when someone grabbed my elbow. It was Hogall, the publican. He told me the soldiers were holding some of our men in the hotel itself, that we were going to force our way in and attempt a rescue. He pulled me back into the line. Now the men were packed too closely for me to get away. Those at each end were armed with rifles, and then we were moving down

Stow Hill, towards the Westgate. The water went beneath us like a torrent. The hotel was completely dark, silent, and looking on it, I was tempted to believe the next few hours would go our way, but reason told me the defenders were inside, waiting. I could feel them.'

Harris nodded. 'I was in that line. We were to capture the men back and take Mayor Phillips.' He chewed harder, then said, 'We didn't know how strong the defences were.'

Arthur continued. 'As we came upon the hotel, Hogall told me to take out my gun, but I pulled free, finally pushing through. The men cheered. They thought I was rushing at the enemy. They thought I was the bravest of them all, when I just wanted to find Barnabas. But I was too late; the bloody business had begun. I could see, even through the rain, that something had happened to provoke a fight. I didn't know exactly what. The order of the column was breaking down, the line turning into a crowd, then a mob. I didn't know, then, what I know now: that some of the first men had gone up the steps, presented themselves, and demanded the prisoners back.' He looked up at Harris. 'Were there even prisoners? I don't think we know, even now.'

Harris shrugged. 'Didn't matter. Doesn't matter. We had to try to take the hotel. The soldiers, the mayor and his men – they were the enemy we had to beat down. They're still our enemy now.'

Arthur hardly heard these quiet words. He was back there, in the fight. 'Then the attackers were swarming the portico. I went half-deaf with the sound of the guns. Barnabas had to be in sight of them, and I had to get to him. The ranks started loosening as men lost their heads. No orders were coming. Some hung back, others forged a course through the middle. I went with them, and won a few yards. I climbed over broken men crying out for their mothers. I nearly lost my footing in the rain, sliding in their blood. But I kept my scything knife in my right hand.' He paused, ashamed to remember how it had shaken. 'I was nearly at the bottom.'

He stopped, picturing the sodden ground as he half-slid down the hill. He did not want to remember what came next.

Then Harris spoke. 'We must have been charging at the same time. Just like you, I never knew who fired first, the defenders or our lot. We just went forward, and soon everyone was firing. I took a shot just here.' He indicated where the bullet had entered, maiming his hand. 'It might have been one of our side, or theirs. I was trampled, and someone pulled me clear.' He paused. 'Was your … Was he in it as well?'

Arthur nodded. 'I still had no sight of him. My eyes stung with the powder. I skidded in a forest of legs and pikestaffs, and hit my head. A man fell next to me with a perfect round hole in his face – a musket ball through his cheek, into his brain. It was Hogall, still in his green coat. The guns were still firing. I looked back up the hill, and those at the rear were slinking away. At last, I saw Barnabas. I shouted to him, but the soldiers warmed to their work, firing through the windows out of the hotel. I stumbled over a man trampled by the crowd, seeing how he clutched his crushed hand to his chest. Then Barnabas saw me.'

He didn't need to recite their exchange, or the betrayal in Barnabas's eyes.

'We're losing!' Arthur had cried.

'Then we'll die honourably!'

'For Christ's sake, see sense—'

'Be with us!'

Returning to the present, Arthur shook his head. 'He stepped away from me. I let him go. At the last, he shouted: "You coward!"' He took deep breaths, not wanting Harris to witness his distress. 'How much of it did you see?'

Harris spat out his tobacco. 'Some. I was the man who stopped in under the eaves, in that rain. I was the man with the crushed hand. Yes, doctor, I saw you run. I wanted to strike you – just once – for that lad. Do you know what happened to him?'

Arthur's nose throbbed where Harris had hit him. 'I went back later.' His voice was weak. Harris knew what it had been like in that time right after the rising, when the word 'Westgate' had been a gaol sentence, with soldiers raiding public houses and hotels, taking up anyone who might have been involved in the march. He didn't need to say it. 'I went back and tried to find him,' he said. He hesitated, then told the entire truth. 'It was weeks later.'

'Why?'

'I was frightened.'

'And?'

'His name was on the list of those taken up. He was in Millbank Prison.' Harris let Arthur's pause stretch out. Eventually Arthur said, 'He was injured at the end of the fight, a shot to the shoulder, but he recovered. The prison was affected with damp, though, and a pneumonia took root in his lungs. He died in the eighth month of his sentence.'

'Where were you then?'

'I … I was in Batavia.' This was the worst part. He quailed under Harris's look. 'They were arresting everyone, hunting down anyone who knew anything about the march, anyone who had been at any meeting, virtually, in the whole of south Wales. My grandfather found a place abroad for me. I planned to come back when Barnabas was released, but when I heard what happened at Millbank, I stayed.'

These weren't excuses. They were just the truth.

'That sounds about right,' Harris said. For a few moments the two men were silent, one spent by telling his tale, the other thoughtful. Arthur wondered whether Harris would get up and leave. But Harris stretched out his right arm. 'Now, will you take my hand in friendship?'

Arthur gripped Harris's crooked fingers. Neither man said much, each being caught in his own recollections. After a while, Harris said, 'Why did you come here?'

Arthur hesitated, then told him the story. 'I'm not going to tell Sir Rowland anything,' he clarified. 'If Dowle was robbing him, it's fair for him to investigate that, but if the men are organising ...' He spread his hands. 'The baronet will have to deal with that himself.'

Harris kicked mud off his boots, saying nothing about whether they were organising or not. 'How am I meant to know you'll keep your word?'

Arthur shrugged. 'Don't tell me anything you don't need to. Or trust me. It's up to you.'

Mulling over this for a while, Harris nodded. 'Bridewell will get what's coming to him. But you should stay out of it, if you can.'

19

The days after the accident passed in a tightness of nerves for Catherine, who felt her position growing more precarious. Someone at Locksley knew who she was. They had her letters. She cursed herself for her foolishness in bringing them at all.

She contemplated what had taken place beneath the yew tree with a mixture of fascination and fear, spending hours poring over the events that day had uncovered. She had believed these memories of her early life lost forever, but even returned, they could not be a comfort. Too many unwelcome thoughts surrounded them, principally whether they were a distortion, or even entirely her own invention. She had seen that possibility in Dr Sidstone's eyes when she had described her feelings the night Mrs Parry had died: his suspicion that she was feeble-minded, suggestible. It gnawed at her, this misgiving. What if her conception of herself was flawed at its deepest root, and she was not vigorous of mind, but defective? Was it possible that, lacking a robust account of its own history, her rebellious consciousness would take matters into its own control, and fabricate one instead?

Yet her most pressing difficulty was in appreciating why she had not yet been exposed. Whoever had the letters in their possession had decided not to act, but she could not work out why. Like her employer, she existed in a state of watchfulness: anxiously passing around every corner; sleeping with her door, and Georgie's, locked. Sleep was no respite. Her dreams remained turbulent, and she rose early and retired after midnight, waiting, with barely checked patience, for some development – a sign or clue to tell her how to proceed.

This unwelcome limbo seemed to affect everyone else as much as her. The disaster had placed a pause on everything at Locksley, and she found herself almost alone. Grizel did not seek out her company, sleeping each afternoon and complaining of her brother's absences. Sir Rowland himself spent more and more of each day out of the house, returning late if he returned at all, and leaving before sunrise. Catherine did not see him for the first several days. Parry, too, was absent, needed at the colliery. Sir Rowland even sent Locksley's cook to assist with meals for the rescuers, putting still more of the work of the Abbey on the beleaguered Edie, who rushed about from before dawn each day, never seeming to be in one place longer than a few seconds.

Anne Bridewell kept to her rooms.

So Catherine's only company was Georgie. The little girl's behaviour did not improve after their venture into the woods. If anything, it got worse. Half Catherine's time was spent chasing her wayward charge from room to room, or persuading her to release yet another spider from the jars she collected in the nursery. Catherine had to scold her often, and began to fret about how to manage her. She wondered what other forms of entertainment might be found to keep her out of trouble.

But Georgie took her scoldings in good grace. She did not seem malicious, and Catherine, liking the child in spite of her naughtiness, became convinced she must look elsewhere for her thief. She was tempted, each day, to try the handle of Sir Rowland's study and search for her letters there, as more likely than not he would be at the colliery, but until she knew his movements for certain, she did not dare; if she were wrong, and was caught, she had no explanation to satisfy him.

The third day after the accident was a Sunday. At around ten in the morning, she found Edie polishing silver in the servants' hall. The housemaid didn't look up as Catherine opened the door, persisting in rubbing her cloth in rapid circles against the mount of a pot. Pausing, Catherine thought something of Edie's plumpness had left her. Even in the low light of the hall she looked tired.

'Good day, Edie,' she said.

'Miss,' said the housemaid, not stopping.

'It's Sunday. Do people in this house not go to church?' Catherine knew they didn't, as Mrs Parry had said so, but needed some excuse to break the silence.

'There's no church to go to, miss,' said Edie stoutly. 'Not to walk to, anyway.'

'I was wondering where they took Mrs Parry,' said Catherine, sitting on the other side of the table facing Edie. She sighed, settling into the chair.

For a few moments Edie kept rubbing, then seemed to realise she had been asked a question. 'They sent a cart over the pass. There's a church in the next village.'

'Is that where members of the family are buried?'

'I wouldn't know, miss,' Edie said, looking up at last, her eyes narrowing in her drawn face.

'I just wondered,' Catherine said lamely. 'Mrs Parry told me there was a church here, and it was in use before the minister took his leave.'

Edie frowned, thinking. 'There's the family chapel on the north side of the wood. But it grows very thick up there. I'd never think of going there to pray.' She seemed to shudder, distracted for a moment from the silver.

Remembering Parry's warnings, and wanting Edie to say more, Catherine said, 'I might walk there this afternoon. It's important to remain close to God. Important for Georgie, too.'

Edie shook her head, vehemently. 'You shouldn't, miss. Not alone. There's no reason for you to be wandering about. Certainly not with that little girl.'

'It's not the first time I've been warned away from the wood,' said Catherine idly. 'Mr Parry seemed to think …' She smiled, as if the thought were foolish.

The rubbing ceased. Edie's expression was stricken. 'What, miss?' she said weakly.

'It was nothing; he just said something about spirits, or ghosts. I found it rather unsophisticated, but he is a simple man, after all.' She was challenging Edie to confirm or deny her agreement with Parry. It wasn't his simplicity she was thinking of at all – Sir Rowland, too, seemed afraid of the wood, and he had ten times Parry's education. What were they frightened of?

Edie's answer came quiet, but determined. 'You stay away, then,' she said, more fiercely than Catherine had heard her say anything before. 'Whatever's there, it's nothing to do with you.'

Whatever's there? What could Edie mean? 'So there *are* legends about the wood?' she asked, trying to sound vaguely interested, as if they were gossiping.

'Some,' said Edie, frowning. 'When I was little my mother would …' She stopped, seeming to think better of it.

'What?'

Placing her dusting cloth on the table, Edie leant in and said solemnly, 'She hated the wood. She'd never let me near it. She said it was full of blood-curdling spirits; restless, if you like. Wild men and their mounts, she'd say, all lusty and …' She hesitated, her cheeks flushed. 'But that's shameful talk.' She seemed unsure of how to explain. 'It was like a hunt. There was a great spirit of the forest, and the men would hunt girls, and the wicked, and make wild music. If you were unlucky and they came across you, you'd be swept up, and never found.'

She gave a strange little laugh. 'Not that I believe any of that. But still, the wood's a dire enough place without any of it.' She began to polish again. 'Anyone might be about. They've not caught Stephen Dowle yet – he might do you a violence.'

'You're right. I should have thought of that. Thank you.'

Edie continued her work and Catherine sat quietly, thinking of the maid's warnings and her own deep sense of unease. She wasn't afraid of Dowle. If she was any judge, he was wily enough to be far from Locksley already.

It was the wood. Its influence had settled on her dreams. Each night as she fell into sleep, she found herself running through its dark groves and thickets. Wolves lurked in the shadows between the tree boles, their bloodied jaws snapping out of the dark places. She ran on, searching, but always the yew loomed over her, or rather over them, for she was not alone. When she looked beside her she was accompanied by another figure. Georgie's delicate features, streaked red with poisonous berries, wavered, and then dissolved into Emily's. Below – though, in the way of dreams, she could not tell how she perceived this – the deep fathoms of the mine stretched eternally. Forty-one men and boys had been crushed and tortured, had choked and died there, but they would not accept their fate; their hands reached hungrily for the surface, or for her, disturbing the earth, resisting some force that pulled them back …

Edie's stories only added to her fear.

She straightened in her chair. She would not think of that now. Nightmares and old wives' tales were for children. She decided she would allow a few more days for Dowle's pursuers to give up on the hunt, then she would venture back into the wood, whatever Edie and Mr Parry thought.

It occurred to her that Edie might be able to help with another problem. 'Would you know if there were any toys or children's trinkets in the house, perhaps put somewhere out of the way?'

Edie thought. 'I can't say I do. There's never been much for the poor mite.'

'Where would they be stored, if there were any?' She thought there might be old things, perhaps belonging to Mrs Wingfield and Sir Rowland when they were growing up here. She didn't care if they had belonged to a boy. Georgie had no girlish pretensions, and even a set of wooden soldiers would alleviate some of her boredom.

Edie said, 'Mrs Parry said there was a lot of old stuff in the attics. You could go up there and look. I don't think it's kept locked.'

She thanked Edie, and returned to the nursery.

Georgie was at her lessons. Before they had completed an hour of French instruction, the little girl began to chew her nails and fidget. When, after several repetitions of one point, the information seemed not to be sinking in, Catherine gently suggested her pupil remove her teeth from her nails, and said they might visit the attics. She did not mention toys – she did not want to raise hopes only to have them dashed. Georgie readily agreed to show her the way. 'They're big,' the child warned. 'They run over this whole section of the house.'

'All the better,' Catherine said wryly. 'They'll keep you occupied for a while.'

The attics were accessed by a rounding staircase, then a door that they found, as Edie had said, unlocked.

Governess and charge stood for a few moments at one end of the long gallery, looking into the dark. Hearing a mournful wind in the rafters, Catherine protected her candle. She had not expected this blackness. She could not help thinking of the mine, a grave for all those unrecovered souls, and much darker, she was certain, than this. Still, the thought gave her pause before, unexpectedly, Georgie's warm fingers closed around hers.

'Come on,' said Georgie. The little girl went along in front of her governess, sure-footed on the uneven planks.

'How often have you been up here?' Catherine asked, placing her boot carefully on a board that seemed to shift beneath her weight. She could not see where she put her feet, and worried about falling through. 'You move like a goat.'

'Lots,' came the confident answer. 'Miss Emily played hide-and-seek with me up here.'

She would, Catherine realised. Such games rarely seemed to occur to her, but she remembered, now, how they had appealed to her younger sister. Emily had loved the hiding even more than the seeking, gaining satisfaction in deceiving her pursuer as long as possible, and in jumping out, Catherine recalled, from the most unlikely places. Once again, these memories seemed to come out of nowhere. She held on to them as they walked further into the long passageway, with Georgie a little ahead.

Just as the windows downstairs had been shuttered and curtained off, so the small windows on this upper floor seemed to have been covered with baize or canvas. A few thin beams of light pierced gaps in the material, cutting across the narrow space. Catherine groped with her spare arm, touching the cobwebbed slant of the roof. She felt webs, dry, no longer sticky. Hoping they were abandoned, she rubbed the strands off on her gown, thinking they were unlikely to find what she looked for here. Perhaps they should return to the nursery.

'Georgie?' Her voice carried down the passage. No response came back. 'Georgie?'

She took another step and stumbled, tripping on something at waist height. She just managed to save herself from a fall, and her outstretched hands struck the object. Their impact produced a low, discordant *thrum* that made her cry out. As she straightened, the notes – for it was a musical sound – reverberated around the attic. She groped more with her fingers, exploring, touching cool wood or ivory. Keys, she realised, as each small motion gave rise to another note, very soft. A pianoforte, she thought, elegant, not quite in proper pitch.

She played a little, the muted sound somehow familiar. Moving over the keys, she became more conscious of the deep chill of the attic, and the prickles mounting on her skin. She shifted to the higher keys – *thrum* – and the notes dredged up something reluctant; half a memory, only. Strangest of all, this recollection, again, was of the wood, of flickering lights between the trees, and something beyond, in the dark, waiting …

These impressions brought her close to panic. What was it that threatened to resurface, so dreadful that her mind resisted? Whatever it was, she could not face it, not yet. She drew back from the instrument.

Georgie's voice seemed to come out of nowhere. 'That was my grandfather's. My father doesn't like music,' she added mournfully. 'He ordered all my grandfather's things removed up here. But now you're here, you could ask if we could take it down—'

'No!' Her voice was too high in the darkness. 'No,' she repeated, more calmly. 'Your father wouldn't like it.' She took a step back. 'Come,' she told Georgie. 'I don't think we're going to find anything here. It's too dark, in any case.'

They returned downstairs. But that night her dreams grew worse.

Six days after the explosion, the inquest began at an inn over the southern pass out of the valley. She learnt from Mrs Wingfield that her employer had put up in rooms there, and wasn't expected for several more days.

On the seventh day, in the afternoon, she decided she had waited long enough, and went alone to Sir Rowland's study. She found it unlocked, with furniture gathering a film of dust. Earlier that day, she had hunted in the service corridor and found a feathered duster. Now she pulled the door closed and ran the feathers negligently over the bookcase, not really cleaning, merely equipping herself with an excuse for her presence here.

The desk was disorderly. Glancing at the door, she leafed through the papers. There were two things she sought. The first was any sign of her letters; if Sir Rowland had them, she would know she was discovered. The second might be anything – a record of a burial; a journal, perhaps. It was possible Emily might have sent Sir Rowland letters of her own. Anything that would help Catherine make sense of what had happened.

Partly covered by a stack of bills, a newspaper lay open at the obituaries page. She looked over the list of names, recognising one: Uriah Caplin. It was brief, and to the point.

Nothing seemed to relate to Emily's death. She tugged at the drawers, but found them locked and turned to the revolving bookcase. Like the desk, it was shambolic, stuffed with fraying newspapers, files and letters. But one heavy file was marked *LP&B*. She remembered these initials, and murmured the names that went with them out loud: *Lewis, Putnam & Bird*.

Quickly, she opened it. Lewis's sedate style was familiar.

Sir:

4th November 1852
Hereford

My condolences on the passing of your father-in-law. As per your instructions, we have applied to the executors, and are informed that probate has been granted. I am sending on records kept by us, relating to what we discussed previously: Mr Uriah Caplin's will stipulates that Lady Anne Bridewell should inherit his property as long as your marriage stands in law. Any children of the marriage must be your only issue. These conditions being fulfilled, the estate will pass into your control once legalities

are completed. We anticipate this taking several weeks. In the
meantime, payments on the line of credit extended to you by
Mr Caplin for the expansion of the Bridewell Colliery should
continue as a matter of form. Once the estate is transferred, we
can revisit these arrangements.

Yours truly,
Fitzhugh Lewis, Attorney at Law
Lewis, Putnam & Bird

So, Sir Rowland had been in debt to his father-in-law. Now not only would it not be repaid, but Sir Rowland had full access to the Caplin fortune. His choices were expanded. He could, if he wished, close the mine, or send his wife away. For Sir Rowland, this changed everything.

But it told her nothing.

Frustrated, she hunted, but found nothing else. She was about to return the desk to its previous state when she heard a soft click. Straightening, she closed her fingers round the handle of the duster and swept one or two strokes, then twisted her head as if she had only just noticed the newcomer.

Grizel Wingfield stood in the doorway.

'Oh!' Catherine exclaimed. 'You startled me ...' She moved so her skirts obscured the papers. 'I thought ... as we are so short-staffed, and I had time to spare ...' She brandished the duster.

Grizel paused with her hand on the knob. Catherine's heart beat erratically as a sly smile played on the tall woman's lips. She took several paces nearer and used her height to see over Catherine's shoulder.

'You lie quite well,' she said. 'But I'm no fool. I know what you're doing in here, why you're looking through papers. You want to know the extent of my brother's fortune. Perhaps ingratiate yourself with him. You wouldn't be the first.' She stared at

Catherine, licking her lips. 'Perhaps you understand, from being with your own husband, how susceptible men can be.'

She knows.

'I have no idea what you mean,' she said coldly.

Grizel's voice rippled. 'Your finger, Miss Symonds. A man might overlook those indentations, but not a woman like me, a woman who has worn the same rings, a woman with nothing to do but observe those around her.' Catherine looked down. The groove in the skin had softened, but was still there. Grizel continued. 'What was it? Was he vicious? Or did he die, leaving you penniless?' She was enjoying her taunting, but her words missed their target, for Catherine was only relieved, realising the other woman had worked out her victim had been married, but no more.

That meant Grizel hadn't taken her letters. She didn't know who Catherine was, or why she was here.

Catherine was thinking furiously, observing Grizel's face, pink with pleasure. Her mouth was curved in a smile. What she had discovered, Catherine realised, had not angered her; she seemed pleased. With distaste, Catherine decided it was a sense of her own power that brought that enjoyment to Grizel's cheek. This was a weak and spiteful woman, overlooked, perhaps always, by the Bridewells. Just knowing something her adopted brother didn't seemed to fill some gnawing need. But what would she do? Would she get more satisfaction from revealing her superior knowledge to Sir Rowland, or from hiding it? And if she did hide it, what would she want from Catherine in return?

Not wanting to risk a denial, Catherine glanced up at Grizel. 'What are you going to tell him?' she asked, with what she hoped was a pleading note. She kept her posture meek, and allowed herself to rub the spot where her rings had been, as if she were in a state of anxiety.

'I'll have to give that some thought,' came the answer, a little airy. 'We can't leap blindly into these things, can we?'

So she would withhold her knowledge, and enjoy her power, Catherine thought. Good. That was a reprieve, if only temporary.

'But if you would rely on my silence,' Grizel continued, pretending regret at what she was about to say, 'I must insist on a favour in return.' Catherine nodded, listening. 'You will promise to stay away from my—from Rowland.'

Catherine, catching the slip, nodded, and, deciding a denial might be more palatable here, said, 'Mrs Wingfield, I never had any intention of—'

The look of self-satisfaction slid from Grizel's face, replaced by contempt as she cut off Catherine's words. 'Do not insult my intelligence. You're all the same, women like you. Fortune hunters, as mercenary as any Swiss grenadier. You were evidently snooping about in here, hoping to discover some way to snare Rowland, just as ...'

She stopped short, and Catherine tried to keep her own rising emotions out of her voice as she said, 'Miss Murphy? Did you mean she—'

'Don't mention that woman's name in front of me!'

Barely controlled fury radiated from her stance and expression; she had hated Emily, Catherine realised. Had she thought she could control her? Had her envy led her to violence? Catherine softened her tone. 'Was her presence a bad influence? Disruptive? Because I can understand if you had to act on that – what good woman would not?'

'Disruptive – that's the very word,' said Grizel, nodding in enthusiastic agreement at the idea. 'She was disruptive from the beginning, I see that now.' She seemed to think, looking Catherine over, seeing only sympathy in her listener. 'I think I will tell you,' she said. 'I'll tell you all, and by the time I'm done, you'll see my advice is for your own good.' She paused. 'And it would please me if you would use my Christian name.'

Before following, Catherine took a chance and snatched up Lewis's letter. With Grizel leading the way, she concealed it in her dress pocket, beneath the silver scissors.

20

In the drawing room, Grizel poured tea from the pot. She sat uneasily in her surroundings, her tall frame exceeding the bounds of her chair. As the tea cooled, words spilled from her mouth.

'I remember nowhere but Locksley. As a girl of six or seven, it was given out that my parents were European nobility. Sir Maurice told his circle how they surrendered my charge and inheritance to him before they died. I was to regard Sir Maurice as my father, though never the Lady Elise as my mother. She hated the sight of me. She did her utmost to keep me out of the view of others, always in the nursery, never allowed to join in with a party of guests, even as I left my girlhood behind me. Lady Elise was from a line of small women, like Lady Anne.' Grizel added a lump of sugar, looking critically at Catherine's figure. 'The top of my head passed her shoulder before I was ten years old. She viewed me as a monster. I never understood why, and was bewildered when Rowland was presented with a new pony and I was not, and my dresses cut from things Lady Elise decided were out of fashion, never bought new. Gradually, I pieced together what I should always have been told. The physical resemblance was too strong not to notice, and before many years had passed, I came to realise Rowland and I shared a father, even if our father didn't care to admit it. I challenged Sir Maurice, and he confessed the truth. There were no Europeans. No inheritance. My mother was a housemaid. He kept me, she kept her character, and Rowland and I were raised in the same nursery. I often wondered whether that was her preference, not his, as my father never seemed particularly satisfied with his end of the bargain.

'When my brother wasn't away at school, he never missed a chance of reminding me how I was not blood. He knew the truth, but preferred to deny it. In letters to his friends, he labelled me the *giantess*. Do you know, Miss Symonds, I have never been called pretty, or charming? But by my own brother, since I was a little girl, I have been called dithering, verbose and dull.' She turned her plump curls towards Catherine, seeming to hint for sympathy. Catherine nodded. It must have been a lonely childhood. Her pity was not feigned.

'Then our father and Lady Elise left for Italy. It was very sudden, on account of his health, and as it became clear that he would not return, and Roland would take the reins of the estate, so my brother turned on me. He was engaged to marry Anne Caplin by that time. Her father was a snob, and public knowledge of my origins would have scuppered the match, so I was to be married away. But I was already past the age when most women are courted. I didn't want to leave Locksley, which, although it had become less of a comfort to me, was still the only home I had ever known. Besides, marriage did not appeal to me. I found the very idea of it ... abhorrent.' She sniffed, straightening her gown about her calves. Catherine waited for her to say more. 'When Rowland started to invite bachelors from his club to dine, at first I took little notice, and simply tried to stay out of their way. But he would insist I join them for dinner, and after several of these excruciating attempts at drawing the luckless guest into discussion of his prospects, I begged Rowland to stop. They could see what he was about, these men. He was never particularly subtle of mind, and it was humiliating how he would try to place me, his father's ungainly ward, in their way. Quite often he would invite them to stay for the weekend and shoot with him, only for them to discover a sudden engagement in town, and be forced to leave without delay.' She reddened, and Catherine saw that she was still ashamed, even all these years later.

She went on. 'But Daniel Wingfield appeared respectable, a retired captain. Rowland said he admired me, and indeed there was nothing in his behaviour to suggest this was untrue. I began to warm to the idea of receiving my own guests in my own home, of being beholden to nobody. He returned to the house several times, and on one occasion asked to speak with me alone. He spoke well enough,' she said, lowering her gaze, remembering. 'In retrospect, I should have seen it for what it was, which was unseemly haste, and known Rowland was concealing something of note, but I didn't, and in a short space we were married. We went to Meath, to my husband's property there.' She stopped, considering. 'The marriage was loathsome in every particular. I discovered, too late, how Wingfield had disgraced himself, and been cashiered. There was debt, and scandal, and … other things. I refrained from going into society, so that his disgrace could reflect on me as little as possible. He died a bankrupt, in the end, of a weak heart. I felt only relief.'

At this, Catherine's own heart fluttered, and she twisted the skin on her ring finger, thinking of William.

Grizel said, 'There was a brief period when I thought I might escape into a respectable, if tedious, widowhood, but even this was denied me. I discovered the house in Meath was mort-gaged to the hilt. My husband left no bequests, just bad credit. The estate was sold off, and, as I had nowhere to go, for my husband's relatives offered me nothing, I returned to Locksley, feeling this to be just another in the long line of mortifications inflicted upon me by my brother. Even so, as Rowland had been married several years by then, I believed things could be differ-ent. He might be as he had always been, but I looked forward to returning home, making a friend of my sister-in-law, and putting the past behind us. I was even willing to mend bridges with Rowland. I decided he couldn't be as dreadful to me now as he had been when we were young.' She smiled without a trace of humour. 'He was worse. Anne Caplin had already become a recluse. I had never been so alone. But, slowly, I began to find my feet. Though as high-handed as ever, Rowland had no real choice while his wife denied us her company, and leant on me to care for Georgiana. This was natural. I was his sister, and her aunt, even if the world did not recognise it. This at least provided me with purpose.'

Catherine understood. Grizel's urge to control Georgie was a way of belonging here, of asserting that Locksley was her home, and the Bridewells her family.

'And then Miss Murphy came, shortly after Michaelmas.'

Catherine couldn't look at her companion without giving herself away. Her hands shook. She held them firmly in her lap.

'At first, I confess, I was resentful. I did not see why Rowland needed to employ her, knowing myself perfectly capable of managing the child, but then ...' She seemed to think of how to word things. 'You must understand, you probably do understand, that this is a dull house. We live without balls, luncheons or picnics. Miss Murphy arrived, and she *glittered*. So clever, with a nimble wit. She had a great talent for mimicry. At Christmas she entertained us with a marionette show in this very room, and even Rowland sat with us and joined in, and it felt like something a true family would do together. Just in that hour, I almost found myself forgetting the disappointments of former years.' She stopped for a few moments, looking about the room, then let out a sigh. 'I could see her drawing Georgiana towards her, and perhaps further away from me, yet I found myself enjoying her company; laughing, even, at her foolish games and occupations.'

She sniffed imperiously, and added, 'All of it rather childish, in retrospect. I should have trusted to my instincts concerning her.

'Just weeks after those enjoyable diversions, perhaps as she had planned since her first days here, it began with Rowland. He drifted from the work of the estate, and followed her about like a puppy. He was fulsome in his praise of her way with Georgiana, and I couldn't help but feel he compared us, with me coming off worse, of course, just as it had always been. When he talked of her, the most bovine expression came over his face, and I wanted to shake him, to tell him not to be such a fool. How could he involve himself with a woman like that, of no background, who could have come from any number of scandalous entanglements?'

Catherine murmured, 'Scandalous, indeed. Did she tell you much about her history?'

'Not much,' admitted Grizel, touching the kettle with a gloved hand. 'She said she had been in Bristol, with a farming family. I remember that conversation one evening, because Rowland hung on her every word. It made me curious, so I followed them. He went to her bedroom, and did not come out.'

A much longer pause followed this revelation. Catherine studied Grizel, seeing that her cheeks were aflame and her breathing somewhat quicker. She wondered how long the other woman had waited for her brother to leave his lover's embrace. She could almost imagine Grizel sinking to her knees, peering through keyholes, her hatred and envy a corrosive thing driving her on, disguised by concern for the reputation of the family that would never accept her. But had it led her to exact revenge on Emily? Surely this story was not leading up to a confession?

Grizel said, 'This situation went on for some time, Miss Murphy cock-a-hoop, my brother her willing cat's paw. It was intolerable, and I thought constantly about the best way to bring it to an end. Finally, I knew I had to share my knowledge with my sister-in-law. I did not want to. It was my duty,' she insisted loftily.

'You told Lady Anne of her husband's unfaithfulness?'

'Yes.'

'When did you go to her?' That the mistress of Locksley Abbey had known of her husband's dalliance was new information, possibly vital. Had *Lady Anne* decided enough was enough, and somehow arranged Emily's death? How would she achieve that? She would have had to have help.

Caught up in her story, Grizel did not register that she was being questioned. 'This was after two or three months, in the early spring, shortly before …' she trailed off, 'before Miss Murphy's death.'

'Did she confront him?'

Grizel's eyes widened with her incredulity. 'No. Imagine my feelings when Anne told me she knew – knew all along! She said, despite her distaste for Miss Murphy's behaviour, that she had no desire for Rowland to return to her bed, and it suited her well enough for him to have his amusements. I asked her – with as much delicacy as possible – what would happen if the governess got herself with child. I remembered my mother, and could not countenance the thought of another illegitimate child at Locksley.'

'What did she say?'

'She admitted it would be an infamous thing if it were to happen, but she seemed strangely unworried. She hinted that Rowland would never allow it, that it was in his own interests to make sure no child was the result of his fickleness. Then she turned away, quite sanguine, and I was dismissed.

'I was at a loss as to how to proceed. It seemed I was the only one who could see Miss Murphy for what she was – an unprincipled, thoroughly venal young woman, who would follow her own selfish wants and bring ruin on us all. But for the time being, there was little I could do. Rowland continued to be infatuated, and the weeks went on.

'Curious about Lady Anne's indulgence of my brother's behaviour, I did some investigating of my own, and discovered that Uriah Caplin, always shrewd in his business dealings, had made my sister-in-law's inheritance contingent on my brother not having any children outside the marriage. If Rowland fathered a child that did not have Caplin's blood, he would lose the Caplin fortune.

'Then in April came that day in the wood. Georgiana was missing, Miss Murphy could not be found either, and then we learnt what had happened. When my brother carried Miss Murphy back to the house, and I looked at her, I experienced a deep fascination to think that one day she was overflowing with life, and the next, there she lay in the boot room, a mere *thing*. I've thought a great deal since of how her neck was discoloured, her face stripped of its intelligence. I decided, after all, perhaps she had not been as in control of my brother as I had thought.

'This is why I warn you, Miss Symonds, to stay away, because he must have killed her, of course. I think she was with child, and he had in mind his purse, and I think, the great fool, that he followed her into the wood, and put that rope around her neck himself. I believe, though,' Grizel concluded, with obvious pleasure, 'that the deed has unsettled him. He suffers as he ought to suffer, and is so far from himself. He talks of spirits moving in the wood, of floating lights that should not be there, of shades of things that were dead. But I suppose,' she said, 'that you cannot account for the effects of guilt on the human mind.'

21

Catherine's head whirled. She made her excuse to go, saying Georgie needed her, but before leaving she approached Grizel's seat, and pressed her hands into the older woman's. 'I promise you,' she said, 'nothing will be repeated. I understand everything you have said. We are now dear friends.'

Grizel, satiated, smiled at this false reassurance.

As Catherine went down the passageway, she considered how far she believed the tale she had been told. Grizel unsettled her, especially in the way she took her feelings out on a child, and her fixation on her brother's affairs. Yet it was unlikely, Catherine decided, that she was a murderess. Her story of a father and a brother with roving eyes was believable enough. It explained why Uriah Caplin would place conditions on his daughter's inheritance.

So perhaps Grizel was right. Emily had been pregnant, and Sir Rowland had murdered his lover to protect his fortune. He staged the scene in the wood and called in Frederick Sidstone to say Emily had taken her own life. It would have been easy enough to overpower her. Perhaps it was even quick.

She fumbled in her front pocket as she walked, comforting herself that she had some evidence for her theory: Lewis's letter.

Soon – if she had her way, tonight – she would use it to prove Rowland Bridewell's guilt.

There was still the matter of her own letters. Neither Grizel nor Georgie had them. That left Sir Rowland: but why did he not expose her? Because, she decided, returning to her room, that was what an innocent man would do. An innocent man would be disturbed to discover an imposter in his household. He would have no qualms about scrutiny from the authorities, and would have her arrested for fraud. Or, if dull enough not to understand the full implications of what he read, he would confront her, and demand an explanation.

But a guilty man? He would know exactly who she was and what she wanted. He might not know, if Emily's body were to be exhumed, what it would tell a coroner, whether it would be clear if she had been strangled by strong hands, or been with child. He might decide to deal with Catherine himself.

Sir Rowland acted like a guilty man. What had Grizel said? Her brother talked of spirits and things that should be dead. He suffered. And what had he said himself, standing amid his father's treasures?

There was no reason anything might be regarded as impossible.

So this was a haunting; or something of the kind, anyway. Consumed by guilt, Sir Rowland was pursued by the ghosts of his own actions. She better understood now why his face was so drained of colour. Why he watched the wood.

He must have been intending to deal with her, but the disaster at the colliery had delayed his decision. It would not do so much longer. She would have to act. Tonight.

As Georgie ate her supper, Catherine made plans. She would leave Locksley on foot, head down the ridge to Hereford, and present herself to the nearest constable. She had no money, and the proof of her identity was gone, but she had Lewis's letter. That proved the Caplin bequest was dependent on Sir Rowland fathering no illegitimate children. She could report Sir Rowland's state of mind, Grizel's testimony that Emily and Sir Rowland had been lovers, and demand to know why there had been no inquest. She was not, after all, nobody. Her staff would vouch for her. It would be a hard walk out of the valley, but the net would close on Sir Rowland eventually.

One thing was certain: she would not wait while it closed on her.

But something remained to be done first. She could not go without seeing Emily's grave. She had come here intending to find her sister again. It was unthinkable to come all this way only to fail.

So she waited. Shortly after sunset Georgie read aloud from her Bible, as Catherine, trying at least to appear obedient to her father's wishes, encouraged her to do each evening. It was a passage from Mark's gospel. Catherine hardly listened as the little girl recounted how the women discovered the rolling back of the stone. At around seven o'clock, she gave Georgie milk and supervised her prayers. As if she could sense her governess's agitation, the child was particularly good. Before Catherine tucked Georgie in, she smoothed the short tufts of her charge's hair with a brush.

'Miss Symonds?' said Georgie.

'Yes?'

'Will you stay?'

Catherine was on her knees, brushing in soft strokes, when this appeal came. Looking up, she caught sight of her reflection in the window, her face white and stricken. 'A governess must find work where she can,' she said gently. 'She can't always stay.' It was not the truth, but she could not explain.

Georgie's voice wavered as she said, 'Miss Murphy said she would always be here.'

Catherine floundered, her throat full. 'What a curious promise,' she said in the end, patting the downy head with her palm. 'Come now, into bed.' She sat, waiting, as Georgie's breathing slowed, until, around twenty minutes later, she slept.

As deeper night fell, she crouched, shivering, in the window. She observed a mist of rain on the pane, and beyond, a bow moon peeping from under a black cloud. It was the eve of St Martin, she realised. The start of winter. Behind the house, a wind swept up the hill and stirred the wood. The dogs bayed, but in her brother's absence Mrs Wingfield had ordered them shut up. It was barbarism, she said, to let them roam the grounds. For several hours, Catherine listened to their howls, not moving from the window until, finally, they lay down to sleep. It was around midnight when she pulled on her gloves and cloak and crept down the back stairs barefoot, carrying boots, tinder-box and a lantern. Fearful of betraying noise, she limited her footfall to the very edges of the boards. She didn't know who might hear. She had not noticed Sir Rowland come back, but he might have abandoned his business at the inquest early, and returned, and though she assumed Grizel would be asleep, she could not be certain.

At the back door, she unfastened the latch, sat down, and laced her boots. For some minutes she stood in the shadow of the house until, confident she was not discovered, she navigated the path past the dying borders and the glasshouses. She breathed in the cold, quiet air with its residue of coal, her senses sharpened by blindness. Other scents – harvested apples, rosemary and devil's daisy – drifted from the raised herb beds. Every few paces she stopped, listening, dreading the howling that would tell her the dogs were abroad. When she moved, each crunch of stones beneath her boots sounded to her like a thunderclap.

Something disturbed the calm. Every muscle in her body went taut. Was it a twig breaking underfoot, or a stone being kicked to the side of the shingle path? When the noise came again, she moved quickly out of the way, sheltering between the glasshouses. As she looked on, a light appeared, shrouded in a halo of mist. The darkness fed her imagination, allowing the presence behind the glow to take terrifying forms. Her first thoughts resurrected Grizel's words: *things that were dead* not staying in their place. She waited, expecting cold dread to flood her veins.

It didn't come. She felt wary, but not terrified. She realised it was the light. It moved with too much purpose. This was not a spirit. It was something more corporeal, she decided: a single person holding a candle lantern.

But not Sir Rowland. He would be on horseback, trotting up the drive in daylight, not stealing through his own gardens in the manner of a thief. She recalled Parry's clumsy tread, nothing like this feline prowl. Even Grizel, if awake, would raise the alarm, but send others to do the searching. And there was weight to the steps. She felt sure they belonged to a man: stealthy, determined not to be heard. She held her breath as the light came closer, then passed her and moved away. She was not safe, just temporarily reprieved. Should she hurry back to the house? The idea was swiftly rejected. Sir Rowland could return at any time. She would miss her chance.

She went on, beginning to shake with the cold. At the cypress boundary, she kindled a flame, then placed the lantern on the other side of the stile before climbing over. She paused, taking stock. The wood grew due west. If she followed the path ahead she would come to the great yew tree, but Edie had said the Bridewell chapel was to the north, where the forest grew thickest. She knew Emily was there, in the vault.

Setting off, the wood seemed vast and her light feeble, dwarfed by the magnitude of her task, and yet, after a few minutes beneath the canopy, she realised, perplexed, that she was not worried about losing her way. She chose her route with surety, and kept climbing, entering the heart of the forest with an unexpected conviction that she would find what she sought. She could not explain why she took or rejected each turn; it was as if some outside agency guided her feet, as if she had been here before, and it produced a sort of fervour to understand that she might be nearing the end of her journey, and, finally, the truth.

The slope ahead was black and dense with trees. Looking behind her, she saw the house was no longer visible. The ground rushed at her steeply, the old branches bowing down like viziers in the glow of the lantern, and it was too quiet, but still, somehow, alive. She had no other word for it. She only felt it, in the sentinel whispering of the trees, and the hoarse rustling breath of the canopy. Keeping on, she walked a broad inclining circle up the side of the valley, cracking dead bracken and sharp bramble canes underfoot.

After a while the ground began to level off and the path widened, becoming more uneven, and sodden. Halfway down a slippery knoll, she lost her footing, and dropped the light. Forcing herself to rise, she leant on a tree trunk, wiping drips of water from her face and neck. She closed her eyes, taking deep breaths, feeling the dark like pressure against her skin.

Black and white shapes flocked against her closed lids. Her mind swarmed with images: the pitiless dark of a mine shaft; forty-one men in their deep crypt, striving, clawing for air ...

Opening her eyes to dispel these pictures, she saw a small number of indistinct lights, like fireflies, hovering between the tree trunks. After several seconds, anxious to determine if they were her own fancy, she blinked hard, then looked again.

They were still there.

She could not tell how far off. They seemed to move uphill, faint, like a stream, but each still distinct. One blinked out of sight as she watched, then another, then another, until all were gone.

They could not really be there. She held on to that thought. Rational people did not see processions of lights appearing and disappearing into nothing. They did not recover memories beneath the boughs of yew trees, or lose years of their lives at a stretch. Again, she was seized by the awful conjecture that she had everything twisted, somehow. There were other things she did not remember. Why didn't she know what happened to separate her from Emily? Why did she hide the truth about her father from William? Had he been right to say her family was polluted by madness?

These chaotic thoughts, along with the biting cold, caused her hands to tremble as she lit her lantern again. But she was not turning back. She could not be discouraged now.

She walked further into the undergrowth. Soon, a steeper mound rose up before her. Limping to its crest, she looked down on a dark outline illuminated by the moon's white belly, and made out toothed eaves and a needle spire. She allowed herself to descend, half-skidding, down the bank, before grappling with an iron railing at the bottom. Fumbling her way, she arrived at a wrought gate, felt for the latch and pulled it across, pushing to dislodge muscular spirals of ivy and allow entry into the tiny precinct. As she put one foot inside, she hesitated. The thought of what she was about to do, this disturbance of the dead, was almost enough to make her retreat.

In that moment's pause, she saw it. There, a light coming through the trees. It couldn't be from the Abbey. She peered, waiting, but now it did not blink or waver. It was a rusty orange glow, growing brighter. Then, from the same direction, came a wild, shapeless noise, a cacophony of which she could make no sense. For long seconds she was consumed by its fearful strangeness, before silence fell again.

Rain dripped through the forest roof, the wind shifted the creaking branches, an owl hooted, and she heard the flutter of its wings through the remaining leaves. On the air came the smell of something rotten, and the baying of hounds.

She had no time to think of the dogs. The lights were back. Faint at first, then stronger, and now accompanied by a din, a hollow sound like a horn meshed with grinding stones and clanging cymbals. A music so strange she could not bear it.

There could be no refuge in the chapel. She couldn't even see the door. She crouched instead in the undergrowth at the bottom of the mound. Above her head it was dense with twisting stems and roots, and soil trickled down the neck of her dress. Behind her, she knew, lay the dead. She could almost feel them, their grasping hands on her, near her throat.

Dark forms moved through the trees. She could only half make them out, her sight wavering between the etched outlines of the trunks, her imagination flooding with low and slouching shapes. The light came closer, and they with it.

A cry escaped her lips as they emerged, horned and horrible, wearing grimaces of ecstatic pleasure. Nearer and nearer it came, a line of braying shapes with rutting beasts at their feet. They appeared armed with forks or branches, and every second or third carried a torch giving off a rank smoke. Some were bearded. Others looked like women, bare-chested, bodies dyed with a dark substance and tangled hair obscuring their features. The hounds seemed to follow them, weaving between their limbs and the tree trunks. They came closer still, and in the orange light cast by their torches, she made out the silhouette of a horse. The dogs had fallen silent, but the horse let out other-worldly snorts, and she imagined fire funnelling from its nostrils, its hooves beating down like rain.

She covered her ears. They had come, they were here, as Sir Rowland had feared: the souls of the restless dead, vengeful, famished. Here to take her.

Or she was mad, like her father. That lunacy had driven her to witness sights nobody else could see, to hear noises nobody else could hear.

The mounted figure edged closer, the horse's breath foetid on her face. She recoiled, sensing it reeked of death. The great head swung, and she saw its neck was covered with ropes, and a drapery of moss.

But then, as she fell and the figure lowered his powerful form and reached for her, so near that the chill from his body sank into hers, the wood revealed its intention, and chose that moment to give something back.

22

'You look ridiculous.' Catherine's voice is as sour as her stomach. The carriage seems to have rumbled along for hours. On the seat opposite her, splayed across a stranger's plush green silk, Gilbert Murphy is asleep, his mouth slack, arms folded over his only decent coat. The carriage is spacious enough, but he still takes up too much room with his legs forked into the corners, forcing his daughters to press close together on the other side. She has no intention of waking him.

Emily, who has pinned her curls with a lavender ribbon and tamed the front strands into spirals, imitating the style of someone older, says nothing, but pats down her hair. The humidity of the long summer evening has ruined the look of it, even if it had suited her to start with, which it didn't. Around her neck hangs the only piece of jewellery remaining to their mother, a silver locket not valuable enough to pawn. Catherine doesn't know how Emily got her hands on it, and wants to tear it off her.

'Why are you preening like that?' she asks, as Emily practises a slight pursing of her lips.

'I'll do as I like. You're only here to keep me company. We'll be there soon, and then no one will take notice of you.'

Would they be there soon? Catherine raises the rolling felt curtain, trying to work out how long they have been travelling. Dusk is approaching. As she pokes her head out of the window, the road's warmed dust rises around the wheels, and she shuts it again, her gaze falling on the coat of arms hanging above the door. A bull and a stag face one another like fighters. She tries to translate the motto. *Nec terra nos tenere potest.* It's something about the earth, but that is all she can glean from it. The lessons of her childhood were all too brief.

She thinks it odd that the track is so quiet. She would expect to be getting close to London. She had pictured a gaslit street, iron railings, the bark and bustle of every form of metropolitan life, like she had seen in paintings. Why is there no line of carriages, no other horses, no noise of packed roads around the huge city?

The carriage had come in the morning. The sisters had stood open-mouthed as it drew to a halt outside the house. It boasted two drivers and a tall footman garbed in blue. Catherine couldn't take her eyes from him. His hat and high, polished boots were like something out of a fairy tale. Their neighbours clearly thought so, too; they came to their doors to gape at the matched copper-coated horses snorting in the traces. The animals pawed the ground as they waited, as if even they knew they did not belong in this place. The drivers did not get down.

After a few moments, Emily seemed to make up her mind. Flicking her ribbons, she sauntered down the front steps. Gilbert straightened his necktie in the mirror, nodded to himself, then followed, leaving Catherine to slam the door.

But that was ages ago. Hours and hours. Now her stomach growls and her mouth is dry as bone. 'They definitely said *Bloomsbury*?' she asks.

'Mr Caplin has a house there,' says Emily positively.

'And that is where we are to go? For certain?' She has a tight knot of anxiety in her stomach. The journey is taking so long, the wheels rumbling on relentlessly, and with every mile her apprehension rises.

Emily looks irritated at the insistent questioning, and blows a crinkled hair out of her eyes.

In another hour or so, Catherine senses the ground changing. She is a town girl, with little feeling for the shape of the land, where it might rise and fall, how steeply, but this just seems wrong. Everything smells too clean.

'This isn't London,' she says softly.

Emily might have heard, but says nothing.

An unknown amount of time later, the wheels begin to slow. Finally, they draw to a halt and the sisters wait, listening to the drivers talk quietly between themselves. After a few minutes the horses are led off.

In the remaining silence, Catherine throws an accusing look at Emily.

See, I warned you.

But there is little time for these recriminations. Someone opens the door. She can't see them; outside the vehicle it is completely dark, too dark for them to be in any city. Her father, at last out of his doze, alights first, clumsily, thumping his head on the frame. Emily, shielded by her sister's body, does not descend right away.

Catherine's senses seem heightened by her deep unease. 'This isn't London,' she says again, tasting the fresh, cool air coming through into the stale interior, making her suddenly too cold. She gathers her cloak close, hearing the low tenor voices of men greeting one another outside. Somewhere a little way off, a dog barks. She has no idea of the hour and no desire at all to leave the shelter of the coach.

'Get out,' hisses Gilbert, realising his daughters have not moved.

Catherine takes Emily's hand in hers. She is surprised to find it clammy. 'Come,' she says, more gently than she might.

She climbs down the steps into the night, and Emily follows.

A small group of men has assembled to meet them. They are three, in frock coats, starched collars and silk neckties. Each holds a lantern. Standing together like that, even as richly dressed as they are, they remind her of clergymen, with the same inviting, watchful quality. She half-expects them to offer her a piece of stale sponge cake. But then she decides they are not like clergymen at all. They are too tense, almost hungry, as if they have been waiting a long time, and the looked-for thing is to happen at last.

She refuses to cower. Let them see her, dusty from the road, tired, hungry, thirsty. Let them explain what they want. Let them try her.

The nearest man breaks the tension. 'Good,' he says, 'you brought them both.' He walks closer, and Catherine gets a better look. He is thin, clean-shaven, his face framed by auburn curls. He could be thirty, handsome if not for a weakness in his chin, and something harder, almost greedy, about the eyes.

'Mr Cox,' says her father fawningly. She cringes as he removes his hat and inclines his head, first towards Cox, then the other two.

Cox looks from Gilbert to his companions, and says, 'This is Gilbert Murphy, the painter. Murphy, this is Sir Maurice Bridewell, our host.'

Bridewell is bigger and a little older than his fellows. Catherine takes in his red face and bushy, greying hair. His features are as opulent as his clothing.

Turning back to his companions, Cox says, 'Never let it be said I don't keep my promises, gentlemen.' He sounds almost relieved.

'You've done well, Cox,' says the third man. He is short, with shrewd dark eyes and black hair. His features are as delicate as a woman's. Catherine would not have recognised him as being English had she passed him in the street, but his voice is polished glass. 'Yet let's not speak prematurely of kept promises. Two birds in the bush, and so on.'

Bridewell laughs, and Cox joins him. From the way the others defer to him, Catherine understands Bridewell is the most important of the three men. 'This way,' he says, his laughter dying abruptly, and walks off.

The two girls follow the men and their swinging lanterns, their steps stiff and halting after the long journey.

'Just so you know,' says Catherine to Emily, through gritted teeth, 'this isn't Bloomsbury.'

Emily's face is pale. She whispers, 'Remember we're here for Mother.'

Catherine is about to counter that their only purpose here is to stroke Emily's vanity, but her father grips her elbow and they are led up a curving gravel drive towards the looming outline of a building. She counts at least ten lit windows before giving up, and many others in darkness. How many in total, she can't tell, but the house is vast, the great country home of a gentleman. Sir Maurice Bridewell. This is his house, she decides. But what does he want?

They approach the door, which opens silently, and the men usher them into an entrance hall with a chandelier and a high vaulted ceiling.

The three men walk quickly, impatiently, their boot heels tapping the stone tiles. Catherine's surroundings almost blur as they are hurried down a passageway, then into a room big enough for twenty. She and Emily are encouraged towards a set of chairs between the fireplace and a ticking bracket clock.

'You'll have a drink?' Bridewell asks their father, who nods with enthusiasm. 'I'm playing butler tonight,' he says, laughing again. 'I've given the staff the night off.'

'Where is Lady Elise?' asks the black-haired man. 'I'm to send Anne's regards.'

'Then I must disappoint you, Caplin. She remains in London; even outside the season, she spends more time travelling about with Rowland than she ever does here.' With a humourless smile, he looks in Catherine's direction. 'Are the young ladies thirsty? Sweet wine, perhaps?'

Emily seems to have regained some of her composure, and accepts. Catherine asks for water.

Bridewell leaves. As they await the drinks, Cox and Caplin stand in the corner and talk just under the reach of her hearing. Gilbert keeps near the walls, appearing to examine the paintings, but perhaps avoiding the condescending looks of the two men.

Catherine observes the room.

Despite its size and lofty ceilings, with painted roundels and an elliptical medallion surrounded by a complex design of ferns, it is done up oddly. There is hardly any furniture. The curtains are drawn. Candles are dotted about and stone dishes set on low tables. Whatever smoulders in them webs everything in a fragrant white smoke that makes her senses reel.

'So lovely,' murmurs Emily.

'Be quiet,' Catherine says, and Emily hisses at her like a cat.

The two men drift closer. 'Both very pretty. Neither unlike my own daughter to look at,' says Caplin to Cox. As he speaks, Bridewell returns with a tray propped high above his shoulder, aping the manner of a servant. He hands a glass of bright green liquid to Gilbert, who smiles appreciatively as he takes it.

'We're not interested in looks, Mr Caplin,' says Cox, frowning. 'We have more serious business tonight.'

'Quite,' agrees Caplin, easily. 'I was just remarking on a resemblance.' Everything about Caplin, she thinks, from his relaxed stance to his careless words, is studied. Despite appearances, he cares very much about this night's business, whatever it is.

Catherine catches a herbaceous smell as her father throws back his drink and accepts another. Bridewell approaches their chairs, and Emily is given a delicate goblet of yellow liquid. Catherine receives a glass of water.

Their host hands port wine to Cox and Caplin, then takes up a position alone in the centre of the room. He commands the attention of the others effortlessly, keeping his voice low. 'As you remind us, Mr Cox, our purpose here tonight is a noble one. Yet you are also correct in what I overheard, Caplin. Occupants of different positions in society can appear so alike, at least when young, that we are duped into thinking they are of the same category, just as when two skulls from different orders of being fool the natural philosophers into thinking they originate from the same class. But the changes that come later in life, I argue, reveal the differences rather better.

'How often, do you think, does a girl like either of these –' he stretches an arm without looking in their direction '– reach forty summers, and resemble a woman of the same age from a higher class? Consider, if you will, how these lovely creatures will appear in thirty years: the mishaps of appearance, of skin, of bones, of carriage, which will befall them. No; it's clear that we change throughout our lives in obedience to the grand plan of the Universe. Some creatures soar while others are spoilt. Regression as well as progression. It's all in Diderot.'

Why her father does not spring up in anger at these insults, Catherine can't understand. Instead, he accepts a third splash of the emerald liquid into his glass. She feels cowed and insignificant. Beside her, Emily seems to regard the gathering with a mixture of fear and excitement. Catherine puts a hand on her sleeve and whispers, 'We need to find a way to leave.'

'It's just a performance,' Emily whispers back. 'Like the theatre. You sigh, you chant what they want you to chant, you take their money. And then we buy more medicine for Mother. So let me be.' She shakes off Catherine's hand.

Their host continues. 'It is many years since I began to collect, strictly as a hobby, at first, specimens of flora and fauna, and mineral life, which might show, as the great thinkers of the last century began to recognise, that life is derived along a chain, transmutating from other shapes. As you know, I have travelled widely, and been privileged to place my feet down in places in this world where life takes the most diverse forms. I cannot agree that many men, even De Maillet or Lamarck, have done more than I, or gone further in their thinking.' He frowns. 'Yet I found I agreed with Lamarck in essence. The life force perpetuates itself. Each form, through struggle, shapes itself to its environment, becoming better fitted to its purpose. As organisms become more complex, each thing – animal or plant – represents a progressive stage in the ultimate plan that shapes our Universe; a narrowing, if you will, of the space between life on Earth, and the Divine.'

He touches his fingers to his mouth, drumming on his moustache. 'Where I departed from Lamarck was where you came in, Mr Cox. Men fear modern knowledge drives them further from God, but I realised as soon as we met that you had touched on something that I – at least at that time – had only instinctively understood: that the Creator might have designed the ladder, but we are not bound to its pattern unless we fail to contemplate our own deific nature.

'One man might place his feet upon his given rung, and be perfectly content, but a bolder one might realise he does not have to stay there. We can transcend what we are. You, as my friends, know my private motto: *Earth cannot hold us*. Cannot be *permitted* to hold us. It is our duty, as gentlemen, as scientists, but most of all as God's own creatures, to place our feet upon a different path. To reach out to the Divine – beginning, of course, with sensible test cases.'

Catherine does not understand everything he says, but there is nothing in it she likes. Especially *test cases*. She glances at Emily. The passion in their host's words, perhaps even the appearance of something forbidden, has impressed her; her eyes are wide and shining. Catherine nudges her elbow. 'He's talking nonsense,' she whispers. 'Don't listen.' She turns to her father, but his glass is empty and his face flaccid as he looks about for more.

Their host has fallen silent. He holds his hands behind his back, straining his waistcoat. 'My first experiments were ...' he hesitates, 'unsuccessful. I understand this, now. I chose the wrong subjects. It was necessary for me to go back to Lamarck, and think. Having chosen from amongst the dispossessed, the barefoot urchins of the Mashriq, I saw I had *nearly* landed upon it: I had judged correctly that the earthly struggles of these creatures had furnished them better for what I needed them to attempt – they were resilient; very, very tough indeed. Each held out for an admirable period. But ultimately, we did not advance. I came in time to see they lacked the raw material.

'To make progress, I needed subjects similar to them in form – youth was a prerequisite, I quickly found – but different in essence. In short, I needed the children of our own nature, but those from whom the appropriate nurture had, for whatever reason, been denied. I looked to my own progeny.' Caplin and Cox visibly start at this. 'Not my son,' comes the swift clarification. 'My natural daughter, who has been with us since birth as my ward. But again, this proved unsatisfactory. Grizel is a dull girl, taking more from her mother than me. I saw, without ever needing to put it to the test, that it would not answer. A void cannot reach into a void,' he adds, with a chuckle. 'And that is when, while in Massachusetts, just as I was at my lowest ebb, I met you, Cox.' He steps to one side, collecting his glass, and sips. 'I'll let you tell Caplin the rest, and then we will proceed to the demonstration.'

Cox clears his throat. 'Thank you, Sir Maurice.' His stance and air are different to his host's. Bridewell is all grandiosity, while Cox, a smaller man, not so well dressed, is more diffident. 'You speak of natural children. You, Sir Maurice, but I think not you, Mr Caplin, are privy to information about my past that I have kept out of the public awareness: the truth is, I am the natural son of Ebenezer Sibley, founder of one of the great lodges of England, and, some say, possessor of occult knowledge.

'I never knew my father intimately, and he has been dead these many years. His life, while fruitful, was cut short, so the knowledge he sought failed to come to light.' Cox's face grows pink with pride. 'I discovered it. Firstly my parentage, then the extent of my father's penetration of the mysteries of transcendental knowledge. You may know, also, that my father studied under Mesmer, though the principles of magnetism were at that time but partly understood. Most believed – and likely still do – that those principles might be employed imprecisely, to make contact with the souls of the dead, or hear them speak. They failed to comprehend the true purpose of that art – to commune with the ultimate truth, the All, and receive the wisdom of the Cosmos into oneself. But it was not enough – my father found the practices to be lacking something, some vital ingredient.'

His voice rises in pitch, taking on the tone of a preacher, as Catherine had first thought of him. 'He continued along his path. He discovered that, by employing certain rituals, and harnessing the imaginative insight of a child – a child of struggle, as perfect as only one born from pain can be – one might enter the transcendental world; that is to say, the world beyond our sight. I extended my father's work, delving deep into the mysteries, and discovered the same truth you did, Sir Maurice: the truth of transmutation; that by changing something within ourselves, we might ascend, quite literally, the *scala naturae*, and meet God in His own Heaven.'

He coughs. 'But all of this you know. I have not brought you here today to reiterate that knowledge, but to demonstrate it.' He pauses. 'To pull aside the veil, so to speak, and reveal to this company, through the medium of artistic discourse, the face of God Himself.'

Catherine has understood even less of Cox's address than Sir Maurice's, but his final sentence makes her shiver.

It introduces a new tension in the others. Caplin's face is set. Even Sir Maurice has lost some of his geniality. For long moments there is silence, until Sir Maurice breaks it. 'No half-measures,' he says, and drains his glass. When he replaces it on the table, the look in his eyes belies his smile. 'Tonight we'll see, one way or the other. A revelation of our own.'

Caplin's dark eyes glitter. 'Very well,' he says. 'Into the wood.'

23

In the absence of servants, the men carried the pianoforte from the house deep into the trees, and into a clearing with a single vast yew at its centre. Now, sitting on a stool before the instrument, Bridewell's demeanour reflects the seriousness of their mood. Upright and silent, he tinkles softly on the keys. The melody, which is complex and unfamiliar to Catherine, is a strange accompaniment to Cox moving about, adjusting his instruments. She catches some of his mutterings, but can make no sense of them: '... stars, the trees, Nature Herself – the only way to proceed! Only a child can see ... in the wood, these plantations of God, perpetual youth ...'

All the while, Caplin leans against the bole of the tree, smoking and smirking.

Catherine can't see what is funny.

The glade is encircled with tall white candles, so many that, in its middle, her hair loose down her back, Emily casts no shadow. Having been guided by Cox to an anteroom to change, she wears linen sheets tied about her chest and waist, skimming the dark undergrowth. A garland of pink amaranth flowers sits at her brow. She looks as though she has just emerged on to the stage for the first time, frightened, and young for her part. But when Cox calls, she steps forward bravely enough.

'Lie down here, young lady,' Cox orders, gesturing to the most peculiar thing in the clearing, a large and roughly circular timber platform, studded with iron rods and draped in ropes. Catherine hadn't seen the men bring it out, and realises it must have been erected before their arrival. As in the house, a gauze of white smoke hangs in the candlelight from something burning in stone dishes. Bridewell has abandoned the ivory keys, and now plays an odd wooden instrument made up of pipes of different lengths; she thinks it is some sort of flute.

Just as she was told, her expression registering both discomfort and a certain pride, Emily reclines against the wood.

'Put that out, Mr Caplin,' says Cox. 'It will interfere with the magnetism.' As Caplin covers the pipe bowl, Cox beckons him. 'Tie her down.' He sounds more confident than before. The drawing room might have been Bridewell's territory, but this ritual is his. Caplin hesitates, but moves to Emily's bare feet and tugs at a complexity of ropes. Soon Emily is secured by her legs to the platform.

'You must grip these,' Cox tells his subject, placing Emily's hands on two of the metal rods. 'Keep hold of them the entire time. The entire time,' he repeats, with gravity.

Emily nods. The sheets can't cover her shivering. She discovered a pot of perfumed oil in the side room and has scented herself with jasmine, but its delicacy is overpowered by the white smoke, the tobacco from Caplin's pipe and the earthy musk of the clearing. Catherine's head feels heavy, but she shakes herself to alertness as Cox approaches Emily with a glass. He takes a small pouch from his pocket and trickles a fine powder into the liquid, stirring it in with his finger.

Catherine knows she should scream and kick, and drag Emily away. But where would they go? Where are they, even? The wood is dense and dark. Their father, left behind at the house with a bottle of the green liquid, can't help them. And the men haven't hurt Emily; they need her to paint something afterwards, don't they? Perhaps it is as Emily said: all theatre. When they are finished they will be paid. They will climb back into the carriage and go home to Mother with enough money for medicine. She holds the final thought close as Cox tips back Emily's head and pours the liquid between her lips. 'Drink. Good girl.' Emily chokes and struggles to sit, and Catherine nearly steps forward, but then Emily clears her throat and settles, moving her hands back to the iron rods. She seems to be working to keep her face expressionless.

Bridewell's melody becomes even quieter, dream-like, while Cox waves his arms, casting them away from his own body as though sweeping something out of himself and into Emily. Nothing appears in the glow of the candles, but he gesticulates as if he is directing a wayward current. He softens his movements, edging closer, and presses his palms to Emily's knuckles, tightening her hands in his own and around the metal rods. He runs his fingers over her face, then lowers them to her abdomen, where he presses and prods, grunting as if to draw something out, or force it in.

Catherine looks away, disgusted, as he reaches his leaping climax. She would rather watch the lights and listen to the soft rustling of creatures beyond the border of the flames. She feels a sudden oneness with everything outside the perimeter; in the circle, there is doubt and fear, but beyond it, between the trees and deep down in the earth, all is as it should be. There, a beauty and order exist, in contrast to this ugliness made by men, that they cannot touch.

As if in response to this thought, something enters her awareness. Though the wood around them is silent apart from Bridewell's delicate tune, she no longer feels alone. She is conscious of a presence. Not a person, not another man. She cannot say how she knows this, but is certain. She stares into the dark until her eyes water, and there! There is movement, nothing clearly defined, just a suggestion of something large and quick, a shadow weaving between the tree boles, growing nearer. Drawn towards them, potent and curious.

Then Emily screams, and Catherine whips her head back.

It takes her a few distraught moments to see that steel glints in Cox's hand. A tiny knife is held low near Emily's navel. Cox whispers something she can't hear. She can't stop herself. She rushes at them and seizes Cox's free arm.

Cox turns but she clings to him. 'Off!' he snarls. His face is puce, contorted with rage. The little knife falls as he staves her off with his other hand, clamping hard fingers to her forehead like a vice.

'Leave her alone!' Catherine shouts.

Bridewell hauls her away. She struggles, but can't break free. On the platform, Emily hasn't moved. Catherine doesn't think the knife touched her, and there is no blood, but she is so still, so terribly still …

Bridewell watches as Cox stands over Emily. Held in a grip of iron, Catherine can't see past Cox to know what he is doing. Her captor waits several moments, then says, agitated, 'It's essentially done. We'll wait and see. I'll take this one back inside.' His face twists with deep concern. 'I say, Cox, this won't impede the magnetism, will it?'

The thin man snaps, 'I don't know. It doesn't help. There's too much ether in her. I need to let a little out. Then I'll bring her back round and we'll see …'

Catherine screams, 'Don't touch her!' But the last thing she sees before being pulled away is Cox leaning over with the knife, nicking Emily's bare white heel, and a shadowy stain on the hem of her dress, growing like an ink blot.

Bridewell drags her back to the house. She scratches his hands as they move through the trees and then the garden. Once back indoors, he throws her roughly on to the stairs. 'Stay there, little wildcat,' he says grimly, rubbing blood and dirt off his hands. 'Until I decide what to do with you.'

On the staircase, rubbing his eyes, is her father. He looks up as Bridewell disappears down the passageway to the drawing room. She knows he craves more drink, and stares at him with contempt. 'You feeble thing,' she spits in his ear. He raises his hand as if to strike her, then grunts, falling back on the bottom stair. His eyes close as he rests his head against a baluster, and she loses track of the minutes, mired in hopelessness.

After a while, a sound from above disturbs her. At the top of the staircase, she sees a female shape with a tall, straight carriage. But just as quickly, the figure is gone. Catherine wonders who it was, and thinks of running upstairs and begging for help. But what good would it do? Everyone here is under Bridewell's thumb.

She shifts in discomfort, eyeing her father with loathing, before voices bring her to her feet.

'... you damned fool!'

Cox's voice comes through. 'It was almost certain to work. You know the theory—'

Then, she thinks, Caplin's. 'Damn your theory! I can't be associated with this, Cox. If it got out in London ... Don't think you have immunity. We would all be finished.'

Ice stills her veins. The door opens and she steps back, straining to see, but Caplin, who hurries past her wordlessly, blocks her view.

Cox stands in the doorway. Emily is in his arms, still draped in linens, now stained dark brown. Her eyes are closed. He holds the knife. Before Catherine can cry out, Caplin, coat and hat in hand, is pushing past Cox to the front door. 'Deal with this. Don't let me hear of it again.'

Striding down the passageway, Bridewell opens the drawing-room door. 'Here,' he orders Cox. Catherine follows, desperate to know what is happening, but Bridewell's bulk is in the way as Cox places his burden down in a seat, and rests the knife on the table nearby. Beyond the two men, the window stands open, its fringed muslins billowing, though the air feels too thick to stir the cloth. After a few moments examining Emily, the big man gives a deep sigh.

Catherine weaves in behind them, trying to make out their words.

She gets close enough to see.

In the shade of the high-backed chair, Emily rests crookedly, like a broken doll. Her head, still crowned with amaranth, for immortality, droops sideways, and what part of her face Catherine can see is white as ash.

'Emily?' she says, her voice trembling.

Bridewell and Cox don't seem to hear. '... best under cover of dark,' says Cox. Bridewell grunts in assent.

'What's wrong with her?' Catherine is only feet away.

The men lock eyes. An unspoken communication passes between them and Bridewell takes a step forward. 'Come, Miss Murphy. Your father needs you.' She stares at his outstretched digits like they are on fire.

'What have you done?' she asks. 'Why won't she wake?' Bewilderment turns her into a little girl. The part of her that retains hope calls out, 'Father!'

'Get her out of here, Cox,' orders Bridewell.

'No!' she cries.

The weakness she saw in Cox's features, the grasping ambition, is transformed into a feral anger. She understands, though doesn't appreciate how, that he has been thwarted. He makes to seize her sleeve but she evades his grasp, moving closer to Emily.

The knife waits on the table. She stares at it for a brief moment.

Then Cox lunges again. She grabs the weapon, and as he takes hold of her, spinning her about with one arm, she lets him pull her close, then rushes, and strikes, burying the blade in his neck. As he cries out, she twists it. She doesn't mean to do it. Her muscles conspire against her. They commit the act. She feels outside herself. Someone is screaming and Bridewell is shouting oaths as he supports Cox from behind. Staggering, his eyes disbelieving, Cox presses his hand to the gaping wound.

Catherine slumps against Emily's chair, and Emily falls from it, just a pile of linen and ribbon. Her eyes are stark and wide, staring at the painted roundels of the ceiling.

PART 2

24

Arthur's hands felt like an old man's. They were overworked, sore and unwilling. Even the light from the candles dotted about the pit lodge so he could see to perform his grisly task pierced his eyes like needles. He knew, from experience, a throbbing headache was on its way. He placed his pen by his notebook and wiped the sweat off his neck, his brow, and out from beneath yellowing cuffs. Rubbing the top of his spine to ease aching bones, he closed his eyes, and determined to focus his attention.

The body on the trestle table was the nineteenth. The examination he conducted now – cutting off the charred clothing, making notes, sponging away earth and blood to expose skin, making further notes, more cutting – was one he had performed on eighteen others. They were reaching the end of what would be recovered. The remaining men and boys entombed beneath the Locksley Colliery would stay there.

Sir Rowland's experiment with coal was over.

He turned back to the victim. This man had been half-crushed by the roof-fall, and badly burnt in the explosion. His flesh was darkened from the extreme heat, most of the hair singed off. Both sections of his jaw were shattered, several of his ribs were broken, and there was considerable damage to the internal organs.

Arthur wasn't confused about how the man died.

What confused him, again, was identification. He had the unhappy duty of trying to name each man and boy so their families could be informed. He and Frederick had set about this task as if solving a puzzle, matching each recovered body to what was known about the missing souls. This was more than a matter of professional obligation. The accident had ripped the heart out of the village. The families were anxious to bury their dead, and what concerned the survivors most was having reassurance that they buried the right person. *But how do we know, doctor?* they asked plaintively, and he was forced to shield them from the truth: he didn't always know. Sometimes, more often than he liked to admit, it was little better than guesswork.

But there was educated guesswork and then there was haphazard guesswork, and his grandfather was making avoidable mistakes.

The tag Frederick had annotated and tied with string to the big toe of this man's right foot had a name scrawled in its centre: *Huw Edwards*. Arthur had written down scrupulous notes from each bereaved family, and they indicated Edwards had been a huge man, everything from his trews to his boots oversized. This man was of average height and build; ergo, not Edwards at all.

Arthur had leafed through his notebook for some time that morning. He recalled what he had read, and decided this man was actually George Tackle. George's wife told him of a long-healed injury to her husband's right foot, sustained when he had been wedged between a pony and a dram in his youth. He was around the right age, from the few teeth still in his head – and the others of George's age or nearabout had been identified – so this was the best guess he had left. It seemed a sensible one.

Yes, he would run with the assumption that this man was Tackle. Sighing, he removed the incorrect tag and wrote out a new one. As he approached the barrel he was using as a paper bin, he examined the strokes of his grandfather's handwriting, feeling an acidic pain in his stomach at the manner in which *Edwards* trailed into a blowsy ink blot. A year ago, Frederick would have disdained this professional untidiness, thrown the tag away and begun again.

This wasn't his grandfather's only error. Arthur thought back to the fourth and tenth victims, and the similar oversights that occurred in those cases. The older man was becoming increasingly fallible. This, combined with his outlandish theories about the Puzzle Wood, gave Arthur concern that the decline he had noticed when he returned from the Indies was accelerating. Frederick had mostly given up his practice, but it was getting to the point where, if he tried to treat any live patient, Arthur would have to intervene. Although deep down he knew this was the natural order of things, that everyone got older and less capable and there was nothing to do but endure it, it hurt more than he had thought possible to see it unfolding.

He put his hand to a cord he had placed around his neck, and a key, dangling like a pendant. This morning he had removed his grandfather's means of unlocking the medicine cabinet, leaving out only the powders and tinctures Frederick might need to treat his own ailments. When Frederick discovered it was gone …

He balled the tag in his fist and flicked it into the barrel. For the moment, at least, things were on an even keel. His grandfather had been at the inquest all day. That was a straightforward affair conducted by the coroner, Baldwin, at the Crossed Keys Inn. As the bodies were examined and identified, they were transported to the inn so the jury could view them. After that, they were driven over the pass to be buried.

So far, the blame for the accident was being placed on Stephen Dowle. It was Dowle who had siphoned off the money that should have made the galleries safe. Everyone knew how much had been ploughed in by Sir Rowland to modernise the operation. The baronet had put his faith in Dowle, and now, his dark scheme known, the overman had absconded. Arthur himself would appear as a witness in due course. He intended to answer Baldwin's questions briefly enough. Yes, the equipment was shoddy. Yes, the bank buildings were run-down. Yes, the accounts, which showed certain large outlays – the cage, the struts – were contravened by the reality, as the coroner would see for himself. No, he had no direct proof Dowle was the thief.

Most evenings, once the work was done, like a salve to the horror of the day, his grandfather would make a pot of tea or uncork a bottle of wine, light the fire and tell stories. Arthur, who usually had limited patience for listening, allowed himself to drift away with the druids and their sacred groves, heard of the coming of Christ and the retreat of this island's many gods, as his grandfather sipped wine and read from the Mabinogion. He told of Math, son of Mathonwhy, conveniently unable to exist unless his feet rested in the lap of a young maiden, and of Arthur's namesake, who hunted the pure white stag.

Ned Parry sometimes joined them, bringing Coke, the dog he had rescued from the levels, which he seemed to have adopted. Arthur had grown pleasurably used to the young miner's presence by the hearth, cross-legged, with his shaggy hair falling in his eyes, covering a sadness that seemed determined to stay. He and his grandfather teased Ned about Edie at the Abbey, and Arthur ignored the tiny thrust of discontent that greeted him each time he thought of Ned and his sweetheart. They were becoming friends, he and Ned, and he diverted his attention from how his gaze was drawn to the younger man.

He washed his hands, then thumbed through the notebook, one of a numbered set belonging to his grandfather. As he sat at the desk, he dipped his nib in ink and copied out his conclusions on George Tackle into the book. When he had finished, he leant back, stretching out his spine against the hard wood of the seat, then made another application of camphor oil to his upper lip and moustache. It had been two weeks since the accident and the conditions underground had slowed some of the decomposition, but the smell was dreadful nonetheless. He saw he was running out of pages in his notebook, and turned to the inside of the front cover to see which number book this was, and which he should take from the stack next. As he flicked through the pages, he registered his grandfather's observations in the neat, careful hand he remembered.

A short entry in April caught his eye.

Emily Murphy. Deceased is a young woman, in appearance in her third decade (age given as twenty-five years by the housekeeper). Weight around 8 stone. Height 5'5". Injuries consistent with hanging by the neck: observed inverted 'v' caused by suspension from a rope, and capillary eruptions on face, eyes and the lower body. Examined 15th April 1852, around eight o'clock in the evening. Incident discovered at four o'clock in the afternoon. Estimated time of death, two hours previous to discovery, around two o'clock in the afternoon.

He had almost forgotten Miss Symonds's dark hints about her predecessor. He read through the short description again, then closed the book. Nothing seemed awry. The observations scribbled down were exactly as Frederick had related. His grandfather had been meticulous – some physicians declined to make notes at all, yet he had whole sets of books containing every professional observation Frederick had ever made. In the case of Miss Murphy, the conclusions were consistent with what Frederick had told him.

So how did he explain his hunch that he had missed something? That there was some connection between these events at the colliery, and the unexplained death at Locksley half a year ago?

The door opened as he tidied up, and his grandfather trod in water from the rain. The distance between the door and the desk allowed him a few seconds to watch Frederick, and see the changes in him since the accident. He was thinner, some of the ebullience had gone out of his step, and he appeared stooped with tiredness. Yet he had dressed well enough in a frock coat and silk top hat, and carried a cane. Behind him, much less polished, came Ned, dragging a tall pine box with plain lead handles and a shining depositum that, as yet, had no inscription. An hour ago, Arthur had watched him drive nails into it in the pit yard.

'It's rough,' Ned said, 'but it will hold.' He levered it down to the floor. 'Who's next?' he asked, rubbing some of the dirt from his hands.

Arthur gestured to the now-covered body. 'George Tackle,' he said. 'He needs to go to the inquest for Monday morning.'

'I can do that,' said Ned. 'I'll drive him over in my father's trap. I'll call on the Tackles on the way.'

'That's good of you,' sighed Arthur, stretching out his back further and closing the notebook. 'Will you come to Hawk's Leap tonight?'

'Not likely. We're clearing out of the gatehouse tomorrow, so there's work to be done.'

Frederick heard. 'That's a shame,' he said. 'I was in receipt of an excellent bottle of Bordeaux from Cardale Musgrave, and he sent a caraway seed cake, too.' Arthur saw, for the first time since the roof-fall, something of his grandfather's old enthusiasm returning. 'He has great faith in my theory of the wood. I'm certain we're drawing near to discovering the lost shrine of—'

Arthur broke in. 'You would be most welcome to share a drink with us,' he told Ned.

'Sorry,' Ned said. 'You'll have to open it without me. Save me a glass, though. I've never tasted fine wine.'

Frederick looked at Arthur. 'What about you, then?' he asked. 'Musgrave sent a list of men we might call on to add their voices against Bridewell's scheme. We could share a bottle together, and write to the great men of Herefordshire – what do you say?'

But Arthur was impatient for his bed. Everything ached. He did not want to face his grandfather's tales tonight. He realised, with a throb of guilt, that if Ned had agreed to come over, he would have put aside the pain in his back and the knowledge that all he needed was to lie down in a darkened room so his headache might recede. But it would just be him and his grandfather, and as much as he loved him, he lacked the stamina.

'Perhaps another night,' he said gently. 'I have to go to Locksley tomorrow for an appointment with Sir Rowland. Best not to do that having spent the best part of the night plotting.'

'Sir Rowland is at Locksley?' asked Ned, with a frown. 'He was at the Crossed Keys Inn. I thought I heard that, anyhow.'

'He returns in the morning. So it's a good night's sleep for me.'

'Your loss,' said Frederick, with a cackle. 'More cake for me.'

Ned turned his eye to the covered body. 'This one is Tackle?' His matter-of-fact tone could not hide his sadness.

'That's him,' said Arthur.

His grandfather frowned. 'I thought ...' But he curtailed what he had intended to say and drifted off, tidying his notes on the overman's desk.

'Do you want me to come?' asked Arthur.

Ned shook his head. 'Harris was his friend. He'd want to do it.'

'I'll fetch him,' said Arthur. 'I need to stretch my legs.' He stood, feeling a crack in his back, and left the lodge. The rain had stopped, but the sky threatened more.

Once the rescue operation was over, most of the men had returned to the village with their wives and sons, but Harris had stayed at the pit yard, saying someone from the village had to oversee what happened to the dead. He had done this silently, soberly, tirelessly, and had become something of a fixture outside the lodge, often to be found sitting on a low wall facing the headgear with a long pipe jammed in his mouth.

Harris saw Arthur approaching and said, 'Long day, doctor? You look all in.'

'It's not the best way to spend an afternoon,' Arthur admitted. 'But it's done now.' He told Harris that the next body was Tackle's and it was ready, and that he understood Harris would want to do the necessary for him.

Harris nodded. 'I worked with George Tackle over ten years. It's only right someone who knew him should be with him.'

'Ned said he'd be going, too.'

Harris nodded and gazed straight ahead.

'You think it should be someone else.'

'I didn't say so, did I?'

'You don't trust him?'

'With the driving I do,' said Harris. He drew on his pipe. 'Ned's a wonder with animals. But he didn't know Tackle well. Or any of them, for that matter.'

'He worked elsewhere for a time, I understand,' said Arthur. 'But what of it?'

Harris clicked his tongue. 'A whole twelve months, he was gone.'

'And that makes him a stranger?' Arthur didn't know why he suddenly felt defensive of Ned.

Another slow nod followed. A hardness straightened the collier's mouth. 'It takes time to be known in a place like this. Time, and steadiness. That's why the mine closing down is such a blow. The men will be forced to go elsewhere, and be strangers. My niece, Edie, she's at the big house. She'll be all right. But the rest …' He whistled through his teeth. 'We'll have to go where the wind takes us.'

Desiring to change the subject, Arthur said, 'I met Edie. I thought she and Ned were … I thought she was his sweetheart, or at least at one time.'

Harris scratched his beard. 'She's always been sweet on him, even before he went to his mother's people. But like I told my brother, she should settle with someone we know better. Someone …' He stopped, standing and putting on his cap.

'What?'

'Nothing.'

'No, you were going to say something.'

'Only that the Parrys have a way of thinking themselves better than everyone else,' said Harris, keeping his voice low. 'I wouldn't speak ill of Ned's aunt, not now, but everyone knows she went to be Bridewell's housekeeper because she thought she was too good for the village. Ned's dad married a woman a bit too good for him as well – but she ran off, and left Ned with ideas. It broke Edie's heart when he went away. Between you and me, Edie's mother – my brother's wife – has always been a bit touched.' He pulled hard on the pipe again. 'Nothing very amiss with her, but just not like others. People sometimes treat Edie like she's the same, though I've never seen much reason for it. It means she's sometimes not looked at the same way as some of the other girls in Hern. Anyhow, Ned told her to wait for him, then he never wrote her, and when he came back he acted like there had been nothing between them.' He hesitated. 'I like the lad, he's a good worker, but you can't trust a family that doesn't know its place.'

To Arthur, that seemed unfair. There was nothing wrong with trying to better oneself. But he believed, unfortunately, that Edie was unlikely to get her way with the young collier. He and Frederick had teased Ned about her, but there had been no heated reaction, just a smiling fondness, as if Edie were a sister or childhood friend. Ned gave little away about what, or who, might be in his heart. Arthur had more than once allowed himself to think that …

No. He would not allow his thoughts down that road.

He changed tack. 'Has anything been heard of Dowle? I know Sir Monty has the constable and his men out scouring the villages. I think they're to turn over the woods next.'

Harris clicked his tongue again. 'They'll not find him at Locksley, nor in the wood. Dowle had his people near Bath. A coven of card sharps, poachers and safe-breakers. A real violent crew. He'll be long gone. No point wasting men's time searching the wood.'

'Better to know that for certain, surely?'

'Better not to use up manpower searching in the wrong place. Dowle's gone. You should tell Bridewell.'

Arthur nodded. 'I go to Locksley tomorrow.' He turned to go before thinking of one more thing. 'I wonder, Harris, did Dowle ever seem to you to have more money than he ought to have had? Did he squander anything on a woman, for example, or cards?'

Harris appeared to think, scratching his beard. 'Can't say he did.'

'But he docked the men's wages?'

'Sometimes,' Harris admitted, kicking the damp earth. 'But show me an overman who doesn't.'

'You never got the impression he worked against Sir Rowland, taking more money out of the colliery than was his due?'

'I thought he was Sir Rowland's man to his bootstraps,' said Harris finally.

'Right. Thank you, Harris. I'll show you Tackle.'

He finished the day believing two things – one firmly, and one with less conviction: first, it was far from a safe conclusion that Dowle alone was stealing from the colliery, and second, Harris wanted to direct someone's attention away from the wood.

25

A rthur trod barefoot through the silent house. It was
Mrs Morgan's day off and his grandfather needed his
sleep. Yet the half-bottle that remained of Cardale Musgrave's
Bordeaux in the parlour told him it might be several hours before
Frederick rose from his bed. Tilting the bottle away, he looked
at the label; an excellent vintage, a noble reward for suggesting
some sites where a creature that never existed might have lived.
It was strange how men could develop a taste for nonsense, he
thought, smiling. Beside the bottle sat half a seed cake. A crumb
had fallen on the plate, and he ate it up absent-mindedly, enjoying the earthy taste. There was no note from Musgrave, but
perhaps his grandfather had put that away somewhere.

He prepared his horse and left after breakfast. A wind snaked
down the valley, stirring up the smoky belt of the river, stripping
the trees of their leaves. Higher up, black clouds furled over the
hills, and the rain fell in a lazy drizzle. The forested slopes rang
with silence, not a sweep of a bird's wing or rustle of a rabbit to
be heard. They traversed the hill and the path got steeper, the
rain more determined. The horse didn't like it any more than he
did, and was slow and unwilling as they crossed the low bridge
over the river, beginning the ascent to Sir Rowland's gates.

He relived his conversation with Harris, and what preceded it.
Nobody had seen or heard from Dowle since the fall-in, but the
net was closing on him. On the way home the previous evening,
Frederick had described Sir Rowland standing in front of the
coroner's jury, explaining how he had laid out almost a thousand

pounds in the last year for new machinery at the works. He had entrusted this sum to Dowle, but the overman had betrayed his faith. There was testimony from the inspecting engineer, too: the roof had collapsed as the result of rotten struts in the levels, and too much rock being removed without the struts being replaced; after that, when the section fell in, the explosion had been close to inevitable. When he was found, Dowle was in the frame for manslaughter.

Yet Arthur was more immediately concerned about the miners. Thirty fatherless families lived in the valley now. All would need food, coal and clothing this winter, if they were allowed to remain in the cottages at all. They would need to be found incomes, and he had little confidence that the master of Locksley intended to put Uriah Caplin's wealth to that purpose. Still, he had to try to persuade him, and that was his intention as he emerged from the trees on to the long drive. As he came up through the avenue of tall cedars, past the gatehouse, he found the Abbey gave him the shivers. He had never liked old buildings, but it was more than that. There were no ordinary human noises, no whistling as a groundsman tended the shrubbery lining the drive, or sounds of doors opening as a maid carried out ash for the heap. The windows were shuttered, as if nobody conducted the business of the morning at all.

But he did not pass entirely undetected. As he went by the kennels, Sir Rowland's dogs howled out a hungry racket. He remembered, with revulsion, how they had torn into the stag. He hated hunting. His feelings were shared by the young governess, Miss Symonds, he recalled, who, presented with offal as her first sight of Locksley Abbey, had been unable to hide her disgust.

He told himself he was not as susceptible as Miss Symonds. The noise of the dogs was not ominous in itself, but why did nobody attend them? He eyed the grounds for Parry, but he was nowhere to be seen, and he decided to take the horse round to the stable block himself, then try the back door. He had just dismounted near the walled garden when he heard quick footsteps. The housemaid was hurrying towards him, her hair undone about her shoulders, not even wearing her pinafore. Her cheeks were bloodless. She spoke so fast he could hardly understand her. Something had happened, he apprehended, but he could not tell what. Then he made out her words.

'I thought no one would come. I thought I would be alone.' She began to sob, crushing her hand to her mouth to hold back a keening noise.

He tied up the horse quickly. 'It's Edie, isn't it?' She nodded miserably. 'What's happened?'

'It's too cruel!' she cried.

'What is it?' She could not answer, and he asked, 'Has Sir Rowland returned?' But the housemaid would not relent in her sobbing. He took her arm and led her inside.

In the entrance hall he found her a handkerchief and asked after the whereabouts of the other staff. This practical question was easier for Edie to answer: she didn't sleep at the Abbey. Sir Rowland's instructions were for her to come at seven o'clock, and she didn't think there was anybody else here. 'On foot? In the dark?' Arthur asked. Edie nodded.

He remembered how Sir Rowland had talked of economies at Locksley. But surely it was no great cost to accommodate a single servant? That was a puzzle, one he put aside for a different moment.

They walked the unlit corridors towards Sir Rowland's study. The house was silent apart from the maid's muffled weeping, and frigidly cold. A strange whistling from behind the closed door of the study confused him; then, as Edie opened the door and he stepped in, a crunch sounded underfoot. His eyes adjusted to the dark. He saw that behind the billowing curtains one of the

French windows was shattered, the fallen glass trodden into the carpet. He noticed more: the room was cluttered with stacks of what looked like storage crates piled high in the corners, and Sir Rowland's desk more disordered, even, than when he had seen it the first time, seething with papers and folders as if its owner had been searching for something.

'An intruder, sir,' Edie managed. 'Someone got in overnight. I wanted to show you so you didn't think I ...'

'That you had done anything wrong?' Arthur finished. She nodded, weeping. He said, 'Well, has anything been taken?' He felt concern at her distress. If nothing worse had happened than a burglary in the night, she would not be this distraught.

Edie shook her head. 'It's not that, sir.'

'Then show me what, I beg you.'

Edie led him up the great stairs unsteadily. She moved with reluctance towards the family rooms, and Arthur thought, suddenly, of Georgie Bridewell. 'Where is Miss Bridewell?' he asked. 'And Miss Symonds?'

'Just let me show you,' said Edie faintly.

One of the doors on the passageway stood ajar. 'It's just as it was this morning, sir,' Edie said. 'I haven't touched nothing. Didn't dare do nothing.' Then, as he placed a palm on the handle, she gripped his wrist. 'Will you speak for me, sir? Tell them how I arrived here and it was done?'

He didn't answer. She stood dumbly as he crossed the threshold.

For the last fortnight he had been surrounded by charred flesh, the putrid gases of death, the reek of decomposition. Unpleasant, but he was accustomed to it, and it did not trouble him.

Here was a different sort of death. The room contained a strange odour, like moist earth, dirt and stale sweat. Like the colliery shaft had smelt as he watched a cageful of brave men dangling over its depths. This room gave him the same untethered feeling. It made him afraid.

It was not lavish, nor one of the principal bedrooms. This was a chamber you might allocate to a guest or distant relative, someone you didn't like much and hoped might leave of their own accord. Other than the bed, the furnishings were cheap, mostly wicker, and the paper outmoded. The carpet was almost shabby. The floral chintz drapes were still drawn across, suggesting they stood as they had the night before, but a single ray of the morning sun came through the slit, angled towards the four-poster bed, to which the eye was inevitably, horrifyingly drawn.

In that first moment, he could not make sense of what Arthur was looking at. As his mind dealt with the scene, he drew back from the doorway in shock and consternation.

Grizel Wingfield was splayed on her back, arms thrown either side, her legs exposed to their flabby, veined knees. The bottom of her nightgown showed its scalloped white hem, but it was impossible to see more of the fabric; all was covered in a thick black coat. A dark blanket covered her from head to mid-section, a blanket that glittered beneath the arrow of sunlight, a field overspreading everything, penetrating everything, and spilling from Grizel Wingfield's mouth, nose, throat and eyes. She had been buried beneath a mountain of coal dust. She had choked on it, become it, died under it.

Arthur stared, and heard Edie whimper behind him. He could not strip his gaze away from the bed. 'Good God,' he said eventually. 'What a devilish thing.'

His tongue felt mutinous and slow. *Devilish* was the only word he could think of. He was hardly religious compared to most men, but the exhibition on the bed, with Mrs Wingfield's arms stretched out, her fingers twisted in pain, her head sagging to the side, flaccidly, appeared blasphemous even to him.

He tasted the black dust in the air. It was bitter as wormwood. Death, he thought. Death had come for her. She had tasted it as it was forced down her throat.

The thought was worse than indecent. It was profane.

Behind him, Edie said weakly, 'You'll tell them it was an intruder? That it wasn't me, and I wasn't here when it happened?'

His own voice sounded dead in his ears as he said, 'Where is Georgie Bridewell?'

She was asleep. Her bedroom door was closed. Arthur opened it with his heart pounding. When he saw the small downy head resting on its pillow undisturbed, he fell back against the doorframe, breathing hard with relief. He crept closer, seeing her chest moving below the eiderdown, evenly, normally. Whoever had broken in, he decided, had not intended to hurt the little girl, or had been interrupted in the attempt, and fled.

'I didn't want to wake her,' said Edie. 'It seemed wicked to stop her dreaming when …' She trailed off.

'Miss Symonds sleeps in the next room?' Arthur said, with urgency. Their rooms were adjoining. If Georgie Bridewell had been left unmolested, perhaps the governess had, too, but if so, why had she not woken by now, and raised the alarm?

Edie stuttered. 'Yes, but …' He had already flung open the door when he heard Edie's bewildered report. 'She's gone.'

He did not need to approach the bed to see she was right; it was empty, and either made or unslept in.

He established that Sir Rowland had not yet returned, though he was expected. 'What about Lady Anne?' he asked. It was easy enough to forget her, but the mistress of Locksley Abbey could not be left in her self-imposed solitude when a murderer had struck. 'Can you fetch her?'

Edie shook her head. 'I'm forbidden to go up to the tower,' she said adamantly. 'I'd lose my place.'

Arthur nodded. With no position to lose, he would have to do that himself. He thought of something else. 'Did anything happen yesterday? Anything of note?'

Edie considered. 'I don't think so.'

'Nobody visited the house?' He wondered whether there had been anything by way of warning, or threat. This was an astonishing crime. Nothing about it made sense – how horrible it was, almost theatrical, and with such an unexpected target. He hesitated to think it of someone who had just been murdered, but if there was one person at Locksley nobody cared for, whose death could bring nobody much benefit, it was Grizel Wingfield.

He reflected on the method again. It pointed in a clear direction: the colliery. Perhaps someone had been provoked by a personal tragedy, holding Sir Rowland responsible for the accident, or the closure of the mine, and this was revenge?

A sinking sensation assailed his stomach as he remembered his grandfather's dark words. *He'll pay.*

With sudden intense feeling, he put aside this thought. Frederick Sidstone would never attack a woman because of a broken promise. He would never kill. No matter how angered he was about the wood, it was unthinkable.

In response to his question, Edie said, 'No one, sir.'

'I'll need to send a note – or ride if nobody can take it – to the Crossed Keys Inn,' he said, frowning. 'We can't wait for Sir Rowland.'

'I can take a note to the village,' offered Edie. 'Then someone could take it on.' She looked about forlornly. 'But I'm needed here ...'

'Do it, but return as soon as you can. And be certain to give it to someone we can trust,' he added. 'Maybe Ned Parry.' Edie shook her head, and when he looked down at her plump face, it was flushed. 'Not Ned, then,' he said, not without frustration.

She said, 'If you have sixpence, I know a boy who'll run it to the inn.'

'That sounds best.' He looked towards Georgie's bedroom. 'But before that, the little girl should be woken and given something to eat. I'll be responsible for her until her father returns.' Thinking for a moment, he said, 'And don't tell her anything. It's for her father to decide when she should know about this.'

A few minutes later, in Sir Rowland's study, he checked over the damaged doors again. The glass appeared to have been smashed from the outside, since the shards had fallen inwards, and the key, still in the lock, had been turned from the inside, too, presumably by means of the intruder donning gloves and twisting their arm through the broken pane. He bent and examined the key, looking for marks or debris. Whoever had entered the study had to have carried some sort of sack, or container, full of the coal dust that had been put to such sinister use. He looked for traces, but discovered none. Realising the room was glacially cold, he pulled the velvet drapes across the breach. Next, he rooted for a blank sheet of paper. Finding one, he scribbled a few lines – *urgent – come at once – inform the constable* – and then added, as a postscript, *Miss Bridewell unharmed*.

He put down the pen. The words wavered. He had stomach cramps, on and off, and the muscles in his legs felt shaky. He would go and find some water in a moment, but first ... What had Sir Rowland been doing with all this? In contrast to its neglected appearance the day before, the room now appeared like a warehouse, its contents piled haphazardly, some of the crates open, others still sealed. It could be nothing – Sir Rowland might be doing no more than organising papers relating to his father-in-law's estate – but he couldn't help thinking the desk seemed particularly chaotic, as if whatever the baronet had been engaged in, he had done it frantically, desperately searching for something. He knew he couldn't open any of the sealed boxes. That would rouse Sir Rowland against him, and prevent him getting any further in discovering what was happening here. But two of the stacks were topped by open crates, with shredded paper sticking out.

Sifting through the ribboned filler, he felt about the contents. They were cold, having sat all night unattended in the freezing room. He drew the first item: a wooden specimen tray, the sort in which an amateur collector might keep curios. He blew it clear of dust, tilted it, and saw it was just an assembly of tiny birds, their feathers shrivelled, each pinned to the base by several needle-like skewers, and labelled beneath a glass casing. There were twelve, arranged by size, the smallest no taller than the space between his knuckle and the tip of his forefinger. He put the tray to one side and dug further. He withdrew another, just the same, and realised the whole crate was full of them: a repository for poor, dead creatures someone had wanted to study, and categorise.

He checked one more crate. This was more carefully packed, the padding protecting a stack of small, wrapped cuboids. He took one out and removed its cushioning to reveal a wooden chest about the size of a travelling medicine cabinet. He unlocked the brass clasp and grunted in recognition, touching the object, following the rounded frontal bone and the twin bulges of the parietal bones, then noted the cut and pinned calvarium, and the meticulous labelling on the inside of the braincase. It was a medical aid, a skull; real, not a replica. Very well preserved. He thought it likely, from its size and supraorbital ridge, and the shape of the eye sockets, that it had belonged to a human male. It was an odd thing for Sir Rowland to have in his possession, but from the appearance and condition of the crates, most of these items had been in storage for years. Arthur imagined they had belonged to his father, as he remembered from his grandfather that Sir Maurice had had an interest in naturalism. He returned the item again as he had found it, put the box back, and took out another, and another, until ten or so of the little cases sat in front of him.

He opened them in turn.

The objects were a little smaller, by degrees, than the first, but all were examples of the same type.

He suspected these skulls had belonged to children.

Closing the boxes, he packed the artefacts away. He had seen such things before, but in this place they were unsettling, affecting him in a way he did not fully understand. He did not want to consider how Sir Maurice had come by them, or why he wanted them. Still, they were of the past. They could have nothing to do with the break-in.

He turned his attention back to the desk. Sir Rowland had upended one of the crates, which stood empty on the floor, and removed its contents, mostly papers. He had perhaps been investigating them when the message arrived about the roof-fall, but it did not look as if he had had a chance to go through everything. In spite of the chaos, at least one pile was dusty and untouched. Arthur picked through it, careful only to touch the edges of the sheets. Most items towards the top of the pile were lists relating to Sir Maurice's natural collection. They detailed specimens, drawings and descriptions of various fossils, molluscs, insects and birds, mostly from the 1830s. Sir Maurice must have had an all-consuming interest in the study of nature. Absently, Arthur wondered why the previous baronet had left it all here.

Then his eye fell on something different – a letterhead. Peering at the design, he recognised a Berkshire address. *The Lowe Hospital for the Insane.*

He had never heard of it. Scanning the writing, he realised he was looking at an invoice for one year's amenities. It was addressed to Sir Maurice Bridewell, under the care of a solicitor's firm, Lewis, Putnam & Bird. The charges were for bed, board and charge of one Gilbert Murphy, billed at one hundred and ten pounds, and the same for one Catherine Murphy, at one hundred and twenty pounds. The year of the first invoice was 1840.

Arthur shuffled more, similar papers, seeing that in 1841 the Lowe Hospital had billed the Locksley estate in the same manner, through the solicitor, for care of Gilbert and Catherine Murphy. Husband and wife? What was their connection to the Bridewells? He shuffled again. In 1842, the invoice was repeated in facsimile, the charges levelled for the man and the woman.

Then something changed. From 1843, and every year until 1848, when the invoices stopped entirely, the hospital had charged the estate, but for the care of Gilbert Murphy only. The second name, Catherine Murphy, disappeared from the records.

He inferred that Lowe was a private hospital. The county asylums would never send out good paper, nor charge such an exorbitant rate. He tapped his fingers against the desk. Why were these documents important to Sir Rowland? Why now? It struck him that Sir Rowland had taken over the estate shortly after the rising, in 1840, when Sir Maurice and his wife had emigrated. The arrangement with Lowe, however, had continued, administered by solicitors. So it was possible Sir Rowland had not known about it, or paid much attention, just filing the paperwork as it came in.

Were the Murphys secret relations? Perhaps lunacy ran in the family. He thought of Grizel, Sir Maurice's ward. Where had she come from, really? Could these poor souls be related to her? This Murphy character might be a brother or uncle, locked up for madness and mistakenly released. If sufficiently deranged, he could have found his way back to Locksley and …

He cursed himself. The morning's horrors had rendered him dull-witted. *Murphy*. These invoices had to connect to the suicide of Emily Murphy, who, far from being a simple, unhappy employee, seemed in some way bound up with the Bridewell family.

He mused on this a few moments, deciding a coincidence was not credible. There was a history here, something hidden. It was impossible to believe that Miss Murphy's arrival at Locksley, and then her death, had no relationship to Grizel Wingfield's. Perhaps Miss Symonds was right, and Emily Murphy was murdered, either by Sir Rowland or – as unlikely as it seemed – Grizel herself.

If that was so, someone knew how Emily Murphy died, and had sought revenge on the Bridewells. He closed his eyes, seeing a mire of black dust and white flesh. A macabre revenge indeed.

Who could have had a reason for it?

At least one person at Locksley knew something: Miss Symonds, on her very first night, shaken from the tragedy of Mrs Parry's fall, had let slip that she believed Emily Murphy's death was no accident.

He considered what he knew of them both. Miss Murphy had been in her mid-twenties when she died. That made her close in age with Miss Symonds. From his grandfather's records, he knew that, like her successor, Miss Murphy had been small, though not tiny, probably about the same height as the present governess.

What was Miss Symonds's Christian name?

A creak from the passageway interrupted his thoughts. Moving swiftly, he took the topmost invoice, folded it twice, and deposited it in his breast pocket.

He was just in time. The door opened. He had expected Edie, or even Sir Rowland returned, but the figure that crossed the threshold was slighter than either, almost spectral in its slenderness. The newcomer was attired in sooty crêpe and the long lace veil of deep mourning. He realised this had to be Lady Anne Bridewell.

Rising, he apologised for his presumption in seating himself at the desk. The mistress of Locksley Abbey waved away the apology and glided towards him. 'It is we who owe you thanks, doctor,' she said. There was a trace of a European intonation in her voice, as if she might prefer to speak French. Her words were cobweb-soft. 'I questioned the housemaid, and it appears that, without your courage, given the terrible events of last night, we would all have been lost.'

He inclined his head. 'That's kind of you, Lady Anne. Though as a doctor – indeed as a man – I could not do otherwise than I have done, and I'm sorry to say, that is not much.'

'You have done a great deal. You have our gratitude. When my husband returns, I have no doubt he will wish to reiterate our appreciation.'

'Miss Bridewell is in the nursery,' he said, wishing to reassure her. 'Will you go to her?'

'Later, perhaps,' said Lady Anne. 'Georgiana must learn to be alone, as I learnt. There is a self-possession, do you not agree, doctor, that can be most useful for a woman, but which cannot be learnt through constant indulgence?'

Carefully, he said, 'I do agree. But Miss Bridewell is just a child, and I'm certain she would want to see her mother.'

He felt he must have overstepped some invisible mark, but Lady Anne did not flinch. She seemed to consider his words in silence. He, who had never much wished to see, or avoid, the face of a woman, women being a matter of indifference to him as they were not to other men, desired, with a sudden intensity that threw him off course, to lift her veil and see her features. It was as if, the sight of her being withheld, he had to see it; a childish inclination, he admitted.

'A man forced his way into this room,' she said, after a few moments' contemplation. 'He walked across the floor, turned the handle, and crept like a shadow to my sister-in-law's chamber. It is a frightening thought, that we are all so vulnerable in our beds. Poor Grizel,' she added, after a while. 'She never really belonged here.'

Arthur nodded. 'It is very frightening.'

'The intruder broke the glass?'

'Yes, with some sort of implement. A hammer or crowbar, I'd assume.'

'Or a mandril?' The word seemed alien on her lips.

'It could be,' he accepted warily.

'My husband will be certain of it,' she said. 'Did you move or touch anything?'

'I disturbed nothing,' he answered hurriedly. 'Only examined the glass with my eyes. It's better left for the constable, I think—'

Lady Anne was already moving towards the window. She pulled aside the curtain, peering through the jagged hole. He heard her murmur to herself, and she bent, as supple as a dancer, and came up from the floor with an exclamation of victory. 'You see?' she said, holding something in her hand.

'What is it?'

She revealed a green square about the size of a postage stamp, folded into quadrants.

Arthur came forward, frowning. Whatever it was, he had missed it. He held out his hand and hers, clad in the finest black wool, passed the item over. He unpicked its folds. It was a wage slip, or similar, covered in figures in black ink. On one side was an amount in tons; on the other, a figure in shillings and pence.

At the top, a name: *John Harris.*

26

S ir Rowland did not return until some time after midday. By then, Lady Anne was back in her rooms, and Arthur was watching over Georgie Bridewell in the dining room, having taken her to the cold pantry and found some cuts and a glass of milk.

She was very quiet, but after a while turned anxious eyes on him and asked, 'Where is Miss Symonds?'

That was certainly one question of the moment. He felt he had acted correctly in not telling her about Mrs Wingfield, as it was not his place, but what could he say now?

'Try not to worry,' he said uneasily. 'Your father will explain everything when he returns.'

But when her father arrived, Georgie fled up the back stairs.

Arthur waited outside the study. As Sir Rowland hurried down the passageway without removing his cloak, Arthur saw, to his slight surprise, the baronet's eyes were full of grief. He understood that Edie had passed on more than his note.

At Arthur's expression, Sir Rowland's face contorted with pain. 'It's true, then?' he said.

'I'm afraid—'

His answer was drowned out by a resounding crash. The baronet had shoved a terracotta bust from a table. The noise echoed round the hall as Sir Rowland rushed towards the stairs. His words were garbled, but Arthur caught some of them – *monster*, *demon* – between inarticulate roars.

Arthur dragged him away and pushed him up against the wall. 'Don't go up there. Don't.' They struggled, the baronet trying to throw him off, but Arthur wrapped his arms about him, holding the bigger man in a bear grip until the fight went out of him and he collapsed, heaving, at the bottom of the stairs. As Sir Rowland's chest rose and fell with ragged breaths, Arthur said, 'Come with me. I'll get you something for the shock.'

In the study, Sir Rowland swilled down a measure of brandy. He did not comment on the chaos around them, and Arthur guessed he was too far undone to note anything missing from his papers.

Once Sir Rowland was calmer, Arthur shared his account of the discovery. He finished, 'I've ascertained, by examining Mrs Wingfield – only as far as was decent – that the intruder choked her of breath.'

'She was strangled?' came the hoarse reply.

'Yes.' He was reluctant to add that she had also been stabbed. He had only realised this himself when he had examined her properly, since the blood had been disguised beneath a clag of black dust, but it was a vigorous blow; the killer had struck just once, with surety, directly through her larynx.

He tried again to explain his thinking. 'What was done, afterwards, with the coal, seems to have been more symbolic, to add to the shock and distress of whoever found the body. That is, it wasn't the cause of death.'

'No. It was for me. I'm being taunted,' whispered Sir Rowland. Before Arthur could ask what he meant, he straightened and said in a clearer voice, 'Nothing was stolen?'

The invoice ticked against Arthur's heart, but he said, 'According to Edie, nothing else was disturbed. Nor was anything obviously missing from Mrs Wingfield's bedroom, although I didn't check for jewellery, or anything of that—'

'She had nothing valuable,' said Sir Rowland, rubbing the sides of his glass with a thumb, almost compulsively. 'This was meant for me. A message.'

Arthur remembered thinking Grizel Wingfield was a strange victim for the crime. Perhaps Sir Rowland was correct – it was more likely he, with his habit of making enemies, was the target, or at least indirectly. 'Do you have any idea what that message would be? Or who would have reason to send it?'

The other man's expression hardened. 'Isn't it obvious?'

Arthur spread his hands wide.

'The coal,' snapped Sir Rowland, as if Arthur were dull. 'The colliery, and me shutting down the mine. This is revenge for dismissing that bastard Dowle. He's in this, just you wait and see.' He poured another measure, muttering, 'Up to his neck.'

Arthur wanted to withhold the green slip, but decided he was honour-bound. He couldn't keep Harris out of it in these circumstances, although he knew his own secrets might be revealed as a result. Reluctantly, he delved into his pocket. 'Lady Anne came down as I searched, and she found—'

'Anne? Here?' The baronet's expression had turned to shock.

'Yes.'

'What did she say?'

'It was more what she did. She has sharp eyes, and found this near the point of entry.' Arthur handed it over. 'I'm sorry to say it may implicate John Harris.'

Sir Rowland examined it. 'It's one of the chits Dowle gave out to the men. This was here?'

'Yes. But if it belonged to Harris, I have to say I can't see him being involved.'

'Why not?'

He thought of Harris at the colliery, his hand gripping his own, his dourness and phlegmatism. 'I don't know. He's too ... straight, I suppose. I feel as though he would come at you more directly.'

Sir Rowland gave a short laugh. 'You feel? Well, I'll be certain to wager my family's safety on your intuitions,' he said sardonically. He held up the chit. 'This makes him suspect.'

Arthur nodded in acknowledgement. Then he hesitated. 'There's more.'

'What?'

'Miss Symonds has gone.'

Sir Rowland looked wholly confused. 'Killed?'

'Vanished.'

Grinding the piece of paper into his palm, the baronet asked, 'No sign of a struggle, or suggestion she was removed by force?'

'Only what you see here. It's possible, of course, that she was taken.'

'No,' came the answer, almost a growl. 'Not taken. It's obvious: they're in it together.'

'Who?'

'Dowle, Harris, the governess. You remember she came the day Mrs Parry died. Who's to say she didn't have to do with that as well?'

Arthur shook his head firmly. 'Miss Symonds was on the lower floors when Mrs Parry fell. What you suggest is impossible.'

'Nothing is impossible!' cried Sir Rowland, in a voice that rose unnaturally high. He catapulted the glass across the desk, spilling the remaining brandy over his papers. 'Nothing.'

Taken aback by this sudden eruption, Arthur reminded himself: the baronet was grieving. 'We should write to the station at Hereford, and have them send over an officer. And we should begin a search of the grounds and the wood,' he began. 'If Miss Symonds is not involved, she may be in danger, or we might find that she has been injured, or worse. I'll search alone if you're indisposed.'

'Eh? No. I'll join you. Two heads are better than one.' Sir Rowland seemed to consider for a moment. 'In fact, as it's urgent, we should find her first, and send for the constable afterwards. We can bring the dogs. They'll find her quick enough.'

Arthur agreed. 'One more thing,' he said, as Sir Rowland was about to move. 'What is Miss Symonds's Christian name?'

The baronet grunted. 'I couldn't say.'

Discovering a gap in the drystone wall, a shortcut, Sir Rowland called to Arthur. 'Here!' He held back one of the mastiffs on its leash. The creature snarled and whined, eager for the scent.

A quarter of an hour earlier, in the barn, as the baronet had wrestled it out of its wrought-iron cage and tightened the leash around its muscular neck, Arthur had declined to take another of the dogs. 'I'm not good with them,' he admitted, eyeing the brindle-coloured animals as they mouthed the bars, their teeth scraping the metal. 'Better off with my cane.'

'Suit yourself,' Sir Rowland said, holding a section of Miss Symonds's eiderdown to the animal's nostrils. When the dog strained, the baronet cuffed it hard, inciting a high whine. He held up a gloved fist and it cringed. Pulling the creature up by the neck, he said, 'Seek, Morpheus. Seek.'

They had followed the gravelled paths through the glasshouses, towards the wood. Arthur had not failed to note, when Edie came downstairs with the cut cloth, that she had been unable to find Miss Symonds's shawl. He filed away the observation that, if the governess had been removed by force, she seemed to have had time to dress warmly first.

'I've been remiss,' he said, as they scaled the rugged slope. 'I haven't offered my condolences.'

There was a pause. 'You'd have no reason to know,' Sir Rowland said eventually, 'and I'd thank you not to spread it about, but

Grizel was my true sister. Well, half-sister. A by-blow of my father's. He paid off the mother, one of the housemaids here.'

'What happened to her?' Arthur asked, thinking of the invoices, and the Lowe Hospital.

Sir Rowland yanked Morpheus, who was hauling so hard the baronet could barely hold him, back by his neck. 'She found a position in Cardiff, according to my father. Died there in 'thirty-eight.'

'And no one ever told Mrs Wingfield?'

The baronet shook his head forcefully. 'Of course not. I don't know why I tell you. I was never fond of my sister. She was always strange, bitter that she was not more beguiling in her youth, and that her husband turned out to be a scoundrel. Still, she didn't deserve this,' he finished bleakly.

The slope levelled off. 'Should we split up?' Arthur suggested.

'No!' The reply was urgent. Confused, Arthur glanced across and caught the look on Sir Rowland's face. Though it was quickly covered, he recognised it as sheer fright. Regaining control, Sir Rowland said, more evenly, 'The sun goes down early in these woods. Neither of us wants to get caught far from the house alone, not with villains like Dowle and Harris about. Let's tend south, then circle round the top to the north side.'

Arthur assented uneasily. He had done more than his share of cowardly things, but Sir Rowland's cravenness embarrassed him. The baronet was accompanied by Morpheus, and armed. What did he have to be afraid of?

They searched methodically over the next hour, quartering the ground as they went up the hill. Their conversation stilled as the physical differences between them became more apparent. Arthur, ten years Sir Rowland's junior and with less weight on him, was also unhampered by the mastiff. He found it easier to clamber over the boulders and trunks littering their way. They couldn't keep to the path without missing a scent, so the canopy glowered over them, and they moved deeper into the wood. The trees here were older, gnarled, covered in lichens and dense mats of moss. Thick boles obscured their way. Finding himself encumbered by low branches and spiky shrubs, Arthur cut through with his cane, but Sir Rowland preferred the longer route. Before long, the two were separated.

For a few seconds Arthur could hear the dog's zealous sniffs and his companion's heavy tread. Then came silence. Even given the events of the morning, and that they chased a murderer, he was not worried by his solitude, but as he picked through the undergrowth, he had no explanation for the sudden, intense feeling that came over him. A feeling of being watched.

He told himself it was paranoia, but his skin prickled and his heart beat faster. There were eyes on him. Someone was here. Someone, perhaps, who ought not to be here, and ...

Before he could finish the thought, out of the near-impassable spread of the trees, a wraith emerged, staggering. He stared, trying to make heads or tails.

The wraith was filthy with the grime of the wood, covered in grasses and dark berry stains. Old man's beard webbed its hair. One of its hands furled around a trunk, and as it reached for him with grasping fingers, forlorn, unintelligible noises left its mouth. As Arthur watched, repelled but unable to look away, something like a short spear of wood dropped from its right hand and, before he could see it properly, rolled away slightly down the hill.

He stared at the apparition. It took several long moments of horrified bewilderment, in which his grandfather's terror of the wood took physical shape, and his mind flooded with evil thoughts, for him to realise, with a strong sense of his own foolishness, that the ghoul was not a ghoul.

It was a woman.

His heart rallied as he recognised Miss Symonds. Then, seeing her dreadful state, he was dismayed again. Trying to reach her before she fell, he pushed aside more shrubs and branches and heard her feverish words. 'I pushed the knife in. I did it. And still she's dead. Dead.'

His spirits sank.

She dropped to her knees in the dirt. Her eyes were closed. Her nails were torn, encrusted with earth, as though she had been digging in the soil. She was sallow and her teeth chattered. He bent to her, wishing she would not say anything. He could not protect her if she did. But she seemed unable to stop. 'I killed William … I lied, and he loved me …'

Who was she talking about now? 'Miss Symonds, save your strength. I—'

Sir Rowland came crashing through the undergrowth, the mastiff barking savagely. 'Do you have Dowle?' the baronet shouted.

'No. I found Miss Symonds.'

'Dead?' came the question. Sir Rowland was still fifteen feet away and could not see them clearly.

'Alive. Hurt,' Arthur called. 'Let's get her back to the house.'

Sir Rowland came closer with the dog loping in front, but was too distant to hear as the governess's eyes opened. 'I'm Catherine. Emily Murphy was my sister.'

But the master of Locksley Abbey was near enough to hear what came next. He gasped as Miss Symonds, her lips bruised with blue, whispered, loudly enough to damn herself, 'And I live in Hell, for I am a murderer.'

27

The two men were ghosts. Their hands on her body and the words exchanged over her head went by like chaff. Nothing of the present moment meant anything. Their faces hovered on either side of her and the dog snarled in front – but she felt nothing.

Nearer, infinitely more alive, was the wood. She knew its beating heart below her feet, the energy of the ground and trees and stream surging through her. It fixed her in its grasp, and in that moment the rough flesh and unyielding bone of men's fingers melted away. It was the wood, not the men, that caught her.

And just as the wood had promised, it had given back her memories. But that gift was not without price. It had taken her mind. It had plucked her from the artificial pattern of her life, the one she had carved out for herself and could reconcile with what others required of her – good daughter, good servant, good wife – and replanted her in older soil, the state of honest raving in which her father died.

She was mad.

The dog wheeled about and snapped its jaws, but it no longer seemed like any domesticated animal. The creature was, like her, part of the greater organism of the forest. It belonged here, and had nothing to do with the men. It answered to some other, wilder master. This struck her as possible, even sensible. For nothing was as she had thought. The world she had understood, the world of discrete sets and binaries – dead, alive, past, present, truth, lies – one moment preceding another in an infinite progression of causes, had been as deceptive as a painted image; almost representative of some underlying reality, but not quite.

Now the puzzle was nearly solved. Its solution would break everything apart.

28

Miss Symonds didn't struggle or complain. Arthur didn't expect her to try to run – the attempt would have been foolish, as Sir Rowland held her in a grip of iron on one side, and Arthur supported her on the other – yet he thought she might protest her innocence. She said nothing, just fell limp all the way back to the house while the mastiff strained at her with yellowed teeth bared and hackles raised.

Sir Rowland held the snarling thing tight by its leather collar. 'Good, Morpheus,' he said, and crowed, 'He knows. He senses she's guilty.'

Arthur said nothing. Why bother with the expense of a jury trial, after all, he thought, if a dog can tell the innocent from the guilty?

Miss Symonds let out murmurs he could not decipher. He feared she had entered a delirium. But why hadn't she run? If Catherine Murphy – he was convinced this was her true identity – was a lunatic who had sought some revenge against Grizel Wingfield, and killed her, why did she roam the wood, and allow herself to be caught?

The invoice in his pocket whispered its conclusions. In 1839 or 1840, this woman, Catherine Murphy, the sister of Emily Murphy, had been incarcerated in the Lowe Hospital. Another man, almost certainly a relative, had been held with her, and then she, but not he, had left the charge of the doctors.

Why? Had she recovered? Or had she escaped? He eyed her. Looking at her now, tangled and encrusted with the dirt of the wood, *escaped lunatic* had a certain credibility. He wondered whether he should tell Sir Rowland what he knew, but something needled him, persuading him not to decide on that. Not yet.

They carried Miss Symonds upstairs, and Sir Rowland locked the inner door to Georgie Bridewell's room before they placed her on the bed and retreated to the doorway.

'Georgie will have to be moved,' Sir Rowland declared. 'Edie will have to manage it. She can't stay here.'

'You'll inform the constables at Hereford?' Arthur took out his pocket watch. 'It's nearly four now. They won't be here this evening.'

Sir Rowland nodded. 'We've apprehended the person responsible, so the urgency is removed. Still, I'll remind them Dowle and Harris are still on the loose.' He clenched a fist and slammed it into the frame. 'That nest of vipers!' He glanced at Miss Symonds, who had turned towards the wall. 'Should she be further restrained?'

'I can't see the need,' said Arthur uncomfortably.

'What if she harms herself to spite me? Then the truth will never come out.' The baronet added vengefully, 'I want them all under lock and key, the whole gang.'

'I'll clear the room of anything she might use to do herself mischief,' Arthur said. He eyed the ceiling and the window. The chamber seemed safe enough.

He couldn't say the same for Sir Rowland's theory. How would Miss Symonds know Harris and Dowle? What connection could they reasonably have?

No. Dowle was a villain, and Harris was hiding something – he had been too keen to direct attention away from the search – but the key to this mystery was here at Locksley. Some aspect of the Bridewell family's past was bound up with the Murphy women. There was a reason the sisters had found their way here, a pattern behind all this death. He would find it.

Meanwhile, Miss Symonds – or Catherine Murphy, whoever she really was – would stay imprisoned until the police arrived. Sir Rowland would tell them she had confessed, and it was true. She had said it plainly: *I am a murderer.*

What would he, Arthur, tell them? If he made it public that Miss Symonds had falsified her identity, that would be enough to condemn her. It might be obvious that she would not have been able to subdue Mrs Wingfield, but Sir Rowland would name Dowle and Harris her cronies. He would say they had worked together.

Then again, would concealing what he knew help her either? Her identity would be uncovered given time. Her documents had to be forgeries. Worse, Sir Rowland was aware of the invoices, so even if he had not linked Emily Murphy to Miss Symonds yet, or to the Lowe Hospital, he would soon, or someone else examining the facts would make the same connection Arthur had made.

He needed to know more. He resolved to return to Hawk's Leap and pen an urgent missive to the Lowe Hospital. His medical credentials might sway them, and he might discover whether Catherine Murphy had absconded, or been judged sane and released. There was a chance he could find out the connection between the sisters and the estate. Then, as soon as he could, he would come back to Locksley: he didn't want to leave Miss Symonds alone any longer than necessary.

All this ran through his mind quickly. He turned to Sir Rowland. 'I think I should examine her. We wouldn't want confusion about when any scrapes or bruises were sustained.'

Sir Rowland frowned, but handed him the key. 'When you're done, return this.' He stared for a moment at the huddled form. 'If she says anything, I want to hear it. Otherwise, I'm back to my desk.'

When they were alone, Arthur closed the door with a gentle click. He did not move immediately, and regarded the governess. She still kept her back to him, her limbs gathered up together. Somewhere in the wood she had abandoned her shawl, and the room was cold. Seeing the mutilated eiderdown crumpled on the floor, he draped it over her, first brushing off the detritus; then, pulling up a chair, considered what to do. It was his usual habit to wait, allowing the patient their rein. He had always found the less he asked, the more was confided. But how to persuade a woman to tell her secrets?

'Miss Symonds? It's Arthur Sidstone.' She didn't acknowledge his presence. He glanced over her, seeing the tears in her gown, and crumbling earth soiling the fabric. She had been kneeling in the mud. Why?

He coughed. 'I'm going to check nothing is broken,' he said. 'I'll run my hands down your arms and legs, and over your head, if you'll let me.' He did so on one side, proceeding in a clinical fashion, palpating the bones and skin, searching for signs of lesions or fractures. She expressed no objection or pain. 'I'm going to turn you towards me, and check your other side, and a few other things.' He felt for her pulse, noting it was a little too rapid, and that her skin was too pale, and clammy beneath the dirt. She had sustained deep scrapes on her hands and torn several fingernails. For a few moments he was uncertain how to proceed. He knelt by the bed, speaking quietly. 'I know about the Lowe Hospital.'

There was not a twitch or a tremor.

'I know you came here to avenge your sister. What I don't know is why she was here. What was the connection between your two families?'

She faced him now, her eyes locked on his, but her gaze was blank and yielding. Her answer was whispered. 'I avenged her.'

He rocked back on his heels, aghast. She was going to talk herself to the gallows.

Urgently, he said, 'Miss Symonds, you must promise not to say anything until I return. Speak to nobody except me. Sir Rowland claims you strangled Grizel Wingfield.' Her eyes were round and wide. He leant in. 'But I know you couldn't have done. These hands don't have the strength. And perhaps the same person hurt your sister.' When she did not reply, he said, 'I'm going to find out what's really happening here.'

He left, locking the door behind him.

29

The rain fell in fits and bursts. These variances in rhythm occupied her thoughts for long minutes. When she was not listening, she stared at the papered wall and its successive revolutions: egg to caterpillar, caterpillar to chrysalis, chrysalis to moth. She thought about change, and the limits of its possibilities.

She was mad, of course.

The knowledge the wood had given squatted in the recesses of her mind like an incubus, allowing her no peace.

Sir Rowland's words hummed in her mind: *no reason anything might be regarded as impossible*.

Perhaps she did kill Grizel Wingfield. Perhaps all this – the bedroom, the creeping nocturnal shapes on the wall, her bleeding fingers – weren't real, and she was somewhere else. Dr Sidstone, concrete as he had appeared, might have been nothing but a figment of her tortured mind.

Only her memories were real.

Catherine. Catherine.

The voice is solicitous, hushed. After several repetitions, it breaks through her fright and pain, and she comes back to herself.

When she opens her eyes, she is on the floor of the drawing room at Locksley. She recognises it now; she and the terrified child are one person. The scene in the wood – the candles, the scents of jasmine and earth – has changed, and the large man,

Sir Maurice, looks down on her with kindly, furrowed concern at his brow.

Next to her, Leonard Cox lies dead. Blood has seeped out of his mouth, and it is that, more than the great spill soaking down into the opulent Eastern carpets, which makes her recoil. He lies on his side, his eyes no longer grasping, only staring. Wherever he is, she wonders if he is disappointed in what he sees, now he has sight of it at last.

Remembering Emily, she tries to rise. 'Where ...' She holds her hand to her head, feeling an angry weal on her right temple. She must have hit her head, or one of the men hit her. The sequence of events is already tattered. 'Where is Emily?'

Sir Maurice's voice grows almost tender. 'Dear me,' he says to himself. 'I think she's quite forgotten.' He frowns and rises, leaving her on the floor. Pacing a circle, he talks aloud. 'The servants are loyal, but nobody's that loyal. This will get out. It could mean disgrace. It could endanger the match with Caplin.'

She can't follow his train of thought. The last thing she remembers is Emily, silent and ... 'I want my sister,' she says. Her voice sounds muted.

Sir Maurice continues as if she has not spoken. 'Murphy's not going to recollect it. He might be susceptible to an offer, but perhaps, after all, it's easier to ...' Seeming now to remember her presence, he turns to her. 'What about your mother, girl?'

'She's dying.' The truth is out before she can stop it. She is frightened by the brief look of satisfaction it produces on his paunchy face.

He takes a step, reaching down to where she lies, and seizes her by the upper arm. 'Come with me.'

She resists, but is dragged across the parquet floor to the door of the same antechamber where, a few hours earlier, Emily changed into the ridiculous linen sheets, and arranged amaranth flowers in her hair. Amaranth, Catherine remembers, for immortality.

He opens the door. 'Stay there until morning, then we can talk. I have every confidence you will understand what is at stake, and choose the path of your own good.'

She throws herself against the frame, pressing the balls of her feet into the corners, trying to stop him getting her over the threshold, but Sir Maurice succeeds in shutting her in the long dark room, and turns the key.

The space is narrow. There is a single window, and within the close confines of the walls, the jasmine scent lingers. She stares at the closed door, breathing erratically. What is he talking about? Why not just give her to the watchman, a murderess who killed a rich man?

She hammers on the door until her fists bruise. 'Let me out! Let me *out*!'

The room brightens as a cloud slides by the moon. She turns in the darkness, sees light beaming through the window, alighting on something white below the sill. Whatever it is, it is long, and thin, and a stream of something fair eddies out behind it, brushed to a sheen, catching the light like tawny glass.

She fights the swaying motion of her body. Her head aches, her vision grows blurred, and the thing at the end of the room falls in and out of focus. She steadies herself against the wall.

She can't be, because ...

But death is ostentatious, and cruel.

Emily, her face pinched in the moonlight, is dead.

Memory floods in, and she remembers Cox, how he manipulated Emily until the life flowed out of her.

Grief and rage break over her like waves. She kneels, holding Emily against her body, feeling the gap between the cold form and her own terrible warmth. She presses her palms against the cool apples of Emily's cheeks, trying to press heat into them, and rests her head on the bones of her ribcage, conscious of a nothingness, an absence inexplicable and dreadful. She moves her head to Emily's feet and forces her body alongside her sister's, burrowing in. 'Your feet are freezing,' she says, and puts her arms around them, kisses them.

They lie for hours, end to end. She does not feel the passage of time, notice the temperature dropping, or sense the slow light blooming outside the window. They might be in their little bed at home, their prayers just said, the sun still setting, the long night ahead.

Near dawn something crows outside.

When Emily moves against her, she knows it's a dream.

The movement is too natural, too much like waking. Emily simply stretches up her arms and yawns. Her toes, to which Catherine has clung throughout the night, flex and curl, are warm, as if, with unknown provenance, some fresh force has been placed behind her blood.

How cruel the dream is! She fights it, squeezing her eyes closed, willing herself awake.

But Emily says, 'I'm thirsty. What is this place?'

30

Arthur huddled into his coat and rode beneath the stable arch. As he dismounted, someone spoke his name in the shadows. 'Who's there?' he said, reaching for his cane.

Ned stepped out of the shelter of the overhanging roof, his lantern swinging by his side. 'You're back.' Coke capered at his feet, yapping. 'Get down,' he said, and the mutt obeyed.

Arthur didn't want to admit it, but he had felt jumpy, somehow watched during the whole ride home. Seeing Ned was a relief. 'Hello, Ned. Have you been inside?'

'No,' said Ned. He patted the horse's neck. 'I came to see you.'

This lifted Arthur, and he rebuked himself. He was too old for these thoughts. 'Well, here I am,' he said.

'You've been at Locksley?'

'Yes.'

Ned took the horse while Arthur hauled on the stable door. Coke settled down just inside, curling up in the dry straw. 'You look tired,' Ned said.

'That would be correct,' he said wryly. Ned led the horse in as Arthur opened up the animal's stall. 'There have been terrible happenings.' As he brushed down the horse, he related the events of the day.

The younger man blew out a breath when he heard how Grizel Wingfield had died. 'It makes you shudder,' he said. 'All laid out like that. Like a sacrifice.'

Arthur hadn't thought of it in that way. 'Yes, that's apt. It was very shocking.'

'And they think the governess did it?'

'Sir Rowland does. I'm less convinced.'

'He'll call the police in, won't he?'

'He'll have to.' When Ned looked worried, Arthur abandoned his strokes and said, 'What is it?'

The collier leant on the stall door, his feet shifting, staring at the straw. 'Well, if there's a constable coming, I might as well get it out. I have a confession. You're not going to like it.'

Arthur paused, putting the brush back in its place. He tethered the horse, then came out into the barn. 'You'd better tell me, then,' he said.

Ned's unbridled cheer had vanished. He spoke soberly. 'You know I've come to see your grandfather a lot. You, too.'

'I do.'

'Well, before you started joining us, in the evenings, you know, we talked a bit about Bridewell.'

'Sir Rowland?'

'That's right. We found we hated the bastard just the same. Different reasons, but we both wanted him paid back, for him to feel a scrap of the way he treated other people.'

Arthur stammered out his next words. 'What are you saying? Not that you – or my grandfather – were involved …'

'No!' Ned said. 'Not him – I used what he told me, but he wasn't …' He stopped. 'I'm going about this all wrong.'

'Then start again.'

They sat together on the straw.

'Your grandfather said Sir Rowland was lily-livered about anything unnatural. Anything his father might have been interested in – unexplained things. Frederick said he only cares about hard things – land and money, see. He hates everything else. So I thought I'd put the frighteners on him.'

'So you did what?'

'Dressed up.'

'What?'

Ned spoke haltingly. 'There were always legends of the wood. Old tales, you know. They grew up all around these parts. My dad told me some, and Edie Harris, so I asked your grandfather. He knew a bit more, and he told me about the hunt, how they'd appear to people in winter, all jangling with chains and screaming, and with burning torches. They were led by a great wild spirit, sort of like a god. They'd take souls with them. Be wicked and greedy and they'd take you first. So me and a few of the lads from the mine would get some of our kit together, and we'd pull out some of the pit ponies – poor little bastards, they were just happy to be above ground – and creep into the woods near Locksley, quite late. Some of the wives would come, too. We did it a few times.'

'That's ridiculous. You can't believe Sir Rowland would—'

'But he did.' There was a suggestion of laughter in Ned's voice, now, but he quickly returned to seriousness. 'Edie helped me. Her being John's niece, she didn't like the way Bridewell treated us at the mine, especially how John kept getting pay docked for wanting things to be fairer. And she liked me, so she helped.'

'That's taking advantage of her feelings, Ned,' Arthur said reprovingly. 'What exactly did she do?'

'Not much. Just signalled with a lantern where he was in the house, where he could see the wood, so he'd see us moving about in the trees. She kept opening the windows so he'd hear our noises even when he'd ordered them closed. She got us some of the old curtains out of the house, and we made robes out of them. We wore sacks and masks, and burnt dung in our torches. I took the keys to the kennels from the gatehouse and took two of the dogs with us. Edie told me,' Ned said, with another, harder laugh, 'he was nearly shitting his trousers. All because of a few ponies and a drum.'

Arthur understood the men's anger towards Sir Rowland. If it hadn't been for the murder and his concern for Miss Symonds, he might have felt more like laughing about something that, as far as revenge went, wasn't strictly harmful. But he was disappointed in Ned. It was a puerile prank. And his grandfather ... He sighed inwardly. Frederick had thought the powers were real, too, and it had driven him into paranoia. He turned away from Ned, wanting to shake him for his foolishness, but reminding himself that the collier was young, and young men often do stupid things without malice.

'Why are you telling me this now? I don't think the police will be interested. They have a murderer to catch.'

'It's the woman. The governess, in the wood.' Ned sounded despondent.

'Miss Symonds?' He began to make the connections. 'She saw you?'

'Last night a few of us were by the old chapel, going towards the house. I don't know what she was doing there. At first I thought it might be Bridewell – and I rode up to her. I didn't mean to frighten her!'

'Of course you didn't,' said Arthur. He placed a hand on Ned's shoulder. The collier glanced down at it, then let it remain for a few seconds until Arthur, seeing no earthly reason to leave it there, withdrew it and placed it in his pocket.

'I didn't even know why she was there. But then she saw us, and it put the fear of Christ into her. She started screaming, trying to get away. I grabbed her and tried to stop her – I was worried she might do herself a mischief – but she took off into the woods.'

'I see. And you were afraid that ...'

'You said she had been locked up, and I thought maybe it was because she said she saw things in the wood. And I wanted you to know ...'

Arthur finished his sentence as he trailed off. '... that you were the things she saw?'

'That's right. I thought, as well, if it got out that I had bad feeling towards Bridewell, I might be blamed for the murder. And worse, if Edie has been leaving windows open, I thought she might get blamed for someone getting in and doing that awful thing to ... to Mrs Wingfield.'

Absently, Arthur said, 'No, the murderer broke the glass to enter.' But still he shook his head in despair. 'This was badly done, Ned.'

'I know,' said Ned dejectedly. 'But he was so ... At first it was a good joke. But then with the mine being shut down, all the men out of work, and there he was, sitting pretty, it made me ... I just wanted to get back at him, you know?'

Yes, Arthur understood. He knew the impotence Ned described all too well. The world was not a fair place. Not for ordinary people.

'What about Harris?' he asked suddenly. 'Did he want to get back at Sir Rowland, too?'

Ned moved the hair out of his eyes and blew air from the side of his mouth. He did not answer.

'I'll find out, one way or another,' warned Arthur. 'I'm Harris's friend. I'd like to protect him if I can.'

'It might be,' said Ned slowly, 'that Harris broke into the Abbey. I can't say for sure.'

'But not to hurt Mrs Wingfield?'

'I can't see it being that way,' came Ned's answer, at last. 'He might have done it to look for something on Sir Rowland and the accident, to put the blame where it belongs. He's got it in for him, all right. But he wouldn't kill anyone.'

Arthur felt the same way, but the chit beneath the window spoke against Harris. He couldn't tell Ned about it, or it might get round the men. He thought, then said, 'What you did was foolish. You're right that the police wouldn't look kindly on it.'

'Yes.'

'But that's only if they find out.'

'You won't tell them?'

He thought again. 'I'll have to tell them something. Miss Symonds's distress was very real, and it's possible it contributed to her ...' struggling for an appropriate word, he settled on: 'episode.'

Ned nodded miserably. 'I know.'

'But there's no reason I have to name names. What you did was stupid, but not criminal.' He decided. 'No. I can describe what happened without putting you in it.'

'Thanks, Arthur.'

'And if there's any doubt about the other – the murder – you know I'll speak for you.'

They sat in silence for a few moments.

The barn grew quieter as the rain slowed to a trickle of water off the roof. The horse nickered, knowing Arthur had left a job half-done, and Coke let out soft snores in the straw.

'I need to speak to my grandfather.' He gave a thin smile, and Ned returned it, deepening the indentation in his left cheek. Arthur was near enough to touch it. He stood. 'I'd better get inside.'

'Frederick's a good man. If he'll still see me after what I did, I'll come over tomorrow.'

'Not now?'

'I need to collect my Aunt Parry's things from the Abbey, and help my dad pack up. Sir Rowland finally gave him that pension. He's off to a cottage near Pantygelli.'

'Generous of Sir Rowland,' said Arthur, surprised the baronet had kept his word.

'Well, my dad's worked hard enough for him. Like a pig in muck, he'll be. But after I've done with the packing, I'll come. Tomorrow.'

'Until tomorrow, then.' Arthur hesitated. 'While you're there, you should tell that young housemaid the truth. Don't let her count on you. Let her find someone else, and be happy.'

Ned nodded. 'I'll do it.'

They parted. Arthur found, as he came to the back door and thought about the next day, that he felt better. Miss Symonds had been undone by a thoughtless prank, and although Ned was an actor in the events, it had not been deliberate.

The house was unlit and silent. As he removed his cloak, he thought more about what he had learnt. His grandfather believed a dark power existed beneath the wood. It had nearly driven him mad. And the colliers' trick had led to Miss Symonds's incarceration, for surely it was seeing the apparitions – really Ned and his foolish friends – that had so unsettled her. Yet he blamed himself. He should have seen her instability before; in fact, he had seen it, at least in part, when Mrs Parry died. Miss Symonds had obviously been on the edge of a nervous collapse. Ned's actions had only been the catalyst.

He had other questions, too. Questions about Emily Murphy. His grandfather had recorded marks on her body consistent with hanging, but did he check for defensive injuries? Scratch marks on the neck or skin beneath the fingernails might suggest a struggle. He was certain unravelling Emily Murphy's fate, including the role of her sister and the Lowe Hospital, was the key, and, as he rehearsed how he would word his letter, he experienced a growing confidence that everything would resolve itself in the coming days.

He removed his gloves, rubbing sore eyes as he passed the stairs. He thought of the coal dust filling Grizel's throat, blinding her, entombing her in rock. There was undeniable hatred in that act – but for her, or for those the killer believed would mourn her? He had been certain, when Sir Rowland had stumbled in his hallway and screamed – *monster*, *demon* – his agonies had been real. But for whom had those words been meant? Dowle and Harris? Surely, if he had been referring to them, he would have used the plural: *monsters*, *demons*. Arthur felt certain he had been speaking of something else.

It might have been the effect of reliving that ghastly scene, but the house felt too cold. He took four or five steps into the parlour before realising something was different. There were no books, papers or empty glasses; his grandfather's typical benign chaos was absent. Old ashes rested in the grate. The curtains were drawn, as he had left them that morning.

'Grandfather?' Where was he? He rarely went abroad after sunset.

'Grandfather?' His voice mingled with the wind's thin moan in the chimney breast as he moved into the kitchen, dark and untidy. Mrs Morgan had not been in. Usually his grandfather would have pottered about, neatening things from the night before, but the bottle sent by Cardale Musgrave, and the remains of the seed cake, were just as they had been when Arthur rode out that morning.

He must be upstairs. Had he risen at all? Perhaps his stomach was plaguing him again. When it was bad, he took to his bed, dosing himself with saleratus powders and making much of his infirmity.

Reaching the upper floor, he found the door to Frederick's bedroom closed. He decided he would not disturb him, but just put his head around and check if he needed anything. Then, when he was up and about again, Arthur would talk to him about Emily Murphy, and Ned's ridiculous antics in the wood.

The door creaked. The curtains were drawn, so he waited a moment, letting his eyes adjust to the gloom of the cloistered room. His nostrils twitched at a sickly smell.

'Grandfather?' He could just make out Frederick lying on his front. There was something unnerving about his position, awkward, free of the quilted blankets he favoured, his hands spread wide on his pillow.

He should have been able to hear the usual rasping snore, the irritated grunts his grandfather made when someone woke him from a comfortable afternoon sleep. Instead, nothing. Steeling himself, he took another step. The blankets were tossed about the bed, damp and stinking. His grandfather had removed his nightgown and, apart from his drawers, was undressed. Arthur approached the bed, his eyes travelling over Frederick's speckled, liver-spotted back, taking in the reddened skin. He heard his voice as if it came from another mouth.

'Grandfather!' The sound was obscene in the still room.

He clambered on to the bed. Heaving, he turned Frederick – he was cold, too cold – then recoiled, hardly able to look at the beloved, swollen face. His throat convulsed as he saw his grandfather's corneas were already flattened. He reached with both hands, ignoring their violent shaking. His fingers found Frederick's eyelids and tried to close them, but rigor had set in. He gave up and stared, thinking of the man who had walked with him through the chirruping woods as a boy, who had done everything for him after Newport, and when he returned to England, had taken him in, and shared his home with him as a man. Who had known his grandson's deepest secrets, and never told, and never judged. He thought of Frederick's endless stories, stories Arthur had not really listened to, and knew he would do anything to hear just one more.

He sat with the dead.

31

Catherine's last conversation with William took place in the orangery on the hottest day of the year. The building was only just completed. William had chosen every bit of masonry and every square inch of glazing himself, and supervised the construction with a hawkish eye. Yet, as with so many of the improvements he made to the estate, though he swelled with pride when he spoke of the orangery, he had little use for it. He had commissioned it because he knew the Burtons, near Lyford, had built one; as soon as it was completed, he let Catherine have the run of it, and she filled the humid space with potted orange, lemon and kumquat trees, treasuring every moment, no longer needing to act the part of mistress or worry about what the servants thought. The flowers, scions and roots did not care if she had been a housekeeper. She thrived in their silence.

But today it was too hot. She felt imprisoned in her silk. All she wanted to do was go to her bedroom, undress, and float in a bath of cool water. Yet, if she wilted, so did the plants, so she filled a can and drenched the gravel around each tree, squeezing the dark green leaves to see how much more they might need.

She was absorbed in her work, and didn't hear the door.

William entered, holding a sheet of paper. She noted a flush above his collar. Like the trees, he suffered in the midday heat.

'Why not sit down?' she suggested. 'I'll call for some lemon water.'

'No,' he said. His lips were taut.

'What's wrong?'

'I should have known,' he said, pacing, half-hidden by twisting columns of bark. 'I should have known I could not be so lucky, not at my time of life.'

'I don't understand—'

He flung the paper on the potting table. 'Because I'm a merchant, because I made my wealth with my own hands, you treated me like a simpleton.'

'I don't know what you—'

'Don't lie to me.'

She picked up the paper. It was a letter. The words rippled on the page. She had to concentrate to hold them in her mind. *Gilbert Murphy, madhouse, died 1848.*

Her stomach heaved. Her gown felt too tight and she sank into a chair. 'Where did you get this?'

He said, 'It didn't make sense. *You* didn't make sense. I should have known. Who could forget so much of their past? I thought I would help,' he said, with a hard laugh. 'I wrote to everyone: business contacts, friends, even men in Parliament. I didn't expect my enquiries to bring back anything significant about a Gilbert Murphy; you were in service, after all, your father was no one important. But I thought there might be *something*. Then I received a letter from a man in the Royal Military Academy. He had happened to share my communication with his brother, a miniaturist, and he, in turn, remembered the name of an obscure artist, a man who painted the gentry – not very successfully, mind, on account of being an inebriate. One day, according to my contact, this Murphy disappeared. Upped and vanished, never to be heard from again.

'I was suspicious. Especially when the letter came from Herefordshire revealing how your sister had died in some conspicuous scandal.'

Catherine fought rising panic. William's anger had cast her adrift. She could focus neither on his feelings, nor the memories they stirred. 'That's unfair, William, we don't know—'

He was relentless. 'So at my request, my contact wrote to a friend in the Grand Lodge. He thought he might have ways of learning what I wanted to know. What came back was ...' William shook his head in repugnance. 'He had heard a rumour involving the Locksley estate, and the death of a man named Cox, sometime in the late thirties. He suggested I write to the madhouses, mentioning Murphy's name. And again, it came back: your father was institutionalised. He killed a man. Of course you didn't want me to know. You knew I wouldn't have married you, wouldn't have wanted my children's mother to be from that stock.' His lip curled in contempt. She had never seen an expression like that on his face before. He was usually so gentle, so eager to please her.

'No, I ...' But the name – Cox – had stirred something, like poking a bees' nest in winter. 'It's not true,' she said desperately, rising, reaching for his hands. 'Or if it is, I have no knowledge of it. Please, you must believe me. I—'

'He was put away as a lunatic.' William stumbled into one of the lemon trees. It swayed in its pot. Catherine reached out to steady it. Her husband saw her hand coming near, and pushed it away. 'I'll lose my reputation,' he said. 'This will destroy me.'

'No one needs to know. People won't—'

'You fool.' The words were spat from his lips. 'I was born in the gutter. I climbed my way up, over others who thought they should have my place. They're all watching me, the county men. They'll love to see me humbled.'

'No, we can—'

'*We* won't do anything. Stay in your rooms for the time being. I'll find out the rest.'

She clung to his elbow as he tried to walk away, but he pushed through the leaves and pots, shaking her off, shouting for her to let him be. 'Please listen,' she cried. 'I didn't know!'

When he turned to look at her, he was purple, overheating. He stared for a few seconds, as if he had never really seen her before. Then he left.

She spent a terrible, sultry night in her rooms. The next morning, they woke her early with the news that William was dead. A sudden collapse. A weak heart, they said.

She put on a high-necked mulberry gown. It wasn't the proper colour, but would do until she could put in an order at Robinson's. As the servants hunted material for a bonnet, she wrapped the mirrors in crêpe, and arranged a wreath for the door. Then she sat with William, and unfurled the fingers of his hand out of a fist. Looking down at him, she wondered what had happened to his reassuring bulk, thinking how death had made him so much smaller. She could not bring herself to speak her regrets out loud. He could not hear her, anyway. For hours she kept her vigil, and clutched Lewis's letter. Emily was dead, and she still did not know why.

Three days later, the will was read. William had left her everything. The house in Abingdon, a second property in St John's Wood, his company, all his interests in the City; all hers. She was rich. Independent. She might shut up the house and become eccentric. She could sell up and take rooms in Naples or Venice. See Charleston, or the Great Wall. She could do anything she wanted.

But if William had had his way, if he had lived, he would have put her aside. She remembered the distaste in his face; he would have divorced her.

Put away as a lunatic.

His words had reduced her to nothing. If her father was mad, and her sister had died scandalously, she would never outrun the stain. One day, lounging in the fierce Italian sun, or rounding the deck of a ship en route to New York, the shadow of the past would reach out and envelop her. She would never be free.

The following day, out of the blue, Lewis's second communication had arrived. It was addressed to William, but now she sat in his study and opened such letters. She had pored over it again and again, feeling sick, trapped in the space between Lewis's professional euphemisms – *the incident*, *the circumstances* – and the brutal fact of the death certificate: *self-inflicted*.

Even then she had known it was a lie.

She made up her mind then and there. She would find out the truth.

But now, her eyes fixed on the stout, peppered body of a painted moth on her bedroom wall, she realised she was back where she had started. If anything, the position was worse, for Dr Sidstone knew about Emily.

And Sir Rowland believed she had killed Grizel Wingfield.

This thought cut through the rest. She remembered Mrs Wingfield. Strangled, the doctor had said. She raised her hands before her face, staring at the soft undulations of her fingers and the deep-set lines of her palms. Were these the hands of a killer?

They were. She remembered everything, now; the unexpected resistance of Cox's flesh against the blade, the heat of his blood on her skin, the rush of feeling as he died – triumph, not guilt.

But she had been wrong, because Cox and his ministrations could not have killed Emily, who had been in a swoon, and not dead at all. Only her own terror had persuaded her otherwise because, when morning came, Catherine had pressed her cold hands against the apples of her sister's cheeks, felt the breath moving in her. Emily had spoken. She had lived.

But then the men had come. There were three orderlies, bulky and deaf to her complaints. First they had taken her father, who, in his deep stupor, hadn't even struggled. When they came back, she had been separated from Emily and placed in a bolted, horse-drawn wagon. Well paid by Sir Maurice, the men had removed her to Lowe, and told her flatly she would stay there, because she was mad.

She had stayed two long years. The doctors' faces were blurred, but not the strait-waistcoats, the manacles, the leather straps compressing the back of her head. She had clawed the walls when they said her mother was dead. As she became more docile, as she stopped mentioning Emily, or the house where the men had hurt her, they became more lenient. She was young, they said, and could recover if she only relinquished her delusions. Nothing was how she recollected it. She had not killed anyone, and nobody had hurt her sister. Emily had gone into service, as she might, too, if she could see things the way they truly were. It was her only path to freedom, and she did as they said, repeating what they told her. The strait-waistcoat was retired. She was given simple tasks to perform, allowed to help with the other inmates. In time, she began to forget things, and to remember other things differently, just as they had predicted, and more and more, she saw that the doctors were right, and everything had happened as they described.

Eventually they had let her go. They gave her a character and found her a place in a house she was told belonged to a friend of Edwin Lowe. On her first day, they said if she worked hard, she might gain a more senior position, and from that day, not a soul spoke to her of the hospital. Nobody mentioned her father or sister. She might have sprung up out of the ground in front of them for all the notice they paid her past. After a few months of back-breaking work, scrubbing floors and carrying out ashes, she was so tired she hardly knew herself, and hardly remembered where she had come from. It was as if someone had reached a hand into her past and snuffed out her former life like a candle.

She understood, now: Sir Maurice had arranged it all. He had placed the blame for Cox's death on her father. She wondered how Sir Maurice had manipulated the evidence, whether Gilbert Murphy had been found with blood on his hands, whether they had taken Cox's pocketbook and placed it in her father's possession.

But in fact she, Catherine, was Cox's killer. Somehow she had hidden that knowledge even from herself, but William had been right. She was tainted.

So maybe it was true. Maybe she had killed Grizel Wingfield because if you could forget one thing, why not another? If she could not trust her recollections, how could she know what she was capable of?

She realised it was growing dark. She had been locked in for hours. Getting to her feet unsteadily, she opened the casement. The rain had gone off. Water dripped off the needled cedars and the late-afternoon sun peeped from behind the clouds, edging them with gold, painting the glasshouse panels burnt orange.

The glasshouse seemed important.

She remembered the man on the gravel path, and the wavering light. She realised there had been someone else here the night Grizel died, an intruder who did not want to be seen. Was it possible she had met the killer?

She unclenched her fists. Her memory might be an unreliable guide, but Dr Sidstone was right: physically, she could not have overpowered Grizel. The hands that choked her had to have belonged to a man. That meant there was still a killer at Locksley.

Facts swarmed her like a covey of tiny birds. She closed her eyes as they came, trying to master herself, clinging to what was solid, but a noise from the nursery disturbed her. Something rattled along the floor. She knelt, then lay, pressing her cheek to the bare boards, realising she could see beneath the doorsill, where an iridescent shape winked from the inside of a glass jar. She blinked, stared, and saw one of Georgie's tiny beetles. As she watched, the tips of the little girl's fingers came into view, and the jar was lifted away.

'Georgie,' she whispered, after a few seconds. 'Can you hear me?'

'I'm not meant to speak to you.' Georgie spoke matter-of-factly.

'I don't want you to get into trouble. Are you well?'

'Nobody will tell me anything.'

'What do you want to know?'

'Why you're locked in.'

'There ... there's something your father thinks I did.'

There came a pause, then, doubtfully, 'I heard Father talking to the doctor. He said the constable will take you away.'

'The constable will come,' Catherine said, trying to brighten her voice. 'He'll get to the bottom of everything.'

'He didn't when Miss Emily died.'

'That was different. They thought she had hurt herself.' She closed her eyes, willing herself not to use the little girl for her own purposes.

'You won't do what she did?' Georgie's voice was almost a whisper.

'No,' Catherine said. 'I promise you that.'

'Miss Emily promised.'

'Promised what?'

'That even if she seemed to go away for a while, she would always be here.'

She searched in desperation for an explanation, recalling how Georgia had insisted this once before. 'Sometimes grown-ups mean what they say at the time, but find they can't keep their word.'

'Can I tell you the greatest secret?'

Catherine's breath came more shallowly. In her mind lingered the impression of Emily's skin against her own, too cold. So cold she shivered. 'Of course,' she said.

'You can't tell a soul.'

'I swear I won't.'

'Miss Emily kept her promise.'

'Whatever do you mean?' She grew colder still. A tightness gripped her spine.

'She's here.'

'That's not possible. She died. Do you not remember?'

Georgie did not answer.

'Who—'

The door to the nursery opened, and Edie scolded Georgie. 'Look at your dress, all that dust! Come away, now! If your father catches sight …' Georgie was hustled off as Catherine rose and squatted on the balls of her feet, breathing deep, stabilising breaths.

She had been trapped as if in a labyrinth, beset by obstacles. Even once she had all the facts at her command, everything she needed to find the truth, it had eluded her.

But now the puzzle had unlocked.

All she had to do was believe in the impossible; believe that one thing could become another.

As she absorbed that thought, and its terrible implications, an unseen hand pushed a key beneath the door.

32

Arthur turned the cottage upside down, clinging to a desperate hope that it had been an accident. People mistook arsenic for flour, weighed out the wrong amounts of ingredients, mislabelled bottles. A year ago, he knew, his grandfather would never have blundered like this – he had always been meticulous about pills and powders – but now? He ransacked cupboards, pulling out every bottle, tub and jar he could lay his hands on, from vinegar to emery powder, soda to rottenstone. He opened anything that could conceivably contain any toxin, and emptied them, one by one, into the deep stone sink. Some had been untouched so long the bottles had crusted tight. He smashed them anyway, rooting in the shattered glass, inhaling the rising scents.

He went into the study and regarded the medicine cabinet. It was locked. The key remained on the cord around his own neck. He ducked to examine the lock, noticing nothing awry. Still he checked, unfastening the case and taking out bottles of castor oil, syrup of ipecac, iodine, spirit of nitre. He stared at the array of potions. The exercise was useless. There were fifty things – a hundred – that might cause a healthy man to sicken if taken in the wrong amounts or combination, but Frederick no longer had access to them, and nothing had been mismanaged.

Next he checked the water. Cases existed where poisoned rats had crept into a well to die, and when their corpses had disintegrated, the substance had entered the supply. But he and his grandfather had shared water, he thought, even as he sniffed and tasted it. He, Arthur, had no symptoms of poisoning, slow or otherwise; in any case, his grandfather's death had been the result of a fast-acting, acute substance, not a lacing over many months.

He hunted anyway, his mind a whirlwind of rage, a tight fury in his soul that this could happen, coupled with a simple disbelief that his grandfather, whose absence was unimaginable, could be gone.

When he had checked everything he could think of, he sank against the wall, cradling his head in his hands, taking inventory of everything he had ruined. Because this was all his fault. While he, Arthur, had walked through the woods with Sir Rowland, trying to find Grizel Wingfield's murderer, as he had tried to save Miss Symonds, his grandfather had died in a pool of his own shit and vomit, and the one person who should have been here to protect him had been far away.

After a while, he seized on what he had missed in his grief, and scrambled to his feet. This poison had been administrated deliberately. He thought he knew how.

At the table, he checked off the items he had left out that morning. A half-bottle of good wine from Cardale Musgrave's cellar. A seed cake, half-eaten. No note. He sniffed the remnants of the wine, holding it up to the light, scanning the bottom for telltale grains or residue. When he found nothing, he examined the cake, remembering how his stomach had ached earlier, how he had eaten crumbs from the plate. It didn't smell unusual, but its peppery scent was vigorous and might be covering something worse. The poison could have been in the sugar or flour. It would have no discernible taste.

His grandfather had thought these gifts came from Cardale Musgrave. Perhaps the wine had been sent by Musgrave, but the cake not, or vice versa. But was the poison meant for him, or for his grandfather?

What could either of them have done, or known, to attract the killer's malice?

His mind whirling, he circled back to his grandfather's only involvements in the strange events at Locksley: his treatment of Anne Bridewell, and his certification of Emily Murphy's suicide. Only a day earlier, Arthur had dismissed the possibility that his grandfather had recorded a suicide when the evidence pointed to murder, but now he had to admit the possibility. Yet why would his grandfather do that? Did Sir Rowland hold something over him? Had Frederick made a medical error he could not afford people to find out about? Perhaps something in his treatment of Lady Anne?

He contemplated the list of the dead. Grizel Wingfield. Mrs Parry. Miss Murphy. Something connected these cases. It must have to do with Miss Symonds. She had come here for a purpose. Was it justice, or revenge? He was still sure she could not have killed Mrs Wingfield, not with her own hands, but Sir Rowland's theory – as unlikely as it had seemed – was not impossible: she might have worked with another, or several others.

But in fact, he decided in frustration, his grandfather's death weakened this theory. Miss Symonds was not going to achieve her ends by attacking Frederick. She was here to solve a mystery – who killed Emily Murphy, and why? If his grandfather had known the answer, now his grandfather could not tell.

So rather than being the poisoner, he decided, Miss Symonds might be in danger.

He had to return to Locksley immediately. He would brook no more excuses. It was time Sir Rowland told him everything.

He could have saddled the horse, but it made more sense to have the beast fresh in case he needed to hurry to Hereford, where a constable might be found. He would go on foot. It would take him an hour or so. Before leaving, he covered Frederick with a clean linen sheet, then said the Lord's Prayer by his bedside. He could not grieve yet. There would be a time for grief, but it was not now.

He wrapped himself warmly and placed his grandfather's blackthorn cudgel in his pocket. He found a storm lantern, and a cloth to wrap about it so he could conceal himself at need, and locked the door behind him.

Hurrying along winding paths through the trees, the wood's carmines and taupes bled unevenly into the gloom. The shadows ran together, the mottled sky lost its edge, and on the thick leafy mould of the forest floor, a mist began to settle.

He was about halfway, deep in the dense thickets above the Abbey, when a sound disturbed the slope above him. He assumed he had unsettled a deer or fox, but then it came again: an earthy squelch, and he stopped below an overhang of jutting roots. He listened, recognising the pattern of stealthy feet on a damp track. No animal showed such fidelity to a man-made route. Someone travelled the path ahead. He hastened to cover his light, then stood alone in the dusk. Reaching into his pocket, he closed his fist around the cudgel, and listened again. The footfall became lighter; they were moving away. Who was his mysterious companion? It was possible Sir Rowland himself had ventured out again, but he could not hear the mastiffs. He felt sure the baronet would not go abroad without their protection; Ned's tricks had done their work too well.

He waited another minute to put off sharp ears, then scrambled up the slope, cursing the telltale noise as he hauled himself up by a thorny branch. Once on the flat, he waited another minute, then picked up speed along the spine of the ridge. The lights of the Abbey winked below.

The other traveller was still ahead, but the distance had closed. He fell back a little. He could not see the person, only detect the light's headway. Whoever it was seemed to be in no hurry. Their movements rather showed a determined caution.

Several minutes of this went by, with Arthur halting behind trunks, weighing every step to avoid gaining in the pursuit, then the light dipped low, and divided. One moment a single, bleary firefly hovered in the dark, and the next he tracked twin lights: one stationary, illuminating the departing contours of a man's legs, the other still drifting away. He watched for a few seconds and inferred that his quarry had placed a lantern on the ground to guarantee his way back, and now carried the other towards his goal.

Climbing a low mound, Arthur entered a glade, where a dark squarish shape rose up before him, ringed by an iron fence. He had never seen this place, but his grandfather had described it: he quickly realised he looked on the Bridewell family chapel. Around it, the wood had been allowed to grow virtually unchecked, except for the fifty or so feet across the clearing.

Arthur was close, the light strong enough that, even with the descending mist, he was able to recognise the man's gait, and make out an impression of studs from heavy boots. Miner's boots. Not noticing he was observed, John Harris moved through the open gate and towards the narrow portico. There, his light was finally still.

The obvious conclusion, though Arthur resented the way it leapt up in his mind, was that Harris was meeting someone. Having dissuaded Dowle's accusers from searching the wood, not because he thought it a waste of time, but because he knew precisely where the fugitive would be found, Harris was here to bring supplies, or news. The chapel was the perfect hiding place for a hunted man: dry, abandoned, with escape routes on all sides.

Arthur took out the cudgel and gripped the sturdy wood. The prospect of fighting both of them weakened his knees, but then he thought of his grandfather and rage flowed through him. Had

Harris sent the poisoned gifts? The collier was cleverer than Dowle. The low wretch had let Arthur think he was his friend. That betrayal fired his belly. Fixing on the figure of Harris in the gloom, he watched as the other man opened the door, and disappeared inside.

Did it make sense to follow, and deal with both men together, or was that to rush the lion's den? If Harris were here only to deliver food and drink, he would depart the same way he had gone in, and Arthur would be able to accost him without being outnumbered. On the other hand, the men might well leave together to put in motion some criminal plan; this might be the last chance Arthur had to stop it. If he stood firm at the doorway, cudgel in hand, he at least would have the advantage of not being trapped in there with them like a rat.

These deliberations were interrupted by a blood-curdling shout from inside the chapel. Whatever was happening, for at least one of the parties, things were not going according to plan.

Harris had closed the oak door fast, and Arthur was not ready to be discovered, so he crept to the east window. He could see nothing within, but as he listened, something crashed down on the stone floor. It was followed by an interregnum of silence, then a string of savage grunts.

He pictured Dowle and Harris grappling with one another, allies turned to mortal enemies, but this idea did not convince him. Why, after all, would Harris work with Dowle? Harris was for the workers, not the overman. He had marched to Newport, and fought bravely there. Arthur could not accept that he would connive to steal the money that should have been invested to keep his comrades safe.

But he had wondered enough. Action was his only path now. He held the cudgel high and turned the latched handle.

The chapel was accessed by a short flight of steps beneath a thick arch leading down to the nave. But he couldn't get there;

the stairs were blocked by a stocky, wheezing figure. His nerves were brittle as he stared, trying to see, before he recognised John Harris.

He looked down, expecting Harris to rush at him with a weapon, but Harris didn't have one. Instead, his hands seemed to claw at his own neck.

Arthur watched in mounting confusion as Harris groped at his collar, near his windpipe. He could not work out what had happened. Harris must have recognised Arthur, because he reached out a hand to him, choking, trying to speak, and then Arthur saw how, beneath Harris's other hand, a dark shadow had begun to spread, and the dreadful truth dawned.

Someone had slit Harris's throat.

Seconds later, Harris's knees collapsed under him. Arthur took several steps closer and knelt at the collier's side. He pushed scratching fingers off as he felt for the wound, trying to knit the slippery flesh back together, but quickly realised it was too late; the gash was from one side of the throat to the other, below the collier's voice box. He couldn't close it, and had no chance of stemming the bleeding. Harris thrashed on the floor, gargling blood for what felt like an age, though must have been no more than half a minute. The dying man's hands fell away as he began to lose consciousness.

Within a minute, Harris was gone. Arthur remained by his side for another minute, holding back furious tears. No man should die alone like this, in such violence, no matter what he had done. He closed Harris's eyes.

He thought.

There was still Dowle.

With a muttered prayer, he placed Harris's lantern near the wall, hefted the cudgel and rose again warily, moving into the nave. If the overman was the killer, he was probably still here. As he cast his own lantern about the shadowy space, he saw, a few feet from him, what had to be Dowle's knife. A crude weapon, nearly ten inches of steel. He had dropped it. But why drop his weapon?

He had no time to think about it, because a second later Dowle was on him. The big man rushed him from the shadows, bowling into his adversary with his superior height and weight, knocking Arthur to the flagstones. They wrestled, and Arthur struck out with the cudgel, sensing that Dowle was grunting in hidden pain, though Arthur was certain, even as he rained down blows on the brute, that he had not inflicted any damage. He managed to raise his arm above his head, and struck Dowle's temple with enough force to see him off for a moment. The overman sagged against the wall. His back was bent, his hands propped against his thighs, supporting his upper body. A blooming stain marred the centre of his chest.

Arthur watched as his enemy's eyelids drooped. There appeared to be no more fight in Dowle, who was thinner than he remembered, his beard heavier, and matted. Still, appearances could be deceptive.

'Dowle,' he said, trying to rouse him. Finally, when the big man fell, he knelt beside him. The overman's shirt was warm and wet, blood soaked through the calico fabric. Arthur felt around the sweating skin, identifying a large laceration in the chest, near the heart. From his shortened breath and the blood at his lips, he suspected the knife had perforated Dowle's lung; he was surprised he had had enough strength in reserve to fight.

He thought he knew what had happened. His suspicions had been wrong.

'Stephen,' Arthur said softly. At this use of his first name, the other man's eyes opened a little wider. 'You worked with Harris to steal from the mine?' Dowle shook his head. 'Don't go to God with lies,' Arthur suggested. 'Tell me what I need to know, and you'll feel better.'

Dowle coughed up blood as he tried to speak. 'With ... Bridewell. His plan.'

Arthur said what he had begun to suspect, what tallied with what he had seen in the mine's ledger, but not immediately recognised. 'You worked with Sir Rowland to embezzle Caplin's investment?' Dowle managed a nod.

'Harris wasn't helping you?'

Dowle said, 'Harris ... hated me. Came to ... find ...' He gasped, his face tight with pain. 'Never knew ...'

A few moments later, Dowle died.

Arthur dropped the overman's head to the flags with care. He looked at the two, side by side in their own blood. Not allies after all. Enemies. Unwilling to leave the man whose duplicity had killed his friends to the law, Harris had gone searching for Dowle himself. When the two came together, a fight had ensued. Yet more death on the conscience of the man who was the ultimate cause of all this horror: Sir Rowland Bridewell.

The overman had been working with Sir Rowland all along. The baronet had used Arthur to put the blame for the accident on Dowle, who, realising he had been manipulated, had fled. The baronet's actions had been a ploy from the start, to get the mine closed down without a workers' revolt. He had known he would soon have his hands on his father-in-law's fortune, and would not have to make the colliery pay to cover his debts. Its cost therefore outweighed its usefulness, and he wanted rid of it. Arthur had been taken in like a babe, blaming Dowle alone, when the culprit had been staring him in the face: Sir Rowland had known from the beginning that there was no new cage, no new struts. He had risked the life of every man who worked for him, and was directly responsible for the loss of forty-one souls. Tommy Cooper's mother had buried her child because of his greed.

It all came back to the Caplin inheritance. It was not impossible, now, to imagine how that inheritance had rested on Sir Rowland being rid of Emily Murphy. If she had been pregnant, or threatened to reveal their affair, Sir Rowland would have had every reason to kill her.

He looked down at the flagstones, stained with blood. The most unwelcome part of his conclusion was inescapable: for some reason, his grandfather had lied about Emily Murphy's cause of death. He had recorded a murder as a suicide.

It was time to find out why.

33

The metal was cool in her hand, heavy and definite. It might have been the only definite thing in the world. For a while, Catherine stared at it, contemplating. After some time had passed – she did not know how much – she made up her mind. She would not stay here, trapped like vermin. She had chosen her path at the start, when she had sat in William's study and refused to resign herself to lies. Now she would complete the course. She would face the truth, however bitter the ending.

She waited. Soon, she heard a footfall; then, a few minutes later, from under the door, Edie's distressed hiss. 'Please, miss, stand still!' Georgie muttered something in reply, and Edie repeated her plea, cajoling. 'You mustn't be so trying, miss – I'll be for it if we keep your father waiting!'

She hovered, listening by the door while Edie ushered Georgie into the passageway. They seemed to progress a few steps from the nursery but, just as Catherine expected their footsteps to die away, she heard a male voice, quite friendly. '… my dad's gone, just now, to Pantygelli.'

'Is that right?' Edie asked coolly.

'I never thought His Lordship would part with a silver penny he didn't have to.' It was Ned Parry. His voice was playful. She remembered how easily he had flirted with her in the wood. He was deploying the same charm against the housemaid. Briefly, she felt sorry for Edie, who, so far, had not shown herself equal to the task of rejecting Ned's variable affections.

But Edie's answer came unexpectedly sharp. 'What are you doing up here?'

'I came for my Aunt Parry's things,' Ned said.

'Well, you've got them, so you can make yourself scarce, can't you?' was the acid reply.

'You're angry with me?'

A long pause followed. Catherine did not know how Edie would respond, but was too distracted by her own troubles to give it much thought when the housemaid's words came through the door, low and furious. 'Trouble with you, Ned Parry, is you think too much of yourself. You cause trouble wherever you go. I go along with all your nonsense, and what for? You tell me to wait for you, and I wait – and look where that gets me! As if I haven't got enough work without you creeping round here. Worse, look at what's happened to—' The servant stopped herself. 'I won't say more in front of the child. But I think you should get out of here – go with your da to wherever it is he's going. And leave me be from now on, I tell you.'

'I'm sorry if I …'

Ned's words faded as he retreated towards the stairs, but Catherine had no time to think of him going off with his tail between his legs. When she was sure they were gone, she twisted the key in the lock. The door swung without a sound. Slipping out, she returned her thoughts to the mystery, reflecting that there were still things she did not know, but they were mostly questions of *why*, not what. The strands, so far resistant to attempts to weave them together, were converging.

What they revealed was nothing short of diabolical.

She knew who had pushed the key beneath the door, allowing her escape. She knew who had taken her letters and rings, and why Mrs Parry and Grizel Wingfield had to die. And she knew, with a terrible certainty, who had placed the rope around Emily's neck.

The person who had done these things waited for her. She would go to them now.

She moved through the silent corridors, past the unlit lamps in their nooks and the windows no one had had time to screen. Outside, evening had fallen and a pinkish mist descended on the valley. As she crept down the stairs and skirted the wainscoting, she heard the dogs yelping and shivered, anticipating the moment when, her flight discovered, Sir Rowland would set them after her. Every passing minute added to her danger.

The Abbey was a shrouded space, swaddled in a hush that extended beyond the house and across the wood, down below the ground, into the sightless roots of the hills. Going beneath the arch and into the west wing, she felt cocooned inside the ancient bones of the building. Its secrets were deep, they travelled in all directions, but she was close to understanding them.

As quickly as this jolt of belief ran through her, it petered out. She staggered against the cool panelling, breathing too fast. She had deceived herself. Nobody could be prepared for this. She could not accept what her intellect told her, the only possible solution to the puzzle.

Yet it was impossible. Fiendish. Her head throbbed and her chest hammered. Leaning back, she pressed her palms to her sides, closed her eyes and waited for her breathing to slow. As she regained control, a brittle resolve grew again inside her — impossible or not, this was the only answer.

The final steps to the double doors were heavy, her earlier determination shaken by her knowledge of what waited for her.

She knew the doors would be unchained. She pulled the handle and went through, thinking, with each stair, round and round, how aptly Grizel Wingfield had described death: a matter of the fleeting instant — one moment here; the next, taken. The way a person, however much the object of adoration, lust, hate or envy, was transformed by death into a *thing*. She thought of Maurice Bridewell, his experiments, his obsessions, and she knew the meaning of his limitless creed.

Nothing ever is. Everything is becoming.

Every single soul on Earth is somewhere along the journey to destiny, she thought, as her foot landed on the top stair. But where does the journey end? What are we becoming? And is the destination identical for us all?

She pushed the door and entered a panelled chamber with high shuttered windows and walls dense with fabrics. It possessed the air of recent occupation, telling of a process begun, but not completed. Her eye was drawn to a stool waiting before an uncovered canvas. By its side sat a palette, untidy with use.

The painting was a family scene. It showed the Bridewells, the canvas dominated by Sir Rowland's wide-legged bulk. He stood sober in a cravat collar, his hand on the back of a chair, which was occupied by a woman. At his feet, a young child made a pretence of embroidery with cloth and a wooden needle. Georgie, she realised, far more obliging in oils than in life.

The seated figure was tiny, with a mane of tawny hair piled on her head, wearing a gown of mazarine blue. Behind her, a glowing light gave an aura of quiet domesticity. The family was harmonious, orderly: here was masterful father, obliging wife, obedient daughter.

The woman in the chair possessed no face. In place of her features, the oval was a cloud of near-white. She had become a ghost, here and yet not here, perfectly invisible.

She had once been Anne Bridewell. No longer.

Now she sat, caught in the act of transformation.

Catherine stopped a foot away from the portrait. She grazed the outline of the ghost and pulled her finger away. The paint was only just dry. Before its application, the peaks and troughs of the original oils had been sanded down with a diligent touch.

She ran her fingers across the sheen again, as if she could give the woman back her voice, her breath, everything that had been taken from her.

Across the room was another doorway. On the other side, screened by deep shadow, a figure was outlined.

Catherine said, 'It was you. All this time it was you.'

34

Arthur breathed the earthy scents of the crypt and held up his lantern. He stood in the freezing well of a walled space without windows, higher and longer than he had expected. To reach it, he had descended a spiral stair anticlockwise, and now looked up at a vaulted ceiling, calculating that he was roughly beneath the chancel. He paced the aisle, noting several low daises on either side. The oldest, nearest the walls, supported massive stone sarcophagi, heavily cobwebbed, likely containing the earliest generations of the Bridewell family. These he ignored; he was looking for something else.

He did not like this place. The dead held no fear for him, but the mausoleum communicated a despondent feeling that had nothing to do with the subterranean air, or its restful occupants. He detested every second spent here, and, although he could not quite explain the feeling, he suspected he suffered the effects of his certainty that something devilish had been concealed. The sensation was so strong, it almost caused him to abandon the venture and run back up into the clean, misty evening air. He could get on his horse and go anywhere, and let Sir Rowland Bridewell and his affairs rot.

He was still hesitating when his light fell on a low, rounded arch, going further into darkness. He moved in its direction and entered a short tunnel carved in stone, seeming to lead into the rock beneath the mound he had crested to reach the chapel. At the tunnel's end, he found what he sought. Against the rear wall, the more recently deceased members of the baronet's family were organised in dusty columns, their caskets stacked on top of one another in niches carved directly into the rock behind, each protected by a small barred door. He raised and lowered the lantern, searching for the newest box, and most likely the cheapest. Sir Rowland might have felt moved to have Emily Murphy buried in his own vault, but he certainly would not have dipped his hand any further into his pocket than necessary.

On the third sweep of the lantern, he found it. He peered into the niche, shining the light closer, and saw plain wood, not sturdy, and a cheap metal depositum. The near-mint condition of the casing suggested the body inside could not have been interred more than a few months. It stood at shoulder height and looked tightly wedged. Testing the door, he was relieved to find it opened easily. There was hardly room to lever the coffin out, but he put down the lantern, gripped the handles, and strained. For a few moments he was afraid it was too heavy, but then it shifted, sliding suddenly, allowing him to take its weight and lower it with care to the flags.

The depositum was etched shallowly: *Emily Murphy, d. 15th April 1852.*

The nails were hammered in close. He struck the wood hard with the cudgel until the end collapsed, then tugged the panel out, opening the contents to the air. Decay, strong and sweet, overwhelmed his senses. He coughed, shining the light, peering inside at the shrunken, shrouded shape. With a short prayer, thinking of bones and creeping, hungry things, he began to pull the corpse from its shell. The wrap, webbed and fragile, disintegrated in his fingers, so he took hold of the body by the shoulder blades, thankful for the thick leather of his gloves as the pads of his fingers sank into the decaying flesh. As she emerged like a moth from her chrysalis, he knew he was too late for some forms of knowledge – the decomposition was too advanced.

Even with more light and more time, he would not be able to ascertain definitively how she died.

Still, it might have something to tell him. He examined the plates of the skull, checking for injuries not recorded in Frederick's notebooks. The necessity of removing his gloves was regrettable, but he did so, and pressed his warm fingers to freezing bone, crêping skin, and a rill of long, dry hair. Nothing. No indentations or breaks. He felt his way along the rest of the body, disturbing her burial clothes. Reaching her feet, he held up one hand, pausing as though he had an audience.

'Wait,' he said.

He counted in inches, estimating, checking.

He thought, and counted again. After he had completed this exercise three times, he was certain. The corpse was roughly sixty inches tall. Five feet.

He thought of his grandfather's meticulousness: his ordered notebooks; the way, despite his recent habits of slovenliness, in the past, no effort was too great to record things correctly.

There was only one conclusion.

He stood, pulling his gloves back on. Though he was alone, and nobody could see him do it, he shook his head in revulsion at the darkness of this deed. He was needed back at Locksley. Miss Symonds was in danger, and what had been hidden here could not be allowed to go undiscovered.

35

Stepping into the room, the newcomer was slight, Catherine's exact height, and rustled faintly in a dark mantle. Though so familiar, known as intimately as Catherine's own reflection, nothing could have been so foreign.

Her own voice echoed thinly. 'You killed Anne Bridewell. You took her place.'

The answer came soft, nonchalant. 'Rowland killed Anne.'

Emily's face was angular and shadowed. She was beautiful, yet haggard in a way that had nothing to do with age. As Catherine looked, she realised something was absent from her sister's demeanour, but it was not sensuousness, or worldliness. Her dark hair was pinned high, her hands bare, and a locket of jet rested at her throat. Her eyes were wild like an animal's, black at their centres, pupils dissolving into lighter rings; and her mouth, with hardly any pink in the lips, was surrounded by a gauze of fine lines.

When Emily spoke again, her voice was hoarse, like someone had scraped away the inside of her throat. 'I tried to warn you. I wanted you to leave.'

'You stole my letters. My rings,' Catherine accused. The charges seemed petty and out of place, the type of thing one levels at a sister when still sharing a room, when neither can secure a space for themselves.

Emily stepped towards her. 'You always did hide things inside stockings.' She was a foot away. The jet gleaming in the hollow of her neck was carved with a rounded eye. Beneath, thin laces of scar tissue hinted at how the rope had scored her skin, and, as if in defiance of it, the space around that vivid blemish shone chalk-white.

'You put the key under my door,' Catherine said. 'Why would you try to help me?'

'It would have been better – easier for everyone – if you had left. But it's no matter. You're here now.' Emily lifted a hand and placed it against her sister's cheek. Catherine was at the same time eager for that contact, and desperate not to flinch. She was surprised to find Emily's touch as warm as her own.

'What did they do to you?' she asked.

'Who?'

'Bridewell and Caplin.'

Emily shrugged. 'You know what they did. You were there.'

'No. After. After they took me away.'

Emily stepped towards the fireplace. She put her arm out to steady herself against the stone. Catherine tracked her gaze; the mantel, like the one downstairs, was inlaid with the Bridewell words.

Nec terra nos tenere potest.

Emily said, 'After that night in the wood, when I came back to myself, I was blind. Sir Maurice said this showed the ritual had worked. My sight would be returned when I translated what I had seen into pictures. For him, it was that literal: a bargain between him and the Universe. I was the vessel into which the knowledge had been poured.' She closed her eyes, using the fingers of her right hand to trace her eyelids, then continued, wearily. 'Sir Maurice wanted to see past the span of his own life, to touch something greater. But he was like an ant trying to play a harpsichord; he didn't understand what he was doing. He should have kept to the domestic sphere, to dogs and horses. Most men are better suited to them.' She stroked the words on the marble, appearing thoughtful. Her nails held a blue-grey tinge. Catherine couldn't look, and turned away.

'What about Sir Rowland?' she asked. 'What did he know of his father's –' she searched for the word '– activities?'

'Nothing,' said Emily. 'I never laid eyes on him until I returned to Locksley. He was married by then, all frustration and resentment. He quickly saw his way to me, complaining of everything but the price of eggs: how Anne wouldn't play her part as his wife, how deeply he was in hock to Caplin, and how he couldn't divorce her – and certainly not replace her – until she inherited.' She glanced at the painting with contempt.

'And he knew what you intended?' Catherine asked disbelievingly.

'I told him how it would be: regardless of what we did, and of any outward appearance, I would not die. As far as the world was concerned, and the law, Anne would still be in her place. When Uriah Caplin died, I would inherit his fortune, and so it would pass to Rowland's control, exactly as he desired, and then to a male heir, when I provided the son Anne Bridewell couldn't.'

'But why would he go along with it?' Catherine asked, bewildered. 'Nobody would believe such a thing could happen.'

And yet it did happen, insisted the voice inside.

Emily continued. 'At first he agreed, but no, I don't think he believed me. Not sincerely. By the spring, he had tired of me. He had no genuine intention of being rid of Anne; her fortune was too bound up with Locksley's. Whatever else he wanted, he always planned to have her money.' She shrugged. 'I had become an inconvenience. I believe on one level he was pleased to think I would no longer be a problem. He likely thought the story I instructed him to tell the authorities – an unhappy governess who took her own life – was how it would be in reality. But he must have been persuaded enough – or curious or greedy enough – to go through with the plan; to see what would come of it.'

'So you went into the wood, and did – that heinous thing – to yourself?' The hubris of it shook Catherine to her centre. 'You have damned yourself.'

The answer was returned full of conviction. 'For another that might be true. Not for me.'

'You let it happen in front of Georgie …'

'Don't be a fool. We didn't intend on her discovering me. She wasn't to know anything about it. It was essential that she accept me as Lady Anne, at least eventually.'

Catherine almost scoffed. 'That's preposterous; she would never forget her mother.'

'Do you remember ours?' Catherine found her jaw fixed closed as Emily waved to the painting. 'Imagine. Three or four years from now, Locksley, its paintings restored to the walls, but where once you would see Anne Bridewell, now you see me. I am her. You have to remember, she was always reclusive. Poor Georgie was motherless from the start. And Locksley was distant from other great houses, so few could testify to my identity with any certainty.' She paused, perhaps thinking of those people, then returned to her tale. 'When it happened as it did before, he finally understood: he could have it all; be rid of the wife he hated, and still have her fortune.

'But Anne had to die. He balked, then, at the last. I thought he wouldn't go through with it, but by then he was so afraid of me, and perhaps even more terrified of the world knowing what he did, and what I was, he would have strangled himself had I ordered it.'

Catherine's blood ran cold. He killed the mother of his child, she thought. 'That's monstrous.'

Emily's eyes glittered. 'She was a Caplin.'

'She was innocent!' Her voice echoed in the draughty space. 'How could she be responsible for what her father did, any more than we were responsible for ours?'

Emily did not take up this question, and Catherine thought of something else. 'One thing I don't understand is how Sir Rowland knew how to find me to send William news. I can't believe you told him the whole story.'

'Of course not. He did what I told him to do. I said I had a sister – Mrs Drake. I simply provided the address and he told Lewis to write to you.'

Catherine thought again. 'But that means you knew,' she accused. 'You knew where I was, and you left me in the dark all that time.'

'Not all the time. I knew about the Lowe Hospital from Sir Maurice. I was able to trace you to the different families where you had a place, and eventually to Drake. It's not every day a man marries his under-housekeeper, after all.'

'Why didn't you write to me, if you knew where I was? Or visit?' *Visit.* It sounded absurd.

'Would you really have wanted a poor relation crawling out of the woodwork? Your fine new husband asking questions?'

'Of course. *Of course,*' Catherine insisted, seeing that Emily's face registered scepticism. 'I always wanted to know.' She didn't think she was believed. After all, was it entirely true? Could she not have found Emily sooner, if she had tried? She wanted to change the subject, and something else now occurred to her. 'What about Sir Rowland?'

'What about him?'

'You wanted Anne Bridewell dead because she was a Caplin. Very well.' Catherine frowned as the thought unfolded. 'But *he's* a Bridewell. Sir Maurice was just as guilty as Uriah Caplin – if not more so. So why revenge yourself on one family, but not the other?'

Emily's fingers ran over the tall male figure on the canvas. 'Rowland fears me. For now that's enough.'

Catherine, feeling there was still something here she didn't understand, turned away. But she understood the baronet better now. His ramblings in the cabinet room took on a terrifying clarity: transmutation, *evolutio*. One thing becoming another. She looked at her sister, watched her dead mouth, how words flowed from it just as they did from her own. It was at once a miracle and a blasphemy. Resurrection and damnation, together, in a single form.

No. She couldn't think about it. She had to concentrate on how the deception was achieved, or she would run mad.

She said, 'What about the other deaths?' Receiving no answer, she pressed on. 'It was you Mrs Parry saw in the passage, wasn't it? She saw you were a—' She didn't know how to continue. Blood pulsed in her ears. 'But you couldn't have killed Grizel. You're not strong enough.' She seized Emily's slender fingers. They were the mirror of her own. 'Did he do that, too?'

Emily pulled away. She took Catherine's arm easily in the crook of her elbow, and talked as if they were never separated, as if they were not quarrelling now. 'Hold, and I will tell you all. But I must go back to the beginning. Sir Maurice sent you to Lowe, but kept me here in this room. Each day he questioned me, exhorting me to paint. He knew that what Caplin refused to countenance was true: that, although the result was not exactly as they had anticipated, Cox's experiment had worked. I had gone beyond our world. I had seen what they thirsted to understand. There was no manipulation to which he would not stoop. He threatened to have me sent to the madhouse like you and Father. He even used Mother, reminding me that he might get good hospital care for her, expensive treatments, but only if I complied. If I painted what I had seen, she would have the very best of attention. If I refused, none.'

There seemed to be a plea for understanding in these words. Catherine could not help softening a fraction. It was as if, all these years, she had somehow etched her knowledge of her mother's death from her mind. Emily had been forced to bear it alone.

Emily went on. 'Sir Maurice paid your bills at Lowe, and he had Mother sent away to a hospital on the sea, near Newhaven. She died the same year, but not in very great pain, he assured me.'

'And you painted?'

'What I remembered.'

Whatever Emily had seen, or thought she had seen, surely only evil could come of it. But the need to know was there, itching at her, and Catherine gave in. 'Show me.'

Emily took her arm again, and guided her into the room beyond.

The next chamber felt more like a tower room, darker, more open to the elements. Tall, narrow windows, a flagged floor and a mean heap burning in the grate dominated her impressions. Shivering, she glimpsed the evening outside, seeing how the grey day subsided. A wind whistled in the chimney breast. She disliked the thought of Emily sitting up here all these months, turning over her revenge. Then, as Emily went about lighting more lamps, Catherine saw how she had employed her time.

The walls were oak panelling carved with bear's breeches and vines, yet little of the wood was visible; any spare inch, it seemed, was mounted with a painting. Emily had had nothing to do here but paint, and as Catherine spun about the middle of the room, every direction revealed some new wonder: a dilapidated castle mourned the end of its rule over a steep-sided valley; winter willows drew bare fingers over a tumbling stream; a convocation of jagged columns serenaded a distant ship; a little shepherdess slumbered in the sun, oblivious of towering thunderheads moving in.

Most of one wall was taken up by a single painting. This scene was unlike the others. For a few moments she stared, trying to make sense of it.

Dust. Held in its vast frame, a red sandstorm marauded across a landscape of immeasurable bleakness. Its shape resisted definition, but it seemed to move out of the frame like a whirlwind, and cruel tongues of sand and rock lashed their path towards her. She felt them colonising the back of her throat, overwhelming her breath, thickening her tongue. Within that maelstrom, the sand was not fine and ephemeral, but muscular and voracious, its voice insidious, whispering of inevitability, telling her the insignificant things of her short life – its loves, memories, fears – were already lost. She looked harder, and as she stared, it seemed the heart of that storm was alive, and shadows occupied its centre, in forms she could not name; but they were purposeful, alive.

Emily continued. 'I was …' She considered, then said, more forcefully, 'I think I was pure spirit. I ached to stay, but that world would not accept me.' She paused, moving away into some private domain, then seemed to come nearer again. 'Then it ended. I saw only dust, dust clouding my sight, stretching forever. Their laughter filled my ears, and their mockery was terrible. I could not have borne it any longer than I had to. That place, that for another might have been a Heaven, for me was Hell.

'But it was worse to be sent back. You can't know how much worse. To walk in the world as just one unintended thing, knowing every blade of grass I crushed, every innocent crawling thing I trod on, should have lived. To be just one thing that should not be, it is too much. It is to walk as a god. Or a devil.'

As Catherine turned away from the picture, she saw, at last, what was missing. It was not her sister's beauty; it was her original, motivating force. She stood here no longer quite alive, though she breathed, and was at once unfinished and corrupted.

'I painted blind,' said Emily flatly, as they gazed up at the canvas. 'I don't even recall doing it. But when I had finished, as Sir Maurice had said, my sight returned.'

'Then what?' Catherine asked. She hated the picture, and turned her back on it.

Emily said, 'I asked Sir Maurice to let me go. I had done what he wanted – surely, I thought, he would send me home, allow me to return to Mother, and to you.' Her mouth twisted in mockery of her hopes. 'He did not. I was his prize. I possessed the knowledge he had spent a lifetime and a fortune trying to acquire. He was never going to let me leave. I had to act for myself.

'Sir Maurice would allow me nothing I might use to hurt myself. I refused food. I wondered, if I were sufficiently determined, whether I might be accepted, finally taken. But I found it did not matter. I did not fade.' She shrugged. 'To this day, although I consume certain things from habit, I need to eat very little. Possibly nothing at all. It didn't work, anyway. It was nearly a year before I could get away.

'I pretended to comply. I told him I had more paintings in me, more knowledge he could squeeze out, but he would have to let me see the sky and the trees. He agreed. I let him think I had accepted my confinement at Locksley, returning again and again to this tower over months, never letting him see my true feelings, until eventually he trusted me enough, when other members of the household were away, or very early in the morning, to allow me to walk alone in the grounds. When I had the chance, I took it, and ran.'

'Where?'

'East. I found work.' She looked at the room's rich trappings. 'I knew I would come back here. The disappointment of losing me – or of losing what I had in my head – must have been too much for him. Several months after I disappeared – or so I know now – he abandoned Locksley for Italy. But I could still get to Rowland. I could still touch his son. First I had to discover everything I could about him. I had to know his weaknesses.'

A hard voice sounded in the doorway. 'And what did you learn?'

The sisters turned.

Sir Rowland stood at the top of the stairs in his shirtsleeves. He was a ghastly shade of white. His gaze fell on Emily, and Catherine was reminded of Mrs Parry's expression in the moment before she fell. Here was no passion, pity or remnant of affection; just undiluted horror.

'You shouldn't have come here,' he told Catherine, without taking his eyes off Emily.

'Sir Rowland—'

He hardly seemed to see Catherine. 'You're … destruction,' he told his lover. 'Everything festering and diseased. Every day since …' The power of coherent speech had been stolen from him. '… unnatural, perverted thing …' He shuddered visibly. 'I've hardly closed my eyes without seeing it.'

His left hand had been steadying his body against the door-frame, but now shifted downwards. It was only then, having felt he was going to take some desperate course, but not knowing which, that Catherine saw the gun in his other hand. She cried out a warning.

Emily, too, got out a word. 'Rowland—'

'Demon,' he said, raising up the gun. His arms shook, but he fired. The barrel flashed white, and her lover's bullet struck Emily high in the chest. As the noise of the shot reverberated, she stared at him for several moments before falling with her dark mantle pooling around her. Catherine let out another cry and dropped to her knees.

Sir Rowland heard the agony in that cry. He perspired in the doorway with the gun against his shoulder, half-obscured by smoke from the barrel. 'What's this?' he said, looking about as if only just realising where he was, and seeing something he did not understand.

Sobbing, Catherine gathered her sister's head in her lap. Moments ago, her feelings had veered between disbelief and terror, but beneath that there had coursed elation, because she had found Emily again.

Now Emily was dying.

Sir Rowland took a step back, muttering, '... the end. Georgie can't stay. We'll go together. Be saved, together.' It hardly registered when he turned and fled down the stairs.

Catherine's hands were pressed to Emily's chest, blood from the wound soaking her fingers. She wondered, half-deliriously, whether the flow might subside – like a miracle. The impossible had happened twice before. Why not again?

But it didn't, and soon Emily's hand gripped hers, pulling it away. Catherine put it back, pressing down insistently. Emily did it again, this time squeezing her sister's hand, forcing stillness. Her lips moved rapidly, trying to form words. Catherine couldn't make sense of it.

She stared, appalled, as Emily's lids closed and her breath grew shallow. It took a minute or so, and when she was gone, Catherine watched for long moments, searching for the other half of herself. The skin over her sister's fine bones was impossibly white, her lashes dark. She looked more alive in death. Catherine released her gently to the floor and folded her hands together at her middle.

Sir Rowland was going to find Georgie.

She could not stay here.

The baronet's words had been dark and turbulent. She was certain what he would do. He would not live in disgrace, or as a petty, defeated man like his father. He would be masterful. He would shape the world the way he wanted it. He would take Georgie with him.

She found herself running.

36

The mastiffs raised a cacophony as Arthur neared the house. He moved at a half-march, the cudgel swinging at his side. As he approached, he shouted, 'Bridewell! Come out, you bastard!'

Sir Rowland had betrayed his own men. He had used Arthur as his dupe, and robbed Frederick of life. And he had done worse. Arthur had measured the corpse beneath the Bridewell chancel. He had compared it to his grandfather's notes. Emily Murphy had been of medium height – five feet and five inches. The body Bridewell had buried under her name was too small, practically childlike. He had realised, thinking back, how his grandfather had described Lady Anne as *tiny*. During the short time in which Arthur conversed with her, or was deceived into thinking so, at Locksley, he had been distracted by Grizel Wingfield's death. He had failed to see what was staring him in the face. The woman he had met, with her lilting French enunciation and sharp eyes, was of average height. He suspected five feet and five inches exactly.

The body in the crypt was Anne Bridewell, and not Emily Murphy at all.

Sir Rowland had killed his wife and replaced her with his lover. Worse, he had compromised Frederick's honour, persuading him to lie to conceal his own crimes. No wonder Frederick had hated him. That act, in Arthur's eyes, loomed largest. As he thought of it, his own courage, long-buried, crept up, combining with a cold rage. His debt to Sir Rowland would be paid, and paid in full.

He skirted the building. As he rounded the east lawn, there was movement in the mist. Bathed in the light from the French windows, Sir Rowland's shape was unmistakeable. At his side stumbled the boyish figure of his daughter. Arthur listened hard, making out a brutish grunt, and her cry as her father dragged her off.

'Bridewell!' he shouted.

Sir Rowland half-turned. Arthur was not trying to hide – it was the opposite – but a cedar blocked the baronet's full view of his pursuer, who emerged from under its dripping branches on to the terrace. Recognising Arthur, Sir Rowland lifted Georgie and carried her towards the drystone boundary. Georgie cried out as he sped up, but the baronet was older and heavier than the doctor, running in darkness with his daughter slung over his shoulder. Arthur, breaking into a sprint, gained on him easily.

The baronet must have realised he could not outpace his pursuer. After a short chase, he turned at bay. 'Get back!' he shouted wildly. 'I warn you! Back!'

Arthur could only see his quarry's outline, but a sound came distinctly: the cock of a hammer. He could not see the little girl, only hear her sobbing. 'It's over,' he said. 'I know everything.'

'You know nothing. You don't know … can't tell what I've done.'

Arthur could not say more in front of the child, but Sir Rowland had to see his deception was discovered. 'I went to the vault. I found her. I know you had my grandfather lie.'

He could not understand Sir Rowland's fevered laugh, or his answer. 'Poor Sidstone. Still as much in the dark as ever.'

'What are you talking about?'

'You know nothing,' he said again. His voice trembled.

Arthur was reshaping his view of what the baronet might do. 'Georgie, can you hear me?' he called.

'Yes,' came the shaky reply.

'Don't speak to her,' barked Sir Rowland.

'I'm not going to move,' Arthur said, keeping his voice level. It was essential Sir Rowland did not feel cornered. 'You have a chance – just one – to get away. But you have to leave her here.'

'She's my blood. She'll do as she's told.'

'No.' Arthur looked for movement in the gloom ahead. 'You have one shot. You could take it, but you'd most likely miss, and then I would be on you. Release her to me and take your chances.'

'Dr Sidstone!' The words came from behind him. A woman's voice, frightened, but with relief at realising he was there.

'Miss Symonds?' he answered.

The call was repeated. In the dark ahead, Arthur heard rustling, then Georgie's cry as she was dragged off again.

'Doctor!' the governess shouted. 'I'm here!'

He retraced several steps, trying to find her. He was torn, knowing Sir Rowland got further away, but feeling he could not leave Miss Symonds alone either. He shouted back, trying to show where he stood.

Then came a high, woeful noise that filled the air, silencing them both.

They each knew what it was.

Someone had released the dogs.

With a deepening horror, Arthur thought of Morpheus, roaming free at the head of the pack.

Miss Symonds reached him. He felt for her in the dark, catching her shaking hands. She was straining for breath.

'I'm sorry. I understand now,' he said.

'He'll kill her,' she warned.

The dogs' howls rose in Arthur's ears. They were closer. He shifted his lantern to illuminate her ashen face. 'You must get indoors,' he said. 'The pack is abroad.'

'I'm coming with you.'

He hesitated, but with every second Sir Rowland drew further away, and the devilish creatures nearer. They were being hunted. A thought needled him: who let the pack out? Sir Rowland? Or Emily, in defence of her lover? These questions whirled about his mind, mingled with the savage sounds of the chase.

'If the dogs come upon us, stay behind—'

She was already moving. 'Follow me,' she said. 'I know where he's going.'

'Where?'

'The yew tree.'

Behind them, more distinct, more terrifying with every second, came the noise of the pack. Sir Rowland was still ahead. Arthur cursed himself for allowing him such a start. Those seconds where he had allowed Miss Symonds to find him had cost him, and now the chase was harder.

'He has a gun,' he gasped.

'I know. He shot her.'

'Who?'

'Emily.'

His head spun. 'But—'

Her words came in bursts. 'He was terrified of her. Eaten up by his fear.'

Arthur had no idea what to make of this. They ran on. At one point Miss Symonds fell and he went back, but she was already scrambling to her feet.

'Don't wait for me,' she ordered. 'Go!' He felt she was different from the woman he had recovered earlier from this same wood. There was nothing wraith-like about her now.

'I must confess something,' he panted, as they went on.

'What?'

'When Grizel Wingfield pinched the child, I saw. I saw her do it, I mean. I lied.'

'I know.'

'I was a coward.'

'You're not now.'

'I should have done better.'

They kept climbing. After a while, the shrubbery thinned. As they emerged into a clearing. With his lantern, it wasn't completely dark. The yew stood stalwart, looming over what he could just make out: a shadow at its roots.

'Miss Symonds!'

It was Georgie. They hurried towards her, but Sir Rowland's growl came out of the dark. 'No closer. I'll kill her.'

Miss Symonds still walked forward. Arthur tried to pull her back but his fingers slid off the fabric of her dress. 'It's done,' she said. 'Emily is dead. Take your own life if you must, but Georgie is innocent.'

Georgie sobbed. 'Father, I don't understand!'

'Don't worry,' said Miss Symonds to the child, her voice very gentle. 'Your father is unwell.'

'Ah ...' Sir Rowland groaned. 'The devilish ensnarements of that smothering demon. My father knew ... knew all things were possible. Knew what could arise from the black pit to walk upon the Earth. A creature, a monster! I did not know myself. I should have killed her at the first ...'

His words were horribly obscure. That Arthur could not see him made them worse. They seemed to be all around them, to come from inside him; he felt filthy, like Sir Rowland's madness could sink into his skin.

'She's dead,' Miss Symonds repeated, taking another step. 'You're safe. There's no need for Georgie to suffer.'

Sir Rowland's harsh breaths were her only answer.

As they waited, Arthur realised, with a sense of deep misgiving, that the dogs had fallen quiet.

He moved a yard, but something disturbed him underfoot. He didn't think, didn't know why he acted, but bent and dug it out.

His gloved hand closed on something rounded, cylindrical, smoother than a stick. He almost threw it aside, but did not have a chance, because just then, a searing whistle broke the silence, and the shadows ran amok.

It took him several seconds to realise what had happened: the pack had been waiting somewhere nearby. Now they had broken the cover of the wood.

As Morpheus stalked out of the night, Arthur tightened his jaw. Never had he felt so exposed, bracing for their attack, and never more like what he was: soft, yielding flesh.

But just as he expected their teeth, the pack went straight past him and Miss Symonds, surging towards Sir Rowland and the child.

A bellow came from beneath the tree: Sir Rowland, his voice rising as he ordered the dogs. What was happening? Why did they not obey him?

The baronet's shouts grew shrill, then turned to shrieks.

Arthur would have groped for Miss Symonds's hand and tried to run if it hadn't been for Georgie Bridewell. He couldn't leave her to the pack.

Dropping his lantern, he ran towards the melee, but stopped at its writhing mass. He couldn't make sense of it – the space where the baronet had stood with his daughter had become a lawless coil, wild with snarls. Steeling himself, he dived in and spun about in the heat of the creatures' breath. Hoarse cries rose around him as the mastiffs shook and tore, seemingly oblivious to the misery of the man who had been, until now, their master.

The smell of blood was sickening. Somewhere to his left the little girl was screaming. He reached out, pushing away the muscular forms of the dogs. Agony flared near his left forearm; one of the beasts clung on as he shook his arm violently, trying to break its grip, but its jaws were iron-locked. Tightening his hold on the cudgel, he struck its broad head, hard, repeating the blow. It fell away, but had torn into the muscle. His left arm hung useless.

He ignored the pain and with his other arm wielded the cudgel, trying to reach the heart of the fight without hitting the child. Somehow he got there and pulled the shaking girl off her feet. She clung to his neck as he scrambled away from the pile-on, burying her in his coat to shield her from the tearing and ripping coming from the huddle that had been Sir Rowland and the pack.

He reached Miss Symonds, who took Georgie from him and set her on the ground. 'Let's go,' she urged.

He looked back. 'I don't understand.' He was breathless, staring as the dogs settled to their work. 'Why would they attack him?'

'Now,' she insisted.

He nodded and slipped the thing he had picked off the ground into his breast pocket, then found his light, just in time to see Ned step out of the treeline.

37

'Ned!' Catherine's heart was still racing, but her stance softened.

Ned had Coke with him. The little dog seemed to cower as the collier raised his hand, holding Catherine in place while he gave a whistle to the others. One by one, the mastiffs, their jaws dripping with gore, abandoned their grisly prize. She stared as they crowded him, whining with a high pleasure, and he put his hands on them. They rubbed against his thighs and did their best to part his knees with their domish heads, and he lavished praise on them.

Georgie whimpered into Catherine's middle. She clutched her governess tightly and Catherine tried to keep her from seeing, but her own gaze was fixed beneath the yew tree where, just visible in the glow of the lantern, no sound rose from the thing huddled in its roots. On her right side, the doctor panted and examined his arm, where she thought he had been bitten. After a few seconds he stood easier.

'You came at the right moment, Ned,' he said. 'You have a talent with them.' He nodded to the pack.

'My dad fed them,' Ned said, watching the creatures. Morpheus directed a snarl at a smaller dog that tried to get near the collier. Chastened, the other animal retreated. 'I'd help him, so they got used to me. They're not that different to people. They'd only tolerate so many of his beatings before they hated him.' He rubbed Morpheus's ears, then gave another short whistle. Obediently, the dogs rested on their haunches before his feet.

'You were collecting your aunt's things?' asked Dr Sidstone.

'Edie said she'd let me in at the back door if I was quick.'

'Well, thank heavens you followed us,' answered the doctor. 'It could have gone badly here otherwise.'

Catherine eyed the mastiffs. Their presence, though they were calm now, frightened her. 'Who released them?' she asked. 'Sir Rowland?'

Before Ned could reply, Georgie dropped down with a soft cry. Catherine called out to Dr Sidstone, who dipped to his knees to feel the little girl's pulse. 'She'll be all right,' he said. 'She's had a shock.' As the doctor laid Georgie on her side, Catherine peered at the dogs, then off in the other direction to where Ned moved towards the yew. He had the lantern, and seemed to be searching for something.

Dr Sidstone's voice drifted up. 'My grandfather is dead. Murdered, by poison.'

She wanted to feel more for him, to acknowledge the grief in his words, but, in the midst of all this death, found she could hardly feel anything. 'I'm sorry,' she said.

'He ... he was deep in Sir Rowland's lie. He identified Anne Bridewell's corpse as being your sister's.'

Catherine said definitely, 'No, that wasn't how it happened.'

'What do you mean?'

She paused. He already thought her mad. He was not going to credit her tale. Nobody would. Shaking her head, she said, 'You have to trust me.'

'Tell me,' he said, distress breaking through his voice.

'Let's just get Georgie back to the house.'

'Yes,' he agreed. 'Ned, will you help me with her?'

Catherine glanced to where the collier's outline was visible beneath the soft, poisonous branches. He appeared to have found what he was looking for, and held something in his hands.

'Ned?' said Dr Sidstone. 'Help me, would you?'

'I'm sorry, Arthur,' said Ned. 'That won't be possible.'

Dr Sidstone raised his head from Georgie to his friend. Ned held the gun loaded and cocked. He pointed the barrel at the doctor.

Rising, with confusion in his voice, Dr Sidstone said, 'Ned, what the—'

The sound was deafening. It took Catherine several seconds to understand, as the explosion was accompanied by Dr Sidstone's violent exhalation of breath, that a bullet had struck him somewhere in his middle. For a few moments the doctor stood staring at his attacker, then he pressed his hand to his body before drawing it away to look. His legs crumpled, and he slumped, letting out anguished moans, curling his tall frame around his abdomen.

The dogs howled. Their master – for Catherine had no doubt now of who that was – silenced them with a loud *tsk*, then whistled long and low, and the pack sidled off into the trees.

Ned took a step towards Dr Sidstone, and stood over him. 'Believe me,' he said. 'I wish I hadn't had to do that. I wish there was another way.'

The doctor wheezed, a high, uneasy noise. Ned stared down, muttering something to himself. Forgotten for the moment, Catherine had a chance to run. The darkness was deep, protective. She might weave through the trees, and ...

She couldn't leave Georgie. She knelt and gripped her charge's listless hand, then lifted her head. 'I don't understand,' she said quietly. 'I don't understand where you fit in this.'

Ned let out a short laugh. 'Why would you? I'm just a hewer.'

'You released the dogs.'

'They come to my command now. Sir Rowland always was careless in how he treated those that served him.'

'But why, Ned? For revenge? For the colliery?'

No.

'You ...'

Even as she spoke, the threads swirled. Somewhere there was a link, something Ned had told her that would explain …

She saw it.

Emily's motivations had remained shrouded in confusion. She had craved revenge on Uriah Caplin, and had taken it – Anne Bridewell, Anne Caplin as she had been, was dead. But to realise her desires, Emily had allied herself to Sir Rowland. That had sat ill with Catherine, not because she pitied Sir Rowland – although now, having heard his torments, she found she did – but because the whole enterprise made no sense. Why would Emily revenge herself on one of her enemies, but not the other? Why shackle herself for life to a man she despised?

The answer? She had not.

Ned was her true ally. Her lover.

'It was you and Emily all along. You met your sweetheart in the West Country,' she said, invoking his words at their first meeting. 'Before all this even began.' She made the next connections. 'You broke into Locksley. You strangled Grizel. Emily d—'

She had stopped herself just in time. Ned didn't know what Sir Rowland had done. He didn't know his accomplice was already dead. If he discovered Emily was gone, she would have nothing with which to influence him. She continued carefully. 'She doesn't have the strength to do what your hands could.'

Ned said flatly, 'Nobody will miss the Wingfield woman. We had no choice.'

'You killed Frederick Sidstone for the same reason,' she said, her thoughts darting to the inescapable conclusion. 'And Mrs Parry – your own blood!'

She did not think she imagined his flinch. But he gathered himself quickly. 'Anyone who knew Emily … We were so nearly clear. Then you came along. I saw it straight away – you moved like her, talked like her. I went to her, and she admitted it.'

'But she wouldn't let you kill me, would she?'

'We just wanted you gone. I worked to get Arthur to see it couldn't have been you who did the killings. If you'd just left, it would have worked out. But you had to keep interfering. Then when I came to finish it, I realised Emily had given you the key herself.' A beat of silence followed. 'She'll see it's for the best in the end.'

'No,' Catherine said, thinking furiously. 'There will be police, an investigation. There's no chance this will end well for you. But if you talk to me, we can find a way ...'

He was so close she could smell the gunpowder, taste his sweat. The endearing plainness of his former intonation had gone. She realised it had been a veneer from the beginning. This was a new person, one she did not know at all. *'Maddened by his grandfather's death of accidental poisoning, willing to blame anybody, the doctor chased Sir Rowland through the wood. Sir Rowland turned his gun on him in self-defence. But the dogs, in a fit of ferocity, attacked the wrong target, and it was all over for the baronet.* It will be in the papers, just as I tell it. Not that you'll see it.'

'You'll be found out. The poisoning—'

He snorted. 'Do you have any idea how many things have arsenic in? How easy it was to take it from Dowle's locker? I'll make that scene look any way I want.' He turned to what had been Sir Rowland. *'The baronet, always too convinced of his own skill, misjudged his control over his dogs. They attacked him.'* He looked down at his feet and said, more softly, 'And poor Arthur. Desperate for a friend, for a lover, desperate to be a good man.'

She shuddered. 'What about Georgie? What about me?'

'You conspired with Dowle and Harris to rob Sir Rowland through the colliery accounts. You had some connection – I don't know exactly what yet. Between you, you murdered Grizel Wingfield; then, when Sir Rowland got wise, you took the little girl and disappeared. She's probably dead. They'll search a while, but here's how it ends: Lady Anne – poor, unlucky woman – keeps her father's fortune. After a while she emigrates, and sometime later, it's rumoured she remarried. The newly-weds stay abroad, of course. Somewhere warm, fat with good things, near the sea. They'll have horses.'

'We disappeared?' Catherine said, desperate to sound scoffing. The truth was that they had thought of everything. She could not tell him his plan already lay in ruins, and Emily was dead, because he would have nothing at all to lose. He would kill them. 'Even if they believe all that, they'll never stop looking for Georgie. She's the heiress to Locksley: they'll search this wood forever.'

'They'll never find her. Not where we're going.'

His words reverberated with dark purpose. She knew he would not be persuaded, and made her choice, grabbing the insensate Georgie by the arm. She tried to lift her, but she was a dead weight. Within seconds, Ned's powerful fingers were at the roots of her hair. She kicked and screamed as he brought her low, trying to prevent him dragging her, but it was no good. She called out to Dr Sidstone, but he was dying, or dead.

They were pulled across rugged ground for what seemed like miles. Eventually, he stopped and forced her to stand. She brushed dirt from her lips and nose and breathed heavily. The terrier, Coke, had disappeared. Their captor looked about and handed her the lantern. 'Carry it,' he grunted. They went on. She had little awareness of time. The trees crowded round, impassive, observing their course through the forest's heart-land. After a distance she could not have measured, he stopped again, and she raised the lantern, searching for the reason. Before them, darkness loomed against the lighter black of the sky. Not more trees, she saw, after a few seconds, but a vertiginous slope, blocking out the moon, shrinking her shaking light to nothing.

He was behind her. She was shoved roughly to her knees. He gripped her shoulders, his thighs hard against her back. She closed her eyes as he bent, his words hot in her ear.

'Run, or do anything unless I say do it, and I'll break her neck.'

She nodded. He tightened his grip, stealing her breath until she thought she would lose consciousness. When he released her, she took in air hungrily. He said, 'Say it out loud.'

'I won't run.'

He placed Georgie on the ground. She checked the little girl, who seemed to be coming round, then sat, listening. The next sound was unfamiliar, but she soon realised what it was: the scrape of wood and metal against rock. He was disbarring a door. The door into the mine, into the mountain itself. Parry had called it the drift road.

The knowledge of what he intended brought a crawling horror over her skin. She anticipated the moment of passing into the darkness, the clean air being snatched away, the mine door closing on them, before being forced down, right to the roots of the Earth. It felt like hands around her throat. There would be no hope of rescue. Nobody knew where they were. Sir Rowland had abandoned the colliery. They would never be found. It was a place for the dead.

She shook Georgie, saying, 'Get up!' The little girl was still drowsy and had started to cry. Catherine thought she might persuade her to run, but Georgie did not seem to understand what she wanted, and Ned returned before another few seconds had gone by. They were hauled to their feet.

He dragged them to the door, which now stood open, and pushed against the small of her back. Her heart quailed before the black cleft in the rock. She stared, but could see nothing. Inhaling deeply, taking in something cold and stale, she looked up and tried to catch sight of the stars winking, or the curve of the slender moon. The mountain loomed too high. Ned shoved her again. Holding Georgie's hand in hers, both shaking, they took their first steps through the door, between the rough tunnel walls. The space was shockingly narrow, its walls seeming to lean closer with every foot they walked. She tasted bile. This wasn't her world. It was his, darker even than in her nightmares.

She tried to stretch, to see whether it was really as tight as she imagined. Her arms were only half-raised before her palms scraped the craggy stone. The passage could be no more than three feet wide. She stopped dead. 'I can't,' she said, a sob rising. 'I can't.' Ned's only answer was another jab in the small of her back, forcing her forward.

Their descent was not obvious at first, but as they went on she realised they were moving downwards with every uneven step. The tunnel twisted in on itself and back again; they passed doorways into other veins carved in the rock, and soon she lost count of the number of turns they had taken. All the time Georgie's hand quivered in hers, and Catherine whispered platitudes she did not believe. *It will be all right. Don't be frightened.*

But there was every reason to be frightened. The doctor was dead. Emily was gone. She and Georgie would sink into this dark, still place, lower even than the rotting things, than the men who had died here, their lungs burning as they gasped for one more breath.

Her own breath came harder. Each took more effort, and she realised it was the air; whether she imagined it or not, it felt polluted, thickening, like she breathed filthy water.

The tunnel got tighter and the roof inclined even more steeply. At the drift door, the passage had been tall enough to allow a man to walk unbowed. Now, behind her, Ned was almost bent double. Her knees ached, and she was no longer able to stand straight. She sucked in air, knowing they had zigzagged so far into the blackness she could not remember the way out. *You won't need to*, said the voice inside.

Ned began to talk. 'This mine is a useless flaccid cock of a thing. Bridewell's lies were the only thing keeping it running. He borrowed so much from Caplin he couldn't turn back. We would hew tons of rock out of the hill, but hardly any coal.'

She was despairing of finding a means to throw him off. He seemed to know his way in the blackness by instinct alone. Part of her believed him inhuman, belonging to this subterranean world as she never could.

But he wasn't inhuman. He was like nearly all men; he wanted to talk. She could use that.

'You always intended to kill him, and for Emily to inherit Caplin's money?' she said.

'We were going to leave it a time. A year, we guessed, until the rumours died down.'

'Yes,' she said, trying to keep her voice level, and panic out of it. 'She's your fortune.' She took Georgie's shoulders in her hands. Could she gamble both their lives on her next words?

She had no choice. 'It's a shame she's dead.'

'What did you say?'

Ten yards ahead, the lantern illuminated another doorway leading off the main tunnel. She thought about how many steps that might be – twenty? Could they – or at least Georgie – get there before he could?

'Dead,' she said flatly. 'Sir Rowland killed her. Unless you really believe the nonsense she spoon-fed you about coming back to life?' She let out a laugh. Big and brittle, it boomed in the tiny space. 'Don't tell me ... Oh, Ned!' She used her other voice, the rich-woman's voice, pouring into it all the derision and condescension she had heard all her life from the sort of woman he hated. The sort of woman he desired. The sort of woman he would ache to own, and to kill.

It worked. He leapt for her throat. As he bellowed with rage, shoving her into a dripping pillar, she pushed Georgie towards the doorway, screaming, 'Run!'

Georgie ran. Catherine counted her steps – five paces, ten – as Ned abandoned her and took off after the little girl.

Even slowed by the low roof, scurrying with the lantern and his knees bent, he was faster.

Catherine heard her charge scream as she was dragged back down the narrow confines of the passageway. Georgie's kicks and shouts had no effect on her captor. She was reunited with her governess, and both were pushed to kneeling.

Her knees rested on churned-up mud and pebbles. She searched behind her for anything she could use. The wall was freezing, damp, thick with fungus. The floor was bare.

'Sometimes they bring the ponies this way,' he said, slumping opposite.

How far had they come? she wondered. How far under the mountain were they?

Ned went on. 'They have to blindfold them otherwise they won't obey. They know what the dark means. Miles of it, years, never feeling the sun on their faces. They hitch them up to those drams and take their money's worth. Poor little bastards pull and pull every day until they die. Thirty-one, they made me shoot. When their legs go and they look at you with so much trust, so much love, and you put the barrel of your gun between their eyes and pull the trigger, it's the worst thing in the world. Nothing loves like a horse.'

She groped in the dirt, but there was nothing, just fragile shards of rock.

He got to his feet again. His voice was conversational, all his anger seemingly vanished. She knew what this meant: he would kill them soon. 'Ever been underground before? Not like this. I don't mean these shallowlands. I mean deep under.

As deep as Govannon. Ever heard the timbers that hold the mountains back from cracking your skull creak with the weight of what's on top, and known, if they break, that even if anyone comes looking for you, all they'll find is dust? Ever known you'd be a slap on the wrist at some inquest years away, another telling-off for some rich fucker, a page in his diary so he can read about himself in front of the fire when he's ninety and his knees feel like mine do now, like they're on fire every time he takes a step, and he's set to hand all you've dug on to the next bastard, so he can do the same? Ever known, if you died, all anyone would have to do is say sorry, and nothing – nothing in the world – would change? That he's taken the very air out of your lungs? Have you ever heard the voices in the dark, telling you it can change, be another way, that they're no different to you, no better, that there's not good blood and bad blood and blue blood? There's blue enough down here, shining. I see it. They can't. But the blood in that fat shite Bridewell's veins was red. You saw it. You were glad to see it. Just like me. A servant. We're the same. You hate them as much as I do.' He took a step nearer.

He was right: she was nobody, just a servant.

And she had the things servants had.

She loosened the string of her front pocket and dug inside. Her hand closed on what she found there. He was still talking. His voice seemed to come from everywhere at once. He knew this place, was part of the underground; he belonged here, and she, who had never really belonged anywhere, did not.

His hands claimed her in the dark, his fingers closing around her neck. His thumbs reached her larynx, and as he squeezed she closed her eyes, trying to hold to Georgie's childlike scent, and fend off his smell, caught up with gunpowder, sweat and blood. Georgie was screaming. He pushed deeper into the flesh, cutting off her breath. She resisted the desperate urge to claw at his skin.

If she gave herself up to that instinct, she would lose her only chance.

She gathered herself, and gave him no warning. In place of panic, her body flooded with satisfaction – no sin or guilt – as she rammed the scissor blades in hard beneath his chin, into the soft, vital parts of him.

Blood sprayed her face. He roared his fury, and his hands fell away from her throat. She drank in greedy breaths of cold air before realising she had not struck deep enough. The gouging points had turned. He was still coming. She twisted, offering up all her rage and terror to whatever lived beneath these hills, and as he raked her skin beneath his nails, she ducked, slipping beneath his reach. His striking elbow cast the scissors from her hand. They clattered down to the rocks and rubble, lost.

She reached blindly and grasped a handful of soft fabric and hot skin. Georgie. Ned had hold of the light now. It sculpted the lines of his face into shadows and ridges; he no longer looked handsome. He grappled with his throat where she had stabbed him, and for a moment she thought he gurgled blood, but as he wiped his mouth with his sleeve and spat, he advanced.

Grabbing Georgie, she pulled the child along. Ned followed. The three of them weaved, stumbling against the rough-hewn walls, through the doorway, deeper into the dark. The road angled downwards and the passage narrowed even further. She wheezed, unable to repel thoughts of the unimaginable mass of rock above. In her mind's eye, it collapsed, entombing them, and she fought the impulse to scream. Turning her head to their pursuer, she saw, closing with every fraction of a second, an orb of light. Blinding against the backdrop, it moved implacably.

With it came Ned's voice.

'… then I'll be the master here, and I'll cut down every tree. I'll have them dig out every cubit of these hills, hollow them out, sell off every rock and speck of dust …'

She and Georgie collided as the corridor tapered. The walls scraped their bodies, tearing skin. Georgie tugged and they lurched forward together. The ceiling came down and down, so close to her crown she smashed her skull against the rock, and reeled in pain. Her lungs screamed.

She looked. The light had nearly caught them.

'Stop!' She did not know what brought her up sharp; perhaps a draught, or a reek of something deeper riding the stale air. She put out her arm and held Georgie stock-still. 'Don't move,' she gasped.

Stars filled her vision. Unseen, a freezing current snaked across her face, and she stared into the blackest black she could imagine. Though she could discern nothing, she knew in her marrow, something had changed. Feeling ahead, her boot hit air, then something hard. Reaching down, she fumbled. What she touched was cold and splintered. With her other hand, she moved across and felt another object, just the same, a stump sticking up out of the rocky ground. Then, as she groped, she realised she clutched the top section of a ladder. Stretching into the dark, she felt further and her flesh met the first mouldy rung. She recoiled. Before them, invisible, was a shaft. They were poised precisely on its edge. She shuddered to think of what would have happened if they had taken another step.

They could not see beyond the pit, or its extent. The opening might have been two feet across, or sixty.

Stay, or run. Down, or across. Climb, or jump into air.

'Hold my hand,' she said.

'Miss Symonds—'

'Listen to me—'

'But—'

Georgie's hand pulled, but she yanked the child close and whispered in her ear. 'We have to go down.'

'No, look!' Georgie's voice rose, determined. 'He's stopped.'

'What?'

Catherine sagged against the wall, and looked again. Georgie was right. The passageway still cradled the light, but it no longer came towards them. Rather, it wavered and waited, illuminating each cleft of the slippery walls, and the shape of the man standing between. Ned had stopped. Why?

She turned towards the pit. The dark space resisted her sight. It was not empty. It made no audible sound, but was not quiet. Something stirred in the arteries of the mountain, something she had always known was here, beneath the wood, since that long-ago night when Sir Maurice had tasked Emily with seeking it out. During all that time, knowledge of its existence had been interred in her memory, buried beneath more comprehensible things, and whatever it was, it rose to meet them now.

Catherine held Georgie's face to her middle.

A vast dark form moved past them, flooding the cramped passageway. For a split second, Ned stood proud, his neck and shoulders ruminant and head thrown back, as an ornamentation of antlers loomed wild and fecund above him. A bellow filled her hearing, but whether it issued from Ned or the thing that now enveloped him, she did not know. It was a lonely and bestial sound, one nobody hearing would have called strictly the noise of an animal, yet nobody could have parsed its words either. It seemed to occupy a different realm of voices; she felt other ears, more like its own, might have understood it better.

Ned was fixed in the light. His arms were elevated in worship or protest, but as the thing that held him grew, he shrank and withered. He released a sigh before the lantern clattered to the ground and went out. He staggered towards them, and as they huddled against the wall, he fell, and was lost to the pit.

There was nowhere to run. Her thoughts turned to Emily's painting, to the muscular things that had advanced through the dust. She thought of the mysteries she would never understand, most of all the stag crashing to the ground before the wood, her hope that life would spark again in its veins. She lived again, in the space of a few seconds, that distant night in the clearing, and knew the most grievous folly of man, who searches out Nature's reaches to harness them for his own ends.

Georgie whimpered into her navel. Then it was all around them, inside them. It vibrated in her skin, in her bones, and she understood its ancient ambivalence, its remoteness. It recognised her: past, present, and all she might do. But this apprehension could never be equal. She and Georgie were flecks of dust in its immutable eye, and as they clung to one another, it rushed past them, down and down, returning to depths they could not fathom.

They crouched, sightless. She stroked Georgie's fuzzy hair, and minutes passed, then more time, as she slowly came back to herself and realised their situation. They would have to move sooner or later, or they would die of cold and hunger, but the bleak knowledge that to go on was likely to see them descend further into the mountain fixed her to the spot.

She held Georgie's head and sang to her. What seemed like hours went by. If morning was approaching outside, they could not know it. The dark was unchanging.

When she first heard it, it brought her out of a half-doze. Distant to start with, the sound came stronger every second, eager and sharp. It could have been coming from any direction. She strained her ears. There it was again. And there. Something was barking.

38

Arthur's right hand was lodged in his inner pocket. His fingers spasmed, seeming to realise before the rest of him that they still possessed the power of movement. He allowed his grip to form around what he found there, clutching it so the blood beneath the skin pulsated, and mingled with a locus of searing pain. Somehow, he worked out that he held in his palm the cylindrical object he had picked up from the forest floor. Realised, too, that he could smell something. It took him a few moments to recognise it: apples. It was cold in the wood, but the smell was warm and bright as a June morning after overnight rain. In his mind there formed a remembrance of his youth, as fresh as his first taste of Welsh water and timorous as the first time he held a certain hand in his. He was injured, shaking, but his limbs were charged with fire.

Memory, his scourge all these years, lost some of its sting. His burden lightened, and thoughts rose up of his grandfather, and then Barnabas. He welcomed those thoughts, savouring the unbidden sweetness of souls walking together in a quiet, beloved place; the trees above became a roof, sheltering them from the coarseness of the world outside – its smoke, and metal, and empty noise – and stealing in behind them came the young thief, Iestin, and the strange promise of the wood.

... if I returned it ... he would put the breath of life back in her. He would give back what was lost.

Thinking of these things, he experienced a pleasure so deep it was almost fearful. Without quite realising why, he let out a great belly laugh, and released the thing he held in his pocket.

He opened his eyes, bringing his hand out and downward, and, wincing, pressed against his upper abdomen where the bullet had entered, and prodded around the wound. His ribcage burnt like someone had run a poker through it. His fingers came away wet.

The voice that brought him fully round was not his. It came from no corporeal thing, and was a mere thrum in the air. *Pressure. Bind it.*

'Pressure,' he repeated, realising the site of the wound, and that he was losing a copious amount of blood. '... pressure ... bind it.' He spoke aloud through his pain, opened his eyes, and worked, coming to his knees, removing his coat to gain access to the bleeding.

The nightmare of the dogs, the torrid chase through the wood, and Ned – *oh, Ned!* – raising up the gun; they had been no fever dream. The scorching pain through his torso was real. The bullet was lodged somewhere near his ribcage. Yet, he discerned, as he felt about with a clinical touch, the breach was not deep either; the projectile had struck something, been turned away from its lethal path. Still, he was bleeding below his arm, and it would need attention. He stripped off his shirt, grimaced as he took a branch from the forest floor and used its point to rip into the dirtied linen before tearing it into strips. He bound these tight around his abdomen, gasping, but stemming the flow of blood. He used what strips remained to dress his arm; it was makeshift, but would suffice until he could reach his bag. When he was certain it was secure, he stopped and breathed deep, accepting the pain, assessing how far he might move.

But he was forgetting something. He squinted into the dawn, knowing he should see others nearby, that he had to remember ... Then it rebounded upon him, and as he tried to stand, the branches and crowns of the trees spun and blurred into a haze.

'Miss Symonds!' he shouted, staggering.

And the Bridewell girl, where was she? Where was Ned? What had he done, and why? He feared his race through the wood and his confrontation with Sir Rowland had been for nothing. He had saved nobody.

Then he felt it, a warmth of breath beside him in the dark flush of morning, accompanied by the impression that he was no longer alone. The steps that had dogged him down the lonely years – on waking, on sleeping, on dreaming, so that he was worn thin with listening, and that would never stay, but faded into echoes just as the desire for them swelled – were here. This was the gift of the wood.

A hand found his.

He would always say, afterwards, when describing that night to his bachelor friends, especially on the cold Christmas Eves of old age when the requirement for a good story did not preclude the inexplicable, that the hand cradled his, and guided him. He would insist an outline went before him, a figure familiar, infinitely dear, knowing each step before he could, showing him the way through the golden-pheasant thickets, down and up the dimples of the land, away from the black tumult of the river, and towards the mountain. He would insist it knew his name, and whispered it over and over, so he had no choice but to follow.

As he went along, even in the greyish pink of the morning, the new light was sharp. His eyes ached with it. The ground was clad in its cloak of brown and yellow, the leaves heavy on the track. With some consternation, he realised the size and wildness of his hunting ground; even if he moved in the right direction, they could be anywhere, and he was weakening every minute, losing blood in spite of the dressing.

Then something yapped. He looked towards the slope, and saw, at first, just shadows, and the fading moon behind.

The presence was drifting away.

Stay. Please. Don't leave me.

But the misery that had accompanied that thought was softening. He looked down in the uncertain light, and saw the lines and hollows of his hand, and beside it, woven through it, the shadow of the hand of another. As he watched – or perhaps it was just that his eyes were not what they were – the two shapes joined, the fingers knitted together, and he found he could regard the whole without shame. He looked about him, and took in the splendour of his surroundings – the firmament above; the high, still slopes; the marvellous disrobed shapes of the trees – and he felt in harmony with them, and at peace with himself.

'Doctor!'

As he stared, two unsteady figures, one taller, one smaller, came down the track. Miss Symonds, holding the girl in front, shepherding her, and behind them, the thing that had made the noise: the little dog, Coke, a scampering black shadow.

'Miss Symonds, thank God,' he breathed. 'What happened? Where's Ned?'

Georgie Bridewell said unceremoniously, 'Dead. Miss Symonds put her scissors in him. Then the monster took him.'

He could not summon the presence of mind to question the child's statement. He regarded the governess a few seconds.

'Dead?' he said, closing his eyes. It hurt, as if his nerves had not kept up with events; his sore intellect knew Ned had been an enemy, but the rest of him did not.

'Dead,' agreed the governess. Her voice was quite steady.

'Then back to Locksley, I think.' With his head hammering, his torso blistering and one arm nearly useless, he could not arrange the night's events in any logical order. He wondered what might await them at the Abbey. 'What about Miss Murphy?' He wanted – needed – to know if his deductions in the crypt had been correct.

Miss Symonds nodded. 'She's there.' Her face contorted with some strong emotion.

'Alive?'

The governess did not answer. Instead, she looked troubled before taking Georgie's hand in hers, and making a start down the path. He decided his questions could wait.

Moving slowly, a few steps behind them, he put his hand in his pocket and took out the mysterious object, the thing he was certain had turned the bullet. It was hard, cartilaginous, with a narrowed point. He turned it over. Deer antler, he thought. Just a single tine. But old, very old. He looked over it for a few seconds and weighed it in his hand, then threw it as far away as he could. It tumbled down the slope for about a hundred yards, then rolled off somewhere out of sight.

EPILOGUE

To Mr Lewis, Hereford:
22nd April 1862
Church Stretton, Shropshire

The circumstances of my deciding to write to you are distinctive, and they are these: Frederick Sidstone, the medical man who passed away almost ten years ago on land belonging to your client, Sir Maurice Bridewell, was my friend. He was a good man and an able one. Whilst it is regrettable that he became preoccupied in later years by ideas which those of a more progressive bent must necessarily reject, he remained a man upon whom one could rely in matters of fact. In particular, he was a principal authority on the archaeological history of Locksley Abbey, including the wider estate on which it stands, and the area of ancient woodland known locally as the Puzzle Wood (this land being now in the control of your firm).

My personal interest thus declared, my gratification at the recent, partial exhumation, with the support of the Monmouthshire Archaeological Association, of the intact foundations of a Romano-Celtic shrine on the site of the Locksley yew felled in the storm of 1861, will not take you by surprise. As things now stand, the Association has uncovered a three-chambered rectangular complex, including a central naos *(the tree being at its rough centre) above the tunnelling below. Harboured within, and near the ruins, have been unearthed (based only on the extent to which*

347

we have been able to dig so far) nearly two dozen artefacts whose nature – coins, marked deer tines, and several carved canine figurines – point to an offertory shrine to the Romano-Celtic figure of Nodens, more latterly his Roman alter ego, Mars, or even the god Pan. We believe the site may have prehistoric significance as a place of defence or pilgrimage, owing firstly to the earthworks over which the wood has sprawled across the centuries, indicating that there was some significant effort taken to defend the place by the enigmatic tribe of the Silures, and secondly to older artefacts found in the vicinity, including a sword button adorned with enamel and cloisonné garnets. We concluded that it was only reconditioned in Roman times, and in its earliest incarnation, we believe the yew tree grew up in an apple orchard. Near to the foundations, after the departure of the Romans, the medieval Abbey rose up, to be replaced, in time, by the current manor house. The extent of modern fascination with these discoveries – and indeed with all such excavations of this type – has driven this news far and wide, to the degree that the Association was honoured with a note of congratulation from the Court of St James itself – a new zenith, I believe you will agree, in popular interest in the sciences!

To return to my friend, for many years at the forefront of the case for the existence of just such a shrine in the vicinity of the ancient Abbey, I am certain recent excavations would have provided him not only with endless diversion, but with a sense of vindication that he, in the face of an unfortunate and stubborn opposition from Sir Maurice's son, Rowland Bridewell, who met with such a violent end nearly on this very spot, was divining on the right lines all along.

The implications of this discovery concern your firm. First, the scheduled sale of the wood and its surrounding acreage to Sir Monty Cottrell, so long detained by the tragedies suffered by the estate a decade ago, including the unexplained disappearance of Anne Bridewell, must come to an immediate halt. The archaeological cost of progressing the transaction, and of permitting deforestation or construction of any description near the site, would be profound, and the two gentlemen concerned should be under no illusions: the learned men of the county, and still more in the country as a whole, would stand against them on this matter. We occupy a different world, in terms of the advancement of the sciences, than the one in which we stood a decade ago. In the second place, the site must be protected. There, the Association is willing to be of use. Please find enclosed details of sketches of the site, and a plan, including proposals both practical and financial, for the careful excavation of the clearing at the earliest convenience, to discover the origins, extent and phases of the activity there, and for its subsequent re-covering, so that future generations might have the same opportunities that now beckon to us. Finally, in order that the site might be better secured against deterioration, we propose the acquisition of the land that would previously have been sold to Sir Monty, by the Monmouthshire Archaeological Association, whose permission I have to act as emissary, with terms to be agreed.

Mr Lewis, you and I stand on the edge of discovery. Let us take our cue from the life's work of my old friend, and not be too cautious in the leaping.

Yours sincerely,
Cardale Musgrave

Intelligence of the death of Sir Maurice Bridewell, master of Locksley Abbey, Herefordshire, reached these parts on Sunday morning last. A telegram arrived from Naples, where Sir Maurice was known to have resided these twenty-two years. Further communications from Naples indicate Sir Maurice was in generally good health at the onset of a sudden illness. By coincidence, the young Miss Georgiana Bridewell, daughter of Sir Maurice's heir, Rowland Bridewell (d. 1852), was known to be in the city, in the company of her guardian, a Mrs Drake, widow of the pottery merchant and philanthropist, William Drake, of Abingdon, England. Miss Bridewell is expected to inherit a substantial landholding in addition to a significant inheritance from her grandfather, Mr Uriah Caplin. In Naples, Mrs Drake and Miss Bridewell, accompanied by a small black dog, were notably in attendance at the showing of a gallery of works by a new artist of the fairer sex, name unknown.

ACKNOWLEDGEMENTS

Heartfelt thanks are due to the many people who contributed, in ways big and small, to the writing of this book. I aim to list them here but the novel was long in the writing and if I have missed mention of any debt, it is not deliberate.

The idea for this story came in several phases, particularly while thinking about the work of Arthur Machen, but also during visits to the Forest of Dean and the real life Puzzlewood; a remarkable ancient woodland site rumoured to have inspired the work of J.R.R. Tolkien. The visit and the name resonated with me and fed into the writing, and eventually provided the title for the novel. This was an involuntary contribution on the part of the owners, but one that should be recognised.

I made other trips to research aspects of landscape and the history of the coal mining industry in England and Wales. I have mild claustrophobia, so the experience of being led underground at the National Coal Mining Museum in Wakefield by a garrulous ex-miner will stay with me for a long time. I am grateful for the memory and for the helpful information provided.

The wider team at Bloomsbury who again have done so much to guide me through the process of a story becoming a proper book: Amy Donegan, Emily Jones, Therese Keating, Ben McCluskey, Grace Nzita-Kiki, Sarah Knight, Joe Roche, Sarah McLean, Faye Robinson, and everyone in the wider sales team, including the field sales managers – I could not be more impressed and grateful. Any errors remaining in the novel are my own. I would add to these acknowledgements all the booksellers who talk to readers, create displays and promote writers' work on social media, generating such enthusiasm for the books they love.

Particular gratitude goes to my wonderful agent Sam Copeland, who works his magic behind the scenes, and to my editor Alison Hennessey, who worked a different form of magic on my drafts. She is so very gifted, the kindest of colleagues and friends.

I repeat my admiration for the cover work of David Mann, who has created another beautiful design that brings out so many of the ideas in the book. I don't know how he does it.

Some early drafts of some chapters of this book were read by others. For those who gave me feedback, it's such a favour. Deepest thanks.

For some time, my brother has been reminding me to mention him in my acknowledgements. I aim to please, and hope he's happy now. He and all my family (including my brilliant in-laws) will always have my thanks.

My husband and my daughter, who put up with me, and my dog, who does his best to stop progress of the work at any cost. I'll never forget my daughter (six, then) expressing surprise at how long all this writing malarkey was taking, and stating her intention to write a better book, and much faster. I hope and have every faith that she will do just that.

A NOTE ON THE TYPE

The text of this book is set in Fournier. Fournier is derived from the *romain du roi*, which was created towards the end of the seventeenth century from designs made by a committee of the Académie of Sciences for the exclusive use of the Imprimerie Royale. The original Fournier types were cut by the famous Paris founder Pierre Simon Fournier in about 1742. These types were some of the most influential designs of the eight and are counted among the earliest examples of the 'transitional' style of typeface. This Monotype version dates from 1924. Fournier is a light, clear face whose distinctive features are capital letters that are quite tall and bold in relation to the lower-case letters, and *decorative italics, which show the influence of the calligraphy of Fournier's time.*